D1096816

Other titles from Riverfeet Press

THIS SIDE OF A WILDERNESS: A Novel (2013), by Daniel J. Rice

THE UNPEOPLED SEASON: *Journal from a North Country Wilderness* (2014), by Daniel J. Rice

WITHIN THESE WOODS (2015), by Timothy Goodwin
A collection of Northwoods nature essays, with original illustrations by the author.

BIRDS OF A FEATHER (2015), by Charles Stone, with original water colors by Eloise Ryan.

THE UNPEOPLED SEASON: Collector's Edition (2015) by Daniel J. Rice
Includes 11 full-color images from the adventure.

available wherever books are sold, or on our webpage:
www.riverfeetpress.com

*You Pay —
We print (anything!)*

Excerpts from the pages:

He never cared too much for parties or people, but misanthropy could easily be cured by several alcoholic drinks. pg 8

This was going to be difficult, because he enjoyed women, but all the ones he has known seemed to have been sent as secret assassins on a mission to destroy his pride and ability. pg 19

The mountains knew the definition of freedom. They provided a place where he could find his mind. pg 26

There was a wildness inside him; someday he would capture it. Not to be tamed, but to be released. For only by understanding his mind could it be freed. pg 31

What man does not seek the power of his dreams, and believe in his ability to match the grace of his illusions. pg 32

The truth of existence was a happiness separated from the easy happy life. There was music in the forest. There was clean air where nobody could hear him breathe. pg 63

...he was sad for all the people he saw who were never free. All the people walking around thinking they were free, but were bonded to so many possessions and responsibilities, so much dispassion and anger, that freedom had become a mirage, like a mythical figure or a god, something they worshiped and followed, but never truly understood. pg 110

It has always been my understanding that truth and freedom can only exist in wild places. pg 143

In our generation of environmental concerns, it seems like every cut branch from a living tree is a disaster. But, looking around me at the abundance of thriving flora, it is easy to forget there is a disappearing world outside of this place. pg 151

Only lost photographs that were never taken know what my mind speaks of when we are alone together. pg 178

The trees show definitions of themselves subtly like the face of a man. pg 181

Every falling leaf reminds me that I too will soon be separated from these trees. Trying to capture freedom is like trying to catch a falling leaf. Occasionally you may grab one out of the air and hold it in your hand, but now what? pg 210

He wasn't really sure what that meant, *recivilize*. Did it mean he had to forget about the forest? Could he pretend like it never happened? Would he be required to wear a tie and speak politely of societal bliss? pg 218

A man without enemies is a dishonest man. pg 235

He felt the freedom of knowing nothing but natural sounds and peaceful walks, the sight of a deer, and the touch of a cool flowing river. pg 264

For Mayana,

The shimmering leaves of autumn have such a magnificent iridescence, that if you stand too close, for too long, you may actually glow in the dark.

You are my Golden Leaf.

THIS SIDE OF A WILDERNESS

Daniel J. Rice

This side
of horse-shit!
An incredibly boring!
and shallow book!

Riverfeet Press
918 4th St SE
Bemidji, MN 56601
www.rivcrfeet.com

THIS SIDE OF A WILDERNESS
Daniel J. Rice
Copyright 2013 © by the author
Edited by Ink Deep Editing
All rights reserved.
ISBN-13: 978-0615779676
LCCN: 2013913620

Cover photo by Mayana Photography
Title page art, *Fallen Leaf*, by Carly Rice
Author photo by John LaTourelle

THIS SIDE OF A WILDERNESS

Part I

From the Outside Looking In

The imagination is a beacon,

and if we follow it long and true,

it will reveal a paradise.

1

His favorite memory was of his father, uncle, and grandfather, sitting beside a campfire, while the moon
glistened off the lake behind them, and he and his younger brother watched through the screen window of a tent.
They looked absolutely free and at peace, as they sat near
the firelight in the dark wilderness. He remembered how
the flames illuminated their faces, and revealed wrinkles
and scars and life experiences. It was many years before he
understood the power of their silence. Now the image lived in
his mind like a painting come to life, and the longer it aged,
the more valuable it became. All he wanted was to touch that
piece of his past, to feel his feet walk through that memory,
and once again see the world as a peaceful uninhabited landscape waiting to be explored.

Often he returned there, through the conduit of wandering thoughts, and felt the cool lake air permeate his
skin, smelled the pinus aroma fill the air, and heard the
soft waves roll against the shore. This remembrance was
never good enough, for reality always interfered, and he got
removed from his daydream and returned to the present. Not
that the present was so bad, his job took him to wild and

scenic locations. But these brief interludes never satisfied, and left him in want of something permanent.

No matter how hard he worked to get what he wanted, he always wanted more. Happiness seemed to be reserved for people willing to sacrifice their dreams and accept something simple. So he decided to think about something simple, like the weather. The weather was what he thought about when he didn't want to be burdened by contemplations of truth.

The season had been hot and dry, which caused the green to fade from the hills by early summer. Eli Sylvan put his palm against the passenger side window and felt the heat outside. The truck rocked back and forth from a powerful wind that rushed down off the mountains and blew across the high plains. Up ahead he saw his home town with oil vapors collected above the city like a translucent satin sheet pulsating in the wind. This was Casper, Wyoming, a boom-and-bust sort of town currently in a state of boom from the oil and natural gas industry.

"Have I told you about my new RV?" asked Ricky, as he gripped the bottom of the steering wheel loosely with one hand. He looked over at Eli through the yellow lenses of his camouflaged sunglasses, "Eli, you listening to me?"

Eli turned his eyes from the prairie freckled with rusty oil rigs churning and grinding into the sandy ground, "Yeah. I mean no, you haven't told me about your new RV."

"Oh man, it's a beaut'. Thirty-two feet long, two bedrooms and sleeps eight, a fully functional kitchen and bathroom, with a forty-two inch flat screen television. Man, the wife and I are going to be camping in luxury."

"That's nice," said Eli, as he turned his head and looked away. The city up ahead was built in a small valley, and through that valley a trout stream cut down off the mountains and began its course to the sea. Eli's eyes followed its serpentine shape from the city up to the foot of the mountains. He thought about how peaceful it was to hear water tumble over cobblestones while he stood waist deep in the river with a fly rod in his hand. From up there this city looked small and lifeless, and its sounds were muted by a comfortable distance. That sense of distance was the happiness he enjoyed most.

Ricky held his cell phone in one hand, while steering with his knee, and said, "Awe hell, my wife just texted me. She wants me to go to the damn grocery store before heading home."

Eli ignored Ricky's statement as if he were alone in a soundless room and could only hear his own thoughts. He watched the city grow larger until they were inside of its walls. He had lived in cities much bigger than this one, but here in Wyoming, the most uncivilized state left in the union, Casper seemed to be the epitome of contemporary America. Sure the fifty-thousand people were isolated on all sides by a hundred or more miles of unpopulated landscapes, but they didn't let that deter them from partaking in the feast of consumerism. Everything was available here, whether it be fanciful name brand clothing, 3-D televisions, fine foreign cuisine, or even sporting goods designed for vanity not pragmatism; if not found in a local shop it could arrive at your doorstep in less than a week.

"That was a good day, the boss will be glad we got it all done," said Ricky, as they returned to the office and got out of the truck.

"Yep, well, have a nice weekend," replied Eli, while he forced a smile and offered an obligatory wave. He couldn't wait to get out of there and put the work week behind him.

"Oh we will. The wife and I are taking the RV up to Echo Mountain. Just need to charge up the battery so we can enjoy that big ol' television."

"See you on Monday," said Eli, and got into his old Ford Ranger pickup truck.

He pulled up to Papa Stephanio's Pizzeria and parked the truck. On the brick wall in front of him was the painted image of a grizzly bear standing beside a mountain stream with a rainbow trout leaping into the air. Eli sat in his truck and stared at the painting, wondering how something artificial, made of acrylic and brick, could create such a sensation of calmness and serenity. He stepped outside and closed his eyes to keep the image in his mind and it made him feel like he was home. He reached out into the empty air and felt the pulse of that cold flowing water as it rushed between his fingers and tickled the hair on top of his hand. Then a muscle car roared by on the street, and he was pulled out of that image by the sound of loud exhaust pipes reflecting off the brick wall. The pavement radiated heat, which caused the soles of his shoes to feel like marshmallows as he walked inside.

"Eli, there you are, come on over and pour yourself a beer," said Kevin, as Eli sat down. "You're running a bit late, get stuck at work?" There were four other people at the table, but only one of them acknowledged his presence, the rest were consumed by an advertisement playing on a digital kiosk mounted on the wall.

"We were working up in the Big Horn Mountains and blew a tire on a rough patch of road," responded Eli.

"That sucks man. You ready to get this weekend started?"

"Yeah, I'm just glad to be off of work."

"Oh man, don't even think about that. Listen, I've got quite the party planned for tonight. There's at least a dozen women coming over, and I just got that new video game *Alien Hero.* So what do you say, you in or what?"

"I'll stop by."

"Yeah, you better."

Eli looked around the room at all the flat screen televisions and pictures of sports icons hanging from the walls. Even though both these mediums presented real life imagery, they seemed artificial. The bear and the trout and the river and the trees on the painted wall outside made more sense to him, those were the type of images that calmed his nerves. All the people in the room made him feel confined, as if they had control over his life and the reality they selected strung around him like a barbwire fence, so he stood up and said, "Alright, well thanks for the beer, but I've got to run home quick."

"You're not gonna wait for the pizza?"

"I'll catch up with you later, just got something else I need to do first."

He walked outside and stood before the giant mural painted on the outer wall of the building. The image began to move, and he saw water droplets rocket off the tail of the fish as it erupted from the surface of the stream and captured a dragonfly in its mouth. The grizzly bear turned its head and looked at Eli, he seemed so real and close, but as Eli brushed his hands across the surface the life faded and was replaced by only abstract colors. He got in his truck and drove away while wondering about the synaesthetic power of inanimate things.

When he returned home he poured dog food into the dish by the backdoor, then shuffled through a stack of mail. Six envelopes were billing statements, the other three were junk. He opened the junk mail first. Two of them were credit card offers, and as he held them both in his hands a mischievous grin crept onto his face. With the kind of money these credit cards offered he could do something crazy and spontaneous like take a cruise ship around the world. Maybe he'd get lucky and maroon on a deserted island as the only survivor. There he could test himself without any human or mechanical interference. Then he would know what he was really made of. Then he would understand.

It would be great to disappear, to create a new identity and become whoever he wanted, to become who he secretly has always been. It invigorated him to think about how it would feel to start a new life with no responsibilities and no burdens from the past. But he knew well enough burdens followed him wherever he went, and responsibilities were a lot like dandelions – no matter how hard he tried to fight them, they always found a way to grow.

The third envelope was a brochure for community education offered at the local college. The *Wilderness First Aid* training sounded appealing, but he figured whatever they were teaching could easily be learned from a book on his own free time. There were six different foreign language classes, but whenever he had been in another country he made do with knowing a few key phrases. Then he saw a course for acrylic painting. As he read through the description, he thought about how he felt after seeing the mural on the side of the wall, like there was an intrinsic power that could only be understood by each pair of eyes that saw it. He set the pamphlet on the table and gazed out the window to imagine his masterpiece. In order to receive this degree he would have to complete eight online classes. This seemed absurd to him, taking online courses to become an artist. It had always been his presumption that artists were born as such, and then refined through hands-on training with a master. Maybe the great ones didn't even need to be trained; they saw a world so magnificent and unique they had to paint it – that was the only way they could understand. He tore it up along with the credit card offers and tossed them into the overflowing garbage can.

Eli retrieved his checkbook from the freezer, and the postage stamps stashed in the silverware drawer. It always seemed like a ridiculous hassle to have to pay these bills. How could he live without the internet, or a cell phone, or electricity, or running water, or heat, or garbage removal? These simple luxuries were the reason he woke up and went to work every day, so he could enjoy a life of comfort.

It was still light outside as he flipped the flag up on his mailbox and hopped into the pickup truck. There were a dozen cars parked outside of Kevin's house as Eli stood in the front yard and prepared to be sociable. Strobe lights flickered in the windows, and he felt the bass from subwoofers vibrate the cartilage in his knees as he walked to the front door and entered. He never cared too much for parties or people, but misanthropy could easily be cured by several alcoholic drinks.

He stood in the doorway and gathered his wit, but nobody seemed to notice he was there. Upstairs was a crowd of people, but Eli only recognized a few faces. In the corner was a minibar with a hired bartender, so he walked over and ordered a drink. He tapped his feet and tried to avoid all the eyes in the room. Everyone seemed so fashionable and important, as though they believed it was their right of birth to be rich and famous. He wondered what Meriwether Lewis would think about this new world he had once explored in its natural state.

Then he noticed something on the far wall. It glowed in vibrant and hypnotic colors, as if it were a portal or passageway into another dimension, and his entranced feet carried him towards the image. Mounted at eye level was a framed painting of a tropical shoreline, where dark skinned women stood topless, and the ocean looked so distorted in its hazy colors it almost seemed real. He rubbed his fingers around the wooden frame, and wiped a smudge off the glass cover with his sleeve. The noise in the room faded and was replaced by the sounds of ocean waves scraping into the sandy beach. He began to hear the women speaking in a language he couldn't understand, but they sounded so exotic he could listen to them forever. Then he felt a tap on his shoulder, and as he blinked several times he saw a young woman in a purple dress with long blonde hair looking at him through curious hazel eyes.

"That's a great piece, isn't it?" she said, and gestured towards the painting.

"Yes, I've been here a dozen times but never noticed it."

"He's had it for a long time. I should know, I'm his cousin."

"Really?" said Eli, as he returned his eyes to the painting.

"It's a Gauguin, you know. Not an original of course," she said with an ostentatious chuckle and flicked the hair from her shoulder, "but it is one of a limited first edition prints. It cost my uncle a small fortune when he bought it for Kevin."

"That so?" replied Eli, while trying to listen to those women speaking in their native tongue.

"So my name's Annette," she leaned in between him and the painting.

"Sorry, I'm Eli."

"Of course. Well this is one of my favorite Gauguin pieces ever. It's the one that made him famous you know."

"No, I didn't."

"Yes, I just love the way he blends colors together to create images that seem almost surreal. He was the master of abstract realism. Ah, it's a shame that great artists only come along once or twice in a generation. If that." She watched him stand there passively with wrinkles on his forehead, as though this were the first piece of art he had ever seen and just now realized human emotions could be justified by a static two-dimensional image. "So, what do you think of it?" she asked.

"It's good."

"Good? Come on, you can do better than that."

"Well, I'd say it's, it's oceanic."

"Oceanic?"

"Yes. You know, deep, fully encompassing, and filled with life and mystery."

"That's an interesting way to explain it," she said, and tilted her head to reacquaint herself with his appearance.

Eli looked at her but only saw a brick wall, a barricade that separated him from his imagination. "It was nice to meet you," he said, and took one last look at the painting then walked away. On the other side of the room was a large flat screen television where a group of guys were gathered around on an L-shaped couch playing video games. As Eli approached he saw Kevin stand up to greet him.

"What's up man, I was beginning to think you weren't going to show. Have you played this game yet? It fucking rocks man. Check it out, you're fighting with a team of aliens who have come to earth to eradicate the zombies. It's awesome, right?"

"Sounds almost, surreal," replied Eli as he looked over his shoulder at the painting on the far wall.

"Yeah, well we're in the middle of a battle right now, but sit down and we'll get you in the next game."

Eli sat down and sank into the couch. He had been here many times and played many games with many beers, but never before had he noticed the sensational imagery on the screen – he had always been wrapped up in the selfless conglomeration of hanging with the guys. Tonight it was different, he saw the game broadcasted on the screen like a million individual paintings with scenery and characters designed by a mind that took the time to create a masterpiece. He drifted off and thought about how great it would feel to design something strangers would admire long after he was gone.

"Yo Eli, it's your turn."

"Huh?"

"Yeah, you're up."

"Alright," he said, and leaned forward in his seat to take the controller. The game played as Eli piloted the device in his hands. No matter how hard he tried, this game couldn't properly design what he saw in his mind. He was trapped in somebody else's imagination and could only exhibit a limited degree of navigation. There must be a way to gain full control of his thoughts, and display them in an accurate and unique form. The people in the room faded from his view, as he became distracted by thoughts of a separate perception. He dropped the controller on the floor and stood up in a bolt, spilling his drink in the process.

"What the hell man!" said the guy who sat next to him on the couch.

"Where you going Eli?" asked Kevin.

"I need to leave."

"What? You can't do that, the party just started. Finish the game at least."

"I gotta go." And he rushed for the door, pushing himself through the crowd.

As he walked down the stairs, Annette stepped in front of him and said, "There you are, I was looking for someone to get into an intellectual conversation with," and placed her hand on his shoulder. He brushed her aside and continued out the front door.

2

Eli sat alone on the front porch of his house and listened to sounds fill the air like a vapor barely distinguishable on the surface of his ears above all his thoughts. Pickup trucks pounded on the freeway pavement only a block away, and the rhythm of their tires sounded like a mountain stream as it plowed over cobblestones and boulders. From the alley he heard dogs, what sounded to be an entire pack of colonized strays, barking with a divided sort of unison, like a crowd of people all talking about different things at the same time, which somehow blended into one incompressible hum. Through the open windows down the street came the buzz of televisions and radios and all the other electrical currents that harmonized around him. There was also a silence.

The silence could be heard within the sound. It was the master of the darkness in the spaces between the leaves on the trees which had become calm in the night. The silence was the power that loomed like a cumulonimbus cloud drifting above the high plains. The silence was the echo he heard most often. The silence was the mediator between the screaming voice of his inner thoughts, and the rampant noises of the ambient world.

The silence was the only place where he could actually hear anything. So that night he listened. He listened to the waves of experiences as they crashed into the shores of his principles and purpose. He heard the sounds these waves made as they slowly, grain by well-defined grain, eroded all the ideals he spent an entire youth developing. He heard the scraping and the splashing of this power equally continuous to the tick tocks of time. It dug away, slowly, constantly, at the barricade of his shores which were built to protect himself from the inevitable truths he always knew these waves would bring. The rejuvenation he found in exploring the bathymetry of these somber thoughts, was the realization of his own perpetual optimism, which could never allow him to sacrifice all his dreams and ethics and surrender to the vacuity of a hopeless existence. There was always hope, even if well hidden, in the possibility of something better being just up ahead, or on the other side of a mountain.

This hunger inside made him realize he needed to be inspired by something again. He longed to feel that anxious discomfort in his heart which told him he was alive by making him ambitious. There was a loss of emotion in the way he now viewed the world. He simply no longer cared. Well, maybe he did care, but the ways of this world forced him to hide emotion, otherwise be forever handicapped by people's arcane ability to take advantage of him. This has made him hard, and some would say strong and mature, but he would give all that up for a chance to relive those juvenile investigations of his heart, to express himself without cares of restraint, and to restore that romantic picture of the world. It seemed everyone went through these investigations, all to the same predictable result; women became inhibited, and men became reserved. But he wanted to be the exception to the rule who never lost his curiosity of youth. So he decided to pursue life, rather than be devoured by it.

He didn't know where to begin. He dug himself into a pit of memory, and slowly but surely lost his optimistic view of the future. He wanted to get all these thoughts out of his head and start fresh. If he developed an image, a wild and untamed world perhaps, then he may start to see the real world with idealistic curiosity again. He was uncertain whether any curiosity remained in his stochastic soul. So he went to sleep that night with the intention of making himself dream up a scene he could paint and then watch which would bring the scope of his heart back into his eyes.

His dreams that night were green, and white, and brown, and black. The images were hazy, all with a blurred fringe, as if the borders had become disfigured, and each single object seeped into the next. There were movements in his dreams, but they were small, barely perceptible movements, like the displacement of air beneath the wings of a falling leaf. He heard nothing. The dreams were silent and obscure, which filled him with a sleeping sense of inspiration. He must fill the void.

The next morning he drove to the nearest arts and crafts store to purchase supplies. He wandered in amazement, meandered through every aisle, and admired every colorful material with newfound curiosity. He realized he didn't know a thing about painting, and had never created a piece of art since boyhood when he drew stick figures with large heads carrying machine guns. The machine guns got most of his attention.

He removed his hat and scratched the top of his head. Pinned to the back of the hat was a colorful fly fishing lure he retired after it caught a spectacular trout. Even though fishing was supposed to be a pragmatic pursuit of capturing a fish, he enjoyed the aesthetic design of flies, and the silence of lonely waters, equally, if not more, than whether or not he actually caught a fish. He tried to focus on the colors and the patterns of his favorite flies he had tied.

Somewhere in the firmament of his mind he had always been fascinated by the arts, though he couldn't remember ever entering a gallery. Those unseen masterpieces on the walls of the galleries he had never entered were created by minds unconcerned with the style or creation of others. The great artists lacked the desire or ability to conform. This is what separated them and left spectators in awe of their performance: mystery. The mystery of simply being different. He also knew the greatest triumph of the arts was to expound on this simplicity. To show the world the way he saw it. To create it as he goes without any laws but his own.

He exited the store with a smile on his face and the sun in his eyes. He pushed a shopping cart full of materials and tools he had never used. As he drove home, the sight of pedestrians and passing cars outside the window of his truck were replaced by images of rivers and trees inside his mind. He felt passionate and strong, and for the first time in his adult life he saw all the colors and shapes that surrounded him in this imaginary world as being tangible.

He returned home and promptly set up a studio in his unused basement. All the cans of paint were organized in a pile ascending from light to dark. The brushes were categorized by both bristle stiffness and width. He aligned the blank canvases along a wall; larger ones to the left, and smaller ones to the right. This reminded him of a mountain range with a long basin stretching out into the horizon.

While he viewed this new studio from the doorway, his mind began to wander, and pretty soon he envisioned brilliant images on those blank canvases like animations from his imagination come to life. The blood in his veins began to shake and jump like water applied to heat. The excitement was exhausting, so he laid down in the center of the room on the cement floor and fell asleep. He dreamt of trees echoing the songs of harmonious birds. The sounds were more visible than the images, and he saw their musical notes leap out from the beaks of the birds like particolored fireworks ricocheting through a long corrugated tunnel.

When he awoke several hours later it was mid-evening. He looked around the room and felt as though still in a dream, a dream void of any creation, with only the tools for him to create it as he chose. He thought he would paint the forest. The forest was his home even though he was imprisoned by the city. His dreams always took him to the trees and lakes and wolves and moose. Could his subconscious sleeping dream be replicated by a conscientious waking dream? All the tools necessary to paint the image were here. He shuffled through the brushes, picked out a paint, then knelt down before a canvas. After staring for a long moment he realized he couldn't fully define the image he wished to paint. He needed more research. He needed a wilderness to conquer the void.

The telephone rang upstairs. Painting could wait. The procrastinators' opportunities make a short list. A short list was alright for now. A short list was easier to manage. The phone was ringing.

"Eli, I've been trying to call you all day, have you been out?" asked a female voice on the line.

"Yes," he responded, still envisioning colors and images draining from his hands and filling the blank canvas.

"Well, you don't have to tell me what you were doing if you don't want to."

"Okay. I've mostly been thinking."

"Thinking? You had to go out to think?"

"Sometimes." Then he remembered his plans to meet with Audrey tonight. She had a beautifully tanned and curvaceous body, but four months into the relationship, the most skin she had revealed was while wearing a bra and panties. They weren't even a G-string. While he admired her sense of continence, he was growing tired of the wait. It's not like she was a virgin saving herself for marriage, she had an eight year old son, whom Eli had taken every measure to be active with.

"What's wrong? Are you telling me the truth?" she asked, sensing his hesitation.

"Of course. Listen babe, I can't talk right now alright."

"Well, if you say so. Are you still coming over tonight? Andrew is at his dad's house so we will finally be alone."

"Sounds like a good time. I'll have to let you know. I may be working all night."

"Working? What work could you possibly have on a Saturday night? Aren't you the man who claims to leave his work at the office every day when he signs out?"

"This is something else." He tried to keep his imagination away from her skin, and focused on his painting.

"You're being very vague. I was so excited we'd have a good time tonight, now you're making me feel unwanted."

"Listen, can't a man have any privacy and still be understood by his woman?"

"Now you're being rude. Just call me when you decide if you want to see me. Will you call me?"

"Sure thing honeydew." He hung up the phone and paced around the house. He considered leaving, going over to see her, feel her naked skin pressed against his, enjoy the comfort that could only come from another warm body. She could wait. She had made him wait all this time.

He removed his socks and slid his bare feet across the carpet trying to remember the way the forest floor felt on the soles of his feet last time he wandered barefoot over the twigs and leaves and moss and dirt of the woods. He wanted to howl. He wanted to give a voice to his longing for solace. He walked downstairs to his empty masterpiece. He saw nothing. There was no vision before his eyes. Somewhere behind all his wandering thoughts was a manifestation, a visage of an idea, a pearl hidden within a gooey substance encapsulated by a shell. In a congestive dizziness he laid his head upon the cement floor and was fast asleep.

• • •

The next morning Eli awoke to sun rays squeezing through the shutters of his basement window. Light seemed magnificent to him. Never before had he noticed its ability to separate and reform, and illuminate an entire space just by sifting through a couple of tiny slits. Light was magical. He understood then that if he were to create a masterpiece, first he had to learn how to capture light. So he watched it. He stood up and followed it to its source at the window. Here the light was thin and singular, like paper coming out of a shredder. He waved his hand before it and watched it stop. Then he removed his hand and saw it flow again. He could control the light by placing the shutters at different angles. With the proper articulation it could be designed however he pleased. He hurried upstairs to a bright room with no light switches on.

Through these wide open windows he could not see the rays. They were joined in a singular force, and collected into one solid illumination. There were shadows on his small confined front yard, narrow little lances where the light was hidden behind yellowing grass.

He began to understand this transient substance of light. This understanding failed to provide a definition. He knew he couldn't paint what he couldn't define. Sometimes definitions were revealed while he thought about something else. This required a distraction. He pushed redial on the telephone.

"Hello."

"Honeydew, how are you today?"

"Eli, why didn't you call me last night?" she said, posing her annoyance as a question.

"Sorry babe, I fell asleep."

"You fell asleep? I thought you were working?"

"I was, then I fell asleep. Listen, let's not argue, last night didn't work out, it's nobody's fault. We've still got today."

"I suppose. You made me very mad though, I stayed up half the night waiting for you to call. Were you with someone?"

"Stop being foolish. What time does Andrew come home?"

"His dad's dropping him off this evening."

"Alright, why don't I come over and we'll make this right."

"You better make it right, I drank that whole bottle of wine all to myself last night. You know how much I hate to drink alone."

"I'll be right over."

• • •

"There you are my little sweet honeydew," said Eli as he entered her home and filled up the space with his presence.

"Don't call me that. You're playful names aren't going to make me forget about last night."

"Somebody sounds ornery. Let's not keep a grudge. Let's make peace instead."

"I am ornery. I already said that you made me upset. You probably shouldn't have come over."

He stepped towards her, lifted her into his arms, and pressed his lips firmly to hers. She succumbed for a moment, and enjoyed the way his hairless upper lip felt as it caressed the tip of her nose. Then she pulled back and said, "Put me down." So he put her down.

"You're not being any fun," he told her.

"Is that the only reason you came over here?"

"Of course not. I wanted to see you. I needed a distraction."

"A distraction!" the words shot from her indignant tongue. "Is that what I am, a distraction! What do you mean anyways, a distraction from what?"

"I've got something important to tell you," he said, beaming in anticipation of her approval.

"I knew it. Last night when I was sitting here all alone wondering where you were, I could just feel something was wrong."

"Anyways," he replied and shook his head, "all I wanted to tell you is that I decided to become a painter."

"A painter?" she laughed, then saw the serious look in his eyes, and said, "I didn't know you could paint."

"Neither do I. I'm going to give it a try though."

"Why on earth would you want to do that? I mean, I like art and all, but that doesn't mean I think I'm an artist."

"I'm not sure that I even like art, at least I never used to. But that's something entirely different. Listen, you're missing the point here. I want to paint because I have something inside that needs to be understood."

"Well, couldn't you just write a journal or something? That would be much easier for you."

"I don't expect anything to be easy, that would make it seem unworthy."

"So is that what you were doing last night, painting?"

"Not really. I was mostly thinking."

She considered this briefly, imagined him sitting alone in his small little house with his chin on his fist. This image seemed both attractive and comical to her. "Well, I thought you just said you wanted to be a painter, not a Buddhist. A Buddhist I could understand, I might even think that was sexy," she stepped closer to him and narrowed her eyes. "You could grow a big old Buddha belly and just lay in my bed all day," as she reached towards his waist.

He pushed her hands away and said, "You're really making a whole dizzy charade out of this. I thought you'd be impressed by having a painter for a lover."

"Not if he'd rather be thinking about painting than actually loving me."

"Wow, you sure know how to tear a man down. Trust me, there's time enough in both our lives for painting and loving you."

"Okay Mister Don Juan Picasso, let me ask you this. If we were getting married, and on our wedding day you had some grand inspiration that you just had to paint, which would you choose?"

He looked directly at her. She began to dissolve. Her solid figure was being erased. There was clarity for him in her new transparency. "That's a very inspiring question. Really, you've filled me with loads of inspiration. Before I answer though, and believe me I want to answer, first I'd like to hear what you think my answer will be."

"That's easy. I think you may be a selfish man, the selfish sort who would choose his work over his woman, and somehow convince himself this was a display of chivalry. Like pursuing your own goal would provide for me and make me happy."

"That so honeydew? Tell ya what, you and me getting married is about as likely to happen as a dinosaur stealing my car. What you need, and listen closely because it's a rare piece of honesty that only comes from opportune circumstances. You need a man who lacks any self-esteem with no original thoughts of his own. You need to find yourself a good lazy coward who will do whatever you say and call you a princess for it. That man isn't me." He turned and shut the door on her scornful teary eyed face.

If the sun had eyes right then it would have been blinded by the brightness of his smile as he stepped outside. He wasn't angered by the events which just occurred. There certainly wasn't any sense of sadness or loss. He felt a satisfying relief. She was supposed to offer him a distraction, but then he realized she was the distraction. Perhaps there wasn't space in his life for painting and loving. He decided never again to get involved with a woman who tried to restrict his potential. This was going to be difficult, because he enjoyed women, but all the ones he has known seemed to have been sent as secret assassins on a mission to destroy his pride and ability.

It seemed as though women searched for what they admired in him, and then stole it away. It was as if they needed to acquire these attributes to make themselves whole. Not for their own use or completion, but of a more subliminal intention to later hand out as gifts to their unborn children. It didn't seem so bad when he thought about it like that, he couldn't blame someone for their sociobiology. But, if anyone were to give pieces of himself as gifts to their unborn children, it would be Eli. So he drove away as a single man.

3

YOUR PASSWORD is
boringwriter...

That next morning Eli wanted to paint the image of a dinosaur stealing an angry old woman's car. The vague depiction of this idea made him laugh as he watched it like a moving picture in his mind. The picture moved too fast to be understood, the details were obscure, with only a fragmental representation being visible. He needed to understand time.

For him, time was a spectral substance. He felt it as an apparition none of his five senses would acknowledge the presence of. But still, he knew it existed. Time was not the tick tocks on a wall or the digital numbers on the bottom right corner of a computer screen. It was not the lost years with the lost idols and joys and glories where he knew time. It was not in those tragic sensations towards all who had come and gone. It was not the preceding myriad of chances and hopes and fortunes that could grow or crumble. It was not the size of his shoe or the length of his hair. It was not the people he knew or the place where he lived. It was the passage.

Time only existed while he was consumed by the instantaneous reactions. Before and after were forever endless voids on the spectrum of memory and possibility, and time was illusory to them. To his memory, time was an open space filled with landmarks. Without the hands of a clock, dates of a calendar, or numbers of a year, he forgot the sequence of events, the location of these landmarks became distorted, jumbled up like a boiling stew, and he lost the reference of what time they occurred. But time was not the clock or calendar or the number of a year. Time was the passage.

Possibility was a request for the future, but to the future time was an unknown possibility. It was filled with predictions, purposes, and plans. But the future did not exist, and never would. It was an unpredictable galaxy whose purpose was transient and plans inchoate. The past and the future were starlight, seemingly so close, but forever out of reach.

Eli felt that starlight, the infinity of knowing nothing but his finite existence.

This was the fear which made him believe time stretched endlessly in all directions. The fear told him time was real. The belief in time told him to fear it.

The clock on the microwave read 7:07 a.m. This was much earlier than he normally arose, except for those five days a week when the incessant scream of his alarm clock told him he had to go to work. It was a good thing he got up so early, this would give him plenty of time to start painting. He looked at the calendar in passing. It was Monday. Just then he heard the alarm clock going off in his bedroom; it was set for Monday through Friday at 7:10 a.m. Painting would have to wait, again.

The routine was easy, it had been memorized and perfected from years of living in the professional work force. As he simultaneously brushed his teeth and scrambled eggs, he also watched the future. Again the future was misperceived as being an inherent link in the chain of time. He coalesced into the structure of what was known as a mature adult; being focused on the future, planning his work day, and convincing himself his work actually mattered, that it somehow bettered the world. It was funny how the mind could fool the man when the man wished to be a fool.

The streets were filled with strangers of the strangest and most fascinating kind, but he only saw them as peripheral distractions. The sun was orange and pink as it crested over the dark mountains, but it may as well have been a colorless void. The only external stimuli perceptible were lines painted on the pavement, and traffic lights. He didn't see the shapes of spinning bicycle wheels, or the colors of withering grass. He saw the clock and it read 7:57. The stop light up ahead turned red. He was going to be late. He should have planned for time better. He cursed the empty air.

When the light turned green, he drove exactly five miles per hour over the indicated speed limit. There was no concern for the scenery he passed through, for this place he would never see replicated exactly as it was. All he saw was the repetition; go to work, say good morning to the secretary, listen to the early bird brown nosing the boss, sit at his desk, then smile and wave hello when the boss passed by for a coffee refill sometime between 8:30 and 9:00.

He entered the door with the sign that said UANT: United Administration of Natural Technology. Everything played out exactly as it did every other morning. The variations were unnoticed by his unfocused eyes. Then there was a catalyst. A subtle moment that could easily be missed and never have any effect at all.

The computer monitor showed the password screen with a flashing icon, but as his fingers rested on the keyboard, he couldn't remember what to type. For five years he had sat in this same chair at this same desk, and looked at this same computer screen and typed the same password. Now it was gone. The inaccessibility of this memory confounded him.

The password was written on a notecard somewhere in his desk. Before it was located, he noticed a red pen on the desk with an ink globule forming at the tip. He picked it up and held it vertically, tip end down. The ink stretched and changed shape. It became long and viscous, as if it were melted rubber. Then it burst free of the pen and traveled downward. During its descent it transitioned through many different shapes. This fall lasted forever. Then with a splash forever ended, and the ink splattered across the laminated desktop. In this new dispersal of shapes and sizes, a new forever was formed. This too seemed to last forever, as the ink scattered and sank into the laminated desktop. These little red amoebas slowly dried and changed color. Now they were trapped in a forever.

Eli spun his chair around and looked out the window. He rubbed his eyes with his fists to clear his vision. Birds roosted on the chain link fence that was tangled with flowering vines.

Insects gathered in clouds subject to the shape of the wind. The sun was so bright and hot that the pavement looked soft enough to pick up a handful and reform it like a snowball. Cottonwood trees spread their enormous canopy over the yard and created flowing shadows that provided shade for the grass. The grass was more than just a yard, but thousands of individual seeds struggling for life. There were so many shapes and colors and depths, and he wanted to understand them all.

• • •

Later that afternoon, Eli was abducted from this new reality and perception by the sound of a voice speaking nearby. His eyes climbed out of that solipsism to see his boss leering at him around the cubicle wall. He sat up straight and tried to remember why he was here.

"You doing alright today, Eli?" asked his boss.

"Yeah, great actually."

"You seem a bit out of sorts. Happen to get that analysis finished?"

"No, honestly I've barely started to write it. But I've been thinking a lot about it."

"Well, we all admire your ability to enter a think tank, but I need that finished first thing tomorrow."

"I'll have it done today."

"That's my man," said the boss while he walked away.

Eli got up to follow him. "Hey Clancy, you got a second?"

"Yeah, what's up?"

"This may be short notice, but I was thinking of taking a three day weekend this week. So either Friday or Monday off?"

"Tell ya what, you get that analysis on my desk by checkout time today, and you can take either or both off."

"Excellent." Eli went back to his cubicle, and rested his fingers on the keyboard. With his mind on thoughts of work, the password came back automatically. He logged in, and then closed the blinds on his window. After laying a piece of scratch paper over the ink blots on his desk, he got focused on the task. The assignment was menial, he could whip out a descriptive analysis on this new Hydrographic Acoustic Doppler Radar in his sleep. All the HADR did was send invisible waves from a transmitter down through the water and back up to a receiver, where it reported the depth and velocity of a river. Elaboration was the easy part.

At 4:42 p.m. the document was finished. He reread it. It was a perfect representation of a descriptive analysis. All the facts were documented with references, and he used all the proper nomenclature. This would be read throughout the professional field, and it would make his boss proud to say he had a man like Eli on his team.

But there was something missing from this technical document. There was nothing unique here. There was no representation of himself in these words. This was something that could be produced by anyone with the proper training. It lacked expression. He imagined some people would be truly proud and satisfied with their ability to write a professional document such as this one, and for a moment he admired that simplicity, that ability to conform to the responsibilities of being a professional adult. He knew this would never be him. He could never write a descriptive analysis to satisfy his soul. This one on his screen was as good as it got. But, being that he wasn't independently wealthy, and he presently had no other means of sustenance, he forced himself to forget about his other abilities, those latent ones hidden from all view except his inner mind, and decided to make the best of what he had now. Someday he would find something better. He would untangle the web and find a passage to where he belonged.

He carried the printed copy into Clancy's office and said, "Here you go. I believe this is a fine piece of technology, and every hydrographer is going to want one."

"Well, it's obviously too late for me to read it today, but I'll check it out first thing tomorrow. Decide what days you're going to take off?"

"Probably just Friday."

"Alright. Send the request through the system and we'll make it official."

4

If you have not touched the rocky wall of a canyon. If you have not heard a rushing river pound over cobblestones. If you have not seen a native trout rise in a crystalline pool beneath a shattering riffle, or a golden eagle spread its wings and cover you in shadow. If you have not seen the tree line recede to the top of a bare crested mountain. If you have not looked into a pair of wild eyes and seen your own reflection. Please, for the good of your soul, travel west.

• • •

Eli woke early and got on the road heading west. His destination was the Wind River Mountains. He didn't know exactly where he would go once he got there, but he had with him several quad maps filled with canyons, rivers, lakes, and unknown passages.

He packed light. Everything needed for three days and two nights fit in his size four Duluth pack and a fly rod tube. In the pockets of his cargo pants was a pouch of long-leaf chewing tobacco, and a pint of Russian vodka. Tobacco and alcohol were his preferred companions on wilderness trips. All he needed now was to get lost for a little while.

He traced his finger along the map on his lap, followed it north from Lander, and then cut west into the mountains on a dirt road. This road would only be considered a road in a place as reclusive as Wyoming. There was no man made surface of any kind. It was only dirt and matted grass. There were long ruts where rain water had cut into the soil. Here and there were deep pockets where truck tires had spun with all their power to free themselves from the mud. Around these pits new roads were made, alternates to the previous road, that cut up through the sage brush of the front range.

The sky was bright and wide. The rearview mirror held a flat and colorless image that stretched out to the distance of an endless basin. He looked up at the long narrow patches of white clouds, soft intangible conglomerates of water; they seemed to be calm as a lentic pond. Then a large shadow approached low outside the passenger window. He watched it advance and grow larger and more distinct. Over the wind-shield came the giant wingspan of a golden eagle. The wings came low above him, wider than the width of his hood, and he saw the soft filaments of feathers highlighted before the sun-bright sky. It soared gracefully above him as he drove slowly beneath it, until a mild mountain breeze steered it aside.

Higher up the mountain, the road disappeared beneath new growth flowers and wild grass. The sage brush receded into tall trembling aspens. The clouds came closer to his touch. This was a State Forest, so he could get out and venture wherever he pleased. The mountains knew the definition of freedom. They provided a place where he could find his mind.

Further up the mountain, this wild road abutted to the bend of a stream. He got out, stretched his legs, and inhaled the fresh oil-free air. This stream was not on any of his maps, so he decided it was the perfect place to start. He placed his full-brimmed hat on top of his head, tilted up so he could feel the sun on his face. The Duluth pack felt light as he strapped it over his shoulders and walked into the mountains.

The sky was filled by jagged rocks and snowcapped peaks. In the crevasses of these cold mountain heads were long narrow glaciers where the snow hadn't melted for thousands of years. As he continued to walk, the groves of aspen trees receded into rows and rows of staggered pines. He followed the gurgling sound of the meandering stream. The stream transitioned be-tween the slow placid surface of a meadow, and the rough rushing rapids of a tight shoreline.

He came out of the green needles of trees and into the purple flowering lupines of an open field. The river was too bright to look at. This meadow stretched out in a long valley from both sides perpendicular to the stream. In this valley, smaller streams trickled down through the flowers and shrubbery, and joined in a confluence on both sides of the larger stream he navigated. All these waters from the same ocean, from the same sky, from the same mountain, met here and became one again; united in a flowing dimension.

He knelt down and put his hands in the cold flowing water. The empty nymphal skin of a stonefly clung to a rock just above the water line. There were darners and damsels in the air and on the grasses. An opaque cloud of mayflies danced above the water. The surface was perforated with concentric ripples of rising trout. He looked across the river and down the valley.

A dark object made a movement in the distance where the trees met the meadow. He dropped his pack and kicked off his boots to cross the stream. He tried to stay silent and hidden as he walked crouched down through the shrubbery. The object ahead stayed in place. It was large and moved slowly, and appeared to be a moose.

He neared the animal and felt an instant rush of elated shock. Less than a hundred feet away stood the muscular figure of a grizzly bear. The blood pounded in his veins, and he fought against his instinct to run. He knelt down beside a boulder and watched the large beast stand up on its hind legs to sniff the air. The slobbery flare of its nostrils as it inhaled and exhaled could be seen like small geysers erupting from its nose. Then it went down on all fours out of his sight. Ten feet from that one, another bear stood up on its hind legs and smelled the air. There were two of them. He felt the simultaneous jolt of fear and excitement.

These animals could kill him if they wanted to. Out here alone with only the knife on his belt as protection, he wouldn't stand a chance. There was no way he could outrun them if they chose to charge. In that moment he felt a primeval urge to rush at them. An image played behind his eyes of a fierce battle between man and beast. But, in this passage of time, they were magnificent. So wild and free, so brave and fierce, so calm and majestic, everything he wished he could be. The longer he looked, the more profound they became.

He watched as the two bears rotated between standing up as a lookout, and going down to munch on wild herbs and berries. What a team these two made, they must've been brothers. It was not often two adult male grizzlies shared each other's company, but only occasionally if they also shared the same mother. In that case they would often live and hunt together throughout the year, only separated during mating season when each went his own way to look for a little alone time with a female. Multiple females if he was clever and bold.

Eli was fascinated by this image before him. He wanted to get closer, to feel it, to understand. He crouched low in the brush and slowly made his way towards them. He knelt on a boulder less than eighty feet away and watched. The second bear stood just inside the tree line, with only its neck up being visible behind the thick branch of a pine tree. Then it turned and looked directly at Eli. They made eye contact. For a reason he would never understand, he felt completely calm in that moment. He knew he belonged amongst the wild as much as these bears. There was no aggression in those big brown eyes, but instead they appeared as curious about him as he did them. He stayed there and watched that bear until it knelt down, and the other one stood up in return, instantly looking directly at Eli, as if they had communicated his presence.

While he enjoyed this silent conversation with the bears, he also knew it was only a matter of time until they took his position as a threat. He took one last look, and added one more moving picture to the photographic journal of his mind. Then he slipped off the boulder and walked back to his boots and pack. As he continued up the stream and into the trees, he took another look back. They were gone.

The sun now crawled through the western half of its daily passage. Eli boulder hopped the river through a steep canyon. The water was loud in shattering white cascades. The sky was blue and the shadows were long. He continued to climb until the river stretched out before him into a flat and calm pond about an acre in size. At the downstream side of this pond was the semi-functional remains of an old dam, and the stream gushed out through the old and cracked cement.

He climbed around the dam and sat on a boulder beside the pond. Pine trees reflected off the quiescent waters, and he thought of northern Minnesota. He had spent many solitary nights canoeing and camping along remote shorelines, listening to loons in the day, and wolves at night. He wanted to relive that memory. He wanted to touch a place not of this space. He set up camp in a small clearing along the shore where the lupines bloomed in bright purples and blues.

He gathered enough wood to make fire for two nights, and then peeled off his boots and assembled his fly rod. He stepped barefoot into the pond, and let the water soak up to his waist. He peeled out line, and stretched the coils between his hands. The rod swung back behind his head, and he held it there until he felt the tug, then guided the line forward. The caddisfly impression landed in a riffle upstream of the pond. He watched it drift down, hold itself on the surface, and bounce around in the current. As soon as it entered the mouth of the pond, a trout rose and took the fly. Eli fought it gently, and kept it on his line until it was ready to be landed. The sight of a native trout in his hands, held up before the background of mountain peaks, was enough to cleanse his mind of any worries. He continued to fish, and each catch brought him greater satisfaction. After a dozen fish he reeled in his line and returned to camp. He kept two and fried them for dinner.

The molting light glowed on the horizon where darkness wriggled itself free and shook off the sun like the nymphal skin of a mayfly. The magenta sky fell down. Golden embers of fire disappeared into darkness. This was a mysterious world and he wanted to paint it. He wanted to capture it the way he saw it now. He crawled into his tent and fell asleep to the thought that we are all painters of a mysterious world, a world of colors only magic could explain, and viewed only through the prismatic distortion of our own eyes.

• • •

The next morning Eli awoke to the smell of burnt nylon. The sun had baked him inside the tent. For breakfast he mixed instant coffee in a mug with cold stream water, and chewed on a large stick of beef jerky. He stuffed a giant wad of long leaf tobacco into his lip, and sat on a log where the river entered the pond. He felt unnerved by the serenity of this place. There was a calm sense of being home, but the emptiness made it difficult to contain his thoughts. Soon this serenity had escaped him. He was now filled with a sense of loneliness and dispassion. Being alone was no bother to him, but the loneliness of having no one to share his mind with filled him with longing and sorrow.

He sat on that log like a statue of Siddhartha for the entirety of the day. Peace entered his mind but just as quickly was gone. He felt so lost he thought his heart may stop. As a distraction from this anxiety, he walked back to camp and started a fire. The sky had dimmed again. Only when his hands were busy could he forget his mind. He needed to find comfort and control of his thoughts. He needed to form an image from the chaos of his mind. It was dark and the fire crackled. He stepped away from its light and into the shadow of a pine tree. In his hand was a full pint of vodka. He knelt down on one knee and tilted the bottle to his lips.

He stared across the laminar lake which possessed the reflection of the infinity of space. He was cold, shivering, and distant from himself. He was alone in the wilderness, a wilderness that seemed deep and forever, but was surrounded by a world filled with people.

He put the mouth of the bottle to his lips, but it was dry. He stumbled back to his campfire and sat down near the warmth of burning pines. He shivered at the thoughts of his distance from what most would call reality. He looked up into the eternity of the night sky and found solace in the fact that he was but a small chemical reaction stranded on a celestial entity not even visible to these bright mysterious lights surrounding him from above. He found peace with this place, his place in this catastrophe, the magnificent catastrophe of coincidental life.

There had been a definitive void in his life, in his heart, in his mind. It was a void he thought would never be replenished. Then he stared into the emptiness of this pristine fertile landscape, and was filled with a strange and alien sensation; it was peace, it was calmness, it was completely unpredicted joy. He smiled then took a piss on the fire to extinguish it. He laid himself down on the granitic lake shore with his feet in the cold water and fell asleep to a dreamless night. No dreams were required once he encountered true joy.

• • •

He broke camp and hiked out while the sun was high in the sky. The Duluth pack felt heavy as it tore into his shoulders. He paused for a moment in the valley of the bears. There was a wildness inside him; someday he would capture it. Not to be tamed, but to be released. For only by understanding his mind could it be freed.

There was sweat on his brow as he tossed his pack into the passenger door. He turned around with his hands on his waist and stared into the trees. Someday he would have a forest of his own, a place to fill up his emptiness. He now had a purpose to life, an esoteric doctrine, of which he was presently the only disciple. It must be protected from all unworthy invaders.

5

Monday mornings became more dreadful to Eli. He didn't want to go to work, not the working man's work anyways. He'd be perfectly happy putting his hands to work on a painting, an expression of substance, a ticket to eternity if he were to achieve the success of his day dreams. What man does not seek the power of his dreams, and believe in his ability to match the grace of his illusions.

The chair at his desk never felt so uncomfortable. Sure it swiveled and had wheels and a softly padded lumbar section, but today it felt more like a snare than a seat. Outside of the window the sun was bright and the pines in the mountains rose up into the sky as though vines climbing to the source. This view was always the same, and Eli inevitably spent much of his work day staring out the window. But today the view was different, he didn't see the outside world. Images flashed rapidly behind his open eyes. Before he recognized an image, it was gone, and replaced by the next. All he could make out were trees, and what appeared to be a river. The final image he saw, before he blinked his eyes and turned away, was his own face; but it was not the face he knew from the mirror this morning. The face in this image was smiling. It was a wide and proud smile bursting with joy and discovery.

At lunch time his coworkers gathered in the dining area; it was only Mondays, birthdays, or holidays when they all ate together. Eli remained at his desk, oblivious to the fact they had gathered without him. They were invisible to him all day.

"What's going on with Eli?" asked Jared, a fit young Scandinavian who sat in the cubicle across from Eli.

"I swear he hasn't done a single thing all day," said Lana, the administrative assistant.

"Yeah boss, we need to get him going on something," chimed in Ricky.

"I could take him out to the garage and make him do some bench presses," added Blake in a deep macho-man voice.

"I think he must be dealing with some personal issues," replied Clancy. "We've all been there. Let's give him some time to figure it out."

"We've got work to do boss. Shoot, I've already written three glorious *Descriptive Analyses* just this morning," continued Ricky.

"He certainly hasn't been himself the past few days," added Jared contemplatively. "Usually I look over at him and he seems to be hard at work, but lately he just dazes out into space."

"I'm telling you guys, all we need to do is get him out there to pump some weights, that'll get his blood working in his brain again," said Blake flexing his forearms.

"Alright," began Clancy, "if he doesn't come to by tomorrow, I'll take him out on a field run, let him test some new equipment. That always brings us back to focus. Besides, he just wrote a very articulated analysis on that HADR last week, probably needs some mental stimulation to get him going again."

"Yeah, you're probably right boss. You sure know how to manage people." In a world full of broken ladders, Ricky had found one to take him directly to the top.

They all filed back into the office. In passing each one took their turn to look over at Eli sitting silently at his desk. He didn't see them. He didn't hear them. Clancy was the only one to speak. "You have a good lunch Eli?"

It took a moment for him to register these sounds as a question, "Yes," was his stoical response.

"He looks so distraught," whispered Lana, after they passed.

Eli, having now been pulled from his waking dream, walked over to join them. "Sorry I didn't eat with you guys today," he said with a somber face.

"Oh that's alright, everyone needs some space once in a while," reassured Clancy.

"You doing alright there partner?" asked Jared as he patted Eli on the back.

"I don't know what you're waiting for man, I've already got three analyses written just this morning. I'm on a roll and it's only Monday. You need to get on your horse and go," Ricky said with a paternal smile on his face.

So Eli obliged, "Actually, that's the only thing holding me down, there's no way any of us could ever match your merit. You are a man amongst men."

"Why don't we take you outside and pump you up with some curls," said Blake, as he punched him in the shoulder.

"I would, but I'm certain it would only be an embarrassment in your presence. What are you lifting now, two-fifty?"

Blake flexed his arms and made his best Rambo face. Eli stared at the floor as the rest joined in a separate conversation. While they talked they secretly studied Eli, wondering where he was and what had happened to him.

To them he seemed to be consumed by an irreversible, inexplicable sadness. His melancholy expressions and soft brief voice indicated a loss of hope; but they were deceived. Deep down inside he was filled with such an explosive happiness that it took all his will power to hide this behind a straight face. He couldn't let them know how much his life had been filled with joy, how much fulfillment he found in every day, every breath. For if they were to discover his secret happiness, they would inevitably become envious, which would lead them to plot against him, and attempt to manipulate ways to bring him down. They were of the type who could never be happy when in the presence of somebody happier than they were. This was an inherent evil found in most men, and he knew if he wanted to be perceived as *one of the guys,* he was required to restrict his behavior so they would feel secure in their false sense of superiority. What did it really matter? As long as he was aware of his happiness, his confidential confidence, then he could silently laugh at their expense while they puffed their chests and tried to step on him like a stone. His confidence was of such magnitude and structure that he was a stone, nothing could break him, and though he found it funny how they could be so easily fooled into a false sense of superiority, he also found joy in giving it to them, for it is what they needed, what they were missing in life.

And so the weeks rolled on. Every weekday Eli sat at his desk, and occasionally got some work done, while his thoughts were of another paradise. In the evenings and weekends he was entranced by the blank canvases in his basement. He stared for hours waiting for the materialization of his thoughts. In his hand would be a dry paintbrush.

• • •

Then one day it happened. Sitting in his atelier on a Wednesday evening, he popped off the lid from a can of paint for the first time. The image in his mind was fleeting, but he wanted to grab it. For a moment it was his thoughts that were blank and the canvas full. He dipped a narrow bristly brush into the creamy substance. As it made contact with the canvas he felt the minute ridges being blanketed with the color of this single stroke. This moment of euphoria was brief. He stopped painting before a recognizable image had emerged. But this was magnificent! There, on that blank canvas, he had created the beginning of an idea. This was cause enough for celebration.

He searched through the contacts list on his cell phone, looking for someone to call. It had been weeks, perhaps months, a seeming eternity, since he made contact with any acquaintance. Had he become the hermit so soon in life? He dialed a number.

"Good evening Eli," said a scraggly voice with a French accent after recognizing Eli's number on caller ID.

"Pierre, long time no see. How ya been?"

"The days are mostly the same, which in my case is fantastic. And yourself?"

"Just been living the dream. Or perhaps in a dream," he laughed. "Have you still been doing the chess club thing?"

"When time does permit. I believe you have not made an appearance in quite some time. They're a boring old bunch of self-congratulatory imbeciles without you."

"I doubt that. I was thinking about getting a game in tonight. Got any plans?"

"That sounds intriguing, but unfortunately I am consumed with work this evening."

"Ah, no worries, some other time then."

"Of course. Now that you mention it, I'm putting on a presentation this weekend, may not be as stimulating as a good game of chess, but if you should care to participate, I could send you the proper invitation."

"Oh yeah? I'll have to see."

"Tell you what, I will take liberty to place your name on the list, if you make it excellent, if not, that shall be your loss."

"Sounds good."

"Until next time then."

"Alright." Eli hung up the phone and paced around the room. Should he try someone else? Perhaps he should stay home and continue to paint. Of all the gifts he was given in life, single moments were the easiest one to waste. Occasionally though, as those moments of waste went fleeting beneath his feet, enigmatic beauties were revealed, unnoticeable to the observant eye, only discovered when he felt lost.

6

May we know hope. May we know love. May we hold them, protect them from any external forces, and carry them tightly in our arms as we walk these dark deceptive passages.

• • •

Beneath the dim lights of a city night, a young woman exited the glass doors of a downtown office building. A brown leather brief case dangled from the strap around her shoulder. She pulled her long black hair out from under her coat and ran her fingernails across her scalp, and then shook her head to clear her thoughts. She locked the door behind her, then turned around and took a deep breath of the cool evening air. Before taking a step further, she fumbled through her purse and pulled out a cigarette. As she brought the lighter towards her face, a young man approached and said, "Here, let me get that for you," as he flicked the mechanism on his gold-plated Zippo and ignited her cigarette.

"Thanks," she said, and raised her blue eyes towards his face. The smile she saw there seemed to be suspended like a great banner in the sky that read *I am happiness.* Forcing her eyes from his face, she quickly took in his appearance. He wore a black suit with a blue tie, which seemed normal enough to her, but then she noticed his perfectly creased slacks tucked into dirty cowboy boots with pointed brass toes, and this seemed odd enough to warrant her curiosity. He continued to stare at her with that giant banner of a smile on his face, which made her knees feel drawn in towards each other. She smiled at him and pulled the zipper up tight on her long coat, and then turned to go. He gently placed his hand on her arm and said, "Don't I know you? You look very familiar to me."

"Sorry, but I don't think so," she said, turning towards him again.

"Oh I am certain that I recognize you. Stick tight a moment and I'll figure it out."

She studied his face and gently tapped her feet on the cracked cement. It was often difficult for her to determine whether a man was trying to seduce her, or just being friendly. She impatiently fumbled through her briefcase, looking for an excuse to leave. Then with big eyes he continued, "That's it, I saw you in that article in *Mountain Life Magazine*, the one about trying to create wildlife sanctuaries on private lands."

She was simultaneously embarrassed and impressed. Embarrassed because this was her first project that provided a public audience, which meant if she succeeded her career would finally start to feel substantial, like she was making a difference, but if she failed, well, she tried not to think about that possibility. Impressed because it seemed most people were too disconnected with actual environmental issues to read an article about the subject, let alone recognize her from one small picture in a local publication. "Yes, you are correct," she answered, while zipping up her briefcase and leaning forward.

"Forgive me, but I can't seem to remember your name. I'm Beau," he reached out with his right hand.

"Oh," she said hesitantly, "I'm Lamara," and shook his hand while her eyes diverted to a car passing on the street.

"There's nothing to be ashamed of, Laura." Lamara cringed slightly at his misuse of her name, but shook it off, as it seemed more people forgot it than remembered. Then Beau, whose eyes were still locked on her, continued, "As a hunter who is also concerned with wildlife conservation, I found that article to be very engaging. It sounds like quite the project to be involved with."

"Yes, well, that is part of our mission, to establish a balance between wildlife populations and human hunting patterns that will ensure sustainability for both into the future."

"That sounds very interesting. I bet you've got a lot of stories to tell on the subject." He looked up at the writing on the door she had exited, *Wyoming Collective of Environmental Engineers*. "You're not just getting off work are you?"

"Actually yes," she sighed, "ever since this project started, I've been working lots of long days."

"Sounds hectic," he said with a smile. "Tell ya what, you look like you could use a break, why don't you let me buy you a drink? I'd be very interested to hear more about this project of yours."

"Oh that sounds nice, but the last thing I want to think about right now is work."

"Alright, I'm sure we can find a million other things to talk about then."

Lamara took a drag from her cigarette and shuffled her feet away from him. "Sorry, not tonight. It's just been a long day."

"I understand. Maybe some other time then?"

"Sure, that would be nice," she replied, as she turned away.

"Laura," he said, placing his hand gently on her shoulder, "if you don't mind, I'm going to need your phone number so we can make this happen."

"Oh," she flicked the ash off her cigarette and stared at him a moment. He may not be the most intellectual man she's ever met – as she often judged a man's intelligence by whether or not he remembered her name – but at least he was handsome. "Certainly. As long as you promise not to ask me about work." She pulled out a business card from her briefcase and handed it to him.

"Maybe we'll talk about the ocean instead."

"The ocean?"

"Yes. I find that being land locked here in Wyoming, talking about the ocean provides a good mental escape. Don't get me wrong, I love Wyoming, lived here my whole life, but talking about faraway places fills me with an exotic sense of mystery."

Lamara smiled. She wanted to touch his hand again. She wanted to change her mind and go sit with him right now and hear everything he has to say. "I actually used to live near the ocean," she replied.

"That so? I suppose you'll be perfect company for me. I'll give you a call sometime." He turned and walked away.

• • •

The next morning Lamara entered her office and sat down behind the L-shaped desk. She sank into the cushiony leather chair and started drumming her fingernails on the oak surface beside the keyboard. Today was going to be a good day. She heard a knock at the door, followed by her secretary entering with a cup of coffee and a bagel.

"Good morning Lamara, how are you today?"

"I'm good. You can set those down over there. Has anyone from the Audubon Society called yet?"

"Yes, a man with a French accent called only a couple minutes ago. I think his name was Jacque Pierre."

"Excellent. Did he leave a message?"

"All he said was that he was calling to verify your lunch meeting at noon."

"Perfect. It will be a big break for us if we can get him to support this project."

"Well, for what it's worth, he sounded excited."

"Thanks Megan."

After the door shut, Lamara began researching this Jacque Pierre fellow who she would meet for the first time today. It had always been her belief you could never get an accurate definition of a person just by meeting them face to face, and asking too many questions made you appear vulnerable, so it was best to go into a meeting with as much knowledge about a person as possible. Luckily for her, the internet was filled with insightful information.

Her chin was pressed firmly into her sweaty palm as she leaned forward in her chair to study the data on the monitor. Jacque Pierre Cristo, born and raised in the French countryside near the Jura plateau, became fascinated with the cycles of life throughout geological timelines after his uncle gave him a copy of *Le Règne Animal* by Georges Cuvier. This passion remained strong into his adult life when he earned his PhD at the Imperial College of London. As a professional Paleontologist who now worked with the University of Wyoming, he has been featured in several highly acclaimed Paleolithic and Archaeological studies, been instrumental in developing high school level paleontology programs, participates in annual international fossil hunts, and was being considered for a video documentary funded by the *Fame and Fossil Magazine.*

Lamara leaned back in her chair, folded her hands behind her head, and tried to take it all in. She didn't feel qualified to sit down for lunch with a man of such esteem, let alone become a professional colleague of his. Then she thought of her own career; she had always been elevated above her peers, and admired as someone destined for success. Just last week she met the governor of Wyoming. He called her up personally and invited her to a conference on wildlife sustainability. She walked right up and shook his hand, and he looked her in the eyes and said he supported her work. It was great living in Wyoming, a state with such large magnificent landscapes that still had a small tight knit community. She could rise to the top of her field, right where she belonged.

Lamara parked her car outside the Sri Lanka Plateau and stuffed her cigarette into the overflowing ashtray. This restaurant was the first Indian cuisine establishment in Casper. The grand opening wasn't until tomorrow night, but she knew the owner, and convinced him she would spread good reviews if he could help her impress a colleague. She entered the tinted glass doorway and was seated at a table with a card folded on the center that read *Reserved VIP* in bold red ink. This seemed unnecessary, since they would be the only ones here, but she decided to leave it as a prop to impress this Mr. Cristo.

As Lamara sipped a green tea and read the menu, the door opened, and Jacque Pierre entered. She held her breath as he approached. All the pictures of him on the internet made him look so professional and demure, but here in person he appeared to be torn from the pages of some handsome comic book. He walked with gaiety and lightness, yet his eyes were focused and unyielding. He pulled a chair out from the table and simultaneously said, "It pleases me greatly that this city finally gets some culture".

Lamara felt a tacit moment uncommon to her loquacious tongue as she studied his face. He had long crinkly gray hair and a shaggy gray beard, both of which betrayed the youthful characteristics of his skin and voice. She cleared her throat and responded, "Yes, I've always been a fan of Indian cuisine."

"Yes, that also," he said, placing his hands firmly on the table and looking around the room.

"Excuse me?" asked Lamara, unsure what he was implying.

"Of course it is a pleasure to dine on foreign foods, that's not exactly the culture I was referring to. I was thinking on my way over here that with Wyoming being the Equality State, there certainly doesn't seem to be many influential women around. You are the culture I was referring to."

"Oh," she looked away as her throat swelled with a swallowed smile.

"There's no reason to be embarrassed. Please, let me try this again," he reached a hand across the table, "you may call me Pierre."

Her hand felt small in his warm grip, "Lamara. Thanks for meeting with me."

"My pleasure Lamara. Now tell me, I am curious about this project of yours, but what is it I can do to help?"

"That's simple. So simple I can answer with just one word. Reputability."

"I see," he used a fork to scrape sand out from under his thumb nail, "actually I'm not quite certain what you mean."

"Let me explain; as I'm sure you're aware, one of the favorite pastimes in Wyoming is big game hunting. Not only is it a pastime, but it also plays a significant role in the local economy. My goal is to provide more habitat for wildlife sanctuaries, which I believe in the long run will enhance this state's hunting resources."

"I understand. You know, and forgive me for speaking bluntly, but you're likely to piss off a lot of hunters by the very use of such words as sanctuary. Wyoming is a wild place and people are defensive against any form of regulation."

"I agree, but I think with the proper planning and support we can help them realize this project will be beneficial. Lots of these people we're talking about have been hunting on the same land their great grandfather's hunted, and both the land and the animals have experienced relatively minimal impact from anthropogenic activities. But that's not going to last forever, and nobody wants to think about arriving at their favorite hunting spot to find a diminished population of game. But that's the way it's going to be if we don't take proactive measures. It's happened to almost every other state, and Wyoming certainly isn't immune."

"That's very interesting. I'm personally not a hunter, so I hope my opinion doesn't come across as biased, but aren't there other reasons to protect wildlife than just for hunting?"

"Of course, but that's the angle that will have greatest impact on most people here. My biggest concern pursuing this issue is to not come across as anti-hunting, which I'm not. In fact, I am impressed by any method employed towards self-sustainability, but I think the present system is going to fail unless we do something about it."

"What is it you plan to do?"

"We want to develop a collaboration of private land owners with significant acreage to adopt a no hunting policy on their property. So much of this state is public lands that there are very few areas for wildlife to find sanctuary. Even a large percentage of private land owners currently allow people to hunt their property. If we could get several of them from each region of the state to agree to this plan, it would provide safe breeding and growing grounds for wildlife, without having any negative impact on the populations of those areas open to hunting."

"Sounds like an admirable plan. What is it you would like me to do?"

"The National Audubon Society is a highly reputable organization, all we want is your support."

"You must know in advance I am in no position to offer any financial support."

"Of course. We only ask for public endorsement."

"I see," he rubbed his hand over a small brass Buddha statue sitting on the table. "So you would print out fliers that say this program is supported by the National Audubon Society?"

"Something along those lines."

"Well, you've convinced me," he reached his hand across the table again.

Lamara wiped the sweat from her palm and shook his hand, and then said with a smile, "I appreciate this greatly Pierre."

"As I said, my pleasure. Shall we eat?" he finished as the waiter placed their food on the table.

"This looks really good."

"So Lamara, tell me, what does a woman like you do for entertainment around here?" he asked, while tearing a piece of naan in two and stuffing one half into his mouth.

"I'm too busy for all that," she waved a hand in front of her face like swatting at a fly.

"Certainly you must have an avocation?" his mouth was full of food, yet somehow his speech was perfectly clear.

"I do enjoy taking long drives through the prairies and up the mountains, if that counts."

"Have you driven east of town, toward the Rochelle Hills?"

"Not yet, I haven't lived here that long though."

"It's some of the most prehistoric landscape I've ever seen. The earth itself looks like the dried and cracked skin of a Jurassic beast," he leaned forward. "What I'm about to tell you is in confidence, but I'm presently working on a dig out there, the type of dig that could make a career."

"It seems like your career has already been made," she instantly pinched her lips together and looked away. With a smile on her face she brought her eyes back to him and said, "I mean you present yourself like someone who has had some success."

"There's no need to be embarrassed about doing your research. Believe me, I read all about you before coming here. I must say, you have a most impressive dossier. It is with this in mind I would like to invite you out to the excavation site with me, if you'd have any interest in that sort of adventure?" She took a large drink from her tea and the skin on her face became taut. "It would be strictly professional, I assure you," he finished.

"That sounds like fun. I do enjoy adventure," she felt her breath getting weak.

"Perfect. I will be presenting an oratory for the Audubon Society this Saturday at the library. I will put your name on the VIP list so we can make arrangements."

"I think I can make it."

"Of course. Now if you'll excuse me, I must be getting back to work."

Lamara looked at his plate still covered with food. "Have a good weekend." She stayed in her seat as Pierre nodded graciously and walked out the door. "Strictly professional," she said out loud, "I wonder if he meant that."

• • •

The next day Lamara decided to take a drive. Country music played loud, and she thought about her drive to Wyoming when she moved here. She traveled alone, with nothing but a few boxes, a chair, an eclectic selection of music, and a carton of cigarettes in her small hybrid car. She felt proud of herself for being able to pack up and leave a life that caused her more pain than pleasure.

Lamara followed her nomadic heart to Wyoming less than a year ago. When anyone asked her the reason for moving to this remote state, she told them it was for the job. But that's not the real reason. Life can chase us, or life can guide us, it depends on the point of view we take. When she left her home centered between the Gulf of Mexico and the Atlantic Ocean, she felt like life was chasing her away. Shortly after arriving in Wyoming, she realized life had guided her here. The wide open grandeur allowed her the space to grow into the woman she always believed herself capable of becoming. Here she had a job with a future in a community she adored, and also enough distance from her past to allow the space for individuality. If ever she became stressed with memories of the past, she took a drive out of town, and within minutes was surrounded by a vast emptiness, emptiness like a vacuum, a vacuum capable of sucking out all the unwanted noise in her mind, and leaving only the tranquility to see the world around her.

So she often drove through the high desert, towards the endless horizon, imagining how powerful that distance would feel if she were a traveler in the days past, making this voyage with horse and carriage. She longed for adventure, and believed time would give her everything she wanted. On the horizon she saw through eternity, and it erupted with beauty.

A herd of antelope rushed across the gravel road in front of her. She pulled over and exited the car to watch them pass. They seemed so free and majestic, so wild yet organized. This was their land, they belonged to it long before these gravel roads boxed in the landscape. It was her goal to help them survive as undisturbed as possible in this machine made world. She lit a cigarette and watched the smoke get swept away by the fierce Wyoming wind.

7

Lamara arrived at the old brick library and walked into the
banquet hall. Jacque Pierre Cristo stood behind a podium
and looked suave and nonchalant. He wore khaki shorts and a
t-shirt beneath a tie and blazer, as he gave a presentation which
included a discourse about a fossil hunt he recently returned
from in Tanzania. His discourse was accompanied by a slide
show of the landscape there, the holes they had dug, the local
people who had helped, along with a showcase of the fossils he
had found; look but do not touch.

The slideshow impressed her greatly, so much she considered
approaching Pierre to arrange a date for attending the fossil hunt
he'd mentioned. She began to plan her approach, but nerves took
control of her body, so she started outside to smoke a cigarette
and collect her thoughts. As she turned to go, she spotted a man
standing in the corner who made her stop in her tracks. He wore
a button up shirt with sleek hair and looked more or less like everyone else. Except for his eyes. His eyes darted around the room,
and at first glance she thought he appeared nervous, but after
watching him for a while, she got the impression he was being
studious, as if he were cataloging all the details in this room. She
decided to stay and watch him from the corner of her eye.

• • •

Eli stood in a corner and watched his friend Pierre speak to the crowd. Pierre was a charismatic man, and had total control of his audience. Eli's eyes darted around the room as he wondered what everyone else was thinking. His hands were tucked deep into his pockets. Then a sudden burst of dissonance struck him like an electric charge, and he realized this was not where he belonged, he should be at home trying to paint, this crowd impeded upon his thoughts, and infiltrated him with unwanted influence. He started to make his way towards the exit, but noticed a woman standing in the crowd who made him stop in his footsteps. Everyone else in the room seemed to be paused like statues or minions wearing concrete shoes, but she was elevated. Her hair looked soft and her eyes were bright, but there was a greater force that radiated from an unknown depth. He stopped paying attention to the presentation, or worrying what others were thinking, and started watching her from the corner of his eyes.

Their eyes met across a room filled with people pretending to know what a *Crocodylus anthropophagus* was, and, like any fairy-tale cliché, the connection was instantaneous. Eli considered his options for displaying that aggressiveness which all women adored, without portraying a sense of desperation that all women despised. This was not as easy as it sounded, for desperation was often the cause of aggression, but such was the paradox of women's wants. The paradox that drove him insane. The paradox that kept his heart pounding and his feet moving. The paradox that made his world spin.

Was he desperate? Yes. Wasn't everyone here desperate for the attainment of that which they seek? It seemed curious to him how he could only obtain that which he seeks at a specific position on his desperation timeline. When his desperation was young, it was all consuming, only focused on what it wanted, not what it deserved. Young desperation was likely to go on romantic tirades pouring out volumes of agony and pride from his bleeding heart. He had not known what a heart break was, yet he would yell and scream of his broken heart as if it could never be healed unless it got what it wanted right now. He knew if desperation became old, without finding fulfillment, it would become a lacuna of emotion, seemingly empty because he had been forced to hide his desires even from himself. Old desperation would be the most dangerous of all because it had lost the most. It would be a manifestation of lost dreams. It would be a broken heart that had gained the wisdom to understand what a broken heart was. The entire spectrum of desperation was likely to produce aggressive behavior, but it was only at that ultra-fine precipice where he could understand his desperation and aggressiveness, and utilize this knowledge to obtain what he seeks.

So he approached her slowly, made his way through the crowd, and tried not to seem obvious. She watched him from the corner of her eye, and smiled as she realized his intentions, but hid her smile from him so as not to seem obvious. She looked at him as though he were somebody she had always known. Eli saw this in her eyes, and for a moment his feet felt suspended in their slow moving steps. Somehow she seemed to already understand him. Lamara quickly looked away, not to hide this fact from him, but from herself.

When he got within arm's reach of her he stopped, slightly behind and to her right side. He tried to untangle his thoughts of failed first encounters from the past. Then he looked at her again. She was like a painting, paused in perfection and surrounded by chaos. Instantly all concerns of his past washed away like chalk markings on the sidewalk after a heavy rain. He seeped through the passages towards her.

True love causes amnesia. She looked back at him and smiled. Her eyes froze him, but it was the most sweat drenching frost he'd ever known. Then she took the smallest possible step towards him with her tiny little feet, attempting to illustrate a mutual interest, except her shoe was untied, and she stumbled, unintentionally falling towards him. He caught her by the hand, held her for the longest micro-second that has ever occurred in this world or any other, then helped her to stand back up. That random touch created a synergy of souls. Everything went calm inside.

"So do you like fossils, or did you just come here for the free food?" he asked, unable to look directly at her.

"I just think science is cool. There's food?"

"Oh yeah, steak, potatoes, cookies, and bottled water. Afterwards we're all going outside to bury the T-bones in the yard for future Paleontologists to discover."

"That's funny," she said, with more of a smirk than a laugh, "I've often wondered what future scientists would think about this era of mankind. I mean, imagine if all of technology got completely destroyed, that means all of our electronic documentation would be wiped out also. Say if it was like a sort of apocalypse, and only a few hundred people survived in the world. It would take hundreds of years to repopulate the earth, right?" Without waiting for a response she continued, "Now imagine this new population would inevitably have its own form of science, and these new scientists would inevitably discover the occasional scattered remnant from our era. Imagine if they found, oh I don't know, say a CD or DVD, and not having the appropriate media player, and having never seen one of these shiny little discs before, they would undoubtedly be perplexed," she was having fun with her elaboration.

"I know what you mean," he responded, trying to keep her beat and defeat the paralysis of his tongue. "They'd probably come up with some paranormal explanation about how aliens or gods left this indecipherable tablet of knowledge for them to discover. I mean, this future society would no doubt have the instrumentation to break down this CD or DVD to its basic elemental composition, if there are scientists anyways, and they'd see it was made of this earth, or a meticulously reorganized composition thereof. However, if they are anything like today's, or even yesterday's scientists, they would believe that if their collective abilities are unable to invent something like this, then it must be impossible for man to achieve," he exhaled deeply, trying to catch his breath up to his thoughts.

"I don't know if I share your same skepticism towards scientists," she replied, trying her best to sound argumentative, "wasn't it Albert Einstein who said, 'To raise new questions, new possibilities, to regard old problems from a new angle, requires creative imagination and marks real advance in science,' or something like that anyways," she blushed at her ability to retain a quote.

"Yes, but I've always considered Einstein more of a philosopher than a scientist, it's just that his outlet for philosophy was through a scientific alley. Besides, didn't he also say, very philosophically I might add, that, 'Gravitation is not responsible for people falling in love,'" as he gave her a subtle wink.

"Oh, is that what you think happened? I assure you, I fell by complete accident."

"I believe you did, but that doesn't change the power gravity had on the moment."

She laughed. Beaten and she knew it. He knew it too. Nothing more needed to be said. They watched the rest of the presentation in silence, then left together, already closer than any other two people who had arrived together.

They stepped into the early hours of a vernal evening. "So," he reached over and placed his hand gently on her lower back, "do you have any plans after this?"

"Yes, as a matter of fact I do," she said, tilting her head up in the air while smirking at him.

"Oh," he said, turning his head and pretending to feel the rejection she was pretending to give.

"I'm going to see a concert actually."

"Oh yeah? Which one?"

"One of my favorite bands, *Murder by Death*."

"*Murder by Death*? That sounds like a death metal band, I didn't really take you for a head banger. Not that I'm saying there's anything wrong with head banging, people's music selections are their own business. I once knew this guy who was a diehard death metal fan, even played in a few small time bands, he was actually pretty good. My point is that just knowing him you wouldn't suspect he was into that kind of music, he was so calm and pacifistic. Sometimes it seems like our music selections are the opposite of our behavior, like if our minds are calm and sincere we need the external stimuli of something aggressive to fuel us through life; and inversely, if our minds are dangerous and explosive we may require soft soothing music to balance us out."

"Which one are you," she asked with lowering eyes.

"Oh I've generally got one foot on each side of the line."

She smiled, "Well that's all very interesting, but they're not actually a death metal band."

"I stand corrected. Wasn't *Murder by Death* a classic movie or something?"

"Not that I'm aware of."

"Yeah I'm quite sure, think it had Truman Capote and Alec Guinness as a matter of fact. It was a regular who-done-it, very similar to that board game *Clue*."

"I believe you, I guess I just don't know how they got their name, but they're a really good band, full of dark emotional lyrics and storytelling. Ooh and they've got this great Cellist named Sarah who's absolutely amazing. They're so lively and intense, I absolutely love their music."

"Sounds like you're gonna have a good time then."

"I know I will, this will be the third time I've seen them live. They always play in small venues, I guess because they've still got the luxury of not being mainstream, and I love that because the small venues are so much more personal, which you really need with musicians who are also great lyricists."

"Well we've got that in common. I mean, I've never been too much into going to concerts, but when it comes to my music selection, I generally prefer a band with good lyrics. My favorite right now is this Irish folk band from Germany singing in English. They're called the *Bushbury Mountain Daredevils*."

"Never heard of them, but sounds interesting."

"Maybe I'll get you a copy of their CD. Just don't go burying it in the name of science." He gave her a wink and she smiled.

"Why don't you come with me? We'll have a blast, maybe I'll even help you change your mind about not liking to go to concerts," she paused for a moment, feeling like maybe she was being too aggressive. It wasn't her style to invite a man she just met out to an entertaining evening. "I mean, if you want to see a good show, and expand your repertoire of music."

"That's always a good thing. What time does it start?"

"About an hour. I know, it's very short notice, you don't have to go or anything, I was just making a suggestion."

"I'll go. Where is it?"

"Actually it's pretty cool; they're playing in this big old barn just outside of city limits."

"Sounds like it could get rowdy, I'm in. Tell ya what, why don't we meet outside the downtown movie theatre in forty minutes, then we can ride together."

"Actually I was going straight there, so if you need to go home first or anything, we could just meet there."

"Alright, where is it?"

She gave him directions, then drove home to change and get ready. She stood in her bedroom with a cigarette burning between her fingers, and picked up clothes from a pile on the floor, smelled them and held them up in front of a mirror, then tossed them onto another pile. She dug through a stack of books and magazines accumulated on her laundry basket. She cursed herself for this lack of organization in her personal life. She wanted to look pretty for him. She picked out an outfit that said sexy and sophisticated, then hurried out the door to beat him to the show.

Eli ran into his house, removed the button up shirt he saved for intellectual events, and put on a plain white t-shirt with faded blue jeans. He wore a black and brown worn out fedora, sprayed on cologne, then looked into the mirror thinking he appeared aesthetic and brave, and hoped this would be the side of him she saw and admired. Most men have more faces than a mirror could ever reveal. He rushed out the door, hoping to have time to buy her a drink before the music started.

Eli drove up the two-track ranch road towards the giant rustic wooden barn in the middle of a sage brush field. There were over two-hundred cars parked at varying angles surrounding the barn. A crowd of young adults flowed into the large open barn doors, and each individual was dressed in attire that made them feel like the coolest one there. They were all rock stars, ready to live vicariously through the music of those who had actually accomplished the goal. That goal was to obtain the idolatry of strangers. That goal was to say, "Look at me, I have something to share, something to say that you will understand. I can give you an answer, or make you forget about your search for answers". Music was delirium, it was a vessel they could ride to escape the passage of time.

Eli stepped from his truck onto the sandy sage brush, removed the wad of chewing tobacco from his lip, and then looked west across that eternal vacuum of open grandeur. In the distance he saw a coyote gallivanting through the fading light. He imagined the silence of being here alone, hearing the coyotes sing, and he wondered if their songs served the same purpose as the ones he was about to hear inside this barn surrounded by strangers and searching for love. He wanted to cross that civilized boundary which confined him to artificial expressions such as clothes and merchandise. He wanted to escape the tangled jungle of societal restrictions. He wanted to be free enough to run through the open field and know the joys of this wild coyote.

He took another look at the glowing plateau of the distant horizon, then paid his toll and entered the barn. Eli stood near the entrance and prepared to search for her through the chaos of loud music and bouncing bodies. His eyes wandered through the crowd while he thought these people were such curious entities, nobody seemed to be themselves here. We are all lost, he thought, more so when in a crowd than while alone. He was surprised when he saw her standing near the entrance, only twenty feet away, waiting for him before disappearing into the frenzied mob.

"There you are," she said as he approached, "I was hoping you'd get here early enough for us to get a good spot on the dance floor."

She looked like an iridescent bouquet glowing in the dark, wearing a purple dress with pink and blue and yellow flowers, surrounded by people in blacks and grays. "You look great," he said, "like a star through a telescope."

"Thanks," she said, looking down and shifting her feet on the loose dirt and scattered hay.

"I thought you said you were coming straight here?"

"Well I spilled a coffee on my shirt so I had to stop home and change quick." A little white lie shouldn't hurt him, not yet anyway.

"I see, good choice. Think we have time to go get a drink before the music starts?"

"Sure, I don't really drink too much, but I will if you promise to dance with me afterwards."

"I don't really dance too much, but I will if you have a drink with me first."

"Okay, should we go to the bar?"

"Come on," he said, and grabbed her hand to guide her through the crowd. As they walked, he turned to her and said, "I haven't gotten your name yet, I understand if you want to retain the mystery, but I need something to call you by."

"My name's Lamara."

"Lamara? Well, very unique name for a very unique woman. I'm Eli"

"Eli, a very majestic name for a very majestic man."

"I suppose so. What do you want to drink?" he asked her as they sat on a stack of hay bales set around a horse trough with a plank across it acting as the bar.

"Oh, whatever you're having will work."

"Two whiskey sours then," he said to the bartender, a young woman who wore pink cowboy boots, chaps, a denim jean jacket, and a straw cowboy hat. "This is a pretty cool place for a show," he said turning towards Lamara.

"Yes, very clever," she shifted her feet, wishing she could light a cigarette, but not sure if he would take offense. "So, you said earlier that you didn't go to many concerts, why is that?"

"Well, in a crowd we are all strangers, and while surrounded by strangers we can be nothing but strange. I mean, everyone, including myself, puts on this persona. To be comfortable in a crowd we all have to be the same, regardless of how much pretending or self-sacrifice is required." For comfort he rubbed his fingers around the can of chewing tobacco stuffed in his sock above the ankle. Most Wyoming women he met weren't disgusted by a man spitting snuff, but he didn't want to take that risk – Lamara seemed more refined.

"Yeah, I agree, that's true. But what's wrong with pretending to be someone else once in a while? Aren't we all strangers even to ourselves, so if all it takes is wearing a disguise to find ourselves, shouldn't we just go with it?"

"Maybe. But why can't we be allowed to know ourselves and then be ourselves?"

"Perhaps we're all afraid of our own boring lives."

"I'm not boring," he said, and smiled with a radiance that made her believe it, "and you definitely don't seem boring."

"I don't know then," she said, trying to change the subject, "I guess we'll just have to agree to disagree for now."

"How about we disagree to agree?"

"Are you always so difficult?" she asked with a smile that was simultaneously playful and scolding.

"I like watching you squirm, and hearing you think."

The band was midway into their first song, and the dance floor erupted with flailing arms and screams of thrill. "If you like watching me squirm so much, why don't you take me out to the dance floor?"

"Let's go then," he said, and grabbed her hand to lead her to the dancing mob. It was a fast galvanic song, so they stood side by side in the crowd, jumped up and down, waved their hands in the air, felt the electricity, and screamed obscure tones as loud as they could. Eli watched the crowd with curious eyes as he tried to fit in, ashamed at his participation in such conforming behavior. They all seemed so strange and so desperate. We are all such precious distortions of our idols, he thought. He did enjoy the band though. The loud music and exhilarating energy filled him with something, he just wasn't sure what it was.

The next song played and Lamara moved closer. Her entire body vibrated. She grabbed him by the hands, jumped up and down, and spun around in front of him. She danced like a rattlesnake as she twirled her hips into a coil and then slithered towards the sky. He looked into her face and saw her joy. Her eyes pierced into him like fangs full of venom. He forgot about the rest of the room, about the confusion of trying to understand the actions of strangers, and found himself dancing carelessly in this place of elation. They stayed on the dance floor until their bodies were exhausted and their clothes were drenched in sweat and spilled drinks.

"Let's get another drink," proposed Eli, as they fought their way through the forest of tangled bodies still lost in the music. "Two more whiskey sours barmaid," he exclaimed boisterously, feeling more alive than he had in a long time.

"You really seemed to enjoy yourself out there," said Lamara, smiling and taking a sip from her straw.

"Yeah, I didn't realize concerts could be so much fun," he replied, pulling out the bent straw and pouring the whiskey into his open throat.

"And that dance you were doing, what was that?"

"What do you mean?"

"It was wild, I dare say comical, like a monkey jumping for pineapples while being beaten on the head with a rubber mallet," she said and placed her hand on his shoulder with a laugh.

He replied magnanimously, "Yeah, but you just wait, next concert you go to everyone will be trying to imitate what you saw perfected first hand tonight."

"Are you always so arrogant?"

"Only when I'm trying to hide my modesty."

"Okay," she said, "but seriously, it looked like you were having fun. I've never seen someone dance with so much energy. It's like there's a demon inside of you you're trying to kick out. Do you have a demon?" she asked with narrow eyes and a wry smile.

Eli dodged the question, and responded, "You were dancing like a woman just freed from the asylum."

Lamara tilted her head quizzically, cocked her eyebrows in contemplation, and then decided to take it as a compliment. She began to reach for a pack of cigarettes in her purse, but then played it off by pulling out some cash and offering to pay for the next round of drinks.

The band played through their last song, while Lamara and Eli remained seated on the bale of hay, and slowly enjoyed their last drink. "Oh, looks like everyone's leaving, guess we should get out of here," said Lamara.

"Yeah, let's drink a water and chill out for a minute, I've already got one DUI, don't want another."

"You've got a DUI?"

"Yeah, well, I wasn't always this well behaved model of outstanding citizenship."

She laughed, and then scooted closer to him. They sat together on that bale of hay and watched the strangers who no longer seemed so strange disperse through the wooden barn doors. They waited in silence, leaned upon each other's weight, comfortable and full of dreams.

"You folks got to get leaving now," said a large man in a tight black t-shirt.

"Alright, here we go," said Eli to Lamara.

"Okay. Wait, let me buy you a copy of their CD before we leave." She stopped at the table in the corner and made her purchase. "Here, something for you to remember tonight by."

"Thanks. Hey listen, what are you doing after this?"

She hesitated. She saw the lust in his eyes and was taken aback. But she also noticed something more in his voice, it sounded like longing filled with compassion, so she replied, "Didn't really have any plans."

"Well," he said, climbing out onto a wavering limb reaching for a fruit, "it's still fairly early, want to come by and listen to this CD with me?"

"Yes," she couldn't believe she was agreeing, "I mean, yeah, that sounds like it could be fun I suppose."

"Excellent," he nodded, "why don't you follow me."

"Actually, since you've already got a DUI, why don't you ride with me?"

"Are you sure? If I'm over the legal limit, than you certainly must be."

"Oh that's alright, I'm a girl, if I get pulled over my breasts will get me out of it," she sat down behind the wheel and quickly shut the overflowing ash tray before he got in.

"Sounds like a pretty cool trick, I almost hope we get pulled over now," he said, stepping into her passenger door.

• • •

Eli opened his unlocked front door and allowed Lamara to enter first. She gazed around the dimly lit room, noticed cobwebs on the ceiling and wads of dog hair that seemed to grow from the carpet. "Do you have a dog?" she asked.

"Yep, a malamute, he's probably out back."

"What's his name?"

"Snowy," he replied. She stood with her hands in her back pockets and her shoulders pulled in tight. "Go ahead and make yourself at home, I'll get some music started." Eli grabbed the two-liter soda bottle that was half-filled with tobacco spit from its normal spot on his desk, and hid it behind the couch.

Lamara stepped in further and noticed homemade plywood bookshelves lining an entire wall, filled with titles and pages that would take a lifetime to read. It reminded her of childhood and long afternoons of reading with her father. She continued to study the rooms as he searched for a CD player. The bedroom door was opened so she peeked in; the clothes were all neatly folded in piles on the floor, but in place of a bed was a pile of sleeping bags with an old dirty camp pillow. The simplicity of this appealed to her, most men would be embarrassed to show a woman they just met their bedroom if there wasn't even a bed. She walked downstairs into a single room. Wood laminate paneling hung loosely off the walls above a cracked cement floor. Paint cans and brushes surrounded a pile of virgin white canvases. Only one canvas had a small indecipherable smudge of paint on it. She wanted to ask him more about that room than the books, but decided not to get too personal tonight.

"I can't seem to find my CD player," said Eli as she returned upstairs, "but we can listen to it on my computer, though the speakers are almost inaudible."

"Oh that's okay, we already heard all those songs tonight. Got any wine?"

"I have vodka and Tang."

• • •

Eli awoke and saw Lamara gathering her clothes from the floor of his bedroom. A smile flashed across his face when he saw her tuck a pack of cigarettes into her purse. He watched her quietly until she was dressed, then said, "Leaving so soon, I expected at least a homemade breakfast.""I'm sorry, I have to go," she said nervously, fretfully pulling on her shoes.

"Is something wrong?"

"No. No nothing's wrong. Except that I just slept with a man who I knew for less than six hours."

"Oh that's alright, it's not like we were drunk. We're perfectly respectable consenting adults. At least, I wasn't drunk. Were you?"

"No I wasn't drunk," she retorted, "I've just never done this before. I'm sure that's what everybody says, but I actually haven't."

"I believe you," and for some reason he did, even though he had heard it from other women, he never believed them, knew they only felt obligated to say it, but with Lamara, he sensed something in her that left no doubt of her continence.

"I know you do," she said, obviously still uncomfortable.

"Listen," he said, standing up and covering himself with the pillow, "you don't have to rush out of here, that will only make it feel like you made a mistake. Let's go get some breakfast."

"Oh, I don't know."

"Come on, I know this place that makes the most amazing strawberry pancakes, I'll even buy you a latte."

She smiled, "I suppose a little breakfast wouldn't seem too peccant."

"I don't believe any girl who ever used a word like peccant could possibly be thought peccable."

"Okay. Let me drop you off at your car first, then I will follow you."

When they got in her car, Eli removed the can of chewing tobacco from his sock and snapped it loudly in his hand to pack the contents. "Care for a dip?" he asked with a smile.

"No thanks, I've heard that stuff is bad for you."

"Probably, but so is any habit worthy of your time. You won't be disturbed if I take a pinch, will you?"

"No, I suppose not. It's just that I recently quit smoking."

"Okay," he chuckled, "I don't want to lead you astray. You wouldn't like this stuff anyways, tastes like dry dirt that's been wetted with cat piss," he opened the lid and stuffed a pinch into his lower lip.

Lamara laughed, "I'm glad to see you have good taste."

• • •

From that day forward they were companions, like two great words that shared the same meaning. Each with their own unique application, and individual definition, but forever bonded by an inherent similitude, a desire for elucidation, the joy of knowing they were not alone.

To make up for lost time, the time before they knew each other, the time while they were waiting for each other, they now moved very fast, not wasting any of the time that time would steal away as it continuously delivered more time and time and time. In six months they lived together, happily in a bright yellow house, on the corner lot of two busy streets, in the most civilized city of the most uncivilized state left in the union.

8

True love causes amnesia. Eli no longer went to work and stared out the window. He no longer used his time on the clock for far away pursuits of a different happiness. He forgot about the pile of canvases and paint that waited beneath a tarp in the corner of their garage. He forgot the single brush stroke across that illimitable white canvas, and the pleasure he received from watching a completely unique creation form from his own hands. Perhaps these sensations still lived somewhere in his mind, but such was the case with amnesia. It all still existed in that matrix of synapses, those sinuous circuits of thought, but it was out of reach, like a misplaced code or map, and required a catalyst to retrieve what had never truly been lost.

Having Lamara in his life filled him with a sense of completion, an ability to procure his place in eternity, an opportunity to fulfill the American Dream. He went to work filled with ambition, completed task upon task, and asked for more. He went home in the early evenings with a long self-made to-do-list, and ninety-nine times out of a hundred, it was all checked off before nightfall.

Lamara too had found a state of secure happiness in their simple life together. She loved to come home from work and see Eli fast at some task. To watch him busy filled her with pride. She enjoyed most of all spending her evenings preparing a magnificent feast, and sitting silently, patiently, across the table, awaiting his compliments of her cookery. She imagined them growing old together, and often giggled to herself at a preconceived notion of him becoming an ornery old man. Their thinning white hair and wrinkly skin would become the definition of a long splendid life together. She was completely happy sharing her life with him exactly as it was now: simple.

After the daily chores were completed, they sat together in the living room, on their micro-fiber furnishings, surrounded by elegant décor, in the glow of an iron cast wood stove, and shared their experiences of the day. These conversations quickly became multi-faceted, branching off into topics neither of them had prepared for, topics neither of them had ever discussed with another human being. There was so much mystery in their minds and it could only be shared in the company of comfort.

Then they retired to the bedroom, sprawled their bodies across the king-sized pillow top mattress, covered in a soft exotic fur, turned on the bedside chandelier, and indulged themselves in fine literature. And that was the standard routine of a typical weekday. They were both happy and could settle in to living like this forever. They only longed for the weekends.

Friday nights were generally spent engaged in a social event of some fashionable kind. Friday nights were Lamara's night to plan. She made phone calls and sent text messages and emails to the sophisticated circles of Casper's elite. And then, upon determining where the spot was to be, whether a downtown restaurant with a gourmet menu and well dressed waitresses, a neon bright cocktail lounge with elegant glassware and marble counters, in the backyard of some classic brick house amongst a fabulous garden with song birds and particolored butterflies, or on occasion in the comfort of their own home where they would prepare a bonfire in their backyard and large coolers filled with drinks, she and Eli then dressed themselves for the occasion, and prepared their wit for an entertaining evening.

Whatever location was selected, when they arrived they were promptly engulfed in a gregarious harmony. There were imported beers, aged red wines, and decorative glass bottles filled with every conceivable potion known to modern man. Everyone wore fashionable attire, button up shirts, slacks, and shining shoes on the men; a slightly revealing skirt or blouse, with colorful heels and blinding necklaces on the women.

The crowd roared with laughter and excitement. The conversation flowed like a mountain stream with the turbulence of politics, the velocity of changing times, the pocket water of economics, the violent cascades of military activities, the erosive shoreline of environmental concerns, and the tranquility of the arts.

Eli had never found himself amongst such a vivacious crowd. Like all new things, he was inspired by the unexplored dimensions. These people all seemed wonderfully amazing to him, like aliens. He knew they were of a foreign species from himself, but he whittled his self out of the equation, and enjoyed the crowd through similar eyes. Perhaps the others felt this as well, this sense of being disconnected from the moment they were engaged in. Not only from the moment, but also from themselves who engaged it.

During the occasional interlude between passing conversations, Eli stared into the sky, or at a neon light, or watched the movement of a woman's feet, and wondered to himself, "What am I doing here?" For in his happiness with Lamara, his pleasure of making her happy, and his enjoyment of exploring these new dimensions and new people, he was lost, this was not his home. His home was a place with no light switches, cultivated plants, name brand clothing, or talk of politics. His home was a place so isolated and remote even he had never lived there. But the crowd roared on. He tumbled along with curious ears.

Perhaps this is how they were born to be, strangers swirled into a friendly mosaic, with nobody lonely and infinity for all. Then he saw them here in their natural state, illuminated beneath a grandiose light, where even the divine stars shed their clothes and revealed themselves to mortal men. And the glory of existence carried them away into that ceaseless universe of twirling clocks. There, in that delirium, was happiness.

But not for Eli. Despite all his efforts for compatibility, despite all his efforts to laugh when he could find no humor, despite all his efforts to be amazed by the self-congratulatory smiles and stories of victory, despite all his efforts to be impressed by the fables of their lives, all he could feel was distance. All he could see was a lacuna, that empty air which existed in the lungs of domesticated men. They were all choking on the toxicity of their own minds. Their minds told them this life was not their own. This life was not the one designed for this body and soul. The truth of existence was a happiness separated from the easy happy life. There was music in the forest. There was clean air where nobody could hear him breathe.

So on Saturdays Eli planned their events. They slept in until the sounds of motor engines and car horns woke them, and dragged them out of their basement bedroom. Lamara then prepared a large salty breakfast with fresh juices to get them lively for an adventure. During this time Eli flipped through maps and planned their destination. After the eating was finished, Lamara filled a cooler with ice and food and drink, while Eli got all the camping and fishing gear in order. There was excitement in the air every Saturday morning with the anticipation of a new adventure.

"Where dost thy wind blow us today, Captain Eli?" Lamara asked with the dialect of a sea mate once they had taken to the road.

"Today, dear lady companion, we go to Moose Creek Canyon."

"I don't think you've ever mentioned that one before? Sounds exciting. Think I'll finally see a moose?"

"I went there once the first summer I lived here, great fishing and lots of Elk tracks, but I never saw a moose then. Doesn't mean we won't today."

"I hope we see a moose, seems like everyone else in Wyoming has seen one but me."

"They are magnificent creatures. I'm sure it's only due time until you cross the path of one."

"I hope so. How far do we go?"

"It's actually pretty close, only about an hour and a half drive to get there."

"If it's so close, won't there be other people?"

"Not likely. Though it's not a far drive, it's well off the beaten path. The last forty-five minutes we will be driving at idle speed over a bumpy two-track ranch road."

"So is it on private land or something?"

"Nope, but there's an easement through private land to get there. Not many people know about it."

"Good. If it's so close, I suppose I'll just read some poetry while you drive, and save my novel until we get there."

"You may want to put the books away until later, the drive's going to be quite amazing, and once we get there we should go for a hike, see if we can find you a moose."

"Sounds good, I can always read later."

• • •

They exited the freeway and drove down a long dirt road headed for the mountains. On both sides of the road were wide open fields where antelope and horses, mule deer and long-horned cattle, all grazed together in the afternoon sun. This road was as winding as the meandering stream they paralleled. Up ahead they saw the deep incision of a canyon on the face of a mountain.

Eli stopped in front of a barbwire fence, and Lamara got out to open the gate. Instantly she was filled with the fresh aromas of sage brush and wild flowers. The sun beamed down on her radiant face with a mild heat. She swung open the gate and stared into the mountain. What was this place? Through what magical portal had life transplanted her here?

Eli pulled through the gate and smiled at her happiness. There was so much serenity in her relaxed shoulders and raised brows. What more could a sane man want? He had a good job, a happy woman, a mountain range, and a trout stream. He could live happily like this and die of old age as a fulfilled man.

As Lamara passed the front of the truck and began to enter the passenger door, everything paused for just an instant. In that microcosm of time Eli saw everything around him; the blinding sun pasted upon a clear blue sky, the shadows of the trees in the mountain, the shadow of the mountain on the prairie, the glistening water rushing around a boulder, the colors, oh so many colors, and all of these shapes and sizes and depths. It all stood still for him to admire, to capture with a single gasp of breath. As she entered the vehicle, Eli made a single arc with an invisible paintbrush across the windshield, and then drove on.

They reached the downstream side of the canyon where the track ended. They stepped outside to stretch and were both filled with a sense of relief. There was not another vehicle, or person, or manmade anything in sight. They were alone to let their lives breathe.

They carried their gear and hiked into the canyon. Along the way they saw the perfect imprint of a mountain lion paw in the sandy shore of the stream. Cliff swallows flew low over the river to gather emerging mayflies. The trout too partook in this feast, and rose to the surface in a vicious display only performed where anglers' hooks seldom touched the water. They made camp at a flat and sandy clearing along the river.

"Do you want to hike upstream with me?" Eli asked.

"Aren't you going to fish?" she responded, since it was usually his custom to take his rod directly to the river after setting camp.

"I thought we could hike up a ways together, then I will fish my way back down after you return."

"Sounds good to me."

Eli put on his fishing vest and walked with his rod and reel in hand. Lamara carried a set of binoculars and a water canteen. They walked along the stream shore through the canyon, through the tangling bushes and over the boulders and water logs. Eli focused on the river with anticipation of catching a trout, while Lamara stopped to view any unrecognizable shape through her binoculars hoping for a moose.

After about two miles, Eli knelt down on a boulder above a riffle. His eyes glazed over with the reflection of the stream. Without a word, Lamara knew this was where he would fish, meaning she would walk back to camp and read a book until he returned. After a few long moments of speculation, Eli tied a parachute-hackle mayfly onto his tippet, then made a delicate cast to the downstream side of a large boulder along the left edge of water. These clandestine trout had the bravery of ignorance where few men ever fished. On that first cast, just before his slack line caught the velocity of the riffle, a trout rose and violently took the artificial fly. Eli raised his rod to tighten the line and set the hook. The fish leapt from the water like a dazzling rainbow silhouette, landed mid-stream, and rushed up against the current. Eli let out line as required, and followed it upstream, stumbling over submerged boulders in the process.

He caught up to the fish in a deep pool where it held to the bottom. He circled around and got in parallel to it. Then he used the rod and forced the fish upstream about ten feet and got directly behind it. Now he raised his rod tip and lifted the fish, then placed his net beneath the water to capture it as it drifted down. He held that magnificent wild creature in both hands, and raised it to the sun to watch it glisten. He removed the hook and placed the fish beneath the air-clear water and watched it swim powerfully from his grasp.

He returned to shore and sat on a boulder to replay the event through his mind. He looked around and saw no other eyes to witness; it was just him and the fish, the way it should be. Just then he heard Lamara scream from somewhere between him and camp. He thought of the mountain lion track. He shouldn't have left her alone; people get killed by mountain lions and never found, only scattered fragments of bones and clothing picked up by the occasional wandering man. He ran towards her, and called out her name in desperation.

When he reached her he was taken aback, for there she stood, holding a large stick in her hand like a sword, swinging it at a bush while cursing under her breath. "What's going on?" he asked with a quizzical grin on his face.

"There's a damn big rattlesnake in here somewhere, it was following me down the trail and hissing its pointed tongue and rattling its tail at me."

"Oh," he said, "I do remember seeing a few last time I was here, suppose I should have warned you."

"Yeah you should've warned me! This thing was huge, like four feet, and it was nearly at my heels before I heard it."

"That's exciting," he said, but she looked upset. "You must have startled it, they don't generally follow people."

"He's just lucky I didn't have a gun, I would have blown its head off."

"Yeah," Eli chuckled, "maybe you should head back to camp now, I'm sure he's run off."

"Do you think there's any more?"

"Probably. Just stick to the way we took up here and keep that stick in your hand. If you hear one again walk faster, they're not going to chase you."

"Alright, I guess I'll be waiting at camp for you then."

He waited and watched her leave. Damn fine woman, he thought, she stood there to fight rather than run in fear. She sure could give him a hard time if she ever chose to. It was difficult to believe she was the same woman he danced with who wore a flowery dress and talked of music on their first date. That unknown depth of people was their most amazing quality. The place which remained hidden from the untrained eye. Only patience and fairness would ever allow him to discover it.

Eli returned to the river and paused for a moment midstream. His feet were balanced upon uneven stones. The current tumbled around him. The canyon walls were steep and jagged and solid. The colors beneath the surface stirred and glittered. He wanted to hold his face under water and breathe in their beauty. He dipped his fingers into the snow-cold transient texture and felt a tingle. He closed his eyes to see this sensation clearly. He breathed. He put his hand up to his face and felt the freshness enter his soul. Water droplets dripped from his skin and returned to the river. He opened his eyes as if they were separate from his body, separate from the tension of life, distant from any distraction. He breathed.

He fished the river all the way back to camp, and caught more trout than he cared to count. The sun was descending beyond the canyon wall. Long shadows crept across the river. A beaver paddled in midstream, and it gave a loud splash with its tail before continuing downstream away from Eli. He entered the river to cross towards camp. There sat Lamara, swamped in a fading light. Killdeer weaved low through the air. He stepped upon dry land, and tried to hide his smile at the perfection of a day. Before he could speak, Lamara looked up from a book, and said with her own joyous smile, "I had the most amazing walk back. I decided to loop around and go halfway up the canyon wall. From there I looked out and saw the entire basin, I never knew my eyes could see so far. Then as I walked back down, a bald eagle came and spread out its wings right above me. It was so amazing. Can we stay right here forever?"

Eli looked around him. They were at the bottom of a deep scar in the landscape, hidden from all judgments of men, protected from the misperceiving eyes of strangers. The shadows started to climb up the canyon to the east, as the sun descended to the west. He let her see his smile.

"So, how was your day?" she asked him.

"I can die happy," he responded.

After a few moments of rest, Eli stood up and asked Lamara if she were ready for a fire. As was their custom, Eli went in search of firewood, while Lamara collected a small bundle of kindling and began the fire. She was great at this task; never had Eli trusted a woman with starting a fire. This was generally a man's task, though he knew not why. It must have remained from the ages when women seldom accompanied men into the dangerous mountains. Even today, most men thought it was their right of manhood to be the supplier of fire, and their pride was noticeably damaged if a woman could perform the same task. Not so with Eli, he enjoyed letting her do it, simply because she enjoyed it so much. She was such a well-rounded woman: professional at work, compassionate at home, and handy at camp. It amazed him just to watch her. He often thought it would have been a pleasant spectacle to have seen her as a child, to watch and know the events that developed her into this amazing woman. But, ironically as it seemed, the knowledge of such events would have stolen away from the mystery required for love.

Lamara retrieved a cigarette from the pack in her shirt pocket, then set fire to it with the glowing tip of a log. She pulled the smoke deep into her lungs, and gazed passionately at the early stars above. The smoke from her cigarette slowly swirled up into the low sky, and became one with the smoke from the fire, like a vine clinging to a royal oak.

"I thought you quit smoking?" said Eli, as he popped the cork off a bottle of champagne.

"Sort of, but sometimes it just feels so right."

"I understand," he said, and poured them each a paper cup full of champagne.

They sat beneath a dark sky. The glowing fire mesmerized them and abducted their thoughts. The gibbous moon peaked out above the canyon. In the distance of that long prairie a band of coyotes yapped their mournful tune. Eli spit a wad of tobacco juice on the fire and listened to it sizzle. In the proximal distance Lamara spoke, but it took him a moment to pull himself from thought and hear her.

"This is really truly perfect, Eli. I mean, ever since I was a little girl and first read *Little House on the Prairie*, this is the life I imagined."

"That's very romantic. We're not exactly in the prairie though," his voice was callous, always slightly irritated at being pulled from his thoughts.

"I know, I know. It's not the exact place so much as it is the freedom. Just being in nature and living however we choose, that's what it's about."

This rang true to Eli. He often dreamt of a life in the deep forest, where there were no artificial responsibilities such as mowing the yard, or dressing respectable, or paying unnecessary bills, or faking kindness to people he despised. A place where there was nothing but the trees and animals and a river. A place where he could find peace. A place where he would be able to unleash the caged canvases and paints from their garage dwelling, and allow them to absorb the beauty of this world, the wonder of his mind. He replied, "I think we share the same dream."

"Well, is it a dream we can make come true someday?"

"I hope so," he said, and stared towards the twilit river. He imagined the splendor of taking her to live in a remote wilderness. He saw her becoming a great naturalist, roaming the woods with her binoculars and camera, learning the cycles of every green and woody, or legged and furry, living thing. Then he considered the price it would cost to make this happen. He knew they didn't have the money, that it would take years to acquire a savings capable of making them self-sufficient.

"So, are we going to make it happen, or is it just going to be one of those dreams everybody has but never follows through on?"

"It would be great, but also very difficult," he said, not wanting to sound negative, but also not wanting to give life to a hope that may be unattainable.

"We wouldn't have to do it for the rest of our lives you know. All I want is to be able to take a year off of work and live in nature before I am too old to enjoy it."

This sounded more plausible to him. A single year. How much would that cost? What provisions were necessary? Where would they live? "I think we can do that. First of all we have to decide where we want to go."

"Where doesn't really matter to me. We could live at a campground and I'd be happy."

"Oh we can do better than that," he thought a moment. "Have you ever been to northern Minnesota?"

"No," she said with curious hesitation.

"Well, if we were to stay in Wyoming, it would be difficult. For starters, we're not going to live at a campground. I suggest we either live out on state land somewhere, which Wyoming does have a lot of, or buy our own piece of land where no one can interfere with our plans. The problem with state land is then you have to obey their regulations, primarily the problem for us would be they only allow you to camp in one place for up to fourteen days. And buying any kind of land we would want to live on in Wyoming is going to be way out of our price range."

"Alright, so tell me about northern Minnesota."

"For starters, there are so many lakes and rivers up there that Minnesota has more total shoreline than Florida, California, and Hawaii all combined. You can hear loons singing in the day, and wolves howling at night. There are more trees up there than people in this country."

"How's the fishing?" she asked, smiling at him.

"The fishing is great," he said with glowing eyes. "Much different than here. As far as trout streams are concerned, it's difficult to beat Wyoming. There are a lot of other opportunities though. I've always wanted to catch a muskie on a fly rod." He imagined those powerful jaws attacking his fly, that strong tail straining his forearm in a long ferocious battle.

"It sounds absolutely wonderful," she said.

"Yeah," he said, realizing it really did, "but how are we going to do it?"

"We could use our savings as a down payment on some land for starters."

"Okay, but then we're going to have to build up enough savings to support ourselves for a year. That means we're going to need to enforce frugality."

"Frugality?"

"Yep, total frugality."

"Alright. We'll also need some extra money for after the adventure, in case it takes us a little while to find new jobs."

"Alright," he said, "let's figure this out."

They sat near the fire and conversed until the moon crossed beyond the other side of the canyon. Eli stood up occasionally to poke the fire and toss on a log. There was no tiring in either pair of eyes. All that existed was excitement.

They came to the conclusion they needed ten-thousand dollars saved for a deposit on land, and also to cover land loan payments for a year. They required fifteen-thousand to live off of, used primarily for gas to fuel the car twice a month to go purchase groceries and incidentals. They also needed another five-thousand as a buffer to move back into civilization. Thirty-thousand dollars total. That sounded like a lot of money, but they already had eight or nine thousand saved between them.

As with the realization of any dream, it must be pursued as soon as possible, so the power of it doesn't fade. They decided in one year, if the money was in order, they would embark on this adventure. They fell asleep as the shadows sunk on the western wall of the canyon.

9

Barely a word was spoken the next morning as they broke camp and hiked out of the canyon. They both lived in a mind of illusions. Illusions were not always confined to the imagination, sometimes they were attainable, and could be manifested through proper planning.

During the drive home, Lamara reached over and put her hand on Eli's lap, then broke the silence and said, "We're really going to do this, right?"

"Absolutely."

She appreciated his short and simple answers most, for she learned during her time with him this meant his mind was occupied with the development of a stratagem. She rode along in peaceful silence. Eli gripped the steering wheel with one firm hand, the other was placed gently on Lamara's thigh.

Once home they immediately initiated frugality. They canceled the internet, movies-by-mail plan, and reduced their cell phones to basic minimal service. There would be no more dining out with friends on Friday nights. Their weekly camping trips got reduced to once a month. Lunches could not be spent on fast food, but would consist of leftovers from the home cooked meal the previous night.

Entertainment and luxuries were all reduced. Their lifestyle was simplified, and probably much healthier. Saturdays were now spent at the library, where they used the free internet services, and checked out movies and books to get them through the week. Their friends stopped contacting them. They began to feel the distance, the isolation, the freedom.

They had a yard sale and tried to sell all their possessions, everything except the essential fundamentals. Everything that wasn't sold was then donated. This included their clothes, that entire wardrobe of fabrics and materials collected throughout the years as a representation of their personality. They only kept what was necessary for work, and for camping. With the money from the sale they purchased more camping supplies.

They moved into a smaller house with lower rent that saved them three-hundred and fifty dollars a month. It was a moldy-brown single-story one-bedroom box, but it had a kitchen, a functional toilet, and a bathtub. There was a small fenced in backyard with a single car garage.

"At least there's a yard for Snowy," said Lamara, trying to sound optimistic.

"Yeah, it sure is small though." Eli knelt down by their dog, who appeared a little confused about his new location, and anxiously ran in and out of every room. "Someday you'll have an entire forest to explore buddy." Then he stood up and removed the can of chewing tobacco from his sock. He snapped it between his fingers and stared off into the distance. He was still snapping it when he realized Lamara watched him. "Why are you looking at me like that?" he asked.

"You've been snapping that thing for over two minutes, I think it should be ready."

"Oh," he said, and looked down at his hand as if surprised by what it held. "You're probably right." He looked off into the distance again, and then returned his eyes to the can of chew. "I suppose if we are going to be faithful to frugality, we should probably quit our tobacco habits."

"Really?"

"I know, I enjoy it too, but it isn't necessary. With the money we spend every week on tobacco, we could probably afford to eat for a month."

"That's a good point. So are we just going to quit?"

Eli snapped the can between his fingers one more time, and then tossed it into the garbage bin. "Done."

"Okay, if you're sure about this." Lamara removed the pack of cigarettes from her purse, and tossed them into the garbage. "So long old friend."

• • •

That spring they drove to northern Minnesota. The snow melted a couple weeks prior, so the rivers were high and the trees had just begun to bud. They had a map marked with half a dozen properties they would explore. The first four were no good, either the ground was too wet, or the land was too close to loud manmade noise.

They wanted a property with enough seclusion to be left alone, and provided the belief they were the only humans in the land. This property should be within ten miles of a grocery store, so the gas bill wouldn't become outrageous when they needed supplies. They wanted trees, animals, and water frontage. All of this they found at their fifth destination.

They pulled down a two-track driveway into the deep woods. Along the way they saw fresh wolf scat and deer tracks. They parked and got out. The air was calm. There were wildflowers in bloom. The trees were tall and the forest was thick. Though there was a paved county road only a mile away, they couldn't hear a sound, for the thick forest wall created a buffer between them and the manmade noises they wished to escape. They walked into the woods.

Lamara sauntered slowly, knelt down to admire a leaf or flower or berry, called out the names of those she knew, and pondered studiously those she didn't. Eli moved gently through the forest as he watched the ground for animal tracks, and anxiously awaited a view of the river.

After a half mile of bushwhacking, they came to the river's edge. It was placid and quiet, with a surface so calm, that if they hadn't known it was a river, it could easily have been mistaken for a long and narrow lake. The trees crowded over the water, which created the illusion of replicates rising from that fluvial world below. This river was a *Scenic State Canoe Route*, so there would be no motorized boats, minimal public access, and regulations that prevented any manmade structure being built within sight from the river. More importantly to Eli, this river had muskie. The elusive fish of ten-thousand casts. The monster of the north. The barracuda of fresh water.

They stood together at a small clearing along the river, beneath the sprawling shade of an old growth cedar, and looked into each other's eyes. Not a word needed to be spoken. This was the spot they dreamed of. They walked back up to the truck where Eli turned on his cell phone to call the real estate agent. There was no reception here, so they drove back out onto the county road. About a mile down a single bar of service appeared. Eli stopped and made the call. After he hung up, he turned to Lamara and said, "He's not going to be able to meet us until tomorrow morning. I suppose we should check out the last property, just in case."

"I agree, though this one does seem perfect," she was so happy, it appeared she never wanted to leave.

"Just to be sure," he said, already knowing this one would be impossible to beat.

Eli put the truck in gear and drove another two hours to the last property on their list. This place was a picturesque landscape that could have been the cover for a scenic magazine. It was on a large lake speckled with islands. There were giant towering pines, with little undergrowth, which allowed an expansive view that reminded him of the mountains. They sat on a boulder along the shoreline and watched a pair of loons diving and flapping their wings. They talked of paddling the waters in a canoe, stopping off to explore an island, and spending many long days just listening to the gentle waves.

Then Lamara noticed something on the far shore. "Does that look like a section of clear cutting to you?"

Eli strained his eyes across the reflective lake. "I think you're right." Then they heard the loud reverberations of a timber truck as it jostled its way down the road. Nothing else needed to be said. They drove away.

That night they camped on a sandy lake shore. Wolves howled beneath the giant pearl moon. The fire smelled of wilderness as it transformed the pine logs into smoke and ash and gas. It was a cool and starry night, but the tent was warm stuffed full of sleeping bags.

The next morning they met the realtor and put in an offer. By that afternoon the seller had agreed. They went to the bank where they had already been preapproved through mail. After making the deposit, they left with a pamphlet of payment vouchers in the glove box, and wildness in their eyes. They were now landowners. The dream was materializing.

"Hello landowner," said Lamara, as Eli put the truck in gear.

"How do you feel, landowner?" replied Eli with a smile.

"Happy."

10

It was a long drive west through the nocturnal tranquility of the high plains. As the sun rose they saw the crest of mountains sketched above the horizon. The highway provided an optical illusion – the mountains looked so close, but it took hours for them to grow beyond the breadth of the windshield. Upon returning to their house in Casper, they settled into a greater degree of frugality. No more ordering pizza delivery on Sunday afternoons, which had become their one culinary debauch. No more bottles of wine on Friday nights to sip in their backyard. No more gourmet spices or high end meats. They could only purchase the generic brand of groceries. They eliminated everything that made them contemporary Americans. But, they couldn't eliminate their single camping trip per month; that was a prerequisite for the adventure.

Their lives may have seemed empty to the onlooker – being void of superfluous possessions, rarely any interaction with friends, and most of their time being spent inside the house – but their minds were filled with another life, a life that possessed them more than they possessed it. These thoughts were so monumental, of such power, that on occasion they needed a vacation from thoughts of their vacation.

They agreed to each be allowed one cheat day per month, to do whatever they pleased, within a very restrictive budget. Lamara generally spent her day at a coffee shop, where she read internet blogs, and enjoyed some good people watching. She truly was fascinated by people. She had the ability to look at a person, and conjure up entertaining stories about their past, and who they were today. On other occasions she called up a girlfriend, and they would meet at a social lounge to sip bottles of wine in a garrulous fashion.

None of her friends understood her new plans. They admired the romance of it all, meeting a complex young man who wanted to take her into the woods, but they worried she hadn't fully thought it through. They reminded her of all her hard work and effort to attain an advanced college degree, and to rise to the elevated position in her career. It seemed preposterous that she would throw it all away just to become a recluse – she had too much potential, too much to offer society.

She tried to ignore them, and reminded them it was only temporary, that it had always been a dream of hers to live in nature. But the more doubts she heard, the more questions she had for herself. What if they moved into the woods togeth-er, and Eli fell out of love with her? What if all the dirt and insects and wild animals became too much to take? What if the time spent away from work tainted her good reputation, and she had to take a job at Walmart afterwards just to get by? What if there was some horrific accident, and they didn't have health insurance? These thoughts all seemed so real and omnipotent, and dampened her spirit. But then she thought of their land, and the look on Eli's face when he first saw the river, and she tried to hold this happiness more powerful than her doubts.

• • •

Eli generally spent his cheat day fishing. He often found himself in the effervescence of a peaceful river, and some days spent more time ruminating on the shoreline than actual-ly trying to catch a fish. On one particular autumn day, he returned in the evening from an afternoon at the river, and found Lamara in the kitchen warming a dish of homemade la-sagna. The smell of spices scattered across the kitchen count-er opened his mind. He peeled his wet wading boots from his feet, his hands were filled with that aroma of the viridity of sage brush. He pulled the full brim fishing hat from his brow, and tossed it onto the couch.

"How was the fishing?" she asked, while stirring the contents of her frying pan.

"I would rather be outside waist deep in water not catching fish, than inside the house on a couch watching television and not catching fish."

Lamara laughed, "It was that good huh?"

"Hard to beat a day on the river. Unless of course it was a day on our very own river." It had become their custom to remind each other verbally that each still thought of the land and living there. For at as great a distance from it as they were, and being consumed with the monotony of daily life, it was easy to get preoccupied with the present life, and wonder if the other still remembered the same dream.

"I was just thinking of our property," replied Lamara. "Do you think we'll have moose there?"

"There's lots of moose up in those woods."

"I can't wait to get back there. Sometimes I get stressed at work, and then come home and worry about losing my job and my friends, or that I've already lost them, but then I think of the property, and our plans, and how wonderful it will be. Then I am happy again."

"We've sure got a good thing going," he said, as he sat down to dinner. The crashing clanging growling rumble of traffic poured through the window. Oh that silence of a stream, where had it gone, and why gone so soon? As Eli held his fork in his hand he became hesitant. A force much stronger than the sight of food pulled at his senses. He got up and walked outside. In the background he heard Lamara saying, "What are you doing?"

He opened up the garage door and stepped inside. It was cool in there. It was like a dungeon. His painting supplies were in the corner beneath a tarp. He wondered why he had imprisoned his imagination in the dark so long.

He threw back the tarp and shuffled through the boards of canvas. He found the one with the single brush stroke. His heart paused as he ran his fingers gently over the smooth dry paint that always maintained a cool wet texture. He thought of his day on the river, but the image was colorless, it was too simple and alone offered him no expression. He picked up a paint brush and held it in his hand. This world was of a malleable concoction; all he had to do was redefine it.

Inside Lamara had finished her dinner and put Eli's dish in the refrigerator. She looked out the backyard window and saw the garage door open. She knew what he must be doing in there. She never asked him about the painting supplies she first saw in the basement of his bachelor pad. She pretended not to notice when he secretively transported them here and packed them away in the garage. She knew he had an aesthetic soul. There was no reason for her to pry into the side of him he wanted to keep private.

In the basement she grabbed a book off of a shelf without even noticing the title. She flipped on the lamp and rolled into bed fully clothed with her shoes still on. The blankets were folded between her chest and elbows. On her lap was a book she gripped firmly with both hands. She flipped the book over on her lap and then looked out the bedroom doorway towards the stairs. A long shadow descended from the kitchen light above. The only sound was the dog breathing at the foot of the bed. She rolled over onto her belly and laid the book upon the pillow, then forced her eyes across the words. The back of her ear began to itch, and her legs felt like running. She tossed the book from her hands and watched it collide with a wall where it fell open on the carpet. She turned off the bedside lamp and squeezed her eyes tightly together and tried to hold them there.

• • •

Late in the evening, Lamara clung to the pillow as though it were a life raft floating on a freezing ocean. Her eyes were open but it was too dark to see anything. Then the backdoor opened, and the stairs creaked beneath the weight of footsteps. Eli slid in quietly beneath the covers, thinking she was asleep. Lamara rolled over and put her head on his shoulders.

"I thought you were asleep," he whispered.

"You know I can never fall asleep without you."

The urge to ask was never more powerful, but she restrained herself. She understood his unspoken longings. She often noticed the way he seemed to disappear, just for a moment, as if fully enraptured by some image no other eyes could see. She put her hand on his, and caressed his fingers, secretly feeling for dried paint. There was none. She knew he needed privacy if he were to ever fulfill this longing. For only in the company of himself could he truly explore his thoughts. They slept the night without a stir.

• • •

Lamara sat in her office at work the next day when a co-worker came in for a chat. She spun her chair around and greeted Krin with a smile. "Good morning Krin, those are very lovely shoes," she said, realizing Krin intentionally drew attention to her feet.

"Why thank you lady friend," replied Krin with a shake of her hips and a tilt of her head. "Me and my husband went down to Denver over the weekend, he took me shopping. Oh how I love shopping in the big city, it seems so glamorous, like starlight in the daytime."

"Sounds like you had a lovely trip. I haven't been down to the big city in so long," she gazed off a second, "seems like I haven't been anywhere in so long."

"Actually, I wanted to ask you about that. Me and my husband have been wondering why we never see you and Eli around town anymore?"

"Oh you know how it is, just get busy with things around the house and never find the time."

"Ooh, I know what that means," said Krin with a mischievous grin, "sounds like someone's getting lots of loving. You guys trying to make babies yet?"

"Oh no, that's not it," replied Lamara blushing. "Actually, we've been planning the purchase of supplies for our property," she added, and then turned to her computer and opened a picture of their river and the trees.

"That looks really nice. I think we'll buy property someday," said Krin, developing a magniloquent tone. "Of course we'll probably have kids first, but then later on it would be great to have a weekend retreat, someplace where we can invite all our friends out and throw big parties. Everybody who's anybody around here owns land."

"Yeah, well that sounds great, but it's not really our plan. We'll probably just build a cabin and use it as a vacation spot, then maybe retire there someday." Lamara felt slightly apprehensive at her ability to distort the truth, but it was in the proximity of truth, and it was all she could tell her coworkers yet.

"Alright, well I'd better get back to work. Want to grab lunch?"

"Not today, sorry, I've got too much work to do."

"Okay girly, you guys should really get out more, we all miss hanging with you two." Krin left, and closed the door behind her.

During her lunch break, Lamara did a job search for openings in northern Minnesota. She hadn't made up her mind yet, and was only curious about what may be available. It amazed her how many well-paying jobs were posted in her field. She narrowed her search to those within a one-hundred mile radius of their property.

She pulled closer to her desk, and leaned in towards the monitor. The city of Beltrami had a listing for a Parks & Recreation Department Manager. She clicked on the link that brought her to a page with all the job specifications. There were eight city parks, three of them on lakeshore properties, and one on the Mississippi River near the headwaters. The pay was a bit less, but she would oversee an office of eight employees, and still be involved with preserving a segment of the outdoors. She leaned back in her chair and put her feet on the desk.

She looked around her office and saw the folder that contained documents for the *Wildlife Sanctuaries on Private Land* project. If she followed it through, this accomplishment would enhance her career. Not only that, but she believed the project mattered, that it truly helped preserve wildlife populations. She sighed as she thumbed through the papers. It would take at least two more years for something like this to be completed, which until recently never seemed like a long time.

A new search for the city of Beltrami brought up images of tall pine trees, quiescent lakes, loons, moose, wolves, and fish. This was all very attractive to her, but they already owned wilderness property. If she were to take a new job in a new city, give up the life she had here, and make a revision to their plans, it had to be in a place with some culture.

She clicked on a link for the chamber of commerce. In a city of twenty-five thousand people, which seemed large for that part of the state, there was a university, a technical college, a multitude of art galleries, live performance theatres, a local winery, and plenty of coffee shops to warm her thoughts on cold winter days. As best as she could figure, it was winter eight months a year up there. She saved the link for the job posting in her computer favorites, and then considered how to present the idea to Eli.

• • •

Eli was at work trying to complete a task his boss asked him to have finished the previous day. The more money in their savings account, and the closer they came to deciding a leave date, the more difficult it was for him to focus at work. He still got his assignments completed, though occasionally a day or two late, but he still maintained the high standard of quality his boss expected from him. It was not easy, because his mind had created a life of its own, and this created life was slowly devouring his real one.

At every break in an assignment, Eli opened the picture folder on his computer, and transported himself into those images of the trees and the river on their property. If a coworker walked by he quickly closed the folder, for he decided not to tell them about his purchase of property until he was ready to give his notice of resignation. It was easy to keep secrets from them, now that he knew they were temporary animations of a life that would soon be changed.

During his lunch breaks he opened up the bank page to assess their money, and made calculations of how soon they would reach their goal. He also checked the local weather for the area of their property, read articles about the local wildlife and fishing conditions, studied online maps, and viewed historical stream flow data for their river. Everything was about planning. No thought existed in his mind that wasn't tinted with plans for the adventure.

He returned home that evening and found Lamara lying on the couch transfixed in thought. "What's going on Blueberry?" he asked, taking a seat beside her.

She sat up and said, "We have to talk."

"Ooh, in my experience it's never a good thing when a woman says that. What's wrong?"

Her eyes darted around the room as she scratched at her jeans with her fingernails. "I could sure use a cigarette first."

"Don't even get me started. Right now I would trade my loyal companion Snowy for one single dip of chew."

"Let's go get some."

"You know we can't. Now tell me what's wrong."

"Nothing's wrong. At least I don't think so. I just hope after I tell you that you agree it's for the best."

Eli was confused. What could she possibly be getting at? Everything was going great, they were on target with their savings, made their monthly land loan payments, and continued to live frugally like they planned. "Well, lay it on me." He was ready for the worst.

"Okay," she hesitated, forming a convincing statement, "I've considered taking a new job when we move to Minnesota."

"Do you mean after our adventure of living on the land?"

"No, more like during."

"So, weekend work or something? That's not a bad idea. We could always get part-time jobs somewhere to help secure ourselves."

"No, not a part-time job. Just listen to me alright. I think it will be best for us if I find a job and let you live out in the woods alone. I've already found one I like in a city that sounds great, and if you agree I will apply for it."

"You don't want to live in the woods?"

"That's not it at all. I'll still be able to come out every weekend, this job's only an hour from the property. You know I want to spend as much time as possible there with you. It's just that, well, I've realized something about myself. I value my career too much to waste a year that could be spent enhancing it. This job will be good for me, the pay's a little less, but I'll get to be a boss, and still be involved with the environment."

Eli was at a loss for words. He wasn't sure what to make of this. On one side he was slightly upset at her for changing the plans, but then he realized his part in the plan wouldn't change. He started to understand her reasoning, and began to understand that being out there alone may give him more opportunity to paint. "So, what city are we talking about?"

"It's called Beltrami. I think it looks great, and it's so close I'll be able to drive out and see you anytime I want."

"Beltrami. I've heard of it but never been." He pondered this for a moment. "On second thoughts, let's go buy some tobacco."

"You already said no."

"You're right. Cursed tongue. So you're saying you'll only come out on the weekends?"

"Yes, I will be out there every weekend."

"Won't you feel like you're being cheated out of your place on the land?"

"I won't ever feel like that." She paused, thinking that if ever she were going to say it, now was the time. "Plus, with me being gone all week, you might be able to focus on painting."

He was surprised. She had never mentioned him painting before. He didn't even know she knew he wanted to paint. "Well," he tried to catch up to his thoughts, "sounds like you've really put a lot of thought into this."

"I have. I know it upsets you to have plans changed, but I really think this will be better for us."

"Alright. So let me get this straight. After all our hard work with frugality, and late nights of planning, you're backing out?" He sensed there was more she wasn't telling him, some secret plan she had developed behind his back.

"Please don't see it like that."

"How should I see it?"

"I still think it's a great opportunity for us."

"You mean a great opportunity for you."

A tear dripped from the corner of her eye. "I'm doing this for us," she said.

"You can't distract me with your tears." Eli walked out of the room and stepped outside. He paced around the yard, picked up sticks and threw them at trees. He leaned against the fence, and looked off into the distance. Beyond the city, emptiness stretched as far as he could see. But there was something inside that emptiness, something tangible yet undiscovered. He wanted to be immersed in it, for only solitude could ever fill the void.

If she wanted to give up her time in the woods to live in a city and work another job, that was her business. He could survive without her. Maybe this wouldn't even wreck what they had. Maybe she would still be in his life on the other side. Alright, he thought, let her chase her career. I will find peace of mind in the forest and paint my masterpiece.

He walked back inside and found Lamara curled up on the couch squeezing a pillow. He approached and wrapped his arms around her, then pulled her tight into his chest and said, "As long as you are part of my life, part of the plan, I am happy."

She looked up and smiled. "That is all I ever want."

And so they agreed, the plans were changed, but the dream stayed the same. They decided to postpone their excitement until she was offered the job. The next morning Lamara arrived at work early and filled out the online application. Now the anxiety of waiting was amongst them.

11

Those capricious seasons of Wyoming shuffled through their lives. The winter days were short and bright and filled with heavy winds. It was nearly a year since they started frugality, and months since the first and only time they visited their property. Lamara filled out the online application over a month ago, and still no calls or emails from anyone to even let her know if she was being considered. She grew concerned about having to change the plans again. Eli reaffirmed her daily with things like, "Don't worry about getting the job, we'll have plenty of money saved to be alright." She knew this was true, but she also sensed he secretly had become fond of the idea of spending the summer alone in a forest. She understood with a feeling of benevolence this wasn't due to any lack of love for her, but that every man should have some time alone; it seemed to be the nature of things.

She thought of the moose, antelope, deer, and the bear. The males of all these species were solitary creatures who wandered the natural world alone, until it was time to find a mate. The difference was these animals had specific mating seasons, which only lasted a short fraction of the year. The human mating season encompassed nearly the entirety of a year, with certain mating rituals being performed out of season. She imagined going to visit him in an isolated forest. After not seeing him for a week, they would adapt to a new mating season, it would be every weekend, and it would be lovely and powerful. She worried about getting lonely during the week without him. She wondered if Eli would get distracted from their love while living alone in the woods.

She considered what to do if she didn't get the job. Eli was going to live in the wild – she wouldn't let him change his mind no matter what happened. So she could either separate from him and stay here in Wyoming, or go with him into a future unknown.

The greatest dilemma for her was wondering if she could actually throw it all away – all her years spent at college, all the professional connections she's made, and her first shot at a respectable career – to live a life without security. The idea of living with nature was so romantic and serene it felt like a dream. She wanted that life like the roots of a tree want fertile soil. It takes years for the soil to develop nutrients capable of sustaining life. There were so many dead trees in the forest. There were also the powerful and grandiose ones reaching towards the sky.

• • •

Eli returned home from work on a Friday afternoon. The first day of spring was near. Every day he watched their savings account closely, withholding his excitement for when it reached fifteen-thousand dollars. At fifteen-thousand he knew they could survive unemployed for a summer or longer, then return to a city as the weather got cold and find jobs. Sure they might not be able to find their dream job right away, but if living the dream of a wilderness required him to take a job below his skill level for a while afterwards, that seemed like a perfectly acceptable exchange. Before he left the office, he checked the bank account – it was just above fifteen-thousand.

He was surprised to see Lamara's car in the driveway; generally he beat her home on Fridays. He went inside and saw her dressed in evening attire; she wore a black evening gown with a pearl necklace and red high heels. "What are you all dressed up for?" he asked, slowly caressing her profile with his eyes.

"I want to take you out tonight."

"That's nice of you. It's difficult for me to say no when you look like that, but you know we've got to stick to frugality."

"Yeah I know, but let me use this as my one cheat for the month. Let me take you out for a change. I've got something important to tell you."

He knew instantly what it must be, but faked ignorance so she could surprise him. "Alright, let me get changed."

They arrived at a sushi bar and ordered some sake. Eli looked through the menu but didn't recognize any of the dishes. "Tell ya what Blueberry," he began, "since this is your treat, I'll let you order for both of us."

"Alright," she giggled, understanding his bemusement of fancy foods.

Eli slugged down his sake and promptly ordered another round. Good news made the drinking easy. Then he considered it could be bad news, perhaps she had changed her mind again. Bad news made the drinking easy also, so he ordered another. Just as he was about to tell her the savings were in order, Lamara exclaimed, "I got the job!"

He didn't often show a visible smile, his smile was usually only apparent in his eyes, but just then he felt his cheek muscles tighten, as his front teeth showed behind a big grin. "That's great! I knew you would. Nobody can resist your charm."

"Oh, I'm so glad you're excited, I wasn't sure if you really wanted me to get it."

He hadn't been sure himself. It was difficult to predict a reaction to something until it had occurred. His eyes glazed over for a moment as he pondered the possibilities of traveling into a forest and putting his mind at ease. "Everything's falling into place," he said, holding up his glass and chiming it against hers.

"Oh it so much is," she replied with a smile as their food arrived.

Eli devoured his plate without even tasting it. His thoughts were congregated around the unfinished aspects of their plan. Would this work, him in the woods with her living and working in a city? Did they have enough money to settle her into town, and provide him enough sustenance for at least several months in the woods?

"You look perplexed," said Lamara, as she looked at his empty plate, "was the food not good?"

"It was delicious. I was just thinking."

"About what?"

"I planned on coming home today to give you the good news that our savings reached the fifteen-thousand dollar mark."

"That's great! So we're all set then."

"Well, probably, but we need to make some reassessments."

"Like what?"

"For starters, we're going to need to figure out your living arrangements in Beltrami."

"Oh I've already thought about that. The housing market is so low right now, I could easily afford a home mortgage loan on my own until you move back and find a job. Or else I could certainly move into a nice cheap apartment, and then when you come off the land we can find a house together."

"Well," he pontificated, "I'm sure you're going to love living in Beltrami, and I doubt we'd ever find you a job more suitable in any other town so close to our property. If housing is as affordable as you say it is, it makes sense to move right into purchasing a house. We'll be homeowners, and won't have to waste any more money on rent."

"It's totally affordable. Believe me, I've already drawn up a spreadsheet."

"I'm sure you have," he chuckled. "I think we have enough money saved to put a down payment on a house, and still have the extra that I'll need for supplies. It could get tight though. When do they want you to start?"

"That's the best part, they don't need me for three more months. So we should be able to save lots of money by then."

"Excellent. It's all coming together."

"I can't believe it's really happening. I'm so excited."

"It's perfect."

12

The days passed quickly as the savings continued to grow. It was a year ago that they started frugality, and seven months since they purchased their property and made the dream obtainable. After the eight-thousand dollars spent on a down payment for the land, they had eighteen-thousand in savings. This was slightly less than their original goal, which should have placed them in the twenty-two-thousand range, but it seemed like enough to support their new plan.

They decided to set aside ten-thousand dollars of savings for a down payment on a house, and spending money to settle in with. All they could take with them from Casper would have to fit in the bed of Eli's pickup truck. This meant they'd be buying all new furniture, and most everything else, at their new home.

Lamara configured another spreadsheet for their new budget. Eli studied it and determined the remaining eight-thousand dollars would be more than enough for him to spend four months living in the woods, after which time there should be enough in savings to support him until he secured an income after the adventure. Still, there were some doubts and uncertainties in both their minds.

Every night Lamara and Eli sat down for dinner, and each night Lamara noticed a greater distance in his pensive eyes. She knew he was making preparations for his time in the woods, and probably thinking about painting, but still, she was concerned. "Is everything alright Eli?"

"Everything's great," he said, looking up from his plate. "I was just thinking."

"About what?"

"Oh you know, our plans and everything."

"Yeah?" she inquired, sensing some hesitation in his voice.

"Well, it's just, I don't ever want to be a burden to you."

"What do you mean, a burden?"

"Just speaking hypothetically. If for some reason I'm not able to find a job soon after coming back from the land, I don't want you to feel like you have to support me."

"Oh you silly man, I'm sure it will all work out perfectly. With your skills and background, you will have no problem finding a job. Besides, I imagine you becoming a great painter, and who knows, you may even be able to sell enough of your work to make a living."

He appreciated the compliment, but didn't like talking about it. Discussing a project before it was finished, or in this case barely started, was bad luck. An image of creation could only exist internally, or externally, never both. Once it traveled from one into the other, it was trapped there forever. So he changed the subject. "It's just that, I keep hearing my father's voice in my head you know. He always tried to instill in me this sense of responsibility. While I have no doubt most of my skills and abilities are owed to him, somehow I never caught on to his idea of responsibility. I mean, I understand it, and respect it, being able to put your head down and make a good career, but I can't seem to allow myself to do it, you know, sacrifice my life for something as combustible as a career."

"If it's what you want then I'm sure you'll do it."

"That's just it, I see everyone around me able to make the sacrifice, maybe it doesn't seem like a sacrifice to them, but to me it's the ultimate sacrifice, giving up your life, likely the only one you'll ever get, just to make some career, to follow in the footsteps of those who have come before. Is that what a man should be, merely a follower of other men? My destiny cannot be aligned to the parallel lives of a conformed society." He stood up in a bolt, prepared to leave the room, surprised by what he had just said. It was never his intention to verbalize complaints. There were so many different congregations of thoughts in his head, sometimes, in moments of distorted clarity, one snuck out as if spoken by a stranger. A man has more voices than his tongue should ever speak.

"Well," she didn't know how to respond, "you will never be a burden to me."

• • •

The next day Eli arrived at work with the intention of giving his notice to resign. It was still a month away from their planned departure date, and he considered the possibility of his employer releasing him on the spot. He was confident they had enough money saved, but he wanted the addition of another month's income. He clocked in early and sat at his desk, waiting for the boss to arrive.

"Clancy, you got a minute?"

"Eli, you're in early."

"Oh, you know, got a lot going on."

"Don't wc all. So what's up?"

"I need to talk to you about something."

"Alright, step into my office."

Eli indulged in a long discourse about the purchase of their property, how wild and beautiful it was, and how he always wanted to live in a wilderness. He told Clancy of their plans, how he would be living as a recluse, while Lamara lived in a house in town and came out to visit on the weekends. He told him all about fishing for muskie, and canoeing, and living amongst wild animals. He told him everything except painting. Every man needed a secret, and painting was his. He presumed Clancy would consider this all ridiculous, and he prepared himself to be mocked and released from duty.

"Wow," said Clancy, after Eli had finished, "I'm shocked."

"I hope I'm not putting you in a difficult position."

"Oh that's not it at all. I've just never heard of someone resigning at the height of their career. I'm surprised."

"Yeah, it wasn't an easy decision for me."

"I bet. I'd be concerned about my financial security if I were you. Have you thought about the future?"

"I'm aware of the possibilities."

"Good. This sounds like a risky endeavor."

"If I don't do it now, I likely never will."

"I understand. And I must admit, it sounds like a great adventure. I wish I could do something like that. I've got too many responsibilities though, there's never the time."

"So I'd like to keep working for the next month," continued Eli, "and during that time I would expect nothing less than for you to throw me the most difficult assignments you can find," he finished with a smile.

"Alright," said Clancy, "we'll see what we can do."

• • •

The nearer the departure date, the more questions that developed in their brains. Would they be happy living in a new dream, or should the dream stay just a dream, never to be known, and so never given the opportunity to disappoint? If they stepped through that metaphysical barrier, and the substance of their dream crumbled like a sand castle at high tide, could they escape, return to the comfort of this easy life? If this dream failed could they ever live another? Was it too late to forget? Was the power of hope strong enough to subdue the fear of failure?

• • •

Lamara entered work on a Monday morning with a trembling uncertainty in her footsteps. As she walked in the front door, the receptionist greeted her with a cheerful smile and said, "Good morning," but Lamara could only look the other way and mumble some incomprehensible syllables under her breath. Today she would give her notice to resign. Up until now everything had been a dream, and like any dream she could wake up and change it if she chose to. But today the dream would merge with the waking life – if she let it.

She walked down the hallway, past the offices of the three shareholders, and thought that with her reputation and work ethic, she could choose to stay here, and one day the plaque on her office door would say *Partner*. It wasn't too late, not yet, she could still rid herself of the uncertainties involved with moving to a new life, and settle into a happy existence here. Was this place really so bad? She didn't think so. Then she sat down at her desk and saw the screensaver pop up, it was a picture of her and Eli standing beneath an old growth cedar, with a wild river in the background, their river, and they were both smiling, and it was real. She realized she wasn't running away from anything, but running towards something.

She opened up her work email and sent a message to the three shareholders, asking them to schedule a meeting with her this morning. Within a few minutes, without having even gotten a response from any of them, and before she could fully develop what she planned to say, all three of them showed up at her doorway.

"Good morning Lamara, you wanted to see us?" said Trevor, the primary shareholder, as they entered.

"Yes, come on in," said Lamara, standing up and pulling out three folding chairs.

"Did you have a good weekend?" asked Shane, attempting to open the conversation.

"My weekends in Wyoming are always grand."

"How's that man of yours doing," added Lee, "is he still catching lots of those trout?"

"Yes, that's about all he ever does, fish."

"Well you tell him I've got this new secret gem of a place, maybe I'll take him there next spring."

"I'm sure he'd love that. Unfortunately," she paused, and tried to calm her rampant breath, "I don't think it's likely to happen." She felt the six eyes pierce into her with questions. "That's actually why I've called this meeting. We've decided to move to northern Minnesota, so today is the beginning of my two weeks' notice."

After an uncomfortable and elongated pause, "Wow, you're really taking us by surprise Lamara," said Shane, with a look of astonishment on his face.

"I can't believe it," added Lee, "I thought you two liked living here?"

"Oh we do, we're not leaving because we don't like it. You know that we bought property up there last year?"

"Right?"

"We've decided it makes more sense for us to be closer, so we can take advantage of our investment."

"I see."

"Lamara," joined in Trevor with a stoical voice, "you know you have been a great asset to our team. In fact, we were just talking the other day about making you a partner. It will be a shame to see you go now. Is there anything we can do to change your mind? You know, the annual review is not that far off, I'm certain with your accomplishments there could be a significant pay raise in the near future."

"I appreciate that Trevor, I really do. Unfortunately my mind is made up."

"I understand. We're going to miss you around here."

"I think a congratulations is in order," said Lee, reaching out a hand. "It's been a pleasure to work with you Lamara."

"Thanks Lee, you too." The other two proceeded to wish her good luck with a handshake, then they filed out door.

As the door was closing she heard Lee say, "I guess we're gonna have to put a hold on that private land sanctuary thing for a while." Lamara sighed as the door shut and concealed her in silence.

She spent the rest of the day hard at work, finishing task upon task, even the seemingly meaningless ones that had been put off. She must leave no room for anyone to doubt she had been a valuable employee. She wanted to leave shoes so large it would take an entire squadron of replacements to fill them.

• • •

Later that evening, on their front porch watching the traffic rumble by, Lamara leaned her head on Eli's shoulder and said, "I'm so happy."

"Good. Me too."

"I mean it. I didn't know how it would feel to give my resignation, and honestly I was a little scared, but now that it's done I can begin to settle my thoughts fully into our new life."

"It's about time," he said, poking her in the ribs with his elbow.

"Oh stop it," she laughed, and squeezed him around the shoulders. "So two weeks, then we are on our way."

"Yep. And you'll have two weeks off before starting the new job?"

"That's right! With everything else going on I almost forgot about that. Oh it's so exciting, we're going to have so much fun. Tell me again about the cabin, I know you've told me before, but it was hard for me to actually visualize anything before today."

"Alright. I've reserved us a log cabin on a lake shore for the first three weeks. We'll literally be able to step out the front door and right into the water. It's only a five minute drive from Beltrami, so it will be convenient for us to go house hunting."

"Do you think we can find a home in that short of time?"

"I have no doubts."

"Good, I want to get settled into a house as quickly as possible so you can get out to the property and enjoy yourself."

Eli looked into the street at the spinning tires of cars passing by. He saw the swirling residue in the air, like the spirals in a large bowl of tomato sauce after it had been stirred with a wooden spoon. His eyebrows tightened, he was perplexed by this substance of empty air. Could emptiness be painted?

"Is something wrong?" he heard Lamara ask.

After a moment he responded, "No, nothing is wrong."

"Alright, it's just, well, you got that look on your face, like something was wrong."

"There's nothing wrong. I was just listening."

"To what?"

"The traffic. I want to remember how annoying this sound is so when I am in the silence of the forest I can appreciate it."

"You're such a silly man," she said, and leaned forward to focus her ears on the street.

"Thank you," he smiled and put his arm around her. "What's for dinner?"

"I wanted to make something special to celebrate giving my notice. I thought I'd make macaroni and cheese."

"Only your mac-n-cheese could be considered special."

"I'll get it started. You hungry?"

"Always." He stayed on the front porch as Lamara entered the kitchen. It was funny, knowing this place was going to disappear, not from existence, but from his perception. He wondered how their departure would affect this place. Would anything change? The landlord will find new tenants to pay the rent and sit on this porch. Their jobs will find new employees to fill their desks and complete their work. Their friends will find new friends and continue living the same life. Will anything change? Will there be no hole that goes unfilled? Has he ever really been here, or will he someday remember this place as a dream, or a movie, unable to decipher the context of truth from fiction. Lamara called him in for dinner. The sun beamed in blinding reflections off the roofs of the neighborhood.

"So," Lamara began as they sat down at the table, "some friends want to throw us a going away party this weekend."

"Friends?" asked Eli, looking up from his plate.

"Yes, we do still have friends here you know. It may not seem like it since we never hang out with them, but they're still our friends."

"Yeah, I know, and they're good people and everything, but I don't want to be the center of attention, you know, answering everybody's questions and explaining everything to them. We could just make a clean break, disappear unknown, leave a tall tale of mystery and whispers behind."

"That does sound exiting. I wonder what kind of stories they would develop? Eli and Lamara disappeared into the mountains, or were abducted by aliens, or were lost at sea, or maybe we became international outlaws. We could even mail random postcards to people, have them postmarked from exotic places around the world to fuel the mystery. This sounds like fun."

"You're right, we should probably go to the party."

"Well, it was their idea after all. Let's let them feel like they're doing the right thing. We'll have a good time, I promise."

"Alright. I suppose there are a few people I'd like to see again."

"We need to celebrate. We're doing something not many people ever accomplish. And we're really making it happen."

"I'm sold, let's celebrate."

13

They arrived at the Wonderland Tavern on a Friday night. Inside the lights were dim and the crowd was loud. The floors showed scuff marks from the old days when men brought their horses inside to join them for a drink. The brass rail along the bar was worn from the thousand-million thirsty hands that had entered the bar for some intoxicating company. In the corner was a large table on a raised platform. Eli and Lamara approached and were greeted with the smiles of familiar faces.

After the customary handshakes and "How's it goin?" they sat down and merged with the conversations. On the table were several pitchers of beer, each of its own unique color and distinct aroma. The large glass mugs never got completely emptied before getting refilled. The faces of the people at the table constantly changed with the light and shadow. A person could spend their entire life painting this image and never get it right.

All these people looked exactly the same to Eli. They all carried the same baggage and burdens. They were all here for the same reason; it wasn't just to say goodbye, but also for the reason anyone entered a tavern: to cure loneliness, to distract themselves from their own company, to drink away their thoughts until all that remained was a smile. To share a smile with someone and call them a friend, without thoughts of transience or permanence, but for happiness and companionship. All the strangers he met and befriended were just as lost and lonely as he. In their company he found solace. Only in solitude could he find peace.

"So," began Kevin, who had lost much hair since the last time Eli saw him, but still lived the philandering life of an early twenties playboy, "I hear you're going Thoreau on us."

Eli clenched his jaw muscles and held his tongue. He didn't like the implication of this comparison. He knew it was intended to be a compliment, so he responded, "Yep, that's what they say."

"Why would you want to do something like that? What are you going to do out there?"

"Well, I suppose I'll do whatever I want to do."

"Yeah, but there's no life out there, no excitement. You should stay in the city. This is where it's at."

Eli wanted to respond, but didn't want to insult, so he took a deep drink from the beer mug and smiled.

"I think it's brave," said Christine, a single and sophisticated looking young woman who sat next to Kevin. "For a man to go out into the woods and live alone, that must take courage. And you too Lamara, I mean, I don't think I could ever move to a new state and a new city and live alone like that."

"I won't be alone, Eli will be just down the street."

"I do envy you two. I wish I could do something exciting like that."

"Why don't you?" asked Eli.

"For starters, I could never afford it. Plus, I never seem to meet anyone I connect with, not enough to go on an adventure with anyways."

Eli noticed all the glamorous jewelry on Christine's wrist and neck and ears. She had a leather purse dazzled with gemstones, her clothes were all new and crisp and clean, and she had a skin more tanned than the natural sun could provide. He looked around the room at all the people, all the possibilities and opportunities right here, ready and waiting to be utilized.

"Oh that's nonsense," replied Lamara, "you're a very attractive young woman with a great job. Eli and I made this plan after only knowing each other for six months. Then it only took a year for us to save the money. If we can do it so could you."

"Oh I don't know, it all sounds so difficult. You know I try, I really do, but there's so many other things I want, so many easy things that make me feel happy, and I don't want to waste the time trying to live out some fantasy that will never come true."

"Not everybody has had the same opportunities as you two," rejoined Kevin, and placed his hand sympathetically on Christine's lap. "You shouldn't rub it in just because you guys got lucky, no sense in making other people feel bad."

"Lucky?" Eli couldn't restrain himself any longer. "You think we got lucky? Let me tell you something, this has nothing to do with luck. We've had to work hard to make this happen. We've had to sacrifice all the desires and temptations you're afraid to. No opportunities were handed to us, we made them happen."

"Oh don't go bragging just because you found a needle in a haystack," responded Kevin, while looking him in the eyes.

"What you don't realize Kevin, is that you're sitting on a haystack full of needles, we all are. But instead of taking the time to dig in and discover this jackpot right beneath you, you sit and complain about the prickly discomfort in your ass. Perhaps you should try standing."

"You don't know what you're talking about man," said Kevin as he shifted his weight and looked away. Eli picked up a pitcher of beer from the table, and leaned across to fill up Kevin's half empty mug. Then he sat down and topped off his half full one.

"Listen," Eli began, "I'm not saying what we're doing is for everyone, we've all got our own idea of happiness, if yours is staying here and living this life then I applaud you for doing it. But that's not ours."

"Eli," Lamara whispered in his ear, "remember, we're here to celebrate."

"Right." Eli lifted his mug, "I'd just like to say cheers and thanks to everyone for coming out tonight. We've had some good times, and even though we are excited to go, it won't be easy for us to leave." Glasses clattered together and beer spilled onto hands.

The night progressed with the emptying and filling of beer mugs and pitchers. Their friend Pierre showed up with a young woman nobody knew. "I'm glad you decided to show," said Eli, standing up and pouring them two beers.

"How could I miss this?" replied Pierre. "If it weren't for me you two crazy kids never would have met in this big old world."

"That is true," said Eli, thinking back to the first night he met Lamara, how lost he had felt, how distorted everything seemed, yet how certain he was that he would find his way. Perhaps he was lucky.

"I'm not sure if I ever thanked you properly," said Lamara, standing up and kissing Pierre on the cheek. "That's for inadvertently introducing me to this marvelous man."

"Oh," said Pierre with a boisterous grin, "that will do the trick."

"So who's your friend?" asked Lamara.

"I'm Vandana," she answered with a friendly smile.

"That's a beautiful name. I'm Lamara."

"Very nice to meet you. Pierre tells me you two are going Thoreau, as the saying goes."

Eli, having had enough beer to separate himself from restraint, responded, "I understand your intentions with that comparison are sincere, and the saying itself is a representation of what we are doing, but I don't agree with its context. The life I'll be living in the woods will be nothing like the one he wrote about. I'm not fleeing from society because I am disgusted with its course of laws. My home has always been in the woods, I'm just now finally going to live at home."

"Our apologies," interrupted Pierre, "we didn't mean to insult you."

"It's no insult, I'm just trying to explain my point. It seems like the very word *Thoreau* is used as a trophy by people in attempt to show they are wilderness savvy. I doubt most people who speak his name in social gatherings have ever read a single page from any of his books. There were so many people during his time of history living much more rudimentary lifestyles. The only reason he is remembered is because he wrote a successful book about it, and so still remains a household name in most of the English speaking world. I don't take the comparison as an insult, I'm just saying that it's not me. I'm not trying to reproduce something somebody else has already accomplished. It's like people get trapped in a cycle, and think they can only do what somebody else has already done, following the footsteps of the past."

"Of course, we didn't mean anything by it."

"I know, I know. It's just that, we are a new generation, why must we limit ourselves to comparisons of those which have passed?" Nobody spoke or would look Eli in the eye. After a moment he continued, "Well, you know you've said something either absolutely brilliant, or completely insane, if everyone in the room goes silent and looks away."

"I see your vision," said Vandana, looking towards him with a smile.

"Alright," said Pierre, assuming a humorous tone, "so you're not Thoreau, big surprise, what shall we call you?"

Eli laughed, "Oh man, call me whatever you want. How about raving lunatic. Listen, I didn't mean to go on a tirade there, it's just I've been hearing a lot of that lately and it got me thinking."

"This is no time to think. Let's drink instead."

"Perfect," said Eli, as he tilted the mug up to his mouth.

"Has Pierre told you the big news?" asked Vandana.

"What's that?" asked Lamara.

"It's really quite exciting. He's discovered the remains of a Stegosaurus, right here in Wyoming."

"You don't say? That is exciting, congratulations."

"Oh it's nothing really," said Pierre. "Just a few bones from some massive beast that lived here many millions of years ago."

"He's being very modest," said Vandana, and placed her hand on Pierre's shoulder. "He's going to be quite famous now."

"Well that's wonderful. I'm so happy for you," said Lamara, smiling at Pierre.

"Really man, that's amazing," added Eli. "Just to think about those massive creatures walking this same ground as we now are, only millions of years ago, makes me dizzy you know. And you of all people happen to find one, it's unreal."

"Yes, but there is no accurate method to justify time," said Pierre as he looked at his watch.

"So, now that you're famous, are you going to finally trim that outrageous beard of yours?" asked Eli with a laugh.

Vandana rubbed her hand through the long grizzled beard and said, "I hope he never shaves it, makes him look like a mountain man or something."

Lamara put her small soft hands on Eli's smooth bald cheeks, "Someday he'll have a big old bushy beard and everyone will know he's my woodsman."

"Yeah, and you'll probably have to pick wood ticks out of it for me," said Eli, as he reached up and wrapped his fingers through hers. They all shared a laugh, the only language with which friends should part.

"It certainly has been great," said Pierre, straightening up his shoulders, "but it's time for our departure."

"So soon?" asked Lamara, with a feeling that everyone she said goodbye to would be for the last time.

"I'm afraid so."

"It was very nice to meet you, I had a lovely time," Vandana gave Lamara a hug and shook Eli's hand.

"It's been great," said Eli, extending his hand to Pierre.

"I wish you two the best of luck, sounds like some great adventure awaits you."

"We wish you the best of luck with your dinosaur fame."

"That was fun," said Lamara after they had gone.

"You know what, it actually was."

"Should we get going?"

"Yeah, I think it's time. We can go home and finish off that bottle of wine on the back porch."

They started to walk towards the backdoor of the tavern. Eli took a look around at the crowd of familiar strangers. How many nights had he been here amongst the same people and only ever known a few by name? How many of those names had been but an allusion to the person he never would know?

The door opened and a man stepped in from the night. "There you two are. I've been in every damn bar in this town looking for you. You're not calling it quits already are you? The bar don't close for another hour, and I've got two full liters of Pendleton out in the truck." He tilted up his ten gallon Stetson cowboy hat so you could see his ginger-red hair. His shoulders were broad and his back was straight. He wore a plaid button up shirt tucked into his jeans which were pulled up to his stomach. On the center of his abdomen was a large brass belt buckle with the engraving of a bull rider. He wore bright white tennis shoes. He looked at them with squinty eyes through his thin wire-framed spectacles. This was Benny Traverski.

"I was wondering when you'd show up," said Eli, gripping him with a firm handshake.

"Shoot, you think I'd miss this."

"I was beginning to wonder."

"So what's your plan?"

"We were actually just getting ready to leave, but now that you're here I suppose we should have another drink."

"Right this way then," said Benny, and marched through the crowd as though he were going to battle. There was a line of thirsty patrons at the bar, but this didn't matter, he pushed them aside and walked right through. "So what do you know?" he asked Eli as they leaned into the brass railing.

"Oh, the less the better."

"I understand. Let's make that happen. Bartender, three shots of Pendleton, and make it quick," he said while twirling his finger through the air like he was spinning a mechanical gear.

Eli looked at Lamara, "Guess we're taking a taxi home."

"Good, I didn't really want to leave yet anyways."

"Here's a cheers to two fools chasing their dream."

"Oh yeah, that's a smooth drink," said Eli, placing his empty shot glass on the table.

"Yep, it's the only whiskey worth shooting."

"I like it, went straight to my head," said Lamara, holding it down with watery eyes.

"Bartender, another round. What do you say Eli, ready to shoot a little stick?"

"If you're ready to be embarrassed again."

"Well alright, let's go."

After a couple games of billiards, Lamara walked up to the bar to collect the tab, while Eli and Benny racked up one more game. Eli watched her in the crowd, she glowed so bright that everyone else was erased in her light.

"What's going on with that?" he heard Benny say.

"What do you mean?"

"Looks like that dude's trying to hit on your woman."

Eli refocused his eyes. Sure enough, a short stocky man with a buzz cut stood close to Lamara and spoke seductively. Eli continued to watch, knowing there was no cause for concern.

"Aren't you gonna go put a stop to that?"

"Nah, I'd rather just watch and see the look on his face when she tells him off."

"Ah, you're too soft. If that were my woman I'd go bust him in the nose."

"No reason to man, it's not like he's got a chance with her."

"Shoot, if you won't do it, I'm going to." Benny marched with furious steps towards the bar. Eli reluctantly followed.

By the time Eli caught up, Benny was already in the guy's face saying, "What do you think you're doing pal," as he pushed the man across the shoulders.

Eli quickly pulled Lamara away, and then jumped in between the two men. The courage of alcohol pushed at him from both sides. The short stocky man wore a black t-shirt with white lettering that read *MMA*. He was coming at Eli trying to get through to Benny. "I bet you think you're some sort of bad ass," said Benny, trying to reach around Eli's shoulders.

"Who do you think you are, John Wayne? Nobody pushes me!"

Eli was quickly engulfed in flying fists. The crowd erupted in a fury. Men rushed in from all directions. Eli swung out with a fist and made contact with a chin. Before he had a chance to see who he hit, he felt a glass mug collide with his cheek. The room started to spin but he stayed on his feet. After several dizzy moments of pushing and yelling and sweating, the fight died down. He saw a group of bouncers dragging Benny out the door as he was yelling, "You ain't seen the last of me!"

Eli found Lamara, grabbed her by the hand, and followed them outside. Benny was nose to nose with a bouncer, "You got no right throwing me out of there, I'm a paying customer!"

"Chill out man," said Eli, putting a hand on Benny's shoulder. "Listen," he turned and said to the bouncer, "I'll take him from here."

"Alright, you get him out of here. And don't come back either!"

"That son of a bitch, you see him try to sucker punch me in there? I got him a good one though."

"Yeah, that was crazy," said Eli.

"Eli, you're bleeding," said Lamara, reaching up to his face.

"Don't worry about it, won't even feel it until the morning."

"Looks like you took the hoof of a broncin' bull to the skull," said Benny.

"I think someone got me with a beer mug. That scene turned violent real quick."

Benny straightened up his back and put his thumbs through the belt loops on his jeans, "Whelp, as my daddy used to say, when it comes to a bar fight most men forget all thoughts of conduct and chivalry soon as the first punch is thrown."

"Don't I know it."

"Shoot, that was fun pardner. Aren't you going to miss all this?"

"Oh, I don't know..."

"Yeah, I can see you now, sitting out there in the middle of nothing but trees, thinking about the good old days with your pal Benny Traverski. Shoot, we've had some fun."

"Yeah, it's been good man."

"You boys are wild," said Lamara, putting her arm around Eli's waist.

"So what's next buddy, you coming over to the house to finish off that whiskey?"

"I think it's time we call it a night."

"You're a drag. Really?"

"Afraid so."

"Alright then, you all have yourselves a good night," said Benny and turned to go.

"Yeah," said Eli to his back, "see you around then."

"You can count on it," replied Benny, turning to look at him without stopping.

Eli watched him leave, thinking that friends can be only strangers, wandering so far away from home. Regardless of our place or our time, we are lost in a sea of desolation.

"That was wild," said Lamara, lifting up on her toes to kiss Eli, "I don't think I've ever seen a real bar fight like that before, at least not from so close."

"It's been awhile for me too." He watched as Benny turned the corner, and heard him whistling a cheerful tune. "That guy has got a whole different kind of wilderness in him."

"Yeah, but I like your wilderness best," she said, and took his hand.

"Shall we go home?"

"I'm ready when you are."

• • •

The taxi pulled up to the curb and they stepped outside. The spring time air had a wintry chill this time of night. They felt unconquerable as they walked towards the house arm in arm. This civilized world embraced them, it was here for them and they could belong to it forever, if they chose to.

"Still want to finish that bottle of wine?" Eli asked her as they opened the back door.

"You know I do. I'm not ready for this night to end."

"Alright, you grab the bottle and I'll set up the music out back."

They sat on those cement steps where they had spent so many nights, beneath those same stars and that same moon; but tonight it all looked different. The music played softly, the same playlist they had listened to so many times, but tonight they heard different words. There were words like *change,* and *life,* and *dreams,* and *lost.* They sat silently, and sipped from the cultivated grapes of a distant valley.

Then Lamara spoke. "We sure meet some interesting people in this life, don't we?"

"I know what you mean."

"There are so many different types too. Just when I think I've got someone figured out, they surprise me. It's ironic, part of me wants to be left alone, out in the woods and free from all this mess, but the other part wants to know as many people as I possibly can. It's like there's two primary options for us; to know ourselves, or to know others."

"That's quite the dilemma."

"I think it defines the two basic sorts of people, those who look inward, or those who look outward."

"Yeah, but then there are some who see both. Like you for instance.

"I don't know, it really makes my head spin. Sometimes I feel like I'm losing my mind," she said with a hint of sadness.

"You lost your mind a long time ago," he said seriously. She looked at him with indignation. "That's a compliment for anyone who knows the freedom and clarity of losing their mind," he reaffirmed her.

"If you say so. All I'm really saying is that I'm glad we're doing what we're doing. I think it's a perfect fit for both of us."

"It's funny, even when I'm alone, and get a chance to sit down and think, it's not really myself I'm thinking about, but other people. Or more directly their place in this puzzle of my life."

"I'm sure you've met some interesting characters."

"Yeah," he swirled the dark purple fluid around in his glass. "Did I ever tell you I once knew this guy, this poet of a young man, who told me he never dreamt in images, only words?" he said and looked up at the stars.

"I don't think you've ever mentioned any poets to me before."

"Well this guy, I remember him clearly, we were sitting at a bench, on a busy city street, just watching people pass by, and out of nowhere he started talking to me about dreams."

"Okay?"

"Yeah, seemed strange to me at first, but then I started listening, you know really listening, and I started to understand something about myself. What he was saying was something about having never seen images in his dreams, that his dreams were filled with words. I thought he was trying to brag at first, like he's such a great poet he even dreams about words. But I kept listening."

"What was his name?"

"I'll get to that. Anyways, he went on about how the entire night he was always in that place of perception, like when you're not fully asleep, but also not quite awake, and he said there were words flowing through him, like narrations for a blind person watching a movie, and the words themselves became the image. Not in the sense that you see a tree or a car or your own reflection, different in the way you can only imagine something that has been explained to you but you have never actually seen."

"That's kinda weird."

"Yeah, I thought so too, but then he said this world is a consummation of words and ideas, that everyone sees the world differently based on their own vocabulary and experience. For example, since you and I spend so much time together, and both like to read similar books, we may look at an object and explain it in analogous terms. But if we picked a random stranger, and asked him or her for an explanation of the same object, it would likely come out completely different."

"I see what you're saying," she thought about it a moment longer. "What are you actually saying?"

"I was thinking about him the other day, I realized that I don't dream in words, I actually dream in images, no descriptions, no narrations, just symbols. This is why I have to paint, because I could never explain something properly with words."

"That makes sense. I can't wait for you to get started, I want to see this work, see what you see in that mysterious mind of yours."

"I'm not sure if I'll be any good, but it's the only resource I have, so I've got to try and use it."

"So what was his name?"

"Huh?"

"Your poet friend."

"Oh, he never actually told me his real name. We were more like acquaintances. Every once in a while we'd bump into each other and end up sitting around somewhere getting into long deep discussions."

"Well, what did you call him?"

"He told me to call him Dazar Freidum. He said that our days are freedom. All of these days, the ones our feet carry us through, any one of them we can choose to be free, we just have to be willing to make it happen. He was such a sad young man, but he wasn't sad for himself, he was the freest person I ever knew. No, he was sad for all the people he saw who were never free. All the people walking around thinking they were free, but were bonded to so many possessions and responsibilities, so much dispassion and anger, that freedom had become a mirage, like a mythical figure or a god, something they worshipped and followed, but never truly understood."

"Sounds like a pretty interesting guy. You ever see him anymore?"

"No, not in a long time. He's probably living in freedom underneath some bridge or in a dumpster right now. But you know what, I bet he's completely happy with it."

"Do you know any of his poems? Was he any good?"

"I've never gotten too much into poetry, but he did give me a book of his poems once, it was alright. I can't say that I have any of his full length poems memorized, but there is a short verse from one I think of occasionally, it went something like:

'To each his own
Disguise for pain
For by thyself
Each own be slain.'"

"That was actually pretty good, kinda sad, but deep."

"Yeah, it's good in the sense that it reminds you of an ancient Chinese proverb or something. Like you've always known it and probably heard it before."

"Or Shakespeare. What was that, 'thyself', it's like an anachronism or something."

"He was an anachronism. A walking talking portrait of an extinct breed of philosophers. Here he was, born backwards into an alien world which did not yet exist. He was a strange character, and I admired him for that. Somehow I think he already knew then what I am only learning now."

"Like what?"

"Oh I don't know, like that being yourself, understanding your place, is more important than any other role you could play in life."

"That's difficult, isn't it?"

"Yes, it is. But I think we're taking the right passage for it."

"I'm so ready to get started."

"Only one more week."

"Tell me about the north woods again."

"Well...

14

They put those mountains in their rearview and drove north. They drove north away from their friends. They drove north away from their jobs. They drove north away from their memories. They drove north away from the place where they met. They drove north away from the only home they had ever known together. The mountains grew smaller in the rearview. There was a wide open horizon of high plains through the windshield. This was all they would see until the trees and lakes of the north woods.

They sold Lamara's car for the extra cash, and now rode in their shared pickup truck. Eli built a topper for the truck bed out of scrap lumber he collected at construction sites, and it creaked and wobbled as they rode up the bumpy freeway. In the truck bed were several garbage bags filled with clothes, some framed photographs of their life in Wyoming, a few small pieces of décor they couldn't part with, half a dozen boxes filled with books, and two large camouflage duffle bags filled with camping and fishing supplies. They drove slowly with the weight in the back, and the hood of the truck tilted up like the nose of a plane preparing for takeoff. Their dog Snowy sat in the front seat between them.

After a few hours they took an exit heading east, and then pulled off on a dirt road to stretch. Snowy bolted out the door and chased a herd of antelope. Eli and Lamara paced around separately, neither of them spoke. Even if they tried to speak, their words would have blown away before reaching the other's ears.

The wind pounded on them like the force of a shifting tide. Their clothes flapped like flags on a pole. Hair fluttered like rampant lightning. Tumbleweeds plowed into their shins like thistly bowling balls. Sand particles blasted their faces, penetrated their eyes, and clung to their hair like water to cotton. This was the Wyoming wind that would carry them east. They would set sail and ride on four wheels until being deposited like glacial till in the forest of Agassiz.

Lamara pinched a handful of sage brush from the hot sandy soil. Eli picked up a multicolored chunk of rock the size of his head. They had each retrieved a piece of Wyoming memorabilia. After Snowy returned from the chase, they got into the truck, placed their items on the passenger side floor, and drove on.

"Did you know ancient people burned sage brush to warn off evil spirits?" said Lamara, rubbing the glaucous leaves between her fingers.

"Did you know that rock is called clinker, and was formed by fire deep beneath the surface of the earth?" said Eli, looking down at the infusion of minerals between Lamara's feet.

They shared an eccentric laugh, then Lamara said, "Let me know if you want me to drive."

"I'm good for now."

• • •

The sun was well into its ascent from the abyss. Eli looked over at Lamara curled up and sleeping with Snowy's head on her lap. He reached over and patted her shoulder, but didn't say a word. She shook the sleep from her head, and then stretched and looked out the window. "Oh my, look at that!" she exclaimed.

The road bended around the bay of a large lake. The water was huge like the ocean, with no distant shore in sight. The edges of the lake erupted with blooms of wildflowers. The trees around the bay were tall and thick; some with large clusters of green needles, others with white peeling bark. Trumpeter

Swans displayed their grace in the open water, and a Great Blue Heron stalked the shallows. Boulders protruded from the surface, painted with green and yellow and white lichens.

"Imagine all the fish in that sea," said Eli, glancing over while driving with one hand on the wheel.

"It's absolutely lovely. We must be getting close?"

"Almost there. Figured I'd wake ya so you can start looking for a moose."

"Oh I'm excited! Let's just pull over and camp right here."

"Sounds like fun, we've already paid for the cabin though."

They drove the winding road, crossed over innumerable rivers, and passed inimitable lakes. "Boy," said Lamara in a breathless voice, "it's like Minnesota isn't even attached to the ground, we're just floating on islands between lakes and rivers."

"It's relaxing, isn't it?"

• • •

It was a sunny afternoon when they arrived at the lake of blue and white and gold. The shoreline was a sandy beach, where canoes, kayaks, and sailboats waited for them. The trees were thinned out so all that remained were tall red pines spaced throughout the yard. The cabin had a wooden terrace up front facing the lake where they stood for a moment and embraced the splendor before they stepped inside.

"This is amazing," said Lamara with delight. "Look at that, we've got a king sized bed, a big kitchen, comfortable couch, and there's actually a shower. Oh how I've missed showers. Baths everyday get so time consuming. How much would it cost for us to just live here forever?" She wrapped herself under Eli's shoulder and pulled him down onto the couch.

"We've got three full weeks here, that's really not much time. We need to focus on finding a house."

"You're always so serious," she said standing up.

He pulled her down and said, "But there's going to be plenty of time for us to have some fun while we're here."

• • •

The next day they drove into town and met with a realtor. They had a list of a dozen houses to view, and knew if they were to stay on schedule, they would have to make a prompt decision. The city of Beltrami bustled with life. For such a small population, it was filled with activities and culture. This pleased Lamara greatly, and she made mental notes of all the restaurants where they would someday dine, the coffee shops where she could sit and gossip with a girlfriend, the theatres where they would join a crowd of friendly people to take in a show, and all the parks she would certainly enhance for the betterment of local residents. The thrill and rush of new discovery was with them.

They scheduled another appointment with the realtor the following day to review their three favorite homes. One of them was a Victorian style house downtown where they could walk to and from all the shops and social events. One of them was a classical white house with a giant park-like yard filled with trees and flowers. The other was a cedar-sided house with forest green trim that had a half-acre yard fully fenced in, and a garden filled with fruits and vegetables and indigenous flowers. Each house was within a four block walk to the lake.

By that afternoon they decided on the cedar house. It was perfect for them, a huge yard for Snowy to run, mature spruce trees surrounded the perimeter and provided privacy, there was a garage for the truck and a detached workshop for storage. The inside was quaint like a cottage home. There were hardwood floors, arched doorways, two full bathrooms, with three bedrooms – one on each story of the house.

"I love it!" said Lamara with joy in her eyes.

"I know, it's great," replied Eli, soaking it all in.

"Seriously, this is the house I would have chosen even if we weren't in a rush. It's my dream home."

"Think you'll be able to live here without me for a few months?"

"Oh definitely. I imagine us growing old in this house."

"Good, I'll go talk to the realtor." Eli put in an offer. Attached to the offer was a contingency that the owners had to be moved out within three weeks. He hoped they were as anxious to leave as Lamara and he were to arrive.

They returned to the cabin and waited for the call. Every several minutes Eli picked up his phone to see if he'd missed it. Lamara checked the classifieds for used furniture. Finally the phone rang. Eli answered while Lamara sat next to him with her fingers crossed.

"Well," he said after hanging up, "we've done it again!"

Lamara jumped up with a bolt of elation, "We're going to be homeowners!"

"Yep, and they've agreed to be moved out the day before we need to leave here."

"Oh I want to move in today."

"That would be nice. Let's enjoy the cabin while we've got it."

The rest of the week was spent in leisure; paddling the waters, laying on the beach, sharing bottles of wine, and just waiting. That weekend they checked out the social atmosphere in town.

"I'm going to have to make some friends if I'm living here all alone this summer," said Lamara with the future in her eyes.

They entered an Irish pub with live music. They walked down to a corner bar that had a classic hockey game playing on a large screen television. They went into a dance hall that was packed with bouncing bodies. They found a college bar where there was a comedian on stage.

"It sure is hard to make friends at our age," said Lamara in the back seat of a taxi on their way to the cabin.

"Don't worry about it, take your time, you'll meet people. You just need the opportunity to work your charm."

• • •

The next week was occupied with retrieving documents and filling out paperwork for the bank. "There's a lot of effort involved to be part of civilization," said Eli, as they sat at the table with stacks of paper in front of them. "Almost seems easier to build a log cabin by hand and farm and hunt for food."

"Someday we'll live that life. You just need to go out and practice for us this summer."

• • •

"Those two weeks really flew bye," said Lamara on a Sunday afternoon.

"It sure did, we had some fun though. You ready to go back to work?"

"Oh yeah, I'm actually excited to start." She looked into a mirror, "Do you think I look too young to be a boss? I mean, imagine you had been working at a job for a long time, and some new young woman showed up and started telling you what to do. Wouldn't that seem strange?"

He saw the trap of words she unintentionally set. If he told her she didn't look too young, she would be insulted and think he was saying she looked old. If he catered to her vanity and told her she was young and beautiful, she would become inse-cure with her position as a boss. So he replied, "You'll do great."

"Oh, I know, it just feels like so much pressure."

"Luckily for you, I've got a magical pressure release potion right here," Eli opened the refrigerator and retrieved a bottle of Sauvignon blanc wine.

"Ooh, that looks very nice. I don't know though, it's only mid-afternoon, I don't want to start the first day with a hangover."

"Alright, I'll just go ahead and put this back for another time then."

"On second thoughts, if we have a couple now I'll still be able to get to bed early and sleep it off."

"I thought you might say that."

They pulled two Adirondack chairs out onto the grass and passed the bottle back and forth. An osprey flew over them with a fish gripped firmly in its talons. On the lake a group of loons flapped their wings and sent echoes of their song across the water. A dragonfly landed on the tip of the bottle as Lamara held it in her hand. "Look at that," she whispered to Eli, trying not to scare it off.

"Looks like you've got an admirer. You know, dragonflies have two-thousand individual pupils in each of their eyes. I bet he still can't see how beautiful you are."

She blushed, and the insect skimmed off through the low sky. "There's so much amazing life in this world, isn't there?" said Lamara, watching it go.

"Certainly is."

"And I think we've got the best of them."

"I agree."

"I can't wait until we move into our new home."

"Home?" he pondered this for a moment, juggling thoughts of their house and their forest. He thought about all the different doorways he had entered and exited in life. All those places his feet had stepped and found a moment of comfort. Without even intending to speak, he asked her, "What is home to you?" After the words escaped, he wished he hadn't said them, and anticipated the result with discomfort.

"What is home to me?" she responded distantly, while her entire body seemed to shrivel. The past like a monster flashed rapidly behind her eyes. She remembered everything lost she had thought would last forever. This new life was great, but every decision seemed to be tainted with previous failures. "All I can tell you is that out of all the things I have given up in life, home was the hardest." Tears started to form in her eyes. She quickly got up and scrambled inside. He thought about following her, trying to comfort her, but some things were better left to be managed alone. So he sat with the bottle in his hand and thought about what she said.

As he drained the last drop from the bottle, she returned and sat beside him. "You alright?" he asked.

"Yes, sorry about that, I'm happy again."

"Good, I love it when you're happy."

They sat in silence and watched the day go by. Eli looked at the world; not just this mystical representation of it right before him, but also the transient one inside his mind. Yes, the world was beautiful, but it was also so confusing if he let himself think about it. He studied all the shapes and colors and depths and movements. He got pulled into another place, a place of misery for all that was lost, for all the images that had disappeared forever. If only he could touch them again, put them all up on a giant billboard and say, 'I have been there, that is me'.

Lamara noticed the twitching of his eyes, and the discomfort in his hands. She was thinking about their new house, her new job, visiting Eli in their wilderness, and growing old together. She got up to separate herself from the place where he traveled. She sensed he needed to be alone to figure out whatever puzzle had formed behind his eyes.

She walked down to the lake as the sun began to set. On the far shore she could almost see their new house. She imagined having children and buying a boat and spending many summer days water skiing and fishing. She wanted more than anything else the opportunity to make somebody happy. She watched the sun set with a smile on her face, then turned back towards Eli who sat on the terrace steps.

She walked barefoot through the grass already damp with nighttime dew. The skin between her toes retained grains of sand from the beach. She looked at him sitting with his elbow on his knee and his chin on his fist, "Are you having a good time here?" she asked. "It seems like you're so distant, as if you're not even present to enjoy it."

"I saw you out there digging your toes into the sand," he looked up into her eyes. "It seemed like you were enjoying yourself. I thought if I were to join you beneath the stars along that shoreline where the white capped waves continuously slap against the sand, if I were to join you in your solace I would find happiness." He paused, and tried to figure out exactly what he wanted to say. Then he looked towards the lake and continued, "But I was hesitant, for isn't happiness the most unapproachable condition in life."

"I thought I felt your eyes on me," began Lamara. "I wanted to turn and ask you over, but I too was hesitant. I didn't want to interrupt your own solace. I understand your distance, that it's not a distance from me, but from the moment. It's more like you're wandering through another realm, someplace I wish I could see and share with you, but I know it's a place you have to go alone. And besides, you usually seem happy. Aren't you happy?"

"I would take you there with me if I could, but I may lack the ability to transport a passenger. How can I take someone else where I go, when I don't know where it is myself most of the time? I'm constantly hopping back and forth over that fine line which separates happiness and discomfort, pleasure and depression, kindness and aggression. I'm continuously falling down a mountain, then climbing back to the peak. I can never predict my balance at any moment, it's a slippery world filled with sublime footings, and despite my constant effort to understand where I am, I generally feel to be like the hands of a compass spinning around some unknown interference. It's like my bearings have all been distorted, and there's no longer any true magnetic force to guide me. I am wandering in thoughts without direction, only an obscure sense of where I want to go." He watched her sit down beside him on the wooden steps. They stared into the northern sky; silent mouths, but heads filled with noise.

Being at the precipice of obtaining their ideal of happiness was a terrifying place. There was melancholy in his eyes as his thoughts wandered into the night sky. How many times in life had he reached for his goals, only to find them just past the tips of his fingers? If he was able to grasp them, the ability to do so made them seem smaller, unworthy of his touch. Perhaps he should have reached further? He was consumed by a fear of wanting too much.

Lamara had long since gone inside, unnoticed to his far off eyes. He spent the entire night outside, trapped in a vortex of ideas, and carried himself through the imaginings of all that could go wrong. He began to doubt his reasoning. Perhaps he should have stayed in the comfort of a good career, the familiarity of friends, the ease of a predictable routine. A future flashed before his eyes like a hallucination; he saw himself a scoundrel, a vagabond, a beggar, resorting to a life of crime and destitution. If he were to take the next step on this adventure, and abandon all social contrivances, then he could become any one of those. He felt hollow and heavy as a ship at the bottom of the sea. But just like the stars as the sun slowly approached the horizon, this too began to fade. When daylight awoke the next morning, he found the world was filled with songs of birds and sunshine, and he was happy.

Lamara woke up just as Eli stepped inside. "Were you out all night?" she asked.

"Yep."

"What's wrong?"

"Nothing. Everything's great and perfect."

"You look like you're ready for the woods."

"I'm trying not to think about it too much, still a couple weeks before I can get there."

"Alright, well if you need to go sooner I understand. I'll be alright here for the next week, and I can get settled into the house if you want to get out to the property."

"I wouldn't think of it. We're moving into that house together. Two less weeks won't matter in the long run, I've still got all summer and fall."

"Okay, I'm going to get ready for work." She showered and put on her professional attire.

Eli laid awake in bed as she passed from the bathroom, "Wow, you look great. Why don't you come back to bed and I'll put you to work all day."

"Oh stop it," she said playfully, "you know I'd like to, but I've got to go to work."

"Alright, I'll see you tonight." He rose from bed and paced around the cabin. He sat down on a chair and stared out the window at a separate world. The walls were thick, and it was quiet inside. From someplace deeper inside his own tabernacle he heard words, silent words being whispered from the waves and the wind. An inaudible voice called him outside. He felt trapped in concrete shoes. He whispered back, "Soon my friend."

15

Lamara put the truck in park and adjusted the rear-view mirror to check her makeup and hair. She thought about how great a cigarette would feel. While staring into the reflection, she pulled her coat tight on her shoulders, straightened up her neck, and said, "This is you now."

Outside of city hall, the bronze statue of a timber wolf had its head tilted back, as though it were offering a last howl of freedom into the distant sky. Lamara paused briefly beside the statue, and then entered front door. The Minnesota flag was painted on the ceramic floor of the lobby, and above her hung a crystalline chandelier with images of hummingbirds, blue jays, chickadees, ravens, and woodpeckers. She walked upstairs and entered the *Parks and Recreation Department*.

Behind the front desk sat a woman who appeared to be in her late twenties, and wore high heels, tight black slacks, and a turquoise blouse. She looked up hastily at Lamara and said, "Sorry, but we don't open for another five minutes."

"Yes I know. Are you always in early?"

"We have a new boss starting today, so I wanted to make a good first impression."

"If you want to accomplish that, I suggest you don't concern yourself too much if someone comes in five minutes before eight-o-clock." Her chest swelled with a swallowed smile. So many front desk personnel had offended her in the past, but she had never been in a position to confront them about it. Now it was her roll; not only her roll, but also her responsibility to make sure anyone who entered the door was treated with respect. "I'm Lamara Grobert, your new boss," she said, and stepped towards the desk to extend a hand while making solid eye contact.

The woman behind the desk paused a moment and studied Lamara from head to foot, then she stood up and said, "Good morning Lamara, my name's Sonya. I didn't mean to be rude, it's just, I expected someone different."

"So much for assumptions," replied Lamara. "Now could you direct me to my office?" She tried to sound stoic and impersonal. Perhaps someday she would make friends with the other staff members, but first they had to see her as someone respectable, somebody admirable, and as a person in charge.

"Of course, right down the hall, first door on the right."

The office was half the size of her previous office, with piles of papers scattered across the top of a cheap wood-laminate desk. Aerial photographs of all the city parks in her district were posted on the walls. The chair felt like it was going to collapse as she sat down and shuffled through the paperwork.

Then she heard a rapping on the door; it was solid and ominous, as if a seven foot man who ate steak three meals a day stood on the other side. Lamara looked up at the clock, it was only 8:17 a.m. "Come in," she said, and laid her palms flat on the desk and scooted her chair in closer.

A tall and slender Native American woman entered the door. She had broad shoulders, focused eyes, and a long braided pony tail that reached to her lower back. She was the epitome of a regal woman. Lamara looked away briefly to clear her thoughts, then she stood up and said, "Good morning, what can I do for you?"

"I am here to speak with you about the hypocrisy of Voyager's Gate Park."

"Of course." Lamara had already taken trips to all of the city parks, and Voyager's Gate was her favorite. It was located on a sparsely wooded grassy knoll where the

Mississippi River flowed out of a large lake and began its route east through the northwoods before cutting south towards the sea. This had been the jumping off point for local fur trader's during the nineteenth century. From here they paddled and portaged into other rivers and lakes to trap beaver and otter and mink. "Go ahead and have a seat. My name's Lamara," she said with a smile and reached out her hand.

"I am Jacquelyn Longwater," replied the woman, without accepting the handshake.

"Of course," Lamara sat down. "You'll have to forgive me, it is my first day on the job, but what exactly is it you wanted to discuss?"

"I represent the *Keep Our Lands Native Coalition*. For many years we have battled your department about the Voyager's Gate Park. It is our belief the park only identifies one side of history. It has always been our way to show respect and civility towards your people; this is why your voyagers were successful here. Without the friendship and support of the native population, these voyagers would not have been able to make a home and hunt and trap in these woods. This is the hypocrisy, for through our friendship the white man has destroyed our forests and pillaged our wildlife. But I am not here to dwell on the past."

Lamara leaned back in her seat and wondered what she had gotten herself into. "Okay, I understand there have been some disagreements, but…"

"These are not disagreements I speak of. We as a people have accepted our place in this new world. But we do not want the memory of our old world erased and replaced with artificial white heroes. Your voyagers were exceptional men, we don't deny that. But what about our great men? All we are requesting," she paused, "no demanding, is that the park be renamed Great Native Waters Park, and that the statue of your canoe be replaced by a majestic image of our ancestors."

"I see. As I mentioned, today is my first day here, so I am unfamiliar with the topic."

"That is why I came today. If I am your first client then you must give this project priority."

Lamara swiveled on her chair which caused the pivot to crack. She caught herself on the desk before falling to the floor. She stood up and brushed herself off, then said,

"I appreciate your candor Miss Longwater. I can assure you I will give this project my full attention."

• • •

Eli walked barefoot through the grass at the resort, and Snowy ran around in front of him. The sky was clear with a mild breeze, and on the breeze he smelled algae blossoming in the lake. His eyes were confused from not sleeping the previous night, and he saw the images around him through the transparent veneer of walking dreams. That fourth dimension of vision was the imaginary place his eyes could see which laminated reality.

It was only alone that he ever saw this separate world. This separate world was the only place he could make sense of his surroundings. His senses were unconcerned with reality for they had discovered something greater, larger, infinite and yet comprehensible.

An angry voice broke through the walls of his contemplation. Eli stopped and looked around. How far had he walked? It seemed like forever. It seemed like he had always been here, moving at a steady pace in a space that always changed. There was a large mechanical crane with a demolition ball attached from a chain. Scaffolding, ladders, ATV's and lawn tools were scattered around the yard. He looked behind him, only two-hundred feet away was their cabin.

"You know all dogs are required to be leashed while on resort property," said a short bald man who wore blue jeans and a flannel shirt.

Eli looked at the man, and then towards Snowy who circled a tree only ten feet away. "Well sir, that just seems unnecessary to me, there are no other dogs around, and he never gets more than ten feet away."

"Regardless, all pets are required to be leashed. It's policy."

"I understand, and if there were any risks imposed by him running freely I would capitulate. Truth is, he's always had difficulty defecating while on a leash."

"You know you are responsible for picking up any waste created by your animal."

"Yep."

"Okay, just make sure you do."

"No problem." Eli whistled for Snowy, and then turned to walk towards their cabin.

"Are you the guests staying in cabin thirty-two?" asked the man.

"Yes."

"My name is Gary, I'm the resort manager."

"Hello," Eli said and continued to walk away.

Gary stopped him, "So you're the Sylvan's?"

"Yes. Well I am, Lamara's last name is Grobert."

"I see. My mistake," Gary looked him over closely. "So what brings you to our resort?"

"We just moved to town and needed a place to stay while we find a house."

"Oh, okay, welcome to Beltrami then," he held out a hand.

Eli shook his hand and said, "What's with all the equipment?"

"We're knocking down six cabins to put up condos for permanent residents."

"That's a shame."

"Actually, it's a great opportunity. So many people love visiting this lake and community that we're offering them a place to live full time. The buildings will all be two story homes with magnificent stucco exterior and all wood facades. Each resident will have their own personal beach and dock. If you and your wife, I mean Miss Grobert, don't find a house, you may want to consider living here. We're anticipating a completion date of early fall."

"We'll see," Eli turned to go.

"Mister Sylvan."

"What?"

"If it's not too personal, I was wondering if you had moved here for a job?"

"Nope."

"Oh I see. So what is it you do for work then?"

"I don't."

Gary tilted his head and put his hands on his hips. "Have you just not found work yet? 'Cause you know we could probably get you on our maintenance crew if you'd like."

"Thanks, but not interested. I am willfully unemployed."

"I see. So does Miss Grobert work then?

"Yes, she does."

"I see," he looked over Eli with paternal scrutiny in his eyes. "Well it's none of my business what a man decides to do with his life."

"Are you sure about that?"

Gary clenched his eyebrows and created rows of wrinkles on his forehead. It had always been his intention to treat guests politely, which meant he kept his personal judgments to himself, but this young man was beginning to test him. He shook his head and was about to speak, but Eli had already turned and walked away.

• • •

That night, Eli and Lamara stood in the living room of the cabin and looked out from the window to watch a storm pass over the lake. The whirling wind pushed white walls of water far upon the shore. Leaves and pine needles twirled and bounced in the low sky. Trees were bent and broken. In the distance a siren howled, but its sound was muffled by the thick tapestry of rain.

Lightning broke the sky and everything went black. Lamara stood tightly pressed against Eli with her arms wrapped around his waist. He put one arm around her shoulder and caressed her hair. They stood in the darkness transfixed by the storm.

Then Lamara spoke. "This job's going to be very challenging for me."

"What do you mean?"

"It was only my first day and it's already gotten political. Not to mention I made enemies with my secretary."

"That could be a good thing."

"Yeah, well, I'm just worried. What if it becomes too much and I can't handle it? I don't want to let you down, we've worked so hard to get here."

"The important thing is whether or not you believe the lifestyle you select is the right one for you."

"I know, and I do, it's just, I want to make sure I don't let you down."

"You won't. There's more between us than the lifestyle we choose. We have the intrinsic attraction of commonalities. You and I are the same, no matter what differences may exist in our lifestyles."

Lamara wiped a tear off her cheek with her shirt sleeve, then squeezed him tightly around the chest. She wanted nothing more than to believe it would all work out. Life was so unpredictable and there had never been anything

127

definite. Carrying the burden of memories made her fear she could hold nothing forever, that she was somehow flawed, and sooner or later anyone she let into her life would discover this. All she wanted was to hold him for as long as she could. She knew from experience anything she held too tightly only became smaller, challenged by her grip.

16

Was this place home? How did they get here? When would they leave? Will they ever know a life of stability, or were they wanderers forever lost in a wandering land? For all the sure-footed steps they took seemed false and misleading. All the rivers they navigated to escape only returned them to the place where they began.

Where was the future? Who lived there in this same space only the passages of time could produce? Will they recognize themselves when old age gets viewed through child eyes? Or will those faces be forgotten like the dreams left stranded along the way, the dreams that could not withstand the storms of time.

• • •

Lamara awoke five minutes before the alarm clock went off, which had become her custom. Eli waited until she was in the shower, then got out of bed and started to brew a strong pot of coffee for a difficult Tuesday morning.

"What's on your mind? You should probably go back to sleep, I know I would if I didn't have to work."

"Actually, I think I'll go fishing this morning. I wonder what fish think of the storms? I'm sure they must experience some subsurface turmoil in the lake."

"You're weird, trying to figure out what a fish thinks."

"To know the mind of nature, that is my only goal," he said with a wink.

"Alright, well you've got all day to figure that out. How does lasagna sound for dinner?"

"That would be great."

"Okay, see you tonight then."

"Don't work too hard."

"You either," she said playfully and walked out the door.

• • •

The water was cold as it smoothed down the leg hair below the knees of his shorts. Eli looked around a moment before he settled his thoughts into fishing. The shoreline was loud with a hustle and bustle of lawn crews and maintenance men as they hurried around with machines and tools cleaning up the mess the storm made. Instead of the sounds of gentle waters slapping into his thighs, accompanied by the call of a loon, and his fly line chirping through the air, he heard chainsaws, ATV's, and foremen barking orders. So he waded out further, until water soaked his shorts and climbed to his lower chest. He felt a healing presence as the pressure of cold water mingled with the rhythm of his breath. He forgot all the ambient noises, and only heard the call of nature guiding him deeper into the water, until he was so deep he had to raise his elbow above his head to make a cast.

It was all quiet for him now; there were no sounds, not even images behind his eyes to disrupt his view. All he saw was the colorful feathers tied to his hook in a Deceiver type fashion as it flew back and forth over his head. He watched it cut through the air like a dragonfly, follow his every stroke, lengthen out behind him, then shoot forward and land softly on the crystalline surface. The lake was so calm and still, the light deflected from every little cornice like a thousand-million tiny suns. He forgot he was fishing. He no longer pursued a catch, and enjoyed the connection with this moment.

Midway through a retrieve his hook stopped solid, mid-column, then pulled with the force of a forty-horse powered boat. He yanked the tip of his rod upright to set the hook, and clenched the forearm of his hand which held the rod. With his other free hand he clung to the line as it screamed out from the reel. "Holy shit!" he extruded audibly, as he imagined the size a fish must be to pull like this. He tightened up the drag on his reel to its maximum force, but line continued to scream out as the fish retreated to deeper darker waters.

He watched helplessly as the chartreuse fly line shot out through the eyelets in his rod, and was followed by the white backing line. He had caught many good sized fish with this rod and reel, but only one fish had gotten down to the backing line. That fish, a thirty-six inch Northern Pike, took fifteen feet of it before Eli was able to reel it in.

This fish was pulling out backing line like it was free dessert at a fat man's buffet; ten feet, twenty feet, fifty feet. Not much remained before the line came to a stop and would be yanked from the reel as the fish swam away with his hook and line as a trailing souvenir from a battle won. He had to make a fight now.

Eli grabbed the backing line between his fingers and palm and pinched it with as much force as he could, but the four-finger-drag only effectively burned a deep white and red line into his hand. He put his palm over the reel handle, slowed its release, and then caught it between his forefinger and thumb. He held it firmly and hoped his knots were tight. Even if his knots were tight, this fish could easily snap his leader material. Eventually the fish realized it could go no further in that direction, so it turned and swam perpendicular to Eli's position. He followed it along the shoreline, in water up to his chin, and cranked in line as fast as he could.

"It must be a muskie," he said to himself. He reeled in enough line until he was at a direct connection with the fish and its force. The fish took an angle towards the shoreline about one-hundred feet away. Eli started to creep into shallower water. From the corner of his eye he saw a crowd of people pointing and watching him from the shore. The men and women who had been working at cleaning up the mess made by the storm were congregated in awe of the battle Eli was engaged in.

He got closer to the fish, with less than eighty feet of line between them. The fish was headed straight for a dock at the resort, so he pulled up as hard as he could on his rod, and forced the fish to turn. He heard the "Ooh's" and "Ahh's" from people on the dock as the fish made a wake in front of them.

One man ran into the water while carrying a lawn rake over his head and shouted, "I'll gaff her for ya!"

"No you won't!" yelled Eli in protest. "You stay there."

Eli cranked in line as fast as he could, while the fish rushed towards him. It brushed by a couple feet from his legs. He saw the hook firmly in its jaw, and the spotted marks decorating its sides, with a body length easily over forty inches. He felt a brief moment of disappointment when he realized it was a northern pike, not a muskie. But disappointment was forgotten when the fish rose violently to the surface thirty feet away.

Fifteen feet between him and the fish. He walked towards shore, into shin deep water. The fish didn't like this, and wasn't ready to give up, so it bolted out towards the deep. It got about thirty feet before Eli was able to hold it again, and again cranked on his reel, slower this time, to let the fish fight and use its own weight to wear it down. As the fish came up towards the surface, Eli knew it was ready to be landed. He reeled in line until it was almost at his leader, then walked the prehistoric creature up to shore.

A crowd of people waited for him, some clapped, some stood with a dropped jaw, and a few others rushed towards the water to help. He brushed them back, and dragged his catch onto dry land. One of the maintenance men on the scene pulled out a tape measure and measured the fish at 46.5 inches. Eli held the fishes head between the bend in his left arm, and reached down with his right hand to remove the hook. The fish shook its head violently, and ferociously snapped its jaw, cutting Eli across the ring and pinky fingers. He held it tighter, grabbed his hook by the shank, and wiggled it free from the mouth of the beast. "Does anyone have a camera?" he asked, looking to the crowd.

"I'll go get one," said one of the housekeeping staff who stood nearby.

"I've never seen a Northern that big." exclaimed a man in coveralls.

"I have, in pictures from Canada," said another.

"You're going to keep him, aren't you?"

"Nope. This one's going back to grow larger."

"Well, if you don't want him, let us take him," said the hotel manager whom Eli met the previous day. "We'll get him stuffed and hang him in the lobby. Could even put a nice little placard with your name under it."

"Not gonna happen." Eli looked at the fish and was reminded of fist fights from his youth. He found it ironic, how his opponent in the battle, regardless of who won or lost, always became a friend after the fight. They developed a mutual respect for each other, even if neither of them had been proven wrong nor right. They would be forever linked by this landmark in time.

Eli looked around for the housekeeper to return with her camera. The fish's breaths got shorter and further apart. If he waited much longer he might have no choice but to kill it. He held that aquatic beast beneath the chin with his left hand, then reached back with his right and grabbed it just above the tail, and walked it out into deeper water.

"What are you doing?" asked the hotel manager nervously, "she'll be back any minute with the camera." He knew even just a picture of this fish on the cover of their travel brochure would increase the angling clientele ten-fold.

"I'm releasing him." Eli walked into waist deep water, and slowly moved the fish front to back to circulate oxygen through its gills. He felt the fish grow stronger in his hands. He held it tight until the fish was strong enough to pull itself free from his grasp. It darted out like a torpedo, and splashed water in his face as it rushed into the deep.

Eli watched the surface of the lake, the surface like the skin of a man with so many mysteries lurking beneath. He waited until the image felt permanent, attached it to his memory, then turned and walked up to shore. The crowd was silent, only one spoke, "I would have kept that fish if it were me." Eli shrugged his shoulders and continued walking. He longed for the day he caught the elusive muskie, and hoped there would be no one around to watch when it happened.

• • •

That evening, Lamara returned from work and cooked her prized lasagna. Eli listened to her across the dinner table. She talked about her day and her coworkers. He smiled and laughed at all the appropriate moments, for even though his thoughts wandered through another realm, he knew this was important to her, so he listened with all the focus his mind could provide.

"I was thinking we could go to the bar at the lodge after dinner, have a couple drinks. It might be fun to talk to some of the other people staying here," she suggested with her usual charm.

"Sounds good to me," he replied, hoping no one who saw his fish would be there to congratulate him. "Maybe they'll have the Stanley Cup Finals on." They finished dinner then dressed in their evening clothes and walked to the bar.

"Mr. Sylvan, please come in, have a seat here with us," said the hotel manager who sat at the bar with several other people Eli didn't recognize. "Eli, I was just telling my friends here about that amazing fish you caught today."

"I heard it was a spectacular fish, and on a fly rod at that," said a man reaching out his hand. "I'm Lyndon," he said as Eli gave it a firm shake.

"It was fun alright. I certainly got lucky."

"I can't believe you didn't keep it," said Gary. "A fish like that would look great as a mantelpiece anywhere."

"Eli, what are they talking about?" asked Lamara.

"Oh, I guess it hadn't come up yet. I told you when you left for work this morning I was going to try some fishing. Turns out I got a pretty lucky catch."

"Your man here is being quite modest," said the manager. "A lucky catch, that's very funny. It was the greatest catch I've ever seen here, and I've been working this resort for over thirty years."

"Let me buy you a beer," said Lyndon. "What will it be?"

"I like their Saison, if you'd be so kind."

"My pleasure. Bartender, bring this man a Saison."

"Thanks," said Eli as he watched the hazy gold liquid get poured into a glass. He felt Lamara looking at him.

"Why didn't you tell me about this fish of yours?"

"It hadn't come up yet, that's all."

"You just let me sit and ramble on about my day at work all through dinner, and didn't even mention you had this amazing experience. That makes me feel selfish. Do you think I talk too much?"

"Absolutely not. I thoroughly enjoy hearing about your day. All the things that can happen in one day on the job are all more exciting than catching some fish."

"So Mister Sylvan," resumed Lyndon from behind him.

"Yes?" said Eli turning around.

"What does a man like you do for work?"

"Well, I suppose you could say I am presently on sabbatical." Last thing he wanted to do now was answer any more questions.

"I see. So you must be in between jobs then?"

"Something like that."

"Well I'm with the Natural Resources Management Bureau, we're always looking for good men willing to get their hands dirty and their feet wet."

"I appreciate that Lyndon, but I'm not looking right now."

"If you say so. Here, take my card in case you change your mind. The pay's good, and it's a federal position, so you know you'll be taken care of."

"I'll think about it," finished Eli, as he took the card and shook hands.

"That was nice of him," said Lamara, as Eli turned towards her.

"Yes, it was. I suppose I could take another job right away, a job that sounds like I would get to spend most of my time outdoors, and then still be able to spend the weekends on our property. But..."

17

They walked into their house and it felt like stepping into a dream. The floors were empty and the walls were bare. It was a blank canvas to cover with whatever they chose.

By end of the week their house was filled with items collected from classified ads, thrift shops, and garage sales. They made a pleasant home from items other people did not want in their home. It amazed them, with all the treasures found second hand, how the manufacturing of new goods stayed in business. It was as if the ghosts of previous owners attached themselves to inanimate objects, and haunted their new proprietor with memories and regret. Eli and Lamara enjoyed this idea as they held each item and wondered where it had been and how many hands it had touched.

Eli was most excited about a giant piece of canvas tarpaulin they bought at a yard sale. It was the color of pine bark, and measured forty feet by thirty-five. He stretched it out on their yard and spent an entire afternoon planning its use.

• • •

The next evening Lamara returned home to find Eli with a reticent grin on his face. "What's going on with you?" she asked cautiously.

"Oh, not much. I was thinking, it's hard for me to imagine leaving you here all alone for the summer."

"Oh don't worry, I'll be fine. You can feel comfortable going into the woods. I want you to. I'll be able to see you every weekend. I'll be so busy with work anyways, the weeks will fly by."

"Yes. But still. I think you need some companionship."

"Oh don't worry, I'll make friends. It's fine, really."

"I don't know. I think a woman like you needs a warm body and a friendly smile to come home to every day."

"Seriously Eli, we've made our plans..." Then she heard the sound of feet shuffling in the bathroom as Eli walked over and opened the door.

"Surprise!" he exclaimed, as a dark little fur ball of a puppy ran to her feet.

"You got me a puppy!"

"I thought you'd be excited."

"And here I thought you were saying..." she trailed off. "Oh, I don't know what I thought you were saying. He's absolutely adorable! Look at that cute little face."

"Yep, he's part Rottweiler, part Malamute. He'll be loyal to you, and objectionable to any trespassers. In fact, I've already trained him to bite any man who comes through that door."

"Stop it now," she said and picked up the puppy. "What's his name?"

"I don't know, he's your dog. You can call him whatever you want."

"Really? I've never had my very own puppy before. How does a person choose a name?"

"You think about it. I'm sure he's going to love you no matter what you call him."

"Maybe I should name him Wyoming, as a reminder of where we met."

"Whatever you like."

"Oh, I don't know. Perhaps something organic, like River? Mountain? Moose? How about Boulder?"

"I like that, Boulder, makes him sound solid."

"That's it, you're my little Boulder. You're going to get so big aren't you? Just look at those paws. Does Snowy like him?"

"I'm sure they'll get along great."

• • •

Saturday evening they put on their finest clothes and went to a pizzeria for dinner. This was Lamara's going away party for Eli. Tomorrow Lamara would be left alone in their new home, with her new job, and a new life.

When they returned home, Eli thanked Lamara for dinner, then told her he needed to wrap up a few things in the workshop. "I'll be waiting up for you," she said as he walked outside.

"It won't be long," he assured her. He walked through their yard, but already his feet were in the forest. There was a silence not actually produced by a lack of sounds. Raccoons, owls, and quivering midnight leaves surrounded him in the dark, and their subtle vibrations filled him with quietude. The silence was a constituent of the void, a complete absence of mechanical noise. In the distance a wolf howled, and he felt the eyes of a bear watch him as he entered the workshop.

He boxed up the cans of paint, and stacked the white canvas boards. To his eyes these canvases were magical windows where he saw through this reality into a solipsistic masterpiece. He pulled out a brush and popped open a can of paint. It was time to capture this image.

Only by finding a place where he became fully enraptured in the passages of moments, did he know himself, see himself clearly, and speak with his own voice. Everywhere else he was a stranger from himself, and viewed this self from a distance, as though reading a third person narrative, never occupying the same space as his body, and never fully understanding the words spoken from his lips. He must step inside of the outside world.

Part II

From the Inside Looking In

The outside is the only place we can truly be

inside the world.

18

If we should journey into a world which is not our own, can we find peace with a place that is not our home? Or can we only and forever be trespassers, always trying to change this world, whichever one it may be, into a place more familiar to our sense of home?

• • •

Lamara pulled the truck alongside a desolate country road. A violent windstorm had passed the previous week, and as they looked down the two-track driveway towards their property, they saw several trees fallen across preventing passage.

"Well, I suppose you'll have to let me out here," said Eli.

"All right, it's going to be a long walk with all those supplies. You sure you don't want to wait and come back with a chainsaw?"

"That's alright, I'm in no rush." There was a presence of hesitation in the space between them. "You sure you don't want to make the first walk down to camp with me?"

"No, I've really got to get back home and prepare for work tomorrow. I've got five public meetings, and I have to give presentations at three of them. Besides, I imagine it will be better for you to make the first trip alone, let your brain settle into the silence. Unless of course you wanted my help carrying supplies in?"

"Oh no, that won't be necessary. I've got all day for that." They stepped out of the truck and started to unload supplies along the side of the road. "I'm really glad we decided on this fiberglass canoe, even though it's a heavy beast. It will be much more dependable," he pulled it off the truck and looked down the long trail.

"Yeah, that's going to be quite the haul down to the river. I can't wait until we get to go paddling together."

"Tell ya what, I'll save her maiden voyage for next weekend so we can both go."

"Alright," she said, and stepped closer to him, "looks like we're all unpacked."

"Yep," he opened up his arms and she dove in.

"I'm going to miss you," she said, and looked up with sad blue eyes.

"I know," he smiled at her.

"I just hope the weeks go by fast, so the weekends together don't seem so far apart."

"They will. You'll hardly even notice I'm gone, and then bam, you'll be here with me."

"Okay," she replied timidly. "I know this will be good for us, being apart will make our love stronger. I can't wait until I come back to see you. Visiting my man in the woods, it just sounds so romantic."

"Yes, I know. It will be a sight for sore eyes every time I see your pretty face walking through the trees."

She got into the truck and started the engine. He put a pack on his shoulders and stood there to watch. She had tears in her eyes as she waved goodbye and drove away. They didn't appear to be sad tears, but happy tears, powered by the realization it had all come true.

The trail was overgrown with tall weeds, thistles, grass, and ferns. In the few open patches of soil he saw fresh tracks of morning deer. Wild flowers bloomed in the deep dark forest as he carried his Duluth pack towards camp.

When he arrived at the clearing where camp would be made, he removed the pack from his shoulders and dropped down to one knee. The sun was bright as he looked into the surrounding forest with squinty eyes. He sat down on the ground, and flattened a patch of wild grasses beneath his weight. On his lap was a red covered notebook. In his hand he held a mechanical pencil...

• • •

Journal entry number 1:

Everything is new and fresh upon arrival. Everything is green and tall and lush. There are flowers and ferns and frogs and birds. This is the arena of life. This is the place where I can smell life's glorious aroma, taste it through my nostrils, inhale and let it fill me with calm satisfaction. This is the jungle of dreams untangled. This is the tangible happiness I always knew I deserved.

I am Eli Sylvan. I am now part of the forest. I have become the recluse. I have decided to keep a journal, but am not yet sure what direction I will take with it. Perhaps I only want to retain a visualization of events, a written account for memory, something more than just a landmark in a spiraling galaxy. The human mind is a fiend for nostalgia, souvenirs we can keep to prove we have lived. I imagine myself as an old man, if ever I live so long, and one day crawling into an attic where I discover a dusty box, inside of that box I find this notebook, and I travel through time simply by scanning the pages. So this notebook will be my time machine.

Placing aside my imagination of a future, I believe keeping a journal will also act as a substitute for conversation and company. It will be for me what the Wilson volleyball was for Chuck Noland in that movie *Cast Away*. There is a common element fundamental to all human ideas. It is the desire to be heard, it is the need to be released from the echoing walls of our mind, it is a smile on the face of someone who will listen, it is a belief that we will be believed. In a word, it is companionship.

Being that I will spend five days a week alone, and the only human I will have contact with until I leave camp is Lamara, this journal will be my primary companion.

Whatever my purpose for this journal may be, it is not intended as an artistic expression. I only wish to describe as simply as I can a catalog of events. If I am able to pursue an aesthetic representation of my mind, which it is my intention to try, I will use the medium of paint and canvas.

All I seek is freedom and space, truth and answers. It has always been my understanding that truth and freedom can only exist in wild places. The comprehension of life's subliminal answers can only be acknowledged in the absence of life's developed distractions. Truth is an answer beyond the reach of a civilized conscience, and must find the space to be released. Space lost within the noise of traffic and electricity requires the freedom to roam in wild places. Freedom is the opportunity to live by my own answers.

Here, in the forest, there is wild harmony. Here there is a dancing green sky that quivers with the clouds. Here there is happiness for all who experience life and death. There are no contradictions. There are no expectations that don't get met. There are no greener pastures to cause discontent. For every member of this sacred system, this is as good as it gets.

I arrive on a sunny afternoon in early summer. It is just under a mile from the country road to camp; about four-thousand feet of overgrown two-track, then eight-hundred-fifty feet of forest. This is all approximated by counting my paces. The amount of gear I have should take me four round trips to retrieve. This will be the project for my first day.

There are no electrical wires, cell phone towers, or windmills in the sky, only trees. There are no fences or windows, nothing to keep me in, and nothing I have to look out from. I journey into the trail, slightly delirious, yet focused.

The trail is unrecognizable to my eyes, but my dog Snowy remembers its course. It's been nearly a year since we partially cleared a narrow trail meandering through the woods. It's overgrown now without constant travelers. Two-thousand feet from the two-track driveway to the river's edge. About halfway down is where I make camp. Here is a high mound that will stay relatively dry. To the north of this mound is a small creek that gathers up water from our property, and the land to the west, and then carries it southeast to the river. The river is broad and beautiful. The shoreline is painted with vegetation and singing with wildlife. The contour of the river bed is uniform and smooth, making the surface appear calm as a lake. Beneath the surface lives many a mighty fish whom I hope to catch. But not today, for today there is work to do.

The sky is so blue today I can't believe it ever will rain. I will walk back up the trail for the next load of supplies. On my first trip down the trail it was unrecognizable. On my return trip I already notice branches bent and broken, and moss and grasses already dislodged. The forest is learning of my presence, recording it for other eyes to see.

How do animals do it? With the number of wildlife I am certain live in this forest, it seems impossible for any vegetation to grow, considering my first passing potentially killed a hundred specimens. Do they hover in secrecy when no human eyes are watching? Like humans, do they rarely leave the routine of a broken trail? Or do they pass so gently through this world they somehow manage to leave it essentially undisturbed?

It's funny, I imagined myself entering the forest and contemplating the unanswered wonders of my civilized life. Yet here I am, contemplating issues I had never previously considered. Enough thinking for today, there will be time later for that. It's time to work.

• • •

After retrieving all of my supplies I am physically exhausted, for each trip weighed between eighty and one-hundred pounds. The small clearing in the trees where I will make camp is already being matted down. When I arrived it was filled with ferns and flowers and grasses. Now there is a distinct trail down the center, with flattened areas around the perimeter similar to the sight of deer beds in a field the morning after. There are still a couple hours of daylight, so I reassess my supplies.

For my home in the woods I brought a large canvas tarpaulin to be used as a pseudo-tent/teepee. I have developed a mental diagram to prepare for this task. I estimate it will take a half days work to cut down enough trees, and then cut those felled trees into appropriate lengths to build the frame for my shelter. I am excited to build my own lodge using nothing but a tarpaulin, rope, hand tools, and natural lumber.

I have brought with me close to two-thousand feet of rope. I spent many hours wandering the aisles of hardware and sporting goods stores to make my selection. My rope supply consists of a multitude of diameters and materials. Even with as much rope as I have, I still want more. It seems I may have a rope obsession.

For tools I brought a wooden handle spade shovel to be used for digging a food cache and a latrine, and maybe a fire pit. I have a twenty-inch carpenter's saw for cutting up my lumber and firewood. I have a fourteen inch Kabar machete for blazing trails, and a fillet knife in hopes of providing a few meals from the river. I also have a five-pound wood splitting axe; though this axe won't fell trees as easily as a wood chopping axe, or split logs as easily as a log splitter, it seemed more efficient to bring one tool with the ability to do both, than to bring two separate tools. On my belt I carry a Leatherman multi-tool, and a wooden handle skinning knife with a seven inch blade.

For entertainment I brought twenty-three books, consisting of classic adventure novels, scientific literature, and naturalist field guides. I have my fly rod and reel, waders, and a compact sample of fly tying tools and materials. Then there is the canoe which is presently stashed in a thicket by the road that I will portage down to the river tomorrow.

Of course, I have also brought my painting supplies. Being here my first day in the forest everything seems so beautiful and complex, I don't know if I will ever be able to reproduce it on canvas. There are so many layers of colors and degrees of light. So many shadows and shapes and subtle movements, with images hidden within images. I could spend the entire summer trying to paint just one single tree, and undoubtedly miss much of its defining characteristics. Do plants have inner beauty the way a person might? If so, can it be captured by a static two-dimensional representation?

For my outdoor enclosures I have a nine-foot by nine-foot screen house; this will act as my sanctuary from the flying buzzing biting insects, while affording me a view of my surroundings not available from inside the dark canvas lodge. In fact, I may choose to set up this sanctuary before the lodge, for I am already being engulfed in a swarm of mosquitoes and horseflies.

I also brought three heavy-duty nylon tarps. One of them is twelve-feet by twenty-feet and will be used as an awning over the fire pit. It's always a pleasing experience to sit by a warm blazing fire outdoors beneath a raining sky. The other two are ten-feet by ten-feet, one of which will be used to cover firewood. As for the other, I haven't decided a purpose yet. I also have a two-man dome tent where I will sleep until my canvas lodging is complete, after which it may be used for storage, or perhaps a dog house for Snowy to get away from the insects; maybe both.

For furnishings I have two camp style folding chairs for Lamara and I to sit by the fire. I also have a single reclining anti-gravity chair where I can kick back and read. I have a cotton-plaid hammock that will be hung with a view of the river – though with the amount of biting insects present today, I don't know if I will ever use it.

For food storage I brought a fifty quart marine grade cooler; this will be placed in a hole in the ground for added insulation and to keep safe from animals. For cooking I have a small single-burner propane stove, though I hope to cook most of my meals over the fire. This will come in handy during poor weather conditions, or if I just don't feel like starting a fire. I have a cast-iron skillet, a standard stove pot, and the minimal essentials for silverware and cooking utensils. I also have an aluminum coffee thermos, with a cap used as a mug.

My first supply of food consists of: canned vegetables, canned meats, packaged pastas, instant coffee, Tang, beef jerky, Clif bars, bread, and shore lunch mix. I didn't bring any cold items for the first week, primarily because I suspect ice won't keep frozen for long until I get the cooler buried in the insulation of soil and out of the warm air and sunlight. On the weekends, Lamara will bring me ice and new food supplies.

For my water supply I have a three-gallon gravity filter. It's quite convenient, I just carry a bucket of water up from the creek, pour it into the upper cylinder, and then let gravity work its magic as it pulls water down through the ceramic micro-filter and into the lower potable cylinder. The small creek, which is presently flowing at approximately one cubic foot per second, is only about one-hundred feet from camp, and assuming it is a perennial supply, it will make obtaining water very convenient. If this creek does go dry, then my daily task of fetching water will be slightly more difficult, as I will have to travel approximately twelve hundred feet to the river and back.

Where there is food, there is waste. For this I have designed a wilderness throne using an aluminum bucket, cutting out the bottom of it, tipping it upside down, and then fastening a porcelain seat. I will need to scout out a location on the opposite side of the creek to dig a latrine pit.

As an additional supply of water, I brought three five-gallon pails. These will be set up at strategic locations off of my tarps to collect rain water. My intentions for this rain water are bathing, washing dishes, cooking, boiling coffee, and a convenient source of drinking water for Snowy. Hopefully it rains frequently.

I decided to experiment with solar power this summer. Though I could survive without it, it will be good preparation for the day when we are able to completely give up our city lives and live in the forest permanently. I purchased a thirty watt polycrystalline panel, which will be ample supply for my minimal uses, a charge controller which prevents the battery from being overcharged or loss of power through reverse charge, a twelve volt deep-cycle battery to store the power, and a three-hundred-and-fifty watt charge inverter capable of powering most small household appliances. Presently, I only have two uses for this system;

recharging batteries for my LED lantern and head lamp, and also to charge my cell phone battery so I can make weekly calls to Lamara – for which I will be required to take the mile and a half walk to reception.

I have other items with me, and though they should seem obvious, it is my intention here to make as accurate a list as possible, so I will note them: tooth brush and tooth paste, body soap and shampoo, dish soap and sponge, three sports bottles, matches, toilet paper, disinfectant wipes, Q-tips, bandages, bath towel, spare clothes, pencil and paper, two pillows, fleece blanket, two flannel-lined sleeping bags, raincoat, mosquito netting, garbage bags, dog dish and food, and of course duct tape.

For the first week I brought a liter of vodka. I do enjoy the fresh clarity this transparent potion provides. Unlike beer, which dulls the senses and makes one forget, vodka has the ability to brighten up the night, and to create an intensity otherwise absent. I intend to only keep a small supply available each week, this is the only way I can discipline myself from its temptation. Are you an alcoholic if you drink every time you go camping? The answer, I suppose, depends on how frequently you are camping.

• • •

I have set up the two-man tent, and prepared enough firewood for tonight. I will heat up a can of beans for dinner, and stay up to watch the stars. It is quite possible I will indulge in consuming the first division of this week's vodka supply. So, loyal journal friend of mine, I suppose this is good night.

• • •

It is still my first night. It must be late, for my firewood supply is getting low, and I am already on my third drink of vodka Tang. I put Snowy into the tent, for I do not want him to disappear into the dark. It may take a while before I am completely comfortable letting him roam freely. I sit here alone beside the dancing fire light. There are many noises surrounding me in the dark forest. It is both exciting and unnerving, the realization that I am the only human within miles.

Day 2:

Today I slept until midmorning, I must rise earlier to take full advantage of my time here. It's difficult without an alarm clock to pull myself from the comfort of sleep. Nevertheless, from here forward I shall attempt to sleep at the first sight of the stars, and awake at the first sight of the sun.

My goal for today is to dig the pit for my food cache, and to set up my screen house sanctuary – these biting insects are becoming ridiculous. First though, I must retrieve the canoe from its hiding place near the road and carry it to the river. I'm going to eat a Clif bar and brew some coffee, then get to it.

• • •

My shoulders are sore. That was a long ways to carry the canoe. It wasn't necessarily the distance so much as it was the thickness of forest I maneuvered through. I could hardly take two steps without getting tangled in branches or tripping over a decaying log hidden beneath the undergrowth. The mosquitoes sure loved it though, taking advantage of my flesh while my hands were occupied with stabilizing the canoe on my shoulders. The most horrific noise these ears ever heard was mosquitoes echoing inside a fiberglass canoe.

Just before I reached the river, the ground took a steep dive of about sixty feet. The trees were so thick I couldn't see water until I was within twenty feet of it. The surface on the hillside was muddy, as though ground water had seeped through from the landscape above. I may have to build a walking platform to prevent returning to camp with muddy feet every time I visit the river.

I haven't seen Snowy since I let him out of the tent this morning. He bolted into the forest after a squirrel, so I decided to let him have some fun. I'm sure he's out there chasing animals, so I will try not to think about it.

• • •

I have completed the setup of my screen house. I am tempted to spend the rest of the day inside this sanctuary. I need to keep working, there's a lot to do. Still no sign of Snowy.

I finished digging the hole for a food cache. It is approximately three feet deep, with a surface area of three feet by two feet. After ten inches of topsoil, the rest of the depth was shoveling sand; perhaps I can come up with a use for my sand supply. My arms and back are sore. I am growing stronger. This wilderness life is going to whip me into shape. The cooler fits nicely into the food cache. I decided to use my spare tarp as a cover to help keep it insulated, deflect sunlight, and hopefully keep insects and small critters away. Still no sign of snowy, though I thought I heard the jangle of his dog tags once.

For efficiency, I heat up a can of corn for dinner using my stove, rather than waste daylight gathering firewood. I will use the rest of the day to start felling trees for my shelter.

• • •

It is getting dark now. I was able to chop down three balsam fir trees, each with a diameter of about six inches at ground level. This axe makes difficult work, but I didn't expect anything to be easy, so I will waste no time complaining. I am going to use my machete to remove the branches, then use the branches to have a small fire tonight. Still no sign of Snowy. I am beginning to grow concerned for him.

Day 3:

I woke up in my tent earlier this morning. There was Snowy, waiting outside for me with a big smile on his panting face. I was tempted to scold him, but it is only fair that he is as free here as I, so I started to pet him and thank him for returning. I quickly realized he was covered in wood ticks, literally infested. They were crawling out of his fur and onto my hands. They were visible on his ears and legs, scrambling for a place to stake their claim in him. They are grotesque little creatures, the blood sucking leeches of dry land.

I reluctantly poured a splash of vodka into one of my sports bottles, and then spent an hour picking the ticks from his fur and dropping them into my liquid companion. I am not sure if this will kill them, or just make them drunk. Eventually they are certain to drown in a happy death, which is much more than they deserve.

As I was enjoying a Clif bar and Tang for breakfast, I had a moment to step out of my thoughts. It's funny, how the forest seems so silent, even though it is filled with sounds. The lack of manmade noises provides the serenity of silence. There is much bird song in the air. One particular song is most intriguing to me, it sounds like soft bells chiming through a long corrugated tunnel. I haven't yet seen the bird that makes this call, but I am anxious to go exploring with my guide books.

My primary task for today is to prepare the lumber for my shelter. I will need to fell four more trees the size of those from yesterday to provide enough material for the frame. I am tempted to put off this task, and just sit here listening to the birds, but I must prepare camp first. I will have plenty of time for the rest later.

Since I don't wear a watch, and am consumed by natural pursuits, I am unaware that it is afternoon, and I haven't eaten a bite since early morning. So I wait until I'm hungry, and even then I find myself occupied with several other tasks that intercept me before making it to food.

I am exhausted and my stomach is grumbling as I sit by the fire heating up a can of beef ravioli. Behind me is a pile of lumber, evidence of my day's labor. I look around and all the ferns and flowers and grasses within camp that were flourishing only three days ago are now trampled and dead from my presence. I have successfully wiped out an ecosystem. I thought this would create a feeling of grief. In our generation of environmental concerns, it seems like every cut branch from a living tree is a disaster. But, looking around me at the abundance of thriving flora, it is easy to forget there is a disappearing world outside of this place. For here I am, one man in a wilderness, and my small little dent is no more than mandatory for survival. Every living creature in the forest creates a dent, and that dent is a direct correlation to the size of the creature. The only problems arise when a particular creature believes it is their right to create a larger dent than they require. Here I view myself as one of the animals of the forest, no better, no worse, so my own dent seems as natural as theirs.

Snowy spent the day in his own pursuit. He has dug a large hole at the base of a tree, presumably chasing a rodent of some kind. Silly civilized dog. He sure enjoyed himself though. Right now he is lying prone in front of the hole with a giant smile on his dirty face. I smile at his happiness, and the fact that despite generations of domestication, the desire for a hunt has not been stolen away from his instincts.

After dinner I decided to use some of my lumber in a practice project. I had to build a platform to get my solar panel up higher so it will reach more sunlight. I started by cutting four legs at approximately six-feet each, just high enough for me to conveniently reach the top without a ladder. I then used the narrow tops from the trees to build the platform, laying out two two-foot pieces three-feet apart, and then eight three-foot pieces perpendicular to those; these were all fastened using a thin twine. I then cut four three-foot pieces, and four two-foot pieces as braces that were fastened horizontally to the legs. After fastening the braces using a quarter-inch diameter rope, I then attached the platform on top using the thinner twine. I stood it up and it felt solid. I lifted myself up on top of it with my arms, dangling my feet, and it only teetered slightly. I think I am ready to secure a tent frame.

It's time to mix myself a vodka Tang in celebration of a hard day's work. I will sleep in my dome tent again tonight, hopefully for the last time. Tomorrow I build my shelter.

Day 4:

I awoke to pouring rain. The sky is dark as far as I can see in all directions, which isn't necessarily that far, for the trees block out most of the horizon. I get the impression this storm will be a daylong event. Building my shelter may be postponed.

Snowy and I had some uninvited company in the tent last night. These companions didn't offer us any body heat or conversation. In fact, they didn't even make a sound. I didn't even know we had company last night until I felt their flat bodies dangling from my skin like scales this morning. I have slept with the wood ticks. I jump out of my tent into the pouring rain. I peel off my clothes and begin picking their tiny little brainless heads from my skin. I spend another twenty minutes picking more off of Snowy. The only consolation I receive is that before diving back into my tent, I realize all the rain barrels are already full.

Back in my tent, with no sound but the contact of rain drops on the awning, I decide that from now on I will not wear outside clothes inside the tent. I will also have to check Snowy every night before allowing him inside. To prevent the wood ticks from getting to my skin, I will tuck my pants into my socks, and my shirt into my pants. I will wear a hat with mosquito netting to repel the paratroopers from tree branches. This should at least limit the number that find their way to my flesh. Nothing is easy out here, even the simple task of going to bed creates a list of chores.

In the afternoon I was growing tired of sitting in this small tent, so I decided to put on my rain coat and go for a walk. I went down to the small creek and found the rain had turned it into a raging torrent of mud and debris. I followed its now high shoreline all the way to the river. The river too had been influenced by the rains. It has come up approximately three feet further upon the land, and the usually reflective laminar surface is now punctuated with churns and ripples. I am glad the canoe is pulled well up the riverbank and secured tightly to a tree.

For the entire day I ate two Clif bars, and drank about three-quarters of a gallon of water. I entertained myself by reading through

Eric Sevareid's *Canoeing with the Cree*. What an amazing adventure. The daring exploits of two intelligent, capable, yet conveniently ignorant boys fresh out of high school. What has happened to that adventurous spirit? Has our courage of ignorance been polluted by horror stories? Is the fear of failure what prevents us from pursuing some tantalizing journey, from which we may not return? So we live out our experiences vicariously through movie screens and video games, rarely gaining any pragmatic knowledge of our own. I hope to break myself from that mold. I know this adventure I am living is but a faint flickering light to what those boys lived, but it is an omnipotent sun compared to how I could be living. I have no grandiose delusion here. I am not Thoreau, or Muir, or Rutstrum, or Meriwether and Henry. I am just a man choosing the chores and solace of the woods over the responsibilities and organized chaos of a city. I am far from the rudimentary existence of the earth-wise Native Americans from years ago. Most of my supplies have been purchased in stores like Walmart, Menards, and Cabela's. I am living with my place in time, it's just that my selection of place is different than others of my time. This is the new wilderness.

Day 5:

I am already losing track of counting the days. If today is day five, that means it must be Thursday. I was supposed to call Lamara last night. Hopefully I didn't cause her any unwarranted concern. I will try to find time to walk up the road and call her today. It seems even alone in a deep forest I have not escaped the necessity of counting time. I considered putting knife marks on a tree as a reminder of the days, but decided the only calendar I need here is the sun and seasons. Plus, my weeks will be noticeably punctuated by the arrival of Lamara on the weekends. I will just have to let her know not to get worried if I miss a call.

Before starting the task of building my shelter, I decided to take a walk to the river. Being up here on the hill surrounded by the thick forest, it is easy to forget I am so close to water. Most of the trail had already dried from the rain just yesterday, but the sloping side of the hill going to the river was still muddy. Here I was stopped short in my footsteps by the sight of a large bear track. It must have passed through earlier this morning. I knelt down to examine it closer. It was about the length of my foot. I rubbed my fingers across and felt the indentation, it was quite deep. I stepped around it and moved on. Only three or four feet away I saw another track, this one was smaller, about the size of my palm. I looked closer, knowing that a single bear makes two different size tracks: the hind paw is large and elongated like that of a man, and the forepaw is short and roundish like a mountain lion – except with five toes instead of four. Sure enough, this second track was also made by a hind foot. So there were two bears of different sizes traveling together, most likely a mother and cub.

The sight of these bear tracks excited me, and helped to solidify my sense of being in the wild. My only concern is they are so close to camp, it is only a matter of time until they smell my food and come to investigate.

I returned to camp with thoughts of bear on my mind. These are black bears, and even though they are omnivores, they make poor hunters. Most of their diet is insects, herbs and berries, carrion, and occasionally they are able to capture a small mammal or bird. Still, every year in North America, several people are attacked, and/or killed, by a black bear. In fact, there have been more deaths caused by black bears than grizzly bears in the last decade. This frequency is most likely due to the fact that more humans live in, and travel through, black bear country than grizzly country. Either way, bear attacks are usually the result of poor planning; for instance, sleeping with a bag of open beef jerky in your tent, or trying to scare away a bear that has already found your food supply and is engaged in consuming it. Other times it involves accidentally getting between a sow and cub, or encountering a feeding bear in thick cover. Occasionally there is the encounter with a sick animal who attacks out of derangement. Sometimes it is simply the character of a particular bear to be aggressive. That's something we as humans often underestimate; we think we can sum up an animal species by studies of a particular group, but the minds of animals are as varied as the minds of men, for which there exists such broad differences that even the summation of psychological studies fail to provide a full-proof predictable system. It is generally agreed that black bears do not approach humans, and if they do they can be deterred by shouting at them. I wonder what I shall shout if the opportunity arrives?

I must convince myself not to think about bears. I must trust in the kinship of the forest. If one approaches I will guide myself on instinct. I certainly doubt one would attack. I've decided to expunge my urine around the perimeter of camp as a deterrent. Between Snowy and myself I think our scent will keep away any predators. It's sad to me, when a bear does attack a human, it is then hunted down and killed. Or correction – euthanized. A bear shouldn't be killed for being a bear. If you are afraid of being attacked by a bear, then you should stay out of bear country. It's simple. I've heard people say there are too many large predators, that they are a risk to our domesticated lives. Perhaps there are just too many people? Forgive me journal, I don't mean to sound cruel, but I wish this world were better designed for coexistence.

It is now late morning, I better get started on my shelter if I am to finish it today.

• • •

I have finished my shelter, and I must say, it looks magnificent. I began the construction by using the dirt and sand removed from my food cache to level out the ground. Then I put my machete to the task of cutting down all the dying ferns and grasses from my clearing to lay above the dirt for both softness and added insulation from the cold ground at night. I then erected the frame. The floor plan is rectangular, about eight-feet wide by ten-feet long. I built walls around the perimeter approximately four-feet high. I then dug a hole in the center and secured a tree pole, extruding upwards approximately eight-feet. I draped the canvas over the center pole; the upper half of my lodge is conical like a teepee, and this tapers down to the squared walls. There was enough canvas for me to cover all the walls and even wrap underneath as a floor to minimize insect intrusion. Every joint of the frame was tied using half-inch rope; it feels solid and secure. The only seam in the enclosure is an overlapping section of canvas on the floor. I used my knife to cut a slit approximately three-feet high for an entrance on the south wall. The only problem is this entrance will not seal shut. After pondering on this I chose to utilize the rain flap from the dome tent, and with the use of duct tape and twine, I fashioned a doorway.

It is completely dark inside, even during the daylight. Faint shadows of trees are barely perceptible, flickering on the walls. I tied a rope around the center pole where I can hang my lantern. I look around and admire my space. I have eighty square feet to get comfortable in. I spent the rest of the day making my bed and settling in my supplies.

This is home now. It is good to be home! It's difficult to know what a home is until you find one. This is my home. It is laced with needles and leaves. It is full of songs and mystery. It is painted with shadow and magic. It is perfumed by aromas no manmade potpourri could reproduce. It is inhabited by strangers and friends. It is the only place I have ever been completely comfortable.

I have tonight and tomorrow night alone to adjust and settle in before Lamara arrives for her first visit. I am anxious to see her and show her what I have accomplished. I am also anxious to settle into my solitary routine. Luckily for me, I have a woman who is comfortable with my balance of both.

Tonight is the first night I sleep in my new home. I have been here four nights camping; but only now am I home. It is dark and mysterious on the other side of these canvas walls. I never step outside at night without my knife, though holding it most likely creates more paranoia than I would otherwise feel. When I hold the smooth wooden handle in one hand, while the other accommodates my need to release urine, I feel ready for battle with any predatory opponent.

I can see a bear, with my imaginations eye, who has been silently stalking my tent, waiting in the darkness, blending with the black of night, then rushing in a blood thirsty attack upon me, even though I know the black bear is seldom known to stalk a human. The word seldom leaves room to imagine. I can envision a mountain lion lying prone just inches from the radius of my light, pouncing on my half-sleeping body with claws and fangs, even though the textbooks say they are uncommon in this part of the country. The word uncommon leaves room to imagine. There is a pack of wolves circling in the darkness, and in a flash of golden eyes I am being eaten alive, even though I know there has never been a reported incident of a healthy wolf attacking a man on this continent. The word reported leaves room to imagine. So I hold my knife, even though my thoughts may be more at ease without it. Perhaps I long for the combat? Perhaps I am willing and eager to trade bodily scars for mental glory. Perhaps I had many a brief encounter with this exchange in the past, and am unwilling to accept the opportunity has passed.

Day 6:

I don't know what time I crawled out of the tent. It stays so dark in there, I would likely still be asleep if the stale air didn't heat up like a sauna.

My camp already feels more like home than any house I put so much effort into making homely. I built my camp on a hill above the valley that the creek flows through. The creek flows to the river. The river flows to a lake, which flows through other rivers and other lakes until it reaches the sea. The sea flows to the sky and back again.

The hill around my camp is filled with Balsam Fir, Quaking Aspen, ferns, flowers, and berries. These colors and scents are nearly enough to distract me from the sound. The sound is like a screw gun. The sound is like a power saw dulling its edge as it tries to cut through steel. The sound is invasive, it pierces my thoughts. The sound is like the rusty rails of a subway train. The sound is like a house built beneath the bridge of a freeway; it is constant. I had mosquitoes for breakfast today. Will I ever hear past their screams and shrills, put them to silence like the cars passing outside of a window on a city street? Or will their sounds still torment me as I swat the empty air inside of a white roomed asylum?

The sound could make me crazy, or it could drive me sane. Whatever the result, I've no reason to complain. Here is where I am. Though talking about mosquitoes with everyone who knew of my plans to live in the forest, while still living in the shelter of a house and the comforts of a city, was much kinder to my senses than actually living with them twenty-four hours a day. The paradox is I wish it would rain. Two days ago when it rained for the entire day, I realized something. Sitting in my wet clothes inside of a cramped nylon tent, listening to the constant tapping of a steady unrelenting drizzle, was the most comfortable discomfort I've known. For while my toes grew shriveled and white in my wet boots and soppy socks, while the bottom of my feet grew coarse like shingles, while my body shivered even though it was nearly seventy degrees Fahrenheit, I could not hear the mosquitoes. Sure I slapped the occasional one from my skin, receiving a small bubble of blood on my palm, but there was no onslaught, there was no air assault that could put Pearl Harbor to shame. The mosquitoes come after the rain.

There is an ancient mythology that says the rain and the mosquito are the same. The mosquitoes are born from the rain. Not the way our modern day science textbooks may explain it; eggs are laid in the water and an aquatic larvae is born then molts into the flying buzzing penetrating insect feared and despised wherever it is known. It's more primeval. It's more mystical. It's more simple and direct. It is possibly more correct.

The raindrops are like parachutes mosquitoes ride down in an assault from that mysterious ethereal place above. Every rain drop carries an assassin. They are on a mission; extracting the blood from our earthly bodies. As soon as that vessel of rain contacts a tree or grass or rock or dirt, it shatters, releasing these alien agents of repugnance. Then they wait for the sun to shine, for they have learned through the eons this is when earthly hemoglobin becomes active. Then they attack. They are sent from a place separate from the realm of good. They are the benefactors of evil here to destroy all blood-pumping bodies who seek to make a home of this heaven. I'm not certain I believe this mythology, perhaps because I don't want to, but the power of these beasts can be quite persuasive.

Today it is sunny and there are more mosquitoes in the air than oxygen. I am tempted to spend the day in my new home, the lodge as I have been referring to it, but there is still much to do. I spent the afternoon digging a latrine pit. I made it slightly over four feet deep, and about thirty inches wide. Then I built a platform over top using sections of timber with diameters between three and four inches. Before assembling the throne I preceded to jump up and down as hard as I could; this is one pit I do not want to fall in to!

I finally took a moment to relax. I went inside my lodge and looked at my painting supplies. It's too dark and isolated in there to paint, I should bring them into the screen house where I can see the ambient world. Instead I sat down for a moment of thought. I've been so consumed with duties of setting camp that I haven't yet had time to pursue the philosophical answers I thought I came here to resolve. I find myself in long moments of wonder about the shape of a damselflies wing, or the direction of a felled tree, or a hole dug into the ground. Perhaps this is the truest answer of all, distraction from the pursuit.

I am not yet certain what the extent of this journal will be. So far my days have been quite active, so I have had plenty to write about each day. Once I settle into camp I may only write once a week, or whenever something exciting happens.

There is a splash of vodka left to get me through the night. Tomorrow my conjugal visitor arrives with supplies.

Day 7:

I started out the day by removing the fallen trees from our driveway so Lamara could drive the truck all the way to the trailhead. I brought my axe and saw for tools. I spent approximately two hours chopping and sawing the trees into small enough pieces to be rolled away. I should have brought a better axe, or a chainsaw. Oh well, I can make do, people survived in the forest long before tools even as good as those I am now complaining about were invented. I need to cure myself from the laziness influenced by technology.

When I returned to camp, sore arms and hunched back, I saw Snowy sitting at the entrance to the lodge with blood on his face. As I approached I realized he had killed a snowshoe hare, which was now lying beneath his forepaws. He must have found its burrow and dug it out, snowshoe hares aren't generally active during daylight. The rabbit was dead, but Snowy had yet to consume the meat. Was he bringing it for me? I quickly got my answer when I knelt down to grab the rabbit's legs, and Snowy growled showing his teeth, like a wolf defending his dinner. I guess he wants the first taste, so I left him alone with his catch while I cleaned up camp. After about an hour he still hadn't eaten a morsel of flesh, just pulled some pieces out with his teeth and looked at them. Was he expecting a grilled steak?

I decided having the fresh blood scent around camp was not a good idea, it may draw bears or wolves in. I attempted again to grab the rabbit from Snowy. This time he promptly stood up with it in his mouth, turned his back to me, and nearly ingested the rabbit whole. Silly dog. I finally got the remains of the rabbit away from him, and buried what was left outside of camp. Then I proceeded to splash bleach on the blood stained soil and leaves. Lamara should be arriving soon. I'd better straighten up camp before she gets here.

After making the bed and stacking a pile of firewood, I pulled out both camp chairs and set them around the fire pit. I began reading the elegant prose of Thomas Wolfe when I heard the drumming of ruffed grouse. The sound is actually startling when unfamiliar with it. It is similar to an old lawn mower engine firing up in the distance. If you don't know what it is it may seem very much out of place. It's amazing how loud this rapid flapping of wings can be. The sound of drums is actually produced by the movement of air under their wings, not from contact with their chest. The forest thunder of blue skies, it sounds like far away war drums banging for battle. But alas, it is the songs of a love struck bird looking for a mate. Did ancient men learn their tricks of seduction from watching birds? The adaptation of their songs and dance can be seen in the eyes of modern women whenever a man is so bold to display himself musically for her.

I heard loud footsteps shuffling down the trail, and Snowy perked up his ears, then bolted into the forest. As soon as I saw Lamara I did a little bird dance by shuffling my feet and bobbing my head. She tried to laugh, but was burdened by a heavy load of supplies. In her arms she carried a crate of four milk cartons filled with ice. That's approximately thirty pounds of frozen water, which will be enough to keep food cold most of the week. Around her shoulders was a pack she unloaded to reveal this week's food supply, a bottle of wine, and a new provision of vodka. What a woman! I was so thrilled at the sight of my new supplies, I almost forgot to pay attention to her. So I decided to start a small afternoon fire for us to enjoy while she told me about her week.

This conversation led us into the lodge, and we didn't reemerge until early evening. After an early dinner we decided to go for a canoe ride. Snowy had been in a canoe several years ago, but Boulder has never even been in the water. We figured it was best to leave the dogs at camp, and take them out some other time.

• • •

That is truly a beautiful river. We covered at least five river miles without seeing another boat, or dock, or beach, or house, or lawn, or manmade object of any kind. It was the definition of relaxation. We maneuvered gently through the swirling mosaic, our paddles pursuing the rhythm of our breath. Bend after tree filled bend. Over the fast gravelly shallows, and above the slow viscous depths. There was too much in the details for our eyes to see anything clearly. The spike of a fir tree over the top of the forest. The silhouette of a maple leaf drifting downstream. The patience of a blueberry bush as it awaits fruition. The dart of a naiad before it ever knows of flight. The wake of a wood duck as it fights against the current. All these sights, and many others, filled our thoughts with the greatest distraction. Oh how fast the strife of a city can be replaced by wild beauty!

There were many animal trails leading down to the water, some of them barely noticeable bends in the grass, others wide obvious clearings with bent branches, trampled undergrowth, and exposed soil. We pulled the canoe up close to shore near one of these larger trails for a better inspection. There, in the soft soil where the water meets the land, was the obvious imprint of a moose track. This made Lamara very excited.

• • •

We now sit by a roaring fire. The air is calm, and the obsidian sky is perforated with star light. Both the dogs have returned from gallivanting in the forest and sit behind us. Our circular positioning and relaxed expressions reminds me of a comfortable family of wolves lying around with full bellies after a hunt.

A moment ago both dogs became alert and stood up with perked ears and serious faces looking towards the direction of the creek. Lamara and I each grabbed one of them by the collar, then knelt down away from the sound of the fire to listen. Sure enough, we heard something large making its way down the creek bed towards the river. We could hear good-sized branches snapping, and then we heard the thumping. It sounded like something bouncing up and down on a felled tree. After determining it was either a large buck deer banging its antlers on a tree, or a bear jumping up and down trying to scare something from a den, we went back to the fire, still holding the dogs tight.

New entry:

I didn't sleep much last night. I was continually disturbed from sleep by the sounds of mice clawing their way up the outside of the lodge. It's as if they would take a running start, reach the vertical walls of the lodge, then scramble up as high as they could before sliding down. Were they trying to get to the top of the tent, or was it just for circus fun? I suppose there is some confusion about the material, for everything else their little paws touch is granular soil, sleek grass, or crisp bark. I hope they grow tired of this activity soon, I don't want to lose sleep all summer over mice.

Today we are going to take an exploratory voyage through our thick jungle of a forest. So far we have only seen a small scratch of it: the trail to camp, the camp area, and the trail to the river. Lamara will carry the guide books and camera, I will carry a water bottle and machete.

• • •

Wow. I am at a loss for words and truly spellbound by the diversity of our property. It's amazing what unspoiled variety exists here. It would take an entire lifetime to learn the names of all these plants. Then there are the birds, mammals, and insects. Today we focused on the trees and flowers. We counted twelve different species of trees visible from the route we took. There were so many flowering plants we didn't bother trying to count them, but our favorite was the Columbine – perhaps because we saw a hummingbird suckling from its nectar. The Latin name for this plant translates into the English word eagle, because its colorful flower produces a shape similar to that of an eagle's talons.

It's easy to quickly get the sensation of being lost in a forest as deep and dark as this one. Even though our feet barely touched a fraction of our twenty acres, we got the impression of being in the center of an intricately designed labyrinth. I remember trips by foot in Wyoming; there, whether on the high plains or up in a mountain, twenty acres seemed small, especially on the sandy plains where you could see much, much further than that. Here, where distance of sight is greatly inhibited, one must be constantly aware of their heading. I chose to use the simple method of directing myself by waypoints. I pick the tallest tree in the direction I am heading, and guide myself to it Once there I choose the tallest tree I can see in the new direction, and go to that, then continue repeating until I get to where I'm going. In different environments a person can easily navigate by the sun, but here the forest canopy is so thick the location of the sun is often obliterated, so this method of waypoints is preferred.

We returned from our voyage for a relaxing afternoon of reading. It's great having Lamara here. Her curious spirit produces a visible world different from my own. Tomorrow morning she has to leave early, and drive back to her city life. She has decided to sleep here Sunday nights, then drive home Monday mornings in time for work. Next week I must focus on getting some painting done. I'm going to cut an ample supply of firewood so we can have a large enough fire tonight for her to smell it the rest of the week. I hope it offers a friendly reminder of both the forest and of me.

Next entry:

I walked Lamara to the truck as the shadows thinned in the early morning. She reluctantly got in and drove away with a wave goodbye. I stood and watched her leave. It appeared as though there were tears in her eyes. I think they were sad tears this time. She didn't want to leave. Neither would I.

Last night we were awakened by a startling sound. In the distance, approximately a half-mile away, though the location of sound is difficult to determine out here, we heard the shrilling screams of a wolf pack. It wasn't the usual serene howls I have heard on autumn nights in the North Country. This wasn't a musical chorus sung soulfully into the darkness. This was different. It was more of a blood thirsty scream. There sounded to be four or five of them at one location, then a moment later we heard the reply of two others not far away. I presume the pack had just made a kill, and was notifying the others to come and join the feast. Oh to see that! To witness the hunt, the kill, the sharing of a meal by a family, that is the wilderness. What have they killed? A deer, a moose, a bear? It must have been something large if they were joining forces like that. It fills me with a deep sense of honor to share this natural kingdom with the wolf.

I have decided to only make entries when something exciting happens, or if there is a thought I need to release. I cannot be distracted with creating a detailed account of every day. I need to start painting. The word need makes it feel like a job, a responsibility, but it is not   it is a desire. I want to start painting. I want to utilize the opportunity I have worked so hard to obtain. I want to stop thinking so I can see clearly. I just thought of something funny; I've had many jobs that paid me but didn't challenge me, this is the first job I've had that doesn't pay me but challenges me.

I spent most of the day organizing my painting supplies in the screen house sanctuary. I wish I could paint noise. Right now that is all I can think of. Whenever I step from this sanctuary I make it as quick and efficient as possible. In fact, I develop a plan of my exact route and actions before even unzipping the doorway. Outside of this screen house my enemies are circling, waiting, ready to devour me. Why so many mosquitoes? Is there no other blood pumping body they can surround and torment than my own? I imagine this is the primary reason most creatures of the forest create underground dens.

New entry:
Last night I thought could be my last night alive. A powerful storm rolled through, with heavy winds blowing down trees, lightning filling the sky, and thunder so close I could feel its vibration in my chest. The rain was like an anvil, so thick and

heavy I thought it would burst right through the ceiling of my lodge. The canvas pulsated and filled with wind like a parachute. I thought I may take off and land in Oz. Needless to say, I didn't get much sleep. I used to enjoy watching storms. It's a completely different experience under the safety of a solid roof. Out here I just wanted it to pass as quickly as possible. It lasted most of the night. My camp survived relatively undamaged. Two of the ropes holding up the tarp over the fire pit were broken, and a large paper birch tree fell only ten feet from my lodge. Oh journal, the only ears who can hear me, if I am to die out here all alone, let it be known that I was happy.

Up above me, at heights only the aspens can reach, is the tail end of wind chasing away the storm. It's amazing how much the rippling wind sifting through the rustling leaves sounds like ocean waves scraping into a sandy beach. The forest is a wall that protects me from the wind. I watch the tops of the aspens way up in the sky swaying about, and I am amazed by their flexibility, to be so tall and narrow, yet bending rather than breaking. They should be known as limber, not lumber. Only a mild breeze permeates the forest walls. With the mild breeze the ferns pulse and wiggle like fingers playing a piano. Even the shadows are magical, shimmering and shaking, always moving, constantly changing, never returning to the same shape or place.

Next entry:

Yesterday I spent the afternoon and into the evening in the sanctuary surrounded by my painting supplies. I never even dipped a brush into a paint can. I need to refine what I wish to define. I need to choose an image from all the images in my mind, from all the images in this world, that can singularly describe what I see. Perhaps I am reaching too far? All I know is there exists in my thoughts something tangible, reproducible, an explanation I can understand. But what is it?

Last night I stepped from the lodge long after dark. I wanted to experience the night. I stood by the doorway until my eyes acclimated, then began to walk. After ten feet I was startled into a defensive position by a loud noise and movement. It was only a badger. He ran right in front of me, making snarling noises as he disappeared into the darkness. I have never seen a badger before in the wild. He was quite comical looking, shuffling his short legs as he waddled along. His movement was similar to a duck on dry land. I wonder if he had ever seen a man? I wonder if he wonders what I am, or why I have appeared in his forest?

I should call Lamara this evening; she got worried last week without it. I don't miss seeing people, but it feels like there's something missing without their presence. It's been nearly two weeks, and the only human I have seen is Lamara. I haven't even looked into a mirror. I feel the fuzz on my cheeks growing thicker. I don't feel lonely, but I wonder how long I can keep myself entertained?

Wednesday: I think?

Last night I heard the wolves again. Their songs were melodious and free, playing just as the sun disappeared from sight. It was a joyous chorus this time. It sounded like two different packs in separate locations. The closer one sounded like it was less than a mile away, to my southwest. The other seemed approximately two miles away to the north. It makes sense that the county road to my north would act as a natural (or unnatural, depending on how one views man's development) territorial perimeter. If this is correct, then my camp is located near the boundary of two neighboring packs – this would explain the frequency of which I hear their howls and see their signs. Hearing their howls fills me with gratitude. I am thankful their calls still exist in wild places. But the paradox is I am simultaneously saddened by the reduction of places wild enough for them to survive. They used to roam freely over most of the North American continent. Now their howls are restricted to isolated locations where their ancestors weren't exterminated by man, or where man has abducted them from their homes and transplanted them miles away as an attempted reclamation. Perhaps this adds to the beauty of their song? A song of remembrance. A song of freedom. A song of survival. A song of defiance. How many men can sing songs so deep?

Next entry:

I spent most of last night lying awake with concerns. There are still some issues with the setup and routine of camp that need to be resolved before I can settle into the undistracted state of mind which will allow me to paint. For starters, so far I have been placing my garbage bag into my Duluth pack every night, then hanging it from a tree. I lay in bed last night, long after dark, listening to all the sounds of the nocturnal forest, and realized this wasn't my best option. Sure, hanging it up in a tree will prevent any animals from getting to it, except maybe a night bird or very resourceful raccoon or weasel. But I'm not really trying to defend my garbage so much as I am trying to keep larger animals out of camp. It seems hanging it up in a tree will only send the scent into the air increasing the radius of its smell. So, I have decided to dig a garbage cache, not to bury trash permanently, but just to minimize the smells wafting through the forest.

• • •

The garbage cache has been dug. I made it approximately two feet cubed. I covered it with a sleeping bag that Boulder had chewed up. I didn't really need it anyways, at least not until it gets colder. When that time comes I will just have to improvise. To help minimize the smells further, I will make my final nightly urination right next to the garbage cache, hopefully disguising any smells permeating through the sleeping bag. Who knew urine was such a multifaceted tool!

I settled into my sanctuary and tried to paint. My mind was wandering in too many directions. I need a distraction. I will try some fishing today. An auxiliary goal of mine while here, besides creating a painting and enjoying nature, is to catch the elusive muskie on a fly rod. The fish of ten-thousand casts. I'd better get started.

• • •

No fish today. I wet waded along the shoreline of our property. It's a nice gravelly bottom there. Next time I will have to take the canoe and explore more water.

While standing waist deep in the river, I was reminded of the trout streams in Wyoming. The scenery here is much different, and each is splendid in their unique way, but there is something common to all flowing waters. Perhaps what I enjoy most is feeling the weight pushing against my legs, and the sound water makes as it separates around me. Inevitably I found myself wishing there were trout in this river. What I wouldn't give to tie on a dry fly and watch it drift in anticipation. I miss the trout streams of Wyoming more than I miss any lover I've ever known, but I feel it in my heart the same way – only more powerful.

No fish were hooked, but I was rewarded with some mammalian company. A mother otter and four young ones were playing in the river. These are truly adorable creatures. They were certainly entertaining to watch, diving and rolling, treading and splashing, whistling and grunting. The mother always had her eyes on me. They were upstream about one-hundred feet, but would drift down with the current until getting about fifty feet away, and swim back up.

I haven't seen Snowy since this morning. I'm not concerned though, he'll return when he wants to. Probably out hunting again. He's been strange about his dog food ever since killing that rabbit. He's all but completely refused to eat it, putting his nose up in the air and turning away, as if to say, 'I can fetch my own dinner thank you very much'. He has taken a few nibbles here and there. I'm interested to see how long this will last. Maybe he'll go wild and won't require my handouts. If a dog doesn't need your food, will he still provide you with companionship? I like to think so.

Next entry:

Snowy returned last night as I was shuffling into bed. This morning, after I let him out of the lodge, I sat down to tie some new flies for my pursuit of the muskie. I've kept all my fly tying materials in a small duffle bag on the floor in the northwest corner of the lodge. As soon as I picked it up, I heard the rustling of mouse paws inside. I carried the bag outside and dumped its contents onto the ground. A momma mouse with two little babies attached to her teat quickly scurried away.

It rained this afternoon. I was able to refill all of my rain barrels. After dinner I took a walk down to the river. There were fresh bear tracks in the same place where I had seen them before. A momma and cub. 'Tis the season for raising young. It must be difficult being an animal in the north woods, with only several months of warm weather to feed your young and prepare them for winter.

Next entry:

Last night I put Snowy in the lodge early and sat outside alone listening to the forest. Just before dark I became confused by a disturbing sound. It started out as a grunting growling moan coming from a couple hundred feet up the creek to my west. I knelt down on the edge of camp and focused my ears. As it got closer it started to make a mooing noise, similar to a dairy cow. There are no cows here. The nearest cow farm is thirty miles away. I listened as it proceeded down the creek bed towards the river.

I lay in bed last night trying to figure out what animal had made that noise. I came to the presumption it was a moose. This morning I walked down to the creek to investigate. I followed its muddy shore upstream and down, but the only tracks I could find were those of deer and rodents. I knew it wasn't a deer or rodent I had heard. As I was about to walk back to camp, I noticed something barely emerging from the shallow creek. It was a big blackish-brown heaving pile of bear scat. He must have been walking right down the center of the channel. This makes sense, for it offers less resistance than trying to plow through the barricade of a dark forest. But then I wondered if there was more to it. I wondered if it was also a strategy to hide his trail and scent from the wolves, being that the wolves are the bear's only natural predator out here.

I came back up to camp and sat thinking about the bears. There is definitely a deep rooted fear of these beasts in the minds of men. There are so many horror stories about them, both true and fictional, that while alone in bear country it is easy to wonder if you will be the next character in a bear fable.

• • •

I had to pause from writing this to go investigate the loud snap of a large branch less than one-hundred feet from camp. My first thought was to zip Snowy up in the dome tent. I stood at the south end of camp, knife in my hand, and looked into the deceptive forest, trying to identify shapes or movements not made by vegetation. I hoped it wasn't a bear. I knew I had to go and investigate though. I hesitated. For some reason I felt safe on the edge of camp, as if this was my home, my territory, but if I took one more step forward, I would be in the bear's home and territory.

I finally calmed the shaking of my hand, and walked across the trail into the forest, towards the direction I heard the sound. I tried to stand tall. I tried to feel bold. I imagined coming upon a bear hiding in thick cover. I have come upon bears before in the wild and felt safe. It is a different story if you spook them in thick cover. I knew I had to portray myself as dominant if I were to deflect him without an attack. I arrived at the approximate location where I heard the sound. I made loud noises and knelt down to see through the underbrush. There was nothing.

I walked back into camp wondering if I had overreacted. I can't get defensive over every cracked branch in the forest. Did I let my imagination get the best of me? Was the fact that I was writing about the bear when I heard the sound a catalyst for exaggeration? I need to secure my thoughts, disable my worries. A man's mind is the beast of him.

Lamara will arrive today. I hope the bears keep their distance. I feel an extra strong sense of protectiveness knowing she will be here. Perhaps I should have brought a gun? That's nonsense though, I knew what I was getting into when I decided no fire-arms were necessary.

Saturday, week three:

Last night we went into the lodge early, just before sunset. We fell asleep to the sounds of coyote songs echoing through the night-silent trees from across the river to the east. Their song is much different than the wolf, and once you have heard both it is easy to distinguish. Coyotes join together in a high pitched shrieking yipping unison. Their voices grow loud as they all sing the same tune. Wolves all sing in a different tune, blending into a more musical orchestra. You can count the number of wolves in a howling pack by the variety of tunes, where it's much more difficult to approximate the number of coyotes yapping together. I like to think this implies the wolf is the more creative and artistic of these two cousin species.

We plan to spend the day relaxing around camp. Tonight we will go down to the river and sit along the shore silently until dark, hoping to spot some wildlife coming down for a drink. After dark we will start a campfire and drink wine beside the quiet water while looking into the night sky. The river corridor offers a much broader view of starlight.

Sunday:

We had ourselves a bit of a thrill last night. I can only laugh about it now. We sat silently along the river's edge, watching for animals in the fading light. We saw a muskrat in the river, and just before dusk, a large buck deer came down on the far shore. I went back up to camp and fetched a couple of brats. When I returned to the river Lamara had a fire burning. We watched the stars and listened to a chorus of frogs as we held our brats over the fire using freshly whittled roasting sticks.

Then we got the scare of our lives. Both of the dogs turned their attention to the forest behind us, up the hill towards camp. We each grabbed one of them and held them tightly by the collar, and placed our brat sticks along the edge of the fire. A loud grumbling vibration started rumbling from the trees. It was very close, but too dark to see anything. I shined my headlamp towards the sound, but the forest was too thick, and the animal was uphill.

We waited silently, hoping whatever it was would pass. Then we heard it again, this time closer and louder. It was now growling and snorting, as if it were taking deep breaths of the air, and either unhappy with what it smelled, or made hungry by it. The dogs were silent, but extremely agitated, and it took all of our force to hold them back. The beast continued its growling and snorting from less than fifty feet away. It sounded to be staying in the same place, so I figured we had just blocked its path to the river, and it would eventually find another route. I forced myself to remain calm, and as a distraction I turned my back towards the animal and continued to roast my brat.

Then a loud rustling came from the branches flanking us to the south, but the growling persisted in the same location uphill to the west. A large animal splashed into the river less than fifty feet away. I explained to Lamara it was probably the mother bear and cub taking turns to get a drink. I told her we just needed to be patient and they would pass. But the growls persisted.

Finally, sensing the discomfort in both Lamara and the dogs, I decided to take action. I tossed both of our perfectly roasted brats into the river, thinking maybe the smell was intriguing to the bears. I used the anchor rope from the canoe to tie up Snowy, while Lamara held Boulder by the collar. I told Lamara if there was a charge, she was to release Boulder and jump into the river. I grabbed a burning log from the fire and walked into the darkness, uphill towards the growling snorting beast.

I stepped with as heavy and as loud of footsteps as possible. I banged on trees with the log in my hand, which sent sparks flickering into the night. In my other hand I held a knife. I turned on my headlamp as soon as I was out of the fire's light. The blood pumped hard in my arms, and my eyes were wide open and focused. I spoke in a deep voice, trying to make myself sound as large as possible, saying things like, "What do you want!" or "Get out of here!" but mostly I just repeated, "Hey! Hey! Hey!"

I climbed the hill now thirty feet from the fire. I hadn't heard a sound since I got up and began my charge. I figured there were two possibilities: either the bears had silently retreated as soon as they saw me approaching, or they were crouched down waiting for me. I hoped for the first option. But still, for reasons beyond my domesticated explanation, I also hoped for a conflict. I wanted to test myself at battle with a bear.

Then I tasted the blood of my heart in the back of my throat. A sudden noise and movement erupted from the darkness just five feet to my right. I threw the fire log at it and cocked my knife back. Two large badgers waddled past me, one on either side of my legs, grumbling their displeasures as they went. For a moment, I considered they were running from the bear who was undoubtedly still there waiting for me. Then the obvious fact that it was only the badgers we had heard sank in, and I laughed.

Lamara was laughing with both panic and relief in her eyes when I returned to the fireside still trying to catch my breath. I sat down and quixotically said, "Yep, I really showed those badgers. That's the last time they try to mess with us." As I replayed the event in my mind, I couldn't believe how large and aggressive two little thirty pound badgers could make themselves sound. I suppose that's a beneficial defensive mechanism for them, sounding as big and ornery as possible, for there are predatory beasts in this forest much larger than them. Then Lamara said, "I can't believe you threw the brats in the river." Neither could I. At the time it seemed like the right thing to do.

Monday:

Lamara is gone and I am alone again. Every man should wake up alone and spend thirty minutes outside. He should spend thirty minutes with the rising sun listening for birds while pacing back and forth in ponderous thought, with a cool breeze on his nose and his arms stretched into the open air. He should spend thirty minutes alone with whatever view is available. Then he should go back to sleep.

Last night I felt as though there were thousands of microscopic insects crawling all over me. There quite possibly was. So far I have been bathing every other day. The word bathing is a vague reference to what I actually do. I've been dipping a sponge into one of my rainwater barrels, lathering myself with soap, and then cupping water in my hands to rinse with. This is a very minimalistic approach to bathing, but I have a minimal supply of rainwater to use. Of course I could bathe in the river, or use water from the creek, but there are so many microorganisms in that water I prefer the fresh water from the sky. I could filter it, but filters have a short enough life span as it is, and I need them for drinking water. I could boil it, but then I'm forced to either use my propane supply, or start a fire every time.

The simplest resolution is to have Lamara bring me a couple more five gallon pails, so that I can collect more rainwater. I will then use one of them to make a shower of sorts, so that I can bathe more thoroughly. Since two of my three barrels are presently full, and it looks like rain tonight, I will use the empty one and start this project.

I made a simple shower, attaching a rolled up section of tarp wrapped with duct tape to a hole in the bottom of a bucket, and then fastened a sock at the bottom of the hose. Now all I have to do wait for rainwater to fill the bucket, then raise it up on a pulley, and stand beneath. I am ready to feel clean again.

Next entry:

I woke up this morning excited to try out my new shower. It rained most of the night. It's sunny and warm now and the birds are singing. Last night I placed my shower bucket at the location of most drainage from the fire tarp, having tied the hose shut with a piece of twine. It is full of crystal clear water now. I tied it up to a tree to test it out. It works very well. There is some leakage from the seal where the hose enters the bucket, and some water drips out along the seam in the hose, but it is fully functional and much better than using a sponge. The water runs down and fills the sock, then starts to squirt out. It's very cold, and there's not a whole lot of pressure, but it gives me five minutes of running water.

The only downside is that I am fully exposed in the forest. Forget about the unlikely possibility of a random stranger choosing this exact moment to enter camp. There is something much worse than a bear finding me unarmed. The mosquitoes love a wet warm naked body. I must have been quite the spectacle, bathing nude in the forest, slapping mosquitoes and cursing while lathering and rinsing.

Next entry:

I spent most of yesterday sitting around and admiring my camp. I am truly enjoying myself here in the forest alone, though it seems as if I am missing something. What good are all these creations if there is no one to share them with? Sure Lamara comes on the weekends, and is excited by whatever additions I have made to camp, but I am missing the company. I convince myself this is for the best, that I need to be alone to clear my head so I can paint. Then I look at my blank canvases and feel discouraged. I can't force it though, when the time is right it will come. Today I will fish.

I had better luck this time. I caught one decent-sized northern pike, and two medium-sized smallmouth bass. No muskie though. I did see a large bald eagle perched on a boulder beside the river. What giant graceful birds they are. His feathers glistened as he flapped his wings furiously into flight.

I just returned from walking up the road to call Lamara. It's difficult for me to judge how she is adapting to living alone in a new city. I wonder to myself if I am being unfair living here without her, but I determine this is what's best for us. It's only a few months and she will be fine. Besides, she's a mature and responsible woman, if she is unhappy she would say something. No, I think she is happy with this arrangement. How many other professional women get to spend every weekend traveling to a wilderness to visit their woodsman?

On my return walk I noticed a large wolf track near our driveway. I had never seen one this large before. At first glance, judging by the size, I thought it was made by a bear. Sure enough, it had four toes, each with a distinct claw mark, and the almost triangular shape of the heal pad. The entire paw print was about the size of my hand. This was one large wolf, probably twice the size of Snowy, who weighs around sixty-five pounds.

I never considered a realistic fear of wolves. I know my nighttime fears walking alone into a dark forest are unrealistic, though at the time they seem exactly the opposite. Still, the sight of that enormous track caused some concern, more for Snowy than myself. How would he react if face to face with his wild cousin? How would the wolf react to this domesticated smaller version living in his territory? So far when we have heard their howls Snowy just perks up his ears, seemingly with only a mild interest. Does he know what they are?

As I sit outside making this journal entry, and the forest becomes one giant shadow, I sense a movement from the corner of my eye. I turn my face to look, but see nothing. Did I imagine it? Maybe it was just a bird, or a bat. Just then I thought of that movie *Predator*, and those alien invaders who have the ability to become invisible. Do I really know, one-hundred percent for certain, that they don't exist in this forest? I shake it off. What nonsense. I have been poisoned by other people's imagination.

Friday, week 4:

I have been here almost a month and still no painting. What am I waiting for? I am continually distracted by these wild and natural surroundings. If I am going to be distracted by something, I would prefer this over the sights and sounds of a city. Maybe I should forget about painting all together? Maybe the idea of painting is distracting me from becoming fully involved with this forest?

Lamara arrives today. It's amazing how much happens in a week between visits. I feel like I am made of a different composition every time she sees me. The location of your space determines the shape of your face. I think we will go canoeing today. It is time we experiment with bringing the dogs.

• • •

It has always been my belief that you can judge the compatibility of two people by the rhythm of their paddle stroke. When Lamara and I are alone in the canoe, our paddles move as fluidly as the tailfins in a school of fish. However, this particular trip had a variable. The variable has a name. Its name is Boulder. Though I do admire his spirit, he sure can make things difficult.

We put both dogs into the canoe and shoved off. Everything was going well for the first couple of miles. While gliding through a deep and narrow section of river, we heard a loud shuffling from the forest. We saw the tops of speckled alders swaying about, so we stopped paddling and waited. Those giant antlers were the first thing visible, rising up above the leaves of the low branches. Then we saw a huge horse-like nose, dark brown and swarming with mosquitoes, reveal itself from the thickets. It was a big old bull of a moose.

Lamara looked so happy. She turned and whispered to me, with as much exclamation that is allowed in a whisper, "There he is, finally!" It took a moment for the moose to see us, but as soon as he did, he raised his head and gave a loud snort. This sent the dogs into a frenzy. By some luck of chance, I was able to grab a hold of Snowy before he leapt from the canoe. It was too late for Boulder. He dove from the canoe with such ambition that he nearly tipped us in the process, which caused the camera Lamara was aiming at the moose to go flying into the river.

The moose, upon realizing Boulder's intentions, gave a couple of stomps with his front hooves, then disappeared silently into the forest. Boulder reached the shore as Lamara and I paddled furiously, yelling at him to stay. I guess he's not a complete rebel, for he did stay put. We reached the shore and boarded all passengers once again.

We anchored off in the approximate location where the camera disappeared and waited for the water to clear. This tannin-rich water has an amber tint to it, so even when all the disturbed material settles, it still has minimal transparency. Needless to say, we didn't find the camera.

"That was magnificent," said Lamara as we paddled upstream.

"I'm glad you finally saw one," I replied, "even gladder it happened on our river." Then I looked at Boulder's soaked fur, as he and Snowy panted profusely, and I said, "I think it's quite possible Boulder here was just as excited as you."

New entry:

It's been a couple days since my previous entry. Lamara is back in the city and probably sitting at a desk in a business suit right now. Snowy is sitting beside me here in the center of camp. I feel as though I should be pursuing an activity, an achievement of some sort, but every time I get started working on something I get drawn back into a meditative position. There's too much here to comprehend. There is so much space for my mind to expand, so much silence for my thoughts to explore.

The sun is amazing today. I look around me at all the life, all the trees and ferns and flowers and birds, and yes, even the mosquitoes. It is all so incredible. How many strokes of the brush to create this masterpiece? I look up at the sun with squinty eyes. The rays flowing down are one powerful and inseparable union of color. The sun is the greatest painter of all. Everything it touches becomes illuminated with magical definition. I should learn to take advice from the sun.

Week 5:

I haven't written since early last week. Not much happened, just a lot of time deep in thought while in a deep forest. Lamara left early today. We had a relaxing weekend filled with reading and silence. The only time I ever feel lonely is the day she departs. I will try to distract myself by fishing.

· · ·

Caught a few fish, but still no muskie. Maybe they don't even live in this river. Maybe the data reports I have read, and the stories I have heard, are all lies. Why so much deception? Why so much cruelty in the world? Even alone in the buffer of a wilderness I cannot escape it.

As I was returning from fishing I saw a tall dying cedar tree down the shore. I walked over and stood beneath it. I found myself distracted in a moment of distortion. How long has it been since this leafless and dismembered tree knew of its own vernal beauty? How many moons have come and gone since the first bud sprouted from the dirt with life in the future? How many nights has it reached for the stars when no one was looking? How many midnight owls have perched in its paternal arms? How many migrating birds have taken comfort here in passing? How many rains and winds and snows has it known, has it battled against, for the patient arrival of sunlight? How many more times will the sun rise before the cement soil releases its grip and sends the top tumbling to the bottom? How many more trips around the sun before every piece of life it has created returns to the hidden world of worms and roots and beetles? How many unknowns before the child of this masterpiece reaches for the same stars, the same sun, in pursuit of the same eternity?

Next day:

I drowned my loneliness last night with a double day's dose of vodka. My head hurts today. I am growing sick of this damn jungle. I can't even defecate in peace. Every trip to the latrine is a voyage to misery. The mosquitoes take advantage of me while I am most vulnerable and defenseless. I stand up slapping my own ass, and pulling up my pants as quickly as I can, simultaneously making a running dive into the sanctuary. Perhaps I should quit this. I could go back to town and find a job. I could still come and visit this property recreationally. I could be a tourist. What I wouldn't give for a fresh baked pizza. What I wouldn't give to sit on a couch and watch a movie. I would trade this entire damn wilderness for one moment of civilization.

It looks like it's going to rain tonight. Let it. I've got enough vodka to get me through. I don't need anyone or anything. I'm going to get drunk and yell at the moon. I'm going to pick up my machete and hunt a bear. I'm going to surrender myself to a pack of wolves. Take my flesh. Take my blood. I don't need any of it, you filthy beasts!

I turn on my lantern to assess my vodka supply – not much left. I stand up and stumble outside for a piss. Take me now forest! Consume me in your wrath. I will not fight it. I am ready.

I sit back inside and watch the lantern shadows. I see images in the light I know aren't really there, but they seem so real I can almost grasp them. Is this epiphany? Is this truth? What world am I in? How have I traveled so far? There is a power inside of me I don't understand.

I thought I knew it all, when I knew nothing but the certainties of ignorance. I thought I had it all figured out when this world was a small little simple place. I thought the few people I knew who were wild and desolate were the definition of life. I thought there was magnificence in their supreme individuality. I thought I belonged amongst the confused and broken-hearted majority. I now realize everything I thought I believed was only fleeting indolence. I now understand these familiar strangers in the world of my memory are just as confused by their loneliness as I. I now see their faces and wonder why I ever believed in them. Where have you gone, oh strangers I used to love? What world do you now consume? What heart do you breathe with in that disaster of your living nightmare? Do you ever think of me when you are lost? Does your clarity supersede that of my own? Can we ever again know the innocence of knowing nothing about our own doubts? Can we ever again feel that power of youth? Where are you, faces I remember? Are you happy? Is this the way we thought it would be, when we were supreme to the requirement of thought? I thought that I loved you. Why does love deceive us? Why are these hearts so frail? Why have you disappeared? Where are the lost and lonely people of my memory? I hope you still know how to smile. I hope the stochastic repetition of days hasn't forged a smile upon your face, and you still remember the freedom we felt, those days when we were, on top of the world. I hope your smile is sincere. You deserve it if ever a day deserved sunlight. You are the gods of my memory.

I thought darkness was only deceiving. I thought sunlight was guaranteed. I thought there would be illumination after the waiting. Haven't I earned it? Haven't I seen all that men are required to see? What else must I prove? What is left before I know my own truth? Where is this world I have waited for? Oh so many nights of loneliness. Oh so many days of pretending to be happy. Oh so many moments of filling up the spaces with people I thought would last forever. It has brought me nothing. There is nothing but an intangible moving picture in my mind. There is nothing I can replicate to prove it all happened. Only lost photographs that were never taken know what my mind speaks of when we are alone together. Who remembers? What other eyes see the same invisible world as I? Are we allowed to reminisce? Are the forceps of the past clinging too tightly to the intentions of a future? Are we ever where we thought we would be? Why this maze? Why so many people as lost as I? Where is the certainty of what we always believed we would be? Have you forgotten? Please, just say you still smile when you think of me. Please, tell me you haven't surrendered all we were capable of. Please, remember those footsteps that took us to places where men will never travel again. That was history. That was our place in eternity. That is all we will ever be when we sit back and wonder if we could have ever been anything more. Please, smile when you think of me. I was as lost and lonely as you. Wasn't it grand! I hope you live there still. As do I.

Another entry:

I saw the sky green and bright and streaked with yellow, then I blinked my eyes and it was gray and dark and filled with sorrow. But now the sun shines. Now the trees grow furiously. Now I am awake. Now I sleep in this waking dream. Now I am too busy to be concerned with what is real and what is not.

I thought I knew what this place was. I thought I would know where I am. I thought there would be something obvious here. I thought there would be understanding in my heart. I thought I could figure all of this out without wondering why. But then I saw a dying tree. I saw this life changing. I saw the cycles repeat themselves into an incomprehensible infinity and I wondered why. I wondered if I would ever understand this rebellion. If ever I would understand this ceaseless change. If ever I would remain stable and fight the differences impounding me. If ever I could know myself. If ever my *self* could know I the way this tree knows its fallen leaves. If ever the change would stop.

I woke up outside with my face in the dirt. This doesn't bother me. I have no recollection of deciding to sleep outside. This doesn't bother me. I feel dizzy when I stand. This doesn't bother me. My stomach is grumbling with hunger. This doesn't bother me. I am alive. My thoughts are clear. So clear are my thoughts I don't even realize I am thinking. I rush into the screen house and open a can of paint.

My hands are flowing like sunlight. The shapes and colors are astounding. I don't understand these images that are empowering me. My brush touches the canvas like photons to the earth, and a new world develops, free from my control, yet intrinsically dependent upon me. I am sweating with elation. I have no idea what I am doing, or what it is my hands are trying to see. There is so much strength in this clarity I am overpowered by the independence of it.

Next day:

The muscles in my hands are sore this morning. My clothes and arms are filled with paint. I can only imagine my face is painted as well, but I have no mirror to verify this. It is strange, sometimes I miss the company of other people, but I just now realized I also miss the company of my own face. It has been over a month since seeing my reflection. I keep the image behind my eyes, but there are no clear defining characteristics to explain my appearance to myself. When I try to picture my face, all I see is a blur of events and symbols, and, oddly enough, other peoples' faces. This is what I will try to paint, my own reflection. Not the exact reproduction of a mirror. Not the superficial view of a stranger's eyes. But my own self, the reflection I see behind my eyes. Not the form of a man, but the form of a mind. Narcissus had his pond. I have my canvas.

And what if I just paint and paint and paint, until the colors wrap around the canvas board like the silky ocean around the fiery earth, until all the waters of my thoughts have engulfed the dry land of my canvas, and even then I paint, I paint because I cannot control my thoughts, because they are vessels of their own design taking form vicariously through my fingertips, until the illusory network of my thoughts creates a visible orientation of my soul.

Next entry:

It is the weekend. I only know this because Lamara arrived this morning. Sorry if I have ignored you journal, but we have another companion at camp who you must share my attention with. I'm not referring to Lamara; when she is here she gets all of my attention, or at least ninety-five percent of it. You know who I'm talking about. Unbelievable, I'm speaking to you as though you're a real person. My pencil is my tongue, this white woven fabric is your ears. I have a real person here today, so you will have to forgive my absence.

Monday:

We had another magnificent weekend. It's so natural when Lamara arrives. She seems to be at peace here. I wonder what her other life is like. She updates me on the details of events that stick out from her week, but I know this is not all. There is another secret world she lives in. A world I will never understand while we are separated.

It is in the details. It is in the minutia. It is in the way she pushes the snooze button on her alarm clock exactly twice every morning, then runs around in a hurried panic preparing for the day, yet always finding time to sit and slowly sip a cup of coffee. It is in the way she must arrive at work every morning with a fresh smile upon her face prepared to repeat a new day. It is in the way she can make the people she meets feel comfortable and important. It is in the way I imagine her returning home from work feeling exhausted, but finding solace in the way her dog greets her with excitement and kisses. It is in the way I imagine her preparing a magnificent feast and wishing someone was there to share it with. It is in the way I can see her lying in bed alone beside the lamplight with a book open on her lap. I can imagine all of these things, and many more, but I cannot see them. All I can do is wonder what new idiosyncrasies have filled her life while she is home alone.

I often feel disconnected from that other life, the one she is living, the one waiting for me, but I never feel disconnected from Lamara. I could go a year without seeing her or hearing her voice, then upon our reunion it would be as though we were never apart. No matter what turmoil this twisting world tosses at me, I know I will be alright, so long as I have the courage of love in my heart.

I haven't been able to focus today. I have spent the last several hours just sitting here staring into the canvas. I think it looks good so far, and I want to keep working on it, but I don't want to risk tainting the image while there is no natural flow in my fingers. Perhaps I will go lie in the hammock by the river and clear my thoughts.

• • •

There are a lot of mosquitoes down by the river today. I had to return to camp and retrieve a sleeping bag, which I used to cover my entire body from head to foot while bundled in the hammock like a cocoon. A few of those little biting bastards still managed to find my flesh from beneath.

I had fallen asleep with a lazy shadow on my face when I heard a loud banging coming from above. I opened my eyes and peeled back the cocoon to see a large Pileated woodpecker clinging to a dying green ash tree and working its chisel. It was a male, for it had an entirely red forehead. I tried to remain still so as not to spook it. Then his mate came swooping down and perched on the next tree over. I was envious for a moment, missing my own mate. They each worked their own tree, drilling long holes and sending small woodchips falling to the ground. Taking intermissions from their work, they would join together in a vivacious chatter that sounded like jungle monkey's dangling from branches at play. Once they had their fill, they gave a loud shrilling bawk, and flew off.

After they departed, I got up to get a closer look. At the base of the trees where they had been working were small piles of saw dust. I wondered why I had never noticed piles like these before. I'm sure I have walked around many a tree that has been hunted on by a wood pecker, but I never before had the clarity to recognize this clue. Now I see more. Now I not only see the tree for its immediacy, but its experiences. The trees show definitions of themselves subtly like the face of a man. I could pass by either many times without any sense of recognition, but once I notice these hidden traits, whether it be the scar on a man's chin, saw dust on the forest floor, the wrinkle beside a woman's eye, or elongated holes in the bark of a tree, I now realize they weren't hidden, but that I just hadn't seen them. These traits become more obvious than before, not because they are any different than they ever were, but because I have the clarity of understanding in my eyes.

I walked back to camp seeing an entirely new world. How have I walked this trail so many times without noticing so many of these little details? There is a vast complexity in this world virgin to my eyes. But now the knot has been tied, and I will pursue consummation. I have returned to my sanctuary. I am going to utilize this new found clarity and try to paint.

New entry:

I spent the majority of last night filling my canvas with new images, images I have never seen the likes of. As I look into these foreign visions, that upon first glance seem so distant from myself, I begin to recognize a familiarity. I now understand the sensation and intention of every brush stroke. I don't mean to brag, dear journal friend, but since your only eyes are my own, I will tell you this is looking pretty damn good. I think I do my best work by lantern light long after dark. It is then the images of the day seep into my imagination like dreams. If I were asleep I would be dreaming. But if I stay awake, I can utilize that dream power through open eyes. This canvas board isn't going to be large enough for everything I now see. I'm going to have to fasten several others to it.

Month 2:

It is good to be working again. I know this painting in the wild is not a real job, but it keeps me busy, and gives me a sense of accomplishment. It gives me something to wake up for every day. What is it about humans – why this inherent desire to produce?

Even when I'm not painting I am busy with all the daily chores around camp. The little creek near camp has gone dry. I don't know if there has been a diversion upstream, or more likely, it has stopped flowing for the season. Either way, I am making more trips to the river to fetch water. The rainwater supplies me for the most part, and when available I prefer filtering this for drinking water.

If my hands are not busy with chores, or my mind not occupied with painting, I generally wander around. Sometimes I practice throwing my knife into the ground, not out of any anticipation for using this technique in combat, but just as an activity to dis-tract myself from my *self*. I have gotten pretty good. I can general-ly hit any target blade-first within fifteen feet. Somehow the sight of my knife penetrating a stump always entertains me. Unfortu-nately, this skill won't offer me any advancement in society, which

I will inevitably have to return to someday. Unless of course I join the circus. I could be a knife thrower for a traveling circus show. They would call me Eli Dagger.

Other times I walk down to the river and sit on a stump to watch the slow moving water. Sometimes on a clear day I notice the nymph of a dragonfly scooting itself beneath the surface. Other days I watch the ducks and otters. They are both playful animals who have figured out how to mix work with pleasure. Occasionally I see a fish dart past me in the shallows. If Snowy is around he dives into the water in pursuit. He hasn't had any luck yet. I wish I could explain better fishing techniques to him. I haven't done much fishing recently, but that's alright, I am continually withdrawn into whatever images pass before my eyes. I never thought my days could seem so full without the daily requirement of going to work. Never a moment of boredom enters my life.

New entry:

During the past couple weeks I have noticed wild raspberries coming into fruit, with some late season wild strawberries still available, and beaked hazel nuts ready to be harvested. This gave me an idea. I called Lamara last night and told her when she comes to visit me not to bring any new supplies, and asked if she'd be alright skipping her visit the following weekend. I want to experiment with a two week duration of living off the land.

She was hesitant at first, I don't think she wanted to skip a week's visit. Finally she agreed, contingent upon me not being too stubborn to walk out to the road and call her if things got difficult, and that I wouldn't eat anything I wasn't one-hundred percent certain of. These both seemed simple and obvious to me.

When she arrived today she wasn't burdened by her typical load of food, ice, and vodka. Perhaps I should have requested more vodka. We have enough food to feed both of us through the weekend. Monday will begin my experiment.

Next entry:

Lamara leaves tomorrow morning. I will have two weeks alone. I will have two weeks without new supplies. Presently in the food cache: two Clif bars, one can of beef ravioli, and a half liter of vodka. Realistically, I could survive for two weeks just off of these items. It wouldn't be a comfortable survival, but I wouldn't die of starvation, as long as I rationed my food properly. But I'm going to go further. I'm going to collect berries and nuts during the day, then take my rod and reel to the river at night in attempt to capture dinner. I could always build traps to capture squirrels, or mice, or maybe even rabbits, if times get tough, but I hope to avoid resorting to that. Not because I have anything against hunting, not hunting for sustenance anyway. Hunting is the most primitive and natural means of securing a meal, and in my opinion killing an animal for food is no different than eating an apple from a tree – both are natural forms of organic energy exchange. It's just that I enjoy keeping my little wilderness as wild as possible, and the more wildlife which exist here, the more wild this land remains.

Next week:

This morning I lay in bed waiting for the rain to pause. On the outside of the canvas wall I saw a small serpentine shadow clinging to the fabric. I was perplexed by its size and its movements. It was too small to be a snake, too narrow to be a worm – about five inches in length, and less than a millimeter in diameter. It slithered and separated into fibrous filaments. It meandered and curled like a caterpillar blindly reaching out for its next footing. It moved up, and it moved down, reaching with both ends, separating in the middle becoming almost transparent, and then reforming into a single solid strand. I was perplexed as I watched its shadow on the canvas wall. Finally my curiosity gained enough momentum for me to step out into the rain and unveil this mysterious creeper. There, on the other side of the shadow, was a half dozen of her hairs slowly dripping down with the rain. I thought to myself: How nice of you to leave me this little mystery.

This afternoon I used my cooking pot to gather berries. I got it about half full with raspberries and strawberries. This is such a beautiful combination of colors and shapes I almost don't want to eat it. But they sure taste good! I ate meat yesterday, so I won't fish tonight.

Next entry:

I stayed up last night painting. The wolves were howling nearby. Snowy ran off so I had to chase him in the dark. I finally found him, digging a hole at the base of a tree and panting with loud excitement. I brought him back to camp and locked him in the dome tent.

This morning I ate one of my Clif bars for breakfast. Figured this would give me some protein for the day. I will go out and collect berries again this afternoon. Tonight I will try to catch a supply of fish.

• • •

I caught one eight inch smallmouth bass. They're not the best fish for eating, and the two small fillets aren't much for sustenance, but it is enough. I washed down my meal with some vodka.

New entry:

I slept late this morning. My skin already feels tight and my muscles feel lean. I think about the days of living in a house when I would consume a large pizza by myself, then follow it with a bag of potato chips. What a waste that seems now. Though a soft dough topped with spicy sauce, melted cheese, and a variety of pork, does sound appealing.

I ate berries for lunch today. I didn't catch any fish, so I decided to eat my final Clif bar for dinner. I may have to spend more time fishing tomorrow. Most of the past few days have been spent gathering berries. Every day I have to travel further from camp to find a new supply.

Next day:

I woke up very hungry, so I waited until late morning and ate my beef ravioli. I think I am going to pass on the gathering of berries, and spend the extra time fishing this afternoon. As enjoyable as fresh wild berries are, they are not the greatest thing for my digestion.

I have revised my fishing technique. Since I am now fishing for food, I have put thoughts of a muskie out of my mind. I need to fish with smaller flies. I want to catch some walleye. I tied up a new fly pattern that most closely resembles a wooly bugger, which is designed to roughly imitate a leech or minnow.

I had some success tonight, I caught a whopper of a walleye. Ooh, a Whopper. Burger King. I can taste that processed meat, and it is delicious! I'm going to eat one of the fillets tonight, then save the other for tomorrow. At least I have no shortage of drinking water since it rained from sunset to sunrise. This makes it easier, I don't know that I've been eating enough protein to support my body carrying buckets of water up from the river. I feel good though.

New entry:

This morning, confident with my new fishing technique, I ate the rest of the walleye for breakfast. I will take another day off from the berries, and catch more fish for dinner. With that settled, I'm going to take a peaceful walk through the woods to clear my mind. Hopefully I can return and get some painting done.

• • •

After returning from the walk I sat in a chair to look at my painting. There was a powerful wind in the low sky all day. I couldn't feel it, but I could hear it. The rustling of leaves and subsequent cracking and falling of branches was loud enough to cover any other sounds. On quieter days, I turn my head curiously toward any crackling of a branch, but today it was just normal white noise, like the sound of traffic outside of a city window. Nearby I heard two loud snaps, one right after the other. These had more intensity than the twigs which had been cracking all day. In the back of my mind I assumed it was just a dead branch that had fallen from up high.

I looked over towards the fern garden about sixty feet away and saw the large black crest of a bear. Its huge round back was breaking through the tops of ferns like the hump of a whale rising from the sea. I felt my body try to jump as I instinctively reached for my knife. But then my mind took over and I restrained myself. Sitting still with a pounding heart, I watched the giant beast. It was about the size of a two-man dome tent, and was shuffling its clumsy feet towards me. It seemed out of place, after all of the smaller creatures – like squirrels, badgers, and mice – to suddenly be confronted with a beast much larger than myself. I was amazed by the sight of it. There it was, after all my waiting and fearing. For some reason he decided to mosey into camp today during daylight hours. Then I thought of Snowy. He was asleep in the dome tent, but I didn't want him to sense the bear and give chase. I quickly stood up to go zip him in, and as I did so the bear saw me and promptly fled. As I watched him scramble into the thickets, a proud smile crept onto my face; today I scared a bear.

I continued over to zip Snowy into his tent, and sure enough he was just lying there completely oblivious in his comfort. Then I rushed back over to the edge of the ferns, hoping to get a better view of the bear. It was then I realized the knife was still in my hand. I stood there silently waiting for a sign of the bear, but could hear or see none. I knelt down to get a look beneath the underbrush, but saw nothing. So I walked into the ferns with hesitant steps. I stood in the approximate location where I had first seen the bear and started to make loud noises. Then the sudden thunder of the bear rising to its feet caused me to swallow my heart in my throat. He was less than twenty feet away where he had gone into the thickets to lie down and hide. I felt the adrenaline of combat as I cocked my knife hand back and yelled obscure sounds in the bear's direction. All I could hear were branches crashing. Then I saw a small dead tree tumble to the ground about thirty feet away. I looked more closely and could see the tops of shrubs parting like the wake of a boat as the bear fled further into the forest. I took a deep breath and smiled; I scared a bear twice today.

It's really no surprise the bear ran from me. I am a man. I represent the species all animals fear most. It is we who have invaded their land and obliterated their homes. It is we who have destroyed their world to make a home for ourselves. It is we who remove them from the wild for study or show. It is we who have hunted them, not for sustenance, but pleasure. It is we who keep body parts of their kin on our walls. There is no bear who collects human skulls and displays them victoriously in a cave. There is no bear who has burned down a man's house. There is no bear who has kidnapped a child for display. There is no surprise the bear was more afraid of me than I was of him. I am a man.

Next entry:

I stayed awake most of the night. Even though the bear fled from me during the day, I imagined him coming back with nocturnal courage on his side. All I have is a thin sheet of canvas separating me from whatever lurks in the darkness. Every sound in the forest picks up volume by night. Every falling leaf is the thundering footstep of a bear.

I feel exhausted and ready for real food. I can't quit now. Perhaps the most difficult part for me is that I could quit this at any time. I am here by choice. All of my discomforts are optional. Of course, by leaving I would only exchange them for different discomforts. This is the life for me. This is the place where the pleasures outweigh the pains.

I think it has been four days. Maybe five. Either way, I am about one-third through this experiment. The squirrels are starting to look appetizing. I could build a spear and hunt grouse. I'm going to collect more berries. Tonight I will fish. My stomach stays full, but it is an uncomfortable full.

New entry:

I have eight or nine days remaining to sustain myself naturally. I am growing tired of fish and berries. Today I will gather hazelnuts.

These hazelnuts are a hassle to eat, seems like I expend more energy gathering and preparing them than I gain by eating them. If I'm going to make this project a success, I will need to find a new source of protein.

Fishing has been unreliable. The hunger in my body affects the perception of my eyes. I no longer see the animals in this forest as artistic representations of freedom, but now I see them as meat. I'm beginning to understand why the Native American's respected and honored the animals they killed. To live amongst these creatures as neighbors, yet rely on them for sustenance, that is the true kinship of the forest.

I have decided to build a trap in attempt to capture a rabbit. I considered a simple lever trap – I could use my cooler, flip it upside down and angle it up with a stick, then bait a rabbit under it with berries and nuts – but then I realized a live rabbit would be trapped under there and would likely escape when I lifted the cooler. So I will need to devise a trap that will either secure the animal, or kill it.

I spent a long time wandering around camp studying tools and materials, waiting for an idea. What I finally came up with seems far-fetched, even to me, but it just might work. I found a rabbit hole near camp, and dug a small pit several feet in front of it. I then cut a small section of tarp to lay over the hole. I used the soil extracted from the pit and placed it in one of my empty rain barrels. I then attached long sections of twine to all four corners of the tarp over the pit, and affixed them all to the handle of the bucket. I then removed the solar panels from their platform, and set the platform near the hole. I placed the bucket filled with soil on the platform directly above the hole, and then balanced it so it will tip directly into the pit if weight is placed on the tarp. I have designed a pulley-type burial pit trap. If a rabbit steps on the tarp, it will fall into the pit pulling the tarp with it, which will, hopefully, create enough force to tip the attached bucket and successfully bury the rabbit. I'm going to collect berries and hazelnuts to place on the tarp as bait.

Next entry:

I painted until dark last night. I am out of vodka so I went to sleep early. I woke up before sunrise to check my trap. Didn't catch anything.

I'm going to gather berries, then paint, then try to fish again tonight. I hope to catch something, I've never known real hunger before this.

New entry:

I woke up this morning feeling the pains of hunger and fatigue, which got me thinking about photographs of Jewish people taken at concentration camps during World War II. I'm not comparing my little experiment with the torment they endured, rather I am thinking of them as inspiration – if they could survive those starving conditions for that amount of time, then certainly I can make do. But that inspiration was quickly replaced by the instinct of hunger, and I now find myself imagining pictures of gourmet pizzas, juicy cheeseburgers, and Lamara's mac-n-cheese.

Then I felt excitement in my veins, and the hope of relief from hunger, as I looked at the trap and saw the bucket inverted on top of a filled pit. I quickly retrieved my shovel and started digging out the pit, my mouth was watering with the idea of savory meat juices.

There, at the bottom of the pit, was a wiry-furred opossum, with enough life left to snarl as it tried to claw its way out of the hole. If only I would have waited until night to dig, then this creature would have suffocated. Now I've got an angry opossum looking at me with beady black eyes and trying to escape. There's no way I'm going to eat this rancorous rodent. This vexatious varmint. I would rather go hungry.

The trapped animal began a valiant effort of escape, and before I knew it I was pounding its head in with the shovel. I retrieved it from the pit by the tail, and carried it into camp. Once Snowy saw what I was carrying he rushed over to me with fierceness in his eyes and tried to snap it out of my hands. After zipping Snowy in the tent I retrieved my fillet knife and extracted as much meat from the vermin as possible.

While the fire was burning and the meat was sizzling, I removed most of the fur from the remains of my kill. I waited until the meat was good and black – the taste of ash sounded more appealing than the taste of vermin – then I ate. The bitter rancid tasting meat went down easy due to my intense hunger. While I will never go to a restaurant and request a fillet of opossum, here alone in the forest and hungry, it was a satisfying meal.

After eating I burned the remains of the animal, and then reset my trap. I am gassy and nauseous, but my belly is full. I'm going to utilize the fur to tie up a couple of new fly fishing lures.

New entry:

The trap was empty this morning, so I ate raspberries and hazelnuts today. I haven't been painting much. I don't know if it's due to this restricted diet, the fact that most of my thoughts are concerned with my next meal, or just a lack of vodka. I am enjoying this experiment, but am ready for it to be finished. I looked through my entries trying to figure out how long it's been, there's still four or five days before Lamara arrives. I'm going to go to the river and test my new opossum flies.

New entry:

I conserved energy this morning. The trap was empty, and I wasn't able to catch any fish last night. I don't want any more damn berries or hazelnuts. Have I really become so spoiled? The squirrels don't complain. Or maybe that's what all their chatter is about. The bears don't complain. But then again they seem to prefer human leftovers when available. I wonder if every animal in the forest grows tired of their routine?

New entry:

Today I am very hungry. Snowy's dog food is looking appetizing. I began walking towards the road to call Lamara, surely she would drive here a couple days early if I needed food. About halfway I stopped to pick raspberries. I looked up the trail and saw two white tailed fawns with freckles on their soft fur. They didn't see me yet. My mouth began to water and my eyes saw a venison burger. I watched them as they playfully rousted with each other. Then momma doe came shuffling across the trail and into the opposite forest. They followed her in, kicking up their heels as they went. I turned around and walked back to camp.

I returned once again feeling inspired. There is no tiresome routine here. This is the only land of the free. This is the lost world waiting to be discovered. I can only hope it never is.

Next entry:

I spent yesterday painting. I think it was some of the best imagery added to the canvas thus far. When I was hungry, I simply got up and found food. There was no pain. There was no hassle. It was right there waiting for me. Living is the easy part. It is only thinking about living that makes life difficult. The curse of a conscience is a confused mind.

I have just returned from fishing, and was able to catch one small walleye with the opossum fly. This fish was so small that under normal conditions I would release it, but I'm too hungry to consider these normal conditions.

New entry:

I've been sitting here trying to paint, but my mind isn't on images, it is on sounds. I hear people talking. Not audibly, but internally. Yes, journal, I am saying there are voices in my head. Please don't think I'm crazy. I've always heard my own voice in my head, and I even sometimes replay conversations with real people. This is different. The voices aren't attached to any faces. There isn't any dialogue. People are telling me things. It's like there's ghosts living in my brain. I have never been entirely alone this long. I need to walk around and rid myself of this spectral thought.

• • •

This afternoon as I walked through the woods looking for berries, I heard an automobile coming down the trail. There is human life here. Lamara is back. I spent a long time just holding her in my arms looking down into her face. She brought me supplies. What a woman! She brought me a steak for tonight. I couldn't wait that long, so I started a fire to fry it up immediately. The smell of steak sizzling over the orange flames made me realize how hungry I actually was. She said I looked pale. I ate with gusto. I felt like a hypocrite, but it was delicious.

The experiment was a success – I didn't die. I realized even though I did survive, it was only for two weeks. If I ever want to truly live off the land, it will take much more planning and preparation.

New entry:

We spent most of yesterday down by the dry creek bed, sometimes talking, mostly listening to the forest, and just enjoying each other. We sat on the mossy log of a decaying elm tree. From our position we could see tracks of bear and deer and badger in the soft creek bottom. Looking up the hill towards camp, the forest was so thick you wouldn't even know a wilderness camp was right there. Inversely, while up at camp I wouldn't know a dry creek bed being used as an animal trail was only a hundred feet away.

New entry:

It was a muggy weekend, with heavy air that smothered my pores like a damp blanket. Lamara left early this morning. She seemed sad all weekend. I got the impression she feels lonely and wonders if she made the right decision leaving the life she had established to embark on this adventure with me. I hope she's doing alright. It must feel lonelier being alone in a city than alone in a forest. If she were here, and if I were capable of speaking the thoughts I have clearly, I may say something like: The new leaves will green and the trees will grow. The sun will sneak away from the clouds and cover the land. The fog will rise and the birds will sing again. You and I will be happy.

I decided to spend the morning painting. When I arrived at my canvas I became distraught. The hot moisture in the air created a deformity in the upper left corner. The paint had absorbed water and dripped down, causing a smeared and blurry image. I was very angry. I considered kicking the painting and cursing the skies. Then I looked closer. The distorted image actually created a better representation of how I view the world. It was foggy and uncertain. Nature had caused an effect I couldn't have done by myself. I liked it.

However, I couldn't risk the entire painting being damaged. I had to figure out a way to prevent this from happening again. I need a dehumidifier. Or even a fan. As I looked around trying to come up with a plan, I realized some of my other materials at camp had become moldy. I wiped all of those off with bleach water, but that same technique couldn't be used on my painting. At a loss for ideas, I decided my best bet was to position the painting above the ground on its back, painted image facing the sky. Transpiration rises, so hopefully this will eliminate the accumulation of water.

New entry:

In the forest there is a battle. Every member is at war, even against members of its own species. Men take up arms and shed blood for land and water and food. The forest fights for sunlight.

The tallest trees have the advantage, but they have had to earn it. Even the tallest trees one day were mice surrounded by bears. Everything green has engaged in this battle. The smallest leafy creatures on the forest floor have evolved with a sense of magnanimous surrender, a modest simplicity that says, "This is all I need, I will never be anything more, but that's alright, my survival requires less greed".

Does my own survival require less greed? I like to think so. I look around at the surrounding forest. I remember shortly after my arrival feeling dismayed by my caused destruction. Now it doesn't look so bad. The initial damage was the worst, nothing much has changed since then. The ferns and flowers and grasses no longer grow within my camp boundary, but the surrounding forest is filled with these and many other plants. I have felled fewer than ten living trees. Sure I ate some berries, the seeds of the plants I picked them from, but if I didn't eat them something else would have.

In a sense I am a hypocrite, for the majority of food I have survived on was produced and gathered in other lands modified for man's benefit. We must survive though. Isn't it our right to use whatever ingenuity exists in the minds of men to survive, to flourish, to procure a place in the future?

Beavers cut trees to build a lodge. Ants displace soil and decrease root structure. Weasels eat up to forty percent of their body weight each day, and cache much more than they will ever consume. Predatory animals kill other predatory animals to defend their hunting ground. Even the sky participates in this battle, sending lightning to burn forests, droughts to dry rivers, winds to wipe away mountains. The world is a battle field. Next to weather humans are the most forceful, and so the most successful. Is it wrong for us to do what we were born capable of doing?

New entry:

I haven't spoken to you in a while, journal. I have been sulking. I am over that now. Today I have been watching butterflies like fluttering flowers. Today the world is beautiful and simple again. Today I am in a state of delirium spawned by the splendor of this forest. Today I am the only man who has ever lived.

I see the maroon-brown needles dying on the lower branches of a fir tree. So much change. I wonder if change can be painted? Can change be a static two dimensional portrait? Or does it require movement, and further dimension? If I can figure out the ultimate source of change, then I may be able to produce it in an image.

New entry:

Hello dear journal friend, I have returned from the night. Sorry if you don't recognize me, for I have changed. Not only the obvious physical differences which have occurred since first making your acquaintance and moving into this wilderness – most noticeably the fur on my face, the tone in my arms, and the definition of my waist – but there is also something more, something permanent, something I don't know if I will ever be able to explain to you. There may not be words for the ideas men use to describe themselves to themselves. So I will stick with simpler topics.

As I said, I have just returned from a wander in the night. There's really nothing quite like walking alone through a dark forest just after sunset. Now the ground is dark so you cannot see your footing. The air is barely bright enough to make out indiscernible shapes. This is the interesting part, for every shape seems to move and conceal other shapes, and the longer you look, the more new possible shapes become revealed. Just when you have fooled yourself into believing that you actually believe this shape is not a beast of the night, the shadows change. Now the forest begins to rattle. There are sounds surrounding you, but you can see nothing. You convince yourself it is but a frog or a mouse, or at worst a badger, but you can never really believe anything you don't see. This is the time when a hidden owl startles you with its blood-curdling scream. There is no other noise in the dark that can influence so much terror. It is an audible representation of evil. Then you remember it is just a little owl, and your nerves find comfort. But in a sudden flash you feel the shutter of wings, never hearing them, only feeling them approach as you look up into the two deep orange glowing eyes growing larger upon you. As the night owl turns and swiftly disappears into darkness, you are glad you weren't born a mouse. Then a lone wolf howls from somewhere behind you, yipping and mournful like a lost dog. As you turn and squint your eyes into the deep shadow, you hear the return chorus of five others coming from what is now your back side. The forest suddenly becomes small and tight. You feel as though you cannot move, but move is all you wish you could do. The hand of the compass in your head is spinning. This isn't claustrophobia, it is blindness. Every unrecognizable shape grows fangs and claws, with broad hunched shoulders shifting in your direction. Now you run, head first into the blindness. But the ground is moving, slithering and squishing beneath your feet. You realize that you cannot run, so you drop down and crawl. You have been reduced to a four-legged beast. You bark and growl in aggressive tones trying to ward off approaching marauders. You snarl and bang a tree with your fist, kick up dirt and give a long intimidating howl into the night. Now the forest recognizes you. You are no longer a man. Now you are safe.

So, journal friend of mine, here we are alone together, again in a deep dark forest. The stars are sporadic flickers above the gentle leaves. My eyes slowly adjust to the darkness enough to know that a tree right before me is a tree. But what is that shape over there? I have never known darkness so complete. We have eight hours to go before the sun spreads the bristles of its brush through the phalanx of trees. During the night every painted image becomes a distortion of black. In the forest there is no color without the sun. But the city burns bright yellow somewhere...

New entry:

I've been fishing every other day during the final hour of sunlight. Sometimes I take the canoe. Other times I wet wade. I only cast large flies in pursuit of a muskie. None yet, though I thought I saw the head of one following my fly. They are the fish of ten-thousand casts for a reason. I think I am about halfway there.

Almost all of the white has been covered on my canvas board. But the painting is far from complete. The image is surreal. There is nothing immediately comprehensive to the eyes. Even I have to spend time thinking about what I see to understand it. It is a visage of my imagination. It is a vivisection with reality. Reality is the imaginations muse.

New entry:

It has been a few days since conversing with you journal. I'm not going to try and recount all of the events, for unlike you, whose memory is engraved with ink, my memory is more fluvial, it is a liquid that constantly changes shape and location. There is one story I want to explain to you though; it just began yesterday, and I want to tell it while it is still fresh.

I was sitting pensively in my sanctuary. I stared through the material of a painted canvas at another world existing in a parallel dimension. I was pulled from thoughts by a powerful wind. In an instant the tops of the trees began swaying violently, and leaves were thrown from their branches and began bouncing in the air. Then I heard the thunder. The thunder shattered the sky and rain began to fall. I packed up my materials and brought them into the lodge so I could continue working by lantern light. The screen house is my sanctuary from the insects, the canvas lodge my sanctuary from the storm. I called Snowy into the lodge, and then settled my materials inside. I put on a rain jacket and stepped outside to watch the storm roll in. The clouds were dark and appeared to be one giant organism, inseparable, joined by the urgency for violence. They were still very high, but the weight of the rain was pulling them lower, getting ready to release a maelstrom. I hoped this storm would pass, for my rain barrels were still full from the previous rain three days ago, and I wanted to spend the evening watching the light and shadows. It appeared as though my plans were about to change.

In the distance I heard voices coming up the trail from the river. Sounds carry in reverberations through the forest, but these sounds were muffled by the approaching storm. I assumed it was my imagination. With the exception of Lamara, I hadn't heard another person's audible voice in many weeks, even months. Then I heard the distinct sound of a damp branch snap beneath a foot, and the voices grew louder. I pulled my knife from its sheath and placed it in the front pocket of my pants, then removed the sheath from my belt and concealed it in my back pocket. I remembered something Lamara said a couple days ago when I walked up the road to call her.

"I have a bad feeling about this week," she had said with a tone of clairvoyance I often underestimate.

I sang her a verse from Bob Marley, "Every lil ting, gonna be awright," but this didn't halt her concern.

"And last night I had this bad dream," she continued after a short laugh. "Homeless people found your camp and took it over."

I laughed, this was preposterous. Then catching myself, and trying to take her seriously, I replied, "That's about the least likely thing to happen here. There's no way some homeless person's going to find this camp. It's too far out of the way. They generally stick to busier areas."

"I know it sounds foolish to you, but the dream seemed so real."

I was imagining a group of rowdy vagabonds carrying rusty axes and pitchforks as I walked towards my camp entrance to confront whoever it was coming up the trail in this storm. I got about twenty feet from the entrance when I saw them already coming in. There were two middle aged men, each carrying a small pack of gear. They stopped about ten feet away. The first was short and stocky like a wrestler, he wore a black trench coat with a hood pulled over his head, and beneath his hood I could see his pale face grizzled with a dark beard, and his green eyes seemed to carry the lightning from the storm. The second man was much taller, with broad shoulders and arms, and a compact torso with long runners' legs. He wore camouflage pants with a red and black checkered flannel shirt, no raincoat. His straight black hair was soaked beneath a pine-green outback hat. His reddened brown face held dark eyes that seemed to be one giant pupil. I noticed each man carried a large hunting knife on their belt.

"Hello there," I said, placing my right hand into my pants pocket and gripping the wooden handle of my knife. I tried to make myself appear bold. I had to make the impression of being in charge so they didn't think I could be taken advantage of. This is my camp after all. These two were trespassers.

"Hello back," said the short stocky Finnish man as he pulled the hood off his head.

"Not a very nice night to be taking a walk in the woods," I told them. The Finn gave a jesting laugh as the Native man continued to stare taciturnly in my direction. Thunder boomed, and I instinctively took a brief look towards the sky. From the corner of my eye I saw the Finn make a sudden movement. My adrenaline kicked in as I quickly shuffled my feet into a defensive stance, cocking my right elbow back ready to remove the blade.

"Whoa, not so fast there buddy," said the short one as he placed his pack on the ground. "We're just here looking for shelter."

I considered this. Here were two middle-aged men, obviously familiar with the backwoods, and they weren't prepared for a storm? It didn't add up. So I began my interrogation. "You fellows mean to tell me you came into the woods without preparations for a storm?"

"I suppose your guess is as good as mine when it comes to predicting the weather round here," said the Finn.

"Where were you heading?"

"We planned to make it to Ontario by the weekend."

Canada? What were they smuggling, or running away from? The native man continued his unflinching stare at me. I understood this was common behavior for people of his origins who spend most of their time in the woods, but it still sent an uneasy feeling to my spine. "Looks like you're going to be held up a bit," I replied. "That's a long ways to go by foot," I was guiding an inquiry without posing a question, for in situations like this it is often the one with the answers who takes the upper hand.

"Nobody said we were walking all the way," said the short man reproachfully. He seemed to not want to tell me much, which in fairness was his right, if in fact what he said was true, and they were just looking for shelter from the storm. The rain was gaining intensity, and the wind began to howl. All our little conversation did was effectively get us soaking wet. I decided to be hospitable.

"You can use that tent to get out of the rain," I said, pointing to the dome tent Snowy has been using to get away from the mosquitoes and flies. I'm sure it was filthy and smelled of wet dog.

Their eyes followed my pointing finger to the tent, then turned back behind me towards my large canvas lodge. "I suppose you don't have room for us in there, huh? We could sit up outta this rain and get to know each other a bit. My quiet friend here," he pointed towards the tall Native, "though he may not look it, he truly is a great story teller."

"I'm sure he is," I said, pretending to consider his request. "I have no doubt you two will be perfectly comfortable in the tent over there. Besides, you're going to want to get some rest if you still plan on making your deadline to Canada."

"If that's what you're offering," was his response as they walked past me and entered the small dome tent.

I stood near the entrance to my lodge clenching the knife handle. I felt my brow remain tight. It didn't look like the storm would let up until next morning. I waited outside until they stopped whispering amongst themselves. When I reentered my room I kept the light off so my eyes would stay adjusted to the dark. I tried to stay awake. The conversation with Lamara kept running through my head. Something seemed wrong about these two. Why had they insisted on keeping mystery about themselves? If I were walking through a forest when a storm rolled in, and was unprepared, and happened to stumble upon a camp, I would be as polite and forthcoming as possible. Were they hiding some malicious intentions? How did they know I was here?

It was hard to hear beyond the raindrops pounding on the canvas roof. Perhaps they were asleep. Perhaps they had already snuck out of their tent and were waiting for me to fall asleep. Perhaps they had already raided my supplies and made a break for it through the soaking forest. The rain kept falling. Pitter-patter, pitter-patter, pitter-patter...

• • •

I awoke this morning with a startled jolt. I had fallen asleep in the chair with my knife handle beneath my palm. Snowy lay silently inside the door, focused on the outside. Did he hear something? My first thought was of the two strangers. I slid my knife back into my pocket and stepped outside. The rain had stopped. Now the sun was beginning to show its pink face below the retreating storm. I didn't see them. I knelt silently, ears focused on the tent where they had slept. Nothing. So I walked over and opened the fly. They were gone.

My next thought was of my supplies. I looked around, everything seemed to be in order. I opened up my food cache, everything was intact, and they hadn't even touched my vodka. There was no evidence but my memory they were ever here. Perhaps I was wrong to be suspecting of two trespassers in a storm? Perhaps my imagination, the devilish wanderer it is, had caused me to assume the worst.

Now I began to wonder what their story really was. Why were two men traveling through a forest with no trail for miles, but my own, and those other faint, barely passable, animal trails? Perhaps they were trappers or traders. This would explain the deadline for their voyage to Canada. But what kind of traders only carry one small pack apiece, and travel by foot, not canoe? This required further investigation.

I started to walk towards the river. On the muddy trail I noticed two sets of tracks, one of them heading up to camp, and another leaving camp. So they had left the same way they arrived, both coming and going from the direction of the river. I followed their tracks all the way to my landing at the water's edge. Here were their tracks leaving the river, and their tracks returning to the river. Were they wading downstream all the way to Canada? That was at least fifty river miles. This seemed unlikely. Presently it was the only hypothesis I had with any sustaining evidence. So I took off my boots and stepped into the river.

Wading downstream I noticed branches broken and bent along the shoreline, indicating they had been used for balance as the two strangers walked through the mucky, boulder strewn river.

So they walked downstream from my camp, but is this how they arrived? I decided I would continue downstream to the end of my property, to verify they weren't camped out down there with nefarious intent.

The sun was now peaking over the trees. The last of the clouds had vanished from the horizon. The river was brilliant this morning; the azure blue of sky being reflected off its swirling mud brown surface. The water is like a chameleon, it knows the colors of its environment, and will change as a replicate from day to day. I paused for a moment of admiration. The leaves were still dripping rain drops beneath the cloudless sky. The transpiration in the hot sun was visible like petroleum vapors rising from a local filling station. There was a reflection on the far shore that seemed metallic, like the scales of a rainbow trout lying caught on a rock in the afternoon sun. This image was radical, it was alien and didn't belong. I swam over to check it out.

I stepped upon the far shore and grabbed the reflection. It appeared to be the aluminum thwart beam of a canoe, bent and mangled with bits of the Kevlar body still clinging to it. The strangers must have capsized in the storm. The river is low enough that large boulders, which at higher water levels are passable, are now just barely below the surface, hard enough to see on a sunny day, let alone during a dark turbulent storm. In fact, about fifteen rods upstream of my landing, I noticed just the other day a large deposit of submerged boulders, giant and jagged, and as I grazed one of them it deflected my fiberglass canoe off at a sharp angle.

Kevlar, though good for making a lighter canoe, and known for its use in a bullet proof vest, could be easily punctured by striking any one of these boulders. They must have been paddling extremely fast, and, blinded by the rain, made head on contact with one of those boulders. I imagine the bow would immediately burst open, and the force would throw them from the canoe. They most likely had more gear in the canoe, probably secured for such a scenario, and as the canoe started taking water and going under they clung to it, grabbing what they could in desperation, naturally taking first what they considered most important. Then the extra weight of their bodies, and the act of two people pulling on the sinking canoe from different ends, would have turned the vessel perpendicular to flow and submerged it faster. They must have struck another boulder, which could have burst the canoe in half length-wise. This would explain the deformed thwart beam with Kevlar still attached. I suppose it would be an embarrassment for two experienced woodsmen to admit to a stranger like myself that they lost control of their canoe and possibly their cargo.

Content with this resolution, I swam back to my side of the river and began walking to camp. They were lucky to have capsized so close to the only human trail within miles on this river. Lucky, maybe, for when they found my camp they were greeted with the hostility of a suspicious stranger. I can only hope that sometime during their walk today they come to the realization my hesitant actions were justified, and are happy to have received the shelter I offered them. Perhaps the moral of this story for me is to be more hospitable and less presumptuous of passing strangers. Still, a man cannot be blamed for taking a stance of hostility when alone in the woods. It often seems like everything is out to get you. I wonder how their voyage is going. I also wonder what was in their packs.

New entry:

I sit up tonight drinking vodka and Tang. I wonder why this world leaves me feeling so estranged. I have lived in a world where men silently judge other men with their eyes. I tried to fit in but was never willing to compromise. Take me for what I am, or cast me aside. In the darkness I am surrounded by beasts made for the forest. Here I am happy. I have seen the beasts made for the city, and they were not made to be kind to man.

New entry:

I am tending to Snowy's wounds this morning. We had a wild encounter last night. I was lying in bed, with images flowing through the darkness before my open eyes. Then I heard a growling grumbling sound outside; it sounded like a bear. I was reminded of the encounter with the deceptive badgers by the river, and not wanting to be made a fool again, assumed this was the source of the sound.

Snowy was alert at the entrance. I slipped out of bed as stealthily as possible, then retrieved my knife and put on my head lamp. I attempted to keep Snowy in the lodge as I opened the door to investigate. He was too curious, and ripped out of my grasp into the darkness. I turned on my headlamp and followed him.

Instantly the night air was filled with snarls and growls. It was a bear alright, he had been digging into my garbage pit. The closest resemblance to a bear Snowy had ever seen was when he chased Black Angus cattle at a ranch in Wyoming. Cattle don't have claws and fangs.

Snowy rushed at the bear as I stepped out from the lodge. The bear had no chance to run, so turned towards him with an aggressive stance. As soon as Snowy was close, the bear swung out with his forepaw. Snowy dodged most of it, but the bear sliced him with several claws across the front shoulder. This sent him yelping in retreat back towards the lodge.

I advanced on the bear, terrified and uncertain about what I was doing. The knife was in my hand as I lifted my arms towards the sky and gave my best prehistoric Tyrannosaurus Rex roar. The bear didn't flinch. Instead he took a couple of steps towards me. Fear causes bravery. I advanced, now hunched over and roaring louder. The bear turned and galloped into the darkness. I couldn't breathe.

I returned to the lodge and saw Snowy shaking on the ground. His front right leg was covered in blood. I grabbed my vodka bottle and poured it on the wound. Blood still seeped out. I went into the lodge and retrieved my pillowcase to use as a bandage. I secured it around his shoulder with duct tape. He was uncomfortable and had panic in his eyes. He is a brave dog though, charging at a beast easily five or six times his size.

We didn't get much sleep after that. I had convinced myself the previous encounter with the bear would keep him away from camp, now that he was aware of my presence. This could have been a different bear, but it seemed to be the same size as the one I had seen in the fern garden. The one last night was also a male. Based on the territorial behaviors of male bears I am going to assume it was the same bear. The smell of garbage was strong enough to erase any fear he had of me. Or maybe he doesn't fear me? It is early autumn now, so the bears are in hyperphagia, taking whatever risks necessary to accumulate enough body fat to survive hibernation. I must take more proactive measures with my garbage.

Snowy is in a lot of pain and doesn't want to move. I reexamined the wound and it is not too bad. He will survive, but it will require some time to heal. I rinsed it with more vodka, which upset him, but he was in too much pain to move.

I have decided to burn all combustible garbage every night. That which cannot be burned will be wrapped in a garbage bag and placed inside of my buried cooler. I do not like the idea of mixing garbage with food, but the cooler is the most scent-locking container I have here.

Now that the bear knows my camp is a source for food, I am certain he will return. The fact that I have been able to chase him away both times I have seen him makes this easier to consider. But the idea of him lurking around camp at night, and possibly smelling my sleeping flesh in the lodge, makes me very uncomfortable. I need a defensive strategy.

I built scarecrows out of timber and placed one at each entrance to camp. I covered them in spare clothes to give a more full-bodied appearance. I will expunge my urine at the base of each one, in hopes that the sight and smell of a man will deter the bear. I am skeptical. What else can I do – leave? I will not. What's the worst that could happen? I get killed by a bear. Let me die happy!

New entry:

I awoke to the indigenous music of sparrow song, raven shrills, and chipmunk chatter. I awoke to the natural gradient of sun and shadows. I awoke to the perforated walls of fir trees, the soft glistening carpet of moss and fern, below the high brilliant green ceiling of aspens. I awoke to a pace of life that requires no race of mind.

It has been several days since the bear attack, and Snowy is almost back to his normal self. I removed the bandage to find pink skin covering the wound. Now that it is exposed he lies down and licks it. Why are humans taught not to lick wounds? It's as if somewhere along this evolutionary escalator we decided to remove anything that could be perceived as animal within us. Who are we kidding?

The forest has become extremely active. The cold nights encourage a hunger in every living creature. I am seeing more animals, and they continue to get closer. The squirrels and chipmunks and birds that all seemed to fear me during the summer months, now ignore me in search for food. Whenever Snowy is in his tent they get very close to me; if he is visible they keep a greater distance.

I am impressed by the wisdom of the forest. Take chipmunks for example; how do this year's newborns know the land will soon be covered with snow, and food will be difficult to find? Is their knowledge inborn, or is it communicated through the generations? Who told the beaver to build a winter lodge, or create a dam to pool up a river? How do birds know it will be warmer farther south, and food will be plentiful? There is wisdom in the forest, wisdom that cannot be explained by the sciences of man.

New entry:

My facial hair is growing out of control. I can't eat without getting mustache whiskers in my teeth. I decided to trim the area surrounding my lip with the fishing scissors. My cheeks are still bushy, so long I can see them without even looking downwards. I wish I could see my reflection, if only because faces are designed to be seen.

The closest thing I have to my reflection out here is the painting. I have ignored it lately. Thoughts of it are constantly on my mind, but I haven't even looked at it recently. I seem to work best in short bursts between long intermissions of contemplation. Perhaps it is time to start again.

I sat for a long while looking at my painting, admiring the colors and textures and shapes and dimensions. My mind was filled with thoughts about the circumstances of my life. As with every other man or woman, my life has seemed unpredictable, erratic, and inimitable. I wish to develop some order out of the chaos. Design a confluence for all the harmony and disorder I have experienced.

Is it not possible to somehow fit it all here in this single static image? Everything. All of it. The good, bad, glorious, and embarrassing. All of those simple and complex events and exchanges which have created this man of multiple faces. Would the definition be recognizable to any eyes but my own? Does it matter if it is or isn't? I have a desire to see myself, so that I may understand this foreign being whom I coexist separately with.

I realized I was thinking too much. I can't paint while thinking. Painting comes after the thoughts.

New entry:

I have been quite stationary this summer. Almost sedentary. The farthest I have strayed from camp is up the county road to call Lamara, or while on the river in the canoe. I need a change of scenery. I need a vacation. Perhaps some new experiences will get me painting again.

Our property is surrounded on all sides, except the west, by tax-forfeited county lands that extend approximately one mile in all directions. On the other side of these county lands, again in every direction except the west, is a vast wilderness of State Forest. Millions of acres of unpopulated lands filled with lakes and rivers and wildlife, and most important – isolation.

Isolation is a sensation much different than loneliness. Isolation, in this case, is optional; it is my own choice. Isolation is an opportunity to find comfort with the company of my *self*. Loneliness is the burden of discomfort with my *self*, most often acquired by missing the company of somebody else. I have experienced both of these sensations during my time here at camp.

I have a few days before Lamara's next visit. I will pack a small bag of gear and take to the woods. It is time to go for a voyage. I will pack light. The mosquitoes are practically nonexistent now, and the nights are still warm enough to sleep comfortably outside, so I will not bring a tent. I will pack a sleeping bag, pillow, raincoat, frying pan, matches, compass, rope, vodka, and food. Snowy has been moving around much better, and I think some exercise will do him good. I am going to leave you at camp for this voyage, journal. I don't want any requirements or distractions.

I will spend two or three nights sleeping outside. I will tie Snowy up next to me so he won't run off during the night, and in hopes that he will alert me to any dangers. I will collect branches small enough to break by hand for a fire, so I don't need to carry a saw. This will be the first time I have spent a night away from camp since my arrival more than three months ago. I'm going to leave a note for Lamara, in case something happens to me out there.

Next entry:

I have returned from the voyage. I should have done this more often during the summer. There is so much amazing land to explore out there. I traveled south up the river bank until I came to a confluence with a smaller stream. I followed this stream up river until I came to a lake. I spent the night on that lentic shore listening to the calls of loons. The next day I headed into the forest, with only natural waypoints and a compass to guide me. I walked all day through thick tangling branches. That was the most isolated I have ever felt.

As the shadows started to merge into darkness, I found a small clearing in a growth of tall red pines where I spent the night.

The next day I reversed my direction and found my way back to the lake where I had slept. Many times I felt lost, but continued to trust my sense of orientation to guide me. Once at the lake, I walked down to the out flowing stream. I followed the outlet down to our river, and spent a night where the waters join into a sea-bound unison. Today I walked back to camp. Lamara should be arriving soon.

New entry:

Lamara and Boulder are here again. She seemed stressed out, so I encouraged her to go for a solo canoe ride. Nothing a little alone time with nature can't fix. I have been spending the afternoon watching Snowy and Boulder play together. Snowy is much more adventurous when his younger stepbrother is here. Boulder, being still a puppy, is quite the wild child. Snowy gets no rest when Boulder is present. Any sound in the forest will be chased enthusiastically. They always return empty handed, but with big boisterous grins.

Lamara returned from her voyage with a smile on her face. She pulled up a chair beside me and sat silently while I wrote this entry. Word to the wise: if ever you want your woman to be tongue tied, simply make her happy. When she is happy, she is not consumed with plans or doubts. When her mind is at peace she is not conversing about her work day or what her friends are doing. What man does not require a little bit of silence? Certainly I get plenty of silence during the week. Most of the time while she is here I am excited by the opportunity for conversation. But still, there is something absolutely serene about two people who are happy enough together to be comfortable in silence.

Enjoying this silence, I decided to take Lamara by the hand and guide her down to the creek bed. I wanted her to experience the world I know when I am here alone, a world without words. We sat for a long time, watching the forest, and listening to the natural voice of the wild.

The forest is most intriguing on a sunny day with a mild breeze. It is then the shadows change most frequently, creating a plethora of indescribable shapes. It is then that an autumn leaf is separated from its parent tree, and sounds like footsteps in the forest as it slowly tumbles through the branches and undergrowth to the soil where it will rest and decay then someday spawn new life and new mystery. Only with a calm mind and patient feet can a person discover such simple splendor. It is only while silent that my eyes and ears know this mystery for what it is, magnificently indescribable. Only the grace of nature will allow me to find peace with my place in this marvelous world of underestimated phenomenon.

And now night approaches. In the distance a wolf sings its joyous tune. As the saturating colors of sunlight fade from sight, the ominous moon reaches out its long arm and applies the dark dyes of night.

New entry:

Lamara is gone again. I walked her to the truck and said goodbye. There were no tears in her eyes this time. This time she said, "Thank you". I think this weekend was the nearest to insight she has had about my life here. It takes a good woman to want to understand her man. An even better one who is willing to share his experiences to gain that personal knowledge.

As I walked to camp, I noticed the forest trail is tiled with golden leaves. The only flowers still in bloom are the purple asters and some goldenrod. The ferns that were a withering brown only a week ago have all but vanished from sight, returned to the soil from whence they came.

New entry:

I decided to take a stroll through the woods today. Wanting to see some wildlife, I zipped Snowy up in his tent before leaving. This disheartened him greatly, and I heard his mournful howl for the first five minutes of my walk. I went down to the river and got on the animal trail heading south, away from the county road. There were a lot of chickadees present, fluttering from tree to tree. Signs of autumn are everywhere.

I made it about a half mile when I came upon a large red fox standing in the trail ahead of me. It was a red fox by species, but this particular animal was of a gray morph, with only a little red being visible on the tips of its fur. He was tall and elegant, and seemed to be in fit shape. We stood about twenty-five feet apart. He gazed at me inquisitively with a cocked head. He seemed to be wondering if I were edible. We stood there in a staring contest for a few minutes before I decided to take a couple of steps towards him. He turned and began to shuffle nonchalantly down the trail. I continued behind him, following in his footsteps for a couple hundred feet before he grew tired of me, looked back one more time, then disappeared into the thick forest. I don't know what he thought about me, but I thought him to be a friendly little critter. How have I lived so long without ever being so close to a fox? Where have I been, when this is my home?

New entry:

Painting was easy last night. I was in a grand state of euphoria; separated from reality and distant from my thoughts. Today I re-examined the image. There is no more empty canvas. In its place is a mirage, a portal into another dimension. In these colors there is clarity of vision like I have never experienced. I have never seen the world make more sense.

But I am not finished with it yet. I need to enhance the defini-tions further. There is something missing. I wonder if I will ever figure out what that is.

New entry:

The nights are getting much colder – so cold that the mornings don't warm up until early afternoon. My time is running out. I intend to stay until snow fall. I hope for an Indian summer. I need to utilize what warm weather remains. I need to soak up any in-spiration this forest has left to offer me. I'm going to wander into the woods, off-trail towards the river. There is still much of our property I have yet to see.

I knelt before a blue bead Lilly, admiring the color of its dying fruits. The berries were of an indescribable blue. They were like little globules of paint, perfectly spherical, dangling vertically from a thin stem. The center was darkest, like the color of the Navy crest, then slightly brighter around the center, like the wings of a Mountain Bluebird, and tapering off to an almost silvery white epidermis freckled with brown and black. In passing they appear to be just a solid blue, but upon closer inspection there are infinite variations of this color all compounded together to create an absolutely unique specimen of reflectivity. I collected a few in my pocket, hoping to imitate their color later.

I stood up and continued through the forest towards the river. My head was down, watching all the amazing specimens pass beside my slow-moving feet. I was amazed and perplexed, not only by the diversity of all the small species which exist wherever sunlight penetrates the forest floor, but also by the confounding differences between all their original colors. Not even two greens were of the same green. No two berries on the same bush had precisely the same shade. This is a particolored world no paintbrush could replicate. I tried to imagine a combination of all the pigments I have in labeled cans back at camp that would somehow do justice to this world of enigmatic images. Then I heard a clanging sound coming from the river.

As I approached the water I saw two men stepping out of a canoe at the landing. I was initially alarmed; not because whoever they were, they were coming unannounced and uninvited, but because the only walking talking person I had seen in months, excluding Lamara's weekend visits, were the two strangers who arrived during a storm many nights ago. I knelt down and waited for them to turn their faces. It was the same two strangers from the storm. What could they possibly want now?

I watched them unload a large duffle bag with a shape inside that appeared to be a heavy weapon. I reached for my knife to regain a sense of security. It wasn't on my belt. I have become too comfortable at camp. I decided to surprise them with a confrontation.

"You boys forget your gear again?" I said with a humorous tone.

The short stocky Finn smiled and said, "Nope, we got plenty of new supplies once we made it to Ontario." The Native smiled and nodded; this was the first friendly gesture I had seen from him. I decided it was either a good sign, or an attempt to conceal their nefarious intentions. "Wasn't sure if you'd still be around here after all this time," continued the Finn, "what with winter gettin' close and all. But my friend here assured me that he knew your character, that you were a man of these woods, and that you'd be in for the long haul."

I wondered what they really wanted. I tried to remember my etiquette of civility, how to treat a stranger kindly and all of that, but I hadn't used those attributes for quite some time. The best I could muster was, "If you fellows need a rest, I can take you up to camp."

"We do appreciate that," resumed the Finn, "but I don't think we've got time for a rest. Need to be making it back to get these supplies unloaded and sold off soon as possible."

"So what brings you here then?" I queried.

The tall Native man began walking towards me carrying the duffle bag. I met him halfway. My curiosity had overpowered any alarm. He unzipped the bag and removed a beautifully polished wood-handle axe, with a sharp bronze blade. It gleamed in the sparkling sun. "I notice you cut your own wood," he said, "those stumps on the trail look like that of a poor axe." He handed it to me handle first. The balance was amazing. I held it up in the air and took a couple of false swings.

"This is great. Why are you giving it to me?"

"You were kind to us first. Now we are even. Perhaps someday you will need my help. Now I can give it to you knowing you will be willing to repay it also."

I was amazed by his simple ability to make a complex point. I said my thanks and helped them shove off. I wish I could say that I will never be suspicious of a stranger entering my camp uninvited again, but I have seen too much falseness in the designs of men to allow one act of kindness to erase those memories. I am glad to know there are still people able and willing to prove me wrong.

New entry:

With every mild breeze more golden leaves are rustled from the tops of trees. Many of the fallen leaves have already turned as brown as the soil they lay upon. The contrast in the sky is amazing; dark green conical fir trees spreading their wings through the tall white bark of aspens. Further above, the remaining golden leaves fill the air with a million suns, suns pasted below a blue sky, a blue sky that carries a thin feathery cloud weightlessly in its arms.

Now I understand the meaning of that saying, "Land of the free". It is not men who are free, not civilized men anyways, but the animations of this wild kingdom. Nobody can tell a leaf where to land.

I comprehend this is as free as I will ever be, while an ephemeral member of this place, this place which continually escapes my words. How can I fully understand this freedom though, while being engaged in it? The sweetness of it all may never make sense until I once again live with that sour taste. How can I hold on, retain this fleeting sensation? Every falling leaf reminds me that I too will soon be separated from these trees. Trying to capture freedom is like trying to catch a falling leaf. Occasionally you may grab one out of the air and hold it in your hand, but now what?

I decided to walk to the river and enjoy the evening. It's funny, before living out here I had it in the back of my mind that a person living in nature would always watch the rising and setting sun. I have not watched enough of them during my time here. So I sat by the river and watched the sky change colors. The autumnal sunset is nature's tranquilizer. It glows in hypnotic colors. It is a magnetic force with the power to pull away any doubts or sadness, and leave me smiling like a fool. I am sedated by the mystery.

New entry:

I am finished with my painting, though the painting itself could never be finished. There is so much remaining in my mind I could never express here. I could continue to add layers on top of layers of paint. I could create the sensation of change by doing this. But I have decided to leave it as it is, eternally wanting more. Not that I am unsatisfied with it in any way. On the contrary, it is the greatest painting I have ever seen. This image helps me understand what I am. Though, unlike Dorian Gray, it is I who am destined to change, while this image forever remains the same.

New entry:

I had to use my knife this morning to break through the solid surface of my rain barrel. I suppose it is time to start packing up camp. I do not intend to leave until the first snowfall. I have camped in the snow many times, and it can be an enjoyable experience. Therefore, I am not leaving due to any anticipated discomfort; it is just the deadline I created for myself. I will carry anything unnecessary up the trail to load in the truck on Lamara's next visit.

New entry:

I spent the final three hours of daylight fishing last night. There was no reward for the stiffness in my casting elbow. I'm going out again today.

With every gust of northern wind, fewer and fewer leaves are falling from the balding trees. I do enjoy standing in the forest beneath a colony of aspen trees, waiting for the wind to blow, watching the fluttering grace of leaves departing the trees, and seeing the leaves throw golden light into the sky like a thousand-million fiery suns.

New entry:

This morning the air was frozen, with a thin layer of frosty haze rising from the cold water into the sunlight. The air was so thick I could touch it. I could feel it oozing through my fingers with the swipe of a hand.

I caught a fairly large northern pike today. I cast every muskie fly I own, but they were all equally dismissed. Perhaps I just haven't put one in front of the right fish yet. Tomorrow is another day. I am going to dream about victory.

New entry:

I walked up the road to call Lamara this morning. Tomorrow she will be driving here. On my return walk I played a game, trying to match the exact paces I took on the way to the road. This was easy, for my footprints were highlighted brightly on the ground. This is the most definition my tracks have had during my time here. I can see the places where animals cut across the trail during the night. Even the muddy soil after a rain does not retain the trace of feet like a fresh layer of white snow.

Camp is all packed up. I miss this place already, it's amazing how settled in I have become. Tonight I will sleep outside. I left a tarp out to lay on, and enough blankets to keep me warm. I gathered a supply of firewood to burn through the night. Still I wonder, will cold sleep be the final experience of my stay here? Not if I catch a muskie tonight!

• • •

A thin layer of ice now forms on the edge of the river. This is the most beautiful landscape I have ever seen. A few stubborn yellow and red and orange leaves still cling to the trees. The firs and cedars are green with a glistening white veneer. The river knows this land is beautiful, and imitates it perfectly on its partially iced surface.

Water was freezing in the eyelets of my rod and on my line. I fished for most of the evening. The action of casting could only keep me warm for so long. There will be other summers when the sun shines and I wade through warm water in shorts and a t-shirt. I will be back for you, muskie. I am allowing you one more season to grow even larger.

I am shivering beneath my blankets. The fire helps, but the ground is very cold. Snowy came over and lay down pressed against me. This is unusual for him, he generally prefers to sleep in his own space. I guess I am not the only body who is cold tonight.

I have been tempted during my entire stay to make a verbal treaty with the wild, to speak in a language it alone can understand. Thus far I have been hesitant; I didn't want to speak out of place. This is my place now. I sit up and lean back on my elbows. I look around at this amazing world of stillness. I think about all the small and simple events which have happened in such a short time. I tilt my head back and see the sparkling icy sky. I open my mouth and bellow a loud soulful howl. I hear its reverberation gallivanting through the trees and up into space. I have said my peace. I slide back into the sleeping bag and try to find some warmth.

Just before I shut my eyes, I heard the pack of wolves singing the most harmonious music I will ever hear. Were they saying goodbye? I smiled.

New entry:

The thin layer of snow is melted in the shape of a circle around my body. Snowy still lies on my feet. I feel as though I have just wakened from the most pleasing dream. The sun is shining on my face. The last golden leaf from an aspen tree ruffles itself free. I watch it flutter down in elliptical movements, seemingly suspended like a puppet, taking its time traveling down a long spiraled staircase. Just before landing on the ground it does a summersault in midair and falls directly on my chest. I pick it up and hold it in my hand. I reach into the sleeping bag and tuck it into my shirt pocket. This is the only item I will remove from the forest that I did not bring in.

All of the gear is loaded into the truck. I am back at camp for the last time this season. Lamara pulled the truck down to the bridge where the river flows beneath the road. She is waiting there for me. I am going to get in the canoe and paddle the two river miles down to her.

I suppose this will be my final entry. It has been good to know you, journal. It has been a pleasure to share this wilderness experiment with you. I hope I can return for a more permanent duration someday. I am glad your memory is better than mine, for I suspect I will want to relive moments from this season in the wilderness for the rest of my life.

I don't want to leave. Now that I know this forest, I want to experience all of its changes. How else will I ever understand? I could get in the canoe and paddle upstream, away from the bridge and Lamara. She is a good woman. She would understand…

Part III

From the Inside Looking Out

All the lost rivers like time unwind

back to the place where they began...

19

Those dreams like the windblown leaves falling to the winter earth, may be lost for a season, but seasons change, and from all that has decayed spawns new life, and new dreams will be born, if only we are patient.

• • •

Trees flowed by with blending velocity. It was difficult to feel attached to this world while he traveled against the current at such high speeds. Eli began to feel dizzy. Was this the right direction? How will he ever know what that other life could have been like if he made a different selection? Was there no way to divide himself in two, and send one each direction? The world moved very fast now. Eli watched it pass through the glass windshield.

"How are you doing over there?" asked Lamara from the driver's seat.

"Good."

"You look kinda pale."

"How fast are you going?"

"Right at the speed limit. Why?"

"Never mind."

"Are you excited to be coming back to town?"

He was silent. He was confused and felt nauseous. He didn't want to think about town or the wild. He wanted to vomit.

"Eli?"

"Yeah."

"You don't look so well. Everything alright?"

"I'm good. Just haven't traveled this fast in a while, feels unnatural."

"That's funny. Do you want me to slow down?"

"No, I'll get used to it."

"So, everybody wants to meet you."

"Everybody?"

"Yeah, I have met people you know."

"I'm sure you have."

"They're all excited to finally meet my woodsman. I told them all about your expedition."

Silence. Eli stared out the window, and wondered if he could ever find words to explain his wilderness experience in a comprehensive sociable fashion.

"I figured you'd want some time to settle in and recover before going out on the town, so I made plans to meet up with a few people on Wednesday."

"What day is today?"

"Friday."

"Alright, that'll work."

"That gives us a few days to be alone and for you to recivilize yourself."

"Sounds good." He wasn't really sure what that meant, *recivilize*. Did it mean he had to forget about the forest? Could he pretend like it never happened? Would he be required to wear a tie and speak politely of societal bliss?

"Don't worry, I'll never ask you to shave your beard. I think it looks good on you."

"What beard?" he chuckled and rubbed his hand across his cheeks. He flipped down the visor and opened the vanity mirror. The reflection was not of a college graduate. This wasn't the professional scientist. This wasn't the self he had memorized in mirrors and photographs. This was somebody else. Another man's face had kidnapped his own. The only bald skin was on his forehead and nose. The shaggy beard completely covered his lips. "No wonder you like it," he began after closing the visor, "it completely hides my face."

She squeezed his fingers tightly and smiled. "I'm so glad you're coming home to me."

"Me too." And he was. It took a good woman to fill the void he felt away from the forest. Ironically though, his fulfillment was tinted with a sense of loss. There were two loves in every man's life, but most often only room for one.

"I've missed you so much," she said, smiling with teary eyes. "But we did it. We actually did it. Now that it's over, it doesn't seem so bad. But there were a few days..." she trailed off. "Well I'm just glad I don't have to feel lonesome anymore."

"I'm very impressed by the way you handled this whole experience. I'm sure it wasn't easy for you."

"Yeah..." she smiled and wiped a tear from her eye.

"There aren't many women who would have been okay with something like this, you know. I am a lucky man."

She squeezed his hand harder. "Are you going to miss the woods?"

He reached into his shirt pocket and felt the golden leaf. He smiled. "Someday both of my loves will be properly introduced, and we can all live happily together."

They continued to drive down the tree-lined country road at exactly the speed limit. Eli slowly acclimated to this fast paced mechanical travel. Then he saw a large pile of bloody fur up ahead on the shoulder of the road. As they passed he realized it was a badger. He thought about seeing the badgers in their wild habitat. He remembered with a sense of comical pride the night he heard their ferocious growls beside a midnight river. Each wild creature in the living forest endured so much turmoil and challenge. So many ways to survive or perish. Was it nature or intrusion that took this wandering badger's life? Four wheels or four feet, everything seemed designed to destroy.

"So, I didn't want to distract you with this while you were out there, but did you end up doing any painting?"

"Yes."

"I bet it's great. Did you enjoy doing it?"

"Absolutely. It was the best thing I've ever done," he tried to hide his prideful smile behind a stoical face.

"When do I get to see it?"

"How about tonight."

"That would be great. I thought I'd make you a homemade pizza for your first civilized dinner back in town."

"You have no idea how many nights I sat up thinking about pizza. It's a good thing I didn't have a vehicle, otherwise I would have certainly driven to the nearest pizzeria on many occasions."

"It's hard for me to believe you've been living without all the things I've been taking for granted every day."

"Yeah, it's hard for me to believe you've been living without all the things I've been taking for granted every day." He smiled at her and gave a wink.

"Oh I've missed that wink," she said. "I think it's amazing how we've each been living such different lives. You know, whenever I'd get stressed at work, or feel lonely, I'd just think about being in the woods with you, and I was happy. It's like, well I'm sure you'll think this sounds like girlish nonsense, but I think we have such a great connection we can actually live through each other's experiences."

"I know what you mean. Believe me, every time you've bitten into a slice of pizza during the last several months, I've tasted it."

• • •

The city was filled with stop lights and honking horns, shopping centers and convenience stores. There was no room for silence amongst this phatic noise. The streets were lined with trees, but their aroma was obsolete, smothered beneath anthropogenic activity. Man's world was a dizzy machine.

They pulled into the driveway which was white with snow. The only animal tracks in the yard were of Boulder's paw prints. Eli knelt beside one and pressed his palm into the cold crisp granular texture. He pretended they were the tracks of a wolf. Lamara watched over his shoulder.

"Do you think we're going to need a snow blower?" she asked.

He looked up at the driveway, "Probably." Then he stood up and paced around the yard, dragging his feet through the snow.

"You sure you're doing alright?" she asked, watching him in befuddlement.

"Yeah. Yes. Why don't you go ahead and go inside where it's warm, I'll get the truck unloaded."

"Alright," she said hesitantly, "I'll just get the pizza started."

Lamara went into the house and turned on the oven. She peeked out the back window and watched Eli kicking around in the snow. It was weird to have him back, he looked almost like a stranger, seemingly so out of place. She smiled and shook her head.

Eli entered the workshop and looked around. This was the first time he had been indoors in months. It seemed so solid and secure. It also seemed isolated. Not isolated in the way he felt in the woods, but a more restrictive and confined isolation. There wasn't enough space for his lungs or his mind to expand to their natural potential. He looked out one of the windows into the yard. On the other side of their fence he saw houses and cars and people. There were telephone poles, electrical wires, and a water tower. He felt trapped.

He pulled the gold leaf from his pocket and rubbed it between his fingers. He looked out at the spruce trees in their yard, still green and plush. He wanted this leaf to stay golden forever. He found a Ziploc bag, sealed the leaf inside, and placed it on the window ledge.

Lamara walked out the back door and saw the truck still full of gear. She entered the workshop and found Eli staring out the window. He appeared almost like a statue, paused into some pensive position. "Dinner's ready," she said, standing right behind him. One of his ears twitched slightly, but otherwise no movement. "Eli?"

"Yeah?" he said, without turning his head.

"Your pizza's ready."

"Alright," he replied, turning around to see her standing there inquisitively. "I'll be right in." He noticed some concern in her eyes, so continued, "Everything's fine, I'm just unwinding. Let's go eat," he finished with a smile and put his arm around her shoulder.

"This is delicious," said Eli, blowing the heat of melted cheese and hot sauce from his full mouth.

"Thanks," said Lamara, calmly waiting for her slice to cool down, "I'm glad you like it."

"What are these toppings, Bavarian sausage?"

"I diced up some brats to remind you of the woods."

He laughed, "I thought after all the brats I've eaten in the past few months, I would never want another. But you've proven me wrong."

"Sorry, I didn't know you were so sick of them."

"I'm not. Not when they're served like this anyways. I've been waiting all summer for something so good."

"What else have you been waiting all summer for?"

He paused, and blew on the steaming slice of pizza in his hand. "I can't think of anything."

"No?"

"Well, I guess you could say I've been waiting all summer for winter to never come. But now it has."

"Are you okay with that?"

"Certainly."

"Good, because I'm glad you're back. No more phone calls once a week, that is, when you'd remember," she smiled at him. "Or only seeing you on the weekends..." she drifted off and stared out the window.

Eli noticed she was looking towards the truck, "Don't worry, I'll get unpacked tomorrow."

"Huh? Oh, that's not what I was thinking about. I was just wondering how strange it must seem to go from being in the woods all alone to this."

"Yeah? It's not so bad."

"Not so bad?"

"Someday I'll figure out a way to explain it to you better."

Eli finished devouring the pizza, then leaned back in the chair and patted his belly, "I haven't been this full in months."

"Good, you look too skinny anyways."

"Yeah?"

"Yeah, but not in a bad way. Don't worry, I'm gonna fatten you up in no time."

He chuckled, "Can't wait to taste that."

"So what do you want to do for your first night back in town?"

"Tell you the truth, I'm exhausted. Thought maybe I'd show you my painting and then get to bed early."

"Alright, do you want to go get it while I clean up?"

"Sure."

It was dim but not quite dark in the sky above the falling sun. Eli climbed into the truck bed and retrieved his painting. He leaned it against the tailgate and admired his masterpiece. He rubbed his fingertips gently across the surface, remembered every stroke of the brush, and every moment of inspiration. There was a life pulse on this inanimate surface. This image could never be created by any hands but his own. No other mind could duplicate this mastery of imagination. He felt his lungs grow large in his chest, as a proud smile covered his face.

"Wow, that's a huge painting," said Lamara, as Eli carried it inside at an angle that only displayed the blank backside. "Where are we going to put it?"

"Well, it's a gift from me to you, so you can put it wherever you'd like."

"Alright," she replied, looking around at the walls as they entered the living room. "We might have to rearrange some stuff."

"Would you mind stepping into the other room a minute while I set it up?"

"Sure," she said, and walked out to the kitchen.

Eli held the painting up on the wall. He admired it for the last time as being only his. Soon it would leave the world of his own creation, and enter into that unpredictable galaxy of other people's perception. It was ready. He was ready to send it out with pride in his eyes.

He set it down on the hardwood floor and leaned it against the wall. He realized there was something missing. Not that he hadn't done everything he could to perfect it. Nothing could ever be finished. There was always a desire to make something better. Every new project was a continuation of the last. Even if he never painted again, this image said enough. He put all of himself into it. He smiled and invited Lamara to come in.

She walked into the room as if entering a surprise birthday party. She was ready to be excited. She saw the beaming smile on Eli's face, and couldn't help but smile in return. Her heart beat rapidly. Eli held his breath.

Lamara stood in front of the painting and felt her heart pause. She studied the lines and shapes and colors. There was an obscure sense of amazement she could feel in her stomach. Her cheeks grew heavy. She blinked and refocused her eyes. None of it made any sense to her. It wasn't even comprehensible in any abstract sort of way. The only words she could think of to describe it were, *hideous*, or *mangled*, or, *what the hell*, but she held her tongue.

She studied it further, trying to find something to complement. Now she felt a laugh boiling up in her cheeks, but restrained it. Perhaps he had intended it to be comical? She looked towards Eli and noticed his proud face becoming anxious. "What happened here?" she asked, pointing to the corner smeared by humidity.

"That was the day nature lent me a helping hand."

"I see." She didn't understand what he meant. It looked like someone had spilled a glass of wine on it. She continued to stare, hoping a sense of his inspiration would present itself. "Are those birds' wings?" she asked patiently, trying to sound studious.

"Yes, they're intended to represent the avian tendency of the human soul."

"I see." It still didn't make any sense to her. The colors were all distorted and out of place. None of the shapes matched each other, or even seemed to be related. "Well, it's absolutely amazing," she finally answered, looking at him with a convincing smile.

"Really? I wasn't sure since it took you so long."

"Definitely. It's a piece of art that requires – no, demands – introspection. I love it!" She knew that a good woman understood how to support her mans delusions.

"Good. I wasn't sure. You know, it's difficult to predict if anyone else will understand a representation of your own mind. I wasn't sure if I'd be able to pull it off."

"You did a great job. So that's what your mind looks like?" she smiled. "Thank you for sharing it with me."

"My pleasure. Now you'll just have to decide where you want to put it."

"Yes," she hesitated, "I'll have to think about that one. I want to find the perfect place for it."

"Okay, I'll just leave it here until you decide."

"Perfect," she said, thinking they better not invite any company over until she could figure out where to properly hide it. "This will give me a chance to look it over for a while and determine which room it matches best."

"Do we have any vodka in the house?" he asked her.

"I don't think so, but I did buy a bottle of champagne, figured we could celebrate your return sometime this weekend."

"How about right now? I didn't realize it would be so unnerving to show you my painting. It is both exciting and a relief to finally let another pair of eyes see it."

She smiled, kissed him on the cheek, and said, "I'll go get the bottle."

They laughed and smiled and conversed with bubbles in their cups. The moon moved slowly across the wintry sky. She fell asleep on the back porch with her head on his lap wrapped up in a fleece blanket. He sat awake and finished the bottle while staring into the starlight. What were these foreign sounds surrounding him? He thought that if life were a writer, it sure wrote him into some funny pages. Last night he fell asleep to the sounds of wolves howling while curled up with freezing feet. This night dogs barked, car engines rattled, and city lights hummed. Tonight his lover shared her heat. What happened to the past after he departed? He laughed and shook his head. The muscles in his neck grew tense.

20

In the kitchen, Lamara had wild rice pancakes ready to be served with blueberry syrup. She had a smile on her face and felt happy. All her hard work was beginning to pay off. She had a good career, a lovely house, and a man she admired. She shook her head and sighed, wondering how she had gotten so lucky. That is a curse of the truly gifted; never believing they deserve what they have, for they never believe they have given their all. And it is most likely they haven't, for there is a whole other layer of skills and abilities waiting for an opportunity to be utilized.

Eli walked past his painting still leaning against the living room wall. For a moment he forgot about the forest. Then he caught the colors of the canvas from the corner of his eye. He paused and knelt down.

"Breakfast is ready," said Lamara, carrying a sizzling piece of bacon to Eli. She stopped short when she saw him kneeling there. He looked up at her with the most ponderous eyes she had ever seen.

"I think I want to paint again. This image," he paused, "there's not enough here. I need to elaborate."

She hesitated, "Well, I think that sounds like a great hobby for you this winter."

"Alright, let's not talk about this right now. It smells delicious in there."

"What do you want to do today?" asked Lamara from across the table.

"Didn't really have any plans, just need to get the gear unloaded and settled back in."

"I thought we could go for a walk. Looks like it could be a gorgeous day," she replied as she pushed the plunger down on the coffee press.

Eli looked outside. The sun was burning hot, and the snow covered yard had turned into wet mud and withering grass. The thermometer outside the window read fifty-two degrees Fahrenheit. "Shoot, if I knew it was going to get this warm I would have stayed at camp."

"We could always go spend the weekend there."

"No, one night would just be a tease. I need to get it out of my mind."

"I've got an idea, something that could help. Why don't we go out on the town tonight? We'll go do some people watching, that will get your mind off of camp."

"I don't know, maybe. Let's just wait and see what happens."

• • •

Lamara sat on a chair and shuffled through her knitting supplies. Eli smiled at her as he walked by, and without saying a word continued outside. The sun was blinding, suspended midway up the southern horizon. He climbed into the truck bed and grabbed an armful of supplies.

After he unloaded the gear and put it in place, he walked over to the windowsill in the workshop. He stared through the glass pane, and his mind returned him to the forest. He picked up the Ziploc bag with the golden leaf inside. The edges had already turned crisp and brown. He wanted to remember the golden luster, so he removed the leaf from the bag and pinned it up on the wall, out of the sunlight.

The fluorescent lights buzzed on the ceiling. The sun poured through the window. Eli had an idea; he knew what was missing from his painting. He unpacked the remaining canvas and paint, and set up a small studio in the corner. He watched the blank canvas, waiting for the right place to start.

The air outside was fresh as he stepped into the sunlight. He wanted to retain the peace he had found in the wild. He scanned the surroundings. Dozens of birds were gathered around a feeder in his neighbor's yard. That was the closest thing to a wild stimulant in view. Unfortunately he couldn't see the feeder while inside the workshop, so he decided to build one.

As he mounted the bird feeder to a back fence post, he noticed the fence line had grown thick with tall weeds. Tall weeds were not acceptable to a civilized life. He considered letting them grow, and engulf his yard in a periphery of uncultivated rebellion. He fetched his machete instead.

He enjoyed this task; as he swiped away weeds it brought him back to the trail. He felt the forest breeze as it sifted through the trees and whisked away his sweat. When his neighbor approached it caught him by surprise.

"Hey, how's it going over there?"

Eli looked up at a thin man with white hair wearing coveralls. "Pretty good," he answered, still swinging away.

"We haven't seen you around all summer. We thought maybe," Eli lowered his eyes at him, "well, we just wondered I guess."

Eli mumbled, "Hope you didn't lose any sleep over it."

"My name's Martin, anyways," said the man, leaning into the fence that separated their yards.

Eli stood up and wiped his brow, "I'm Eli."

"You know, I've got a weed whacker in the garage there that you could borrow, make that job you're doing a lot easier."

"No thanks."

"Alright, suit yourself. If you change your mind just come on over." He walked away and looked over his shoulder towards Eli.

After finishing the task with his machete, Eli walked back into the house to clean up. Lamara sat on the couch with a book on her lap. "What are you reading?"

"Oh, just some trashy mystery novel to get me through the day. You all done out there?"

"For now. I just met our neighbor."

"Which one?"

"The older guy next door."

"Martin?"

"I guess so."

"He's a nice guy. His grandson mowed our yard this summer."

"How much did he charge you for that?"

"Twenty-five. Why?"

"He didn't do a very good job."

"Oh, are you upset?"

"Nope, just saying."

"Okay. You still want to go for a walk?"

"That sounds good."

They attached the dogs to leashes and voyaged out onto the pavement. As far as cities were concerned, this one was quite scenic. Every yard had tall trees. The front of every house was decorated to look as natural in a deep forest as here in town. Their neighborhood streets had minimal traffic. The only wildlife were dogs, cats, squirrels, and birds. And people.

They made it to the lake and followed a paved trail with painted lines. The edge of the trail was groomed with non-native trees and shrubs. People flew past them on bicycles and rollerblades. Eli stared into the lake which was a deeper blue than the sky had ever been. Lamara reached over and held his hand.

"It's nice living so close to the lake," she said.

"Yeah, it is," replied Eli, kicking aside an empty pop bottle.

"I'm not saying it compares to our river in any way, but it's still a good supplement. For now."

"Did you ever walk down here during the summer?"

"Occasionally. Every time I did all I could think about was building a cabin on our property so we could live there full time."

"I can't wait for that. I mean, during the warm months the canvas lodge worked great, and maybe we'll continue to live out of that for the summers, but we'll definitely want a cabin of some sorts if we are to survive the winters out there."

"I've got some great ideas. I spent a lot of time researching cabin kits, and I think it will be totally affordable for us."

"How's our savings account looking? I haven't had a chance to check since I got back."

"It's doing good. After your expenses, and including the little bit I've been able to add, we're at about half what it was when we moved here."

"That's great. We kick ass at this frugality thing."

"I think we're doing good. And I developed a spread sheet..."

"I'm sure you have," interrupted Eli, pinching her elbow.

She laughed, "So anyways, I figured even if we lived just off my salary, we'd have enough money saved to build a cabin and survive with part-time jobs in five to seven years."

"Oh yeah? Well it will go even quicker once I start making money again."

"That's true. What I'm saying is, I don't want you to feel rushed into some job you won't enjoy."

"We'll see," said Eli, as they entered the sprawling meadow of a city park.

"So this is Loon Echo Park," said Lamara, as she stood up straight and assumed the tone of a tourist guide. "You see that building over there?" she pointed towards an old cement structure covered in graffiti and looked ready to collapse. "We're going to restore it, not in a modern sort of way, but just to make it look like it did originally."

"What will it be used for?"

"Some of the board members have suggested putting a coffee shop or ice cream parlor there, but I think it should be used as a small museum to show off local artifacts and tell the story of regional history."

"I like your idea better."

"It's so much fun to be involved with projects that have a visible impact on the community."

"I'm sure it is," said Eli, as he knelt down and pinched a handful of yellow grass. "I wish we could let the dogs off the leash, Snowy isn't used to this anymore."

"You boys are both going to have to get used to leashes again," said Lamara, and nudged him in the ribs with her elbow.

Eli laughed, "Yeah, I guess so."

"But aren't you glad you did it?"

"Of course. I just hope someday we can all go back for a much longer duration."

"That would be lovely."

• • •

That evening, after much convincing from Lamara, they left the house and drove to a small neighborhood restaurant. This was the kind of place where people stopped after work for happy hour, then stayed for dinner, and often remained trapped in conversation and drinks until closing time. There were hockey sticks and fishing poles on the walls. Above the bar was an old birch bark canoe. They walked past a group of people standing outside the front door holding cigarettes in cold shivering hands.

They stepped inside and found a booth along the far wall. The booth in front of them was filled with a group of college girls all dressed in fashionably revealing attire, whose loud conversation and exotic body movement's commanded attention from everyone in the room. Three young men were seated behind them, dressed in camouflage and wearing bright orange hats, speaking softly in gruff voices, with intermittent bellows of masculine laughter. Eli and Lamara sat silently for a moment and soaked in their surroundings.

"Care to split a pitcher of beer?" asked Eli as he saw the waitress approaching.

"I could probably drink a glass or two," replied Lamara with a smile.

They placed their order, then sat silently, while Lamara patiently waited for Eli to adjust. He looked like a man just released from prison, with his neck retreating into his shoulders, looking around cautiously at this suspicious world surrounding him. Absentmindedly, she began to draw a heart on the frosty window beside their booth. Eli noticed, smiled, and drew wolf tracks. Lamara laughed, then sighed and said, "You know I miss our property too. I mean, I didn't get as attached to it as you did, I'm sure, but it was still great having that to look forward to every weekend."

"I know. We'll get it again, just need to be patient."

"I guess it's like they say, you never know what you got until it's gone."

"No," Eli said retrospectively, "you never know what you got until you get it."

"There you go again, being disagreeable," she smiled at him with a cocked head and a twinkle in her eyes.

He laughed, "I just like watching you squirm and hearing you think." He reached across the table and took her cold hands in his.

A large disheveled woman approached their table with heavy steps. Lamara moaned and shuffled in her seat, then turned her head to look out the window. The woman wore dirty hiking boots, cargo pants, and a Carhartt jacket, with frizzy brown hair that looked like a rotting brush pile. The large woman leaned on their table nearly spilling the beers in the process, and said, "We're very upset with you Lamara. Voyager's Gate Park is a local emblem of our regional history. How dare you change the name and remove our statue!"

"I'm sorry you feel that way Joan," replied Lamara, looking up at her. "The park and the history still exist, but after considering both sides we decided the title and statue belonged to our Native American heritage."

"You've done a great dishonor to the community. I'm going to see to it that you are removed from your position and the park is returned to its proper status." With that, Joan turned to go, making a noise that could only be compared to the grunting growl of a badger.

"I can't stand that woman," said Lamara after she'd gone.

"Who is she?"

"Somehow that woman got elected as a board member on the Minnesota Historical Society. You'd think someone with that position would hold reverence for the Native American culture."

"She sure seemed ornery."

"Ugh, she's always like that. Nothing ever makes her satisfied."

"Well, don't worry about her, I'm sure there are many more people happy with your decision to change the park than those who are upset about it."

"Yeah, it's hard to ever know if I'm doing the right thing."

The men at the booth behind them had gotten louder and more boisterous with every new pitcher of beer. Eli became irritated. Lamara noticed and said, "Don't worry about it, you're in a public place now, just enjoy the entertainment."

"Yeah," said Eli as he looked over his shoulder, "do you hear what they're saying though?"

Lamara refocused her ears.

"I shot that big old bitch right in the head," said one of the men. "It was hilarious, her skull split open, and there were brains all over the trees. Somehow she still managed to stumble around for another fifty feet before falling."

"Oh man, that's awesome," said one of his buddies.

"Yeah, and that stupid cub just circled around her dead body. I swear I could hear it saying, 'Mommy mommy, what happened to your head?'" he slammed his fist on the table and they all roared with laughter. "I woulda shot that little bastard too, but I only had one permit."

"When has that ever stopped you!"

"Shut up man. Shooting a wolf without a permit is one thing, they're mangy little mutts, but you can't get away with shooting a bear like that."

Eli began to turn around, but Lamara stopped him by saying, "Just ignore them, we can go sit somewhere else." He turned towards her and put his fists up on the table. He looked like an upset school child whose cookies were just stolen by the local bully. There was both anger and sadness on his face. Like every repressed school child, eventually it becomes too much, and they lash out.

"So how much did she weigh?"

"Just over two-fifty, which is pretty big for a female around here."

"You sissy, last year I shot a male that was pushing four-hundred. That was a thrill! I hit him in the chest with a solid shot, then he came charging at me. I probably would have been bear bait if it wasn't for that safety cage I was standing in."

"It's a dangerous game we play."

"Not many men got the guts, it's certainly not for your average city boy."

Eli turned towards them. Lamara reached across the table, grabbed his arm and said, "Don't," but it was too late.

"Excuse me gentlemen," said Eli, attempting an artificial tone of civility, "I couldn't help but overhear you. I was wondering if you might have some bear meat for sale?"

"Bear meat? Who the hell keeps the meat! Don't you know anything man? If you want some meat go shoot a deer."

"Oh, my mistake. I thought you said you shot a bear?"

"Damn right, it was a clean shot straight to the head."

"I see. So what did you do with it, if you don't mind my asking?"

"Well if it was a male, I would have shot him in the chest, so I could mount the head. But since it was just a bitch I blew her head off. She's over at the taxidermist making a fine rug as we speak."

"A rug?" Eli clenched his jaw muscles to restrain his temper. Every good man wishes to defend his neighbors. Some men travel across oceans for this cause. Eli's battle was closer to home. "I must admit, sir, that is the most amazing story of cowardice I have ever heard."

"Excuse me!" said the man and turned around to put his face in Eli's. "What would you know about it?"

"About killing an animal for sport? Honestly, I must say I lack that experience."

"That's right! And I bet you've never even seen a bear except on TV. Let me tell you something, when you're out there, face to face with a bear, and you see that wild rage in their eyes, you have to shoot. If it would have seen me first it would have attacked. That's the way of the world."

"If you say so. But let me ask you this, if you're so afraid of bears, why do you even bother going into their forest?"

"I'll go wherever I damn well please! What do you think, you're some kind of tough guy who wouldn't be afraid of a bear in the wild? Shoot, I bet you'd crumble like a cracker then lay down to die."

"I'm certainly as susceptible to fear as anyone else. But killing your fear isn't a sign of bravery, only a sign of more fear. The real challenge is allowing your fear to exist and accept it."

The man stood up and walked to Eli's table. "You're lucky your woman's sitting here, otherwise you'd be in trouble."

"Yeah," Eli chuckled, "I guess she's my safety cage."

"Oh, that's it!" exclaimed the man flaring up at the nostrils.

"Hey man," said one of his buddies, walking over and putting a hand on his shoulder, "don't worry about it, this guy's obviously just some liberal tree hugger who doesn't know what he's talking about. Let it go."

"Alright. You're lucky this time," he said, looking down at Eli. "If I ever see you again I'll show you what a coward looks like."

"I bet you will," Eli winked and looked the man directly in the eyes.

The man growled and punched the empty air, then walked furiously outside. His buddies followed, pointing at Eli as they stepped out the door.

Eli had a big grin on his face when he turned towards Lamara and said, "Now that's entertainment."

"I don't understand why you insist on making enemies here. You could have just ignored them."

"A man without enemies is a dishonest man."

Lamara developed a contemplative look on her face, "Is that same rule true for women?"

Eli looked towards the door where they had exited, then without answering her continued, "Besides, they weren't going to do anything."

"I know. And I agree with what you were saying and all..." she hesitated.

"Go ahead and say it, I won't be offended."

"I just don't think you're going to change anyone's opinion by being hostile with them. People are going to do whatever they want."

"Yeah, you're probably right."

"Listen," she said, noticing his mood dropping, "we've got our giant piece of wilderness property. We may not be able to decide what the rest of the world does, but we can keep that place as natural as we want. It can be our wildlife sanctuary."

"I like that idea."

"Alright, good. Now that you've got that out of your system, can I trust you'll be civil if I take you out to public places again?"

"I can't make any promises," he smiled.

21

Honk! Honk! Honk! "What are you doing ass hole!" yelled a man out the window of his pickup truck. A man walked down the middle of the street in nothing but a robe, and just ahead of him was a dog zig-zagging from curb to curb. The man in the street turned his head slightly, then veered towards the sidewalk and called his dog to him. The man in the truck slowed down in passing long enough to say, "Put on some clothes, you damn hippie!" before putting the pedal to the floor and leaving a long tail of exhaust wagging in the walking man's face.

Eli shook his head and continued walking. Why should he care? He no longer lived in this world. All he wanted was to wake up and walk down the trail to the river. There were fox and deer and fish waiting for him. The river would be brilliant this morning, surrounded by bare branches and frosty needles.

Consciously, Eli knew he was no longer in the forest. His mind was aware of the pavement. He understood his time alone in the wild had passed. But his eyes deceived him. His open eyes could see this real world in front of him, but his closed eyes could see another real world, one more marvelous and serene, but was intangible like a dream. He realized the concept of time was more conducive when viewed from the past. He had been wrong to try and focus on the now. The past was more powerful and should be given more attention. He wanted to live there still.

Perhaps this is where he had erred on his painting. He tried to capture the image of himself at the moment, but moments were unstable and impetuous. He needed to capture a static image, something permanent and perpetual. He whistled for Snowy, then turned and began jogging towards the house.

Lamara sat at the kitchen table with a newspaper opened in her hands. Eggs sizzled in a frying pan. The morning sun cut angles through the room. She heard a door slam shut outside, and looked out the window to see Snowy lying in front of the workshop. She sighed, then continued reading the news.

The cement was cold on Eli's knees as he dipped his paintbrush into an open can. He had the luck of being burdened by an imagination so vivid and distinct, he always believed whatever it conceived. There were no ulterior motives in the way his brush caressed the canvas. He had no intention of creating a masterpiece to win the admiration of strangers. All he wanted was a visual stimulant for self-satisfaction. All he wanted was a time machine to take him away from this world of manmade scenes.

There was more to the forest than just animals and trees. There was something sacred and profound in the empty spaces. It was a sensation none of his five senses could register alone. It was a synaesthetic absorption of his inner world. Somehow, as mysterious as it seemed, the natural world understood his personal greatness, but only shared this wisdom when he was alone to hear it.

"What have you been doing out there?" asked Lamara, as Eli entered the back door and walked over to the kitchen sink. "Looks like you've been painting?" she asked, noticing the colors dripping from his hands and twirling down the drain.

"Yeah, well I got started on something anyways."

"That's good," she said, standing up and shuffling through the newspaper.

"Everything okay in here?"

"Yeah, everything's fine. I'm just gonna throw away the paper. Unless you wanted to read it?"

"How is the world anyways?" he asked smiling at her.

"I'd tell you, but I don't want to ruin it for you."

"That good, huh?"

"I just don't understand the things people do. I often wonder if anybody is actually conscious of their actions. All this crime and politics and gossip, it seems like it's all for show. Nobody really thinks about the big picture, like what it's going to do for their lives, or the lives of others. They seem to get trapped in the cycle, pick a role and then follow it."

"Yeah, I've often wondered if secretly everyone goes home and wonders the same thing. It's like sitting on top of a mountain and watching a storm pass through the prairie. From up there it looks so small and weak, like you could just avoid it if you wanted to. But once you're inside of that storm the power is so overwhelming, so tempestuous, that you can't control it, you just have to accept it, and try to adapt accordingly."

"I wish we could live on top of that mountain," she stated with dreamy eyes. "It seems much more enjoyable to laugh and mock this disaster from a distance. Is that wrong?"

"Absolutely not. And that's what we're going to do, you and I, escape to a place where we won't even know there's a storm unless we decide to read the papers for entertainment."

"And we can just live there, you and me, without having to impress people with our knowledge of worldly affairs, or who's dating who, or what the score was last night?"

"Sounds perfect."

"So what will we talk about?"

"Who said we have to talk," he replied and gave her a wink.

"Oh I get it now, you're trying to take me to a place where I'll be quiet," she laughed. "I suppose I'll have to talk to the birds and the trees."

"I hope that's enlightening for you."

"Uh huh. So what do you want to do today?"

"I was going to take a break, then try to paint some more."

"Alright, what do you say to going to the movies? We could still make an afternoon matinée."

"The movies? I have no idea what's even playing."

"Me neither, but it sounds like fun."

"Alright, let's do it."

• • •

They pulled up to the cinema complex and found a parking spot in the far corner. Soft feathery snow filled the air like cobwebs. Lamara put on her stocking cap and mittens, then they stepped outside.

"Look at all these people," said Eli in amazement.

"Yeah, a snowy Sunday afternoon, what else is there to do?"

"Have a fire."

"Maybe we can do that tonight."

The line of movie-goers stretched out the glass doors and down the sidewalk. People shivered and huddled together. Everyone talked about what movie they saw last week, or who was nominated for awards, and what big name stars were in the film they were about to watch. They spoke these names as if they were familiar faces they knew personally. They talked about the plots of the movies as though it were the story of their lives. Civilization was a vicarious world of other people's imagination.

Eli was tempted to turn around and leave. He wanted to escape while he still could. Inside those doors were not people, but humanoids, unaware they had lost their humanity. An inextricable force pulled him inside. There was mystery through these doors. There were experiences he could learn from without leaving his seat. This was the unified knowledge of mass media entertainment. This was the success and destruction of the modern world.

"One large popcorn and two medium drinks," said Eli to the concessions clerk.

"This is going to be fun," said Lamara, as they filled their thirty-two ounce sodas.

"Yeah, but for the price of tickets and snacks we could have bought a couple wooden paddles for the canoe."

"Oh please don't think about that. Let's just enjoy ourselves. Okay?"

"Alright."

The lights were dim as they entered the theater. An advertisement for the latest action video game played on the screen. They walked up halfway and found two seats in the middle. Strangers fought for elbow space on both sides. The lights faded and the movie began. Cell phone screens glowed in the room like an inverted planetarium.

• • •

Sunlight dangled on the horizon as though it were ooze seeping from the trees. The snow had stopped, and the clouds had disappeared, which revealed the first faint stars burning through the firmament. They walked towards their car, high spirited and arm in arm.

"That was a great film," said Lamara, with the wide open emptiness in her eyes that can only come from pure entertainment.

"I agree, I truly enjoyed it. That was a very engaging story."

"I just love that actress, she's so good."

"I know. She pulled it off perfectly."

"I'm sure she's going to get an Oscar for that performance."

"That's indisputable. I think it should also win best screen-play hands down."

"What was that writers name?"

"Oh I don't remember. Whoever pays attention to that?"

"True. It was such a deep thought provoking movie, I wonder what else he's written."

"I'm sure we could find out."

"Perfect, I'll get online as soon as we get home and do an internet search. Maybe we can pick up some of his other movies next weekend."

"That sounds like fun."

As they drove home, the thrill of the movie faded from Eli's mind. He began to feel ashamed he went at all. Such a hypoc-risy, he thought, knowing he had been aware of the diabolical intrigue, but ultimately too weak to avoid it.

When they arrived home he went into the workshop and tried to realign his thoughts. The gravity of temptation, even in small things, has a deceptive power. Even if aware of its presence, and consciously determined to avoid it, once within its proximity it has the power to seduce the most highly com-posed man. He had to find the forest again.

Eli looked at the image he began painting earlier that day. He closed his eyes in search of the same inspiration. Behind his eyelids was a movie screen where he played the charac-ter of somebody else's life. He walked over to the window and looked outside.

A congregation of birds was at the feeder he had built. This will do, he thought, as he tried to remember their melo-dious songs of freedom. But these birds outside his window were not free creatures, they were manmade illusions. These were clones, no different than the characters on the movie screen, designed as an artificial representation of their natural archetypes. Flying from feeder to feeder, eating seeds cultivated in gardens, and living in boxes built with saws and nails. Man has not only domesticated himself, but also every inch of the world he has touched.

Eli walked inside with his head down. He passed Lamara who already had her face in a book. He walked upstairs and opened his journal. He needed to remember. He needed to split himself in two so he could accept this civilization and secure a successful future. He picked up a pencil.

New entry:

Hello journal. I have not forgotten you. I have not forgotten all the experiences we shared, that only you and I will ever know and understand. But I live in another world now. This new world requires me to surrender imagination to the inactive background, if ever I will have a chance to succeed, to survive. You will have to be my secret affair. I hope you are okay with this. It's much more mysterious, don't you think? I cannot let this new world know that I secretly live in another. My attentions must be of pragmatic pursuits. I must make myself appear normal. The more normal I am able to make myself appear, the greater my success shall be. Don't laugh, I know I am a hypocrite. What else can I do? Someday we will run away together again, my friend. Perhaps we will be able to take Lamara next time? For now our encounters must be brief. I hope you understand that us having a future together depends upon my present ability to ignore you.

22

The alarm clock screamed from the bedside table. Lamara reached over and pushed the snooze button, then turned around and wrapped an arm over Eli's chest. She felt his beard soft on the skin of her forehead, and exhaled passionately then closed her eyes. Eli opened his eyes and put his hands behind his head, wondering what he would do with the day. They lay like that until the alarm went off again. This time Lamara jumped from bed and began her Monday routine.

Eli yawned and reluctantly rose. He put on his robe and brewed coffee while Lamara showered. Lamara stepped from the bathroom in a tight black business skirt that went to her knees. She wore a red button-up shirt with a silk vest. Her dark hair was straight and her face was decorated with a modest amount of makeup.

"You look great," said Eli, "I wish you were coming to work in my office."

"Oh stop it," she said blushing, "I just have to look professional."

"You pull it off well."

"Thanks. So what are you going to do today?"

"I don't know, suppose I'll work on my painting."

"That will be good for you. Maybe you can sell the next one." She wanted this to be true, because she had yet to find a place to hide his previous painting.

"Yeah, let's hope so. I need to start making some money so we can get on with our lives."

"Don't worry about it so much, take your time."

"Yeah..."

"Okay, well I'll see you tonight."

"Have a good day," he said, and closed the door behind her.

He paced around the house, trying to find something to do. There was never urgency or boredom in the forest, but now they both hung from his shoulders and told him it was time for a plan. He filled a cup of coffee and went to the workshop.

The new painting laid face up on the cement floor. The long branch of a fir tree swept across the center with florescent green new growth needles on the tip. The can of green paint sat open and empty beside the canvas board. He would have to buy more paint. That thought disturbed him, and he began to consider whether this painting would be good enough to sell for profit. His creativity was dampened by pragmatism.

The side of his head began to itch, and as he scratched it, he walked over to the windowsill. The leaf tacked to the wall was now speckled with brown spots that covered most of its surface, with only small freckles of faded gold still visible. In frustration he shuffled through one of the duffle bags filled with camping supplies.

Eli stepped outside into the cool morning air. He wanted to slice open a passageway through this barrier which restrained him from imagination. He pulled the dagger from its sheath and juggled it in the air, and then paced around the yard tossing it into the ground. Only one in five throws struck blade first, the rest sent the dagger skidding across the yard leaving trails in the snow.

The woman who lived next door stepped into her backyard to feed her dog. She looked over and started to wave at Eli. Then she noticed the knife blade gleaming in his hand, and the absentminded expression on his face.

Eli knelt down and removed the blade from the soil with a victorious grin on his face, and then twirled it in his hand. He was surprised to see a woman standing in the yard next door, and walked over to introduce himself. The woman took a step back, towards her house. Eli sheathed his knife, waved, then returned to the workshop.

There was nothing for him to do in this place. All of the moments he spent here felt wasted. The forest still lived inside of him, but he would never again live inside of it unless he developed a plan. He walked into the house and dressed himself in brown slacks, woven sweater, and a fedora hat. To remember his place in this civilized world he needed to submerse himself in it. He walked outside, carrying a laptop beneath his arm. He didn't know where he was going.

Giant yellow plow trucks ruled the streets, pouring out salt and sand on the pavement. The engines sounded aggressive, like futuristic beasts sent back in time to destroy his sanity. Eli shook his head in annoyance, then closed his eyes and searched for a silence lost. He wondered how anyone found time to think with all these disturbances. He continued down the sidewalk, stopping to pet every barking dog that greeted him at a fence. It didn't take long for his nose to become red and his toes to numb. Up ahead was a coffee shop, so he went inside for some heat.

He stared at the billboard menu in bewilderment, and finally asked for a black coffee. A book on a table caught his eye; it was a copy of *Backwoods Survival for the Modern Family*. He looked around at the contemporary art on the walls, the furniture looked as though it had traveled back in time to get here, and the people all appeared sophisticated in their civilized roles. This book seemed out of place to him. What was it doing here? Did everyone share the same dream of escaping to a simple, natural life? He tried to imagine the regular customers of this place flipping through the pages and contemplating the design of a cabin or bear box.

The brown leather chair with fur arm rests felt comfortable as he kicked his feet out onto the ceramic hearth. The artificial flames from the gas burning fireplace stole away his thoughts and silenced the room. Outside of the window a thin layer of ice had formed around the edge of the lake. He began to day dream. The song of a loon played so vivid and distinct it must be real. He turned around and saw a man holding a cell phone in his hand, and as soon as the man pushed the answer button, the song of the loon died.

The screen on his laptop turned bright and he looked at the desktop image of a mountain stream paused in perfection. So many days his feet had touched the bottom of that stream and many like it. He wondered if the fish still hid in the same pockets of water, beneath the same reflection of mountain peaks. It would have been easy for him to stay and live like that forever, but forever has changed like an image from a dream. Now he is trapped in a reality whose future is guided by memory.

Eli shuffled in his seat, then signed on to the internet to open his email account. It had been months since he logged in and checked his messages. There were three-hundred and sixty-seven unread messages. He pushed the *delete all* button to start fresh. Just then a young man approached who wore baggy straight-cut black jeans, a bright red sports coat, and a tall blue wool stocking cap.

"Yeah dude," began the young man, looking around nervously and lowering his voice, "you know where I can score a bag?"

"Excuse me?"

"Yeah man, I know it's weird that you don't know me and all, it's just that my dealer's out of town. I just need a small bag to get me through a few days until he returns. So what do you say, can you hook me up?"

"Sorry pal, can't help you there."

"Shit man, you're obviously a fellow stoner. I'm not going to tell anyone. Just help me out. I'll make it worth your while."

"Not gonna happen. Now if you don't mind, I was working on something here."

"Damn man, you're a drag. Can you at least smoke me up? I'll give you ten bucks to share a joint."

"Get out of here."

"Mr. Bogarting..." said the young man as he walked away with a huff of disgust.

Eli got up and walked into the men's room. He looked into the mirror and thought about his days of teenage rebellion when it was common behavior to ride around with friends getting stoned. He never dressed like this back then, and he certainly didn't have a beard. He shook it off, grabbed his laptop, and walked home.

• • •

He entered the house and felt more confused and alone than ever. Downstairs there must be a change of scenery to distract him. Centered on the back wall was a flat screen television. All he had to do was sit down and his boredom and loneliness would be resolved. It took all of his will power to turn and walk away. Upstairs the afternoon melted away as he picked up books from the shelf, read a few passages, and then exchanged them for another. Nothing could distract him enough to keep his attention.

Finally Lamara returned home. After the thirty minutes required to discuss each other's day, and eat a simple dinner, they walked downstairs. Here they sat for hours flipping through TV stations while sharing a bag of potato chips.

"Do you prefer the flat or folded ones?" asked Eli, watching her selective hands sort through the bag.

"I prefer the folded ones, they're crunchier."

Neither of them was satisfied with this form of entertainment, but it was easy and comfortable, and at least they were together. Tomorrow would be another day. Tomorrow always sounded more productive. They stayed on the couch until it was late enough to reasonably go to bed.

23

New entry:

There is something missing from the sky. The shape is different, like a void. The clouds have too much room to roam. Where have the mountains gone? Whose eyes watch them now? Whose hands grasp the rocky ledge? Whose feet tramp the earthly pinnacle? Whose lungs breathe that occidental sky?

This world I see it is not real. These people with eyes all seem so blind. The pavement echoes of time before. Vinyl houses are happiness. Here I sit, watching them all so busy. I wonder what their objective is. I wonder what secrets they have learned that I have missed. I wish that ignorance was bliss.

There is something missing from these streets. I've walked the sidewalks up and down. So many people with smiles and frowns. I see their eyes through glassy walls. They look at me as though I don't belong. Where has the river gone? What trees have fallen without a sound? Whose fresh footprints are to be found? I wonder if the forest waits for me as I wait for it. This narrow distance of space and time, is separated by the greatest rift.

Here I sit, with you again. Light blue lines and gray leaded friend. I need your help, if you should be so kind. My way of life must be redefined. There is happiness here that others have found, though it must be floating on the dreams they've drowned. I shall live my life with buoyancy. My hopes and dreams wait ahead of me.

• • •

Eli folded up the notebook in his hand, and tapped it gently against his thigh in the rhythm of a joyous song. He entered the house and removed his winter coat. Snow fell outside the window and the floors in the house felt cold on his feet. He turned up the dial on the thermostat and considered how lucky he was to find warmth so easily. Civilization must be for the betterment of man's longevity.

He stood before the kitchen window with a cup of coffee cooling in his hand. Outside the frozen clouds crumbled into inimitable flakes that tumbled to the ground. In this narrow sphere of air they were free, unique, and erratic individuals. Only in this brief eternity were they identifiable. Perhaps this was why they moved so slowly. Soon they would reach their destination, rejoin in a selfless conglomeration, and once again become as obscure as a raindrop in the ocean.

Here in the organized rituals and routines of society was the peace and simplicity of babbittry. Here he could put his head down and let life pass by him with nonchalance. There would always be weekends for debauchery. All he needed was a routine. All his routine required was a paycheck.

He picked up the phone and dialed a long distance number. His mind ran rampant with the presence of the past. Torrents of words were dammed by his tongue. A voice answered and he opened the gate.

"United Administration of Natural Technology, this is Lana speaking, how may I help you?"

"Must be a busy day, I almost got three full rings before you answered," said Eli in an energetic voice.

"Oh, we're always busy around here. Is this Eli?"

"You got it. How are things out west? Get any snow yet?"

"Nope. Not in town anyways. You can see snow up in the mountains though. It's just been real windy here. Most of the guys are out in the field today. I told them they shouldn't go, we're supposed to get freezing rain this afternoon. I don't need to tell you what that does to the roads."

"I'm sure they'll be fine. That's what those big trucks are for. So, you holding down the fort alone?"

"Just me and Clancy here today.

"Would you mind putting him on?"

"I'll see if he's busy."

"This is Clancy."

"Hey, how's it going?"

"Eli? Wow, surprised to hear from you. We were beginning to think you fell off the face of the earth."

"I almost did," he said with a chuckle.

"So what's up? How is life in, uh, Minnesota?"

"Going good. I just did a lot of camping this summer, you know, and now I'm settling back into our house."

"Sounds like some adventure."

"It definitely was," replied Eli, trying to be direct through abbreviation. "So what's going on out there, tested any clever new equipment lately?"

"Oh there's always some new gadget on the market. All we can do is roll with it."

"Yeah, sounds good for business."

"Certainly is. You know me though, I often think all these new gadgets are a waste of time. None of them really enhance the capabilities of old models, just make it more complicated so people feel intelligent by using them."

"I hear the guys are out in the field testing something today?" asked Eli as he paced around the house blind to his surroundings. He pictured Clancy sitting in his office with his feet up on the desk. Out through that office door was Eli's old desk, and he remembered staring out that window at an imaginary future which was now his past.

"Yep, we got this new optical radar meter," replied Clancy. "They claim it can quantify all field parameters in the cross section of a river just by holding it submerged on one edge for five seconds. I must say, I'm a bit skeptical."

"Sounds like a talented piece of equipment. They probably won't even have to get in the water to use it?"

"That's just it, every new piece of hydrological equipment we see is designed to keep the users feet dry. I feel sorry for the next generation of hydrographers who will never know the pleasures of fighting against a current. There is no real sense of victory in laziness."

"It's a shame. All I can say is that I'm glad to have worked there while we were still putting on waders."

"Yeah, you got out of here at the right time. Next thing you know, none of us will leave the office. We'll be testing all new equipment remotely with satellites and robots."

"This may sound crazy of me to say," said Eli, slowing down his speech, "but I actually miss it sometimes. Just driving up to some hidden mountain, finding a reclusive stretch of river, and spending the day there, all while getting paid. That's an opportunity not many people get."

"Yeah, it's not as good as it used to be. In the old days it seemed like eighty percent of our time was out in the field. Now-a-days it's more like eighty percent office time."

"Still, I'm not sure I ever thanked you properly." Clancy waited quietly on the other end of the line. "I learned a lot there. When people ask what I did for work, I can never find a way to explain it to them in a form they understand. I guess what I'm saying is, I appreciate the opportunity you gave me. I hope you don't think I took it for granted because I left."

"Oh no, everybody's got to do what they got to do. Can't expect someone to stay forever if their life changes. Besides, like I said, you got out at the right time."

"I suppose so," said Eli softly.

"So," resumed Clancy, "got any work lined up yet?"

"Nope, like I said, just getting settled back in town. Probably start that task next week."

"Well, if you ever need a good reference..."

"Will do, thanks."

"Alright, good luck."

"See ya."

• • •

That night Lamara and Eli shared a bottle of wine. They fought the temptation of the television screen. They made a photographic slideshow of their lives together. Eli watched in a silent state of remembrance, while Lamara shed happy tears. Their dogs curled up at their feet. Outside these walls, a city full of people lived their lives. The barstools were warm and the movie theaters were loud. The restaurants were full and the shopping centers had sales. It snowed harder and the night glowed in white.

24

"Wednesday night, oh how I wish it was Friday already," said Lamara as she stood in front of a full-body mirror and held up two evening dresses.

"You're going to get cold if you wear either of those," said Eli as he entered the bedroom.

"We'll be inside most of the night. Which one of these do you like best?"

"They both look nice," he said and reached into his closet.

Lamara gave a disgruntled sigh. Eli walked up behind her, put his hands on her waist, and said, "The brown one matches your skin tone best."

Lamara smiled and said, "Yes, I think you're right."

"So how many people are going to be there?"

"Let's see, I only invited six, but you never know who will make it or who will bring somebody else. What are you going to wear?"

"I thought my camouflage pants with a red checkered flannel shirt would be appropriate."

"That would be perfect," she said playing along. "People are going to want to see the woodsman tonight."

Eli pulled a pair of dress slacks and a black button-up shirt from their hangers in the closet. "Listen," he began patiently,

"I appreciate you throwing this party for me, and I'm excited to meet some new people, but let's not make the whole night about me. I just don't want to be the one talking about myself, and trying to explain what it's like to live in the woods, you know."

"Of course not. I doubt if it will even get brought up. You know how people are. Let's just go and have a good time."

"You look great," he told her, as he pulled on his gray tweed jacket. "Ready beautiful?"

"Whenever you are, handsome."

• • •

The stars reached out behind the dwindling daylight. The sun painted its departure with elegance. The moon was most amazing pasted upon a blue velvet sky. In the surrounding fabric were various tones of pink, barely perceptible. It was the saddest tone of pink ever seen, surrounded by blues and paled by the moon.

It was warm inside and the bar room pulsated with energy. The nocturnal forces had taken control of these bodies. Their minds lagged behind, still focused on their daylight lives. With a few more drinks and a little more darkness, these worlds would converge into a spectacular eruption of ecstatic delirium. Caution exchanged for chaos. Confusion exchanged for nonchalance. Anxiety replaced by comfort.

"What'll it be?" shouted the bartender from two feet away.

"How about a whiskey sour for the lady, and an Avalon for myself," responded Eli as he leaned into the bar rail.

"Can do. Only problem is we don't carry the Finlandia vodka. Something else?"

"That's alright," said Eli as he looked across the counter at the shelf of transparent potions, "Van Gogh Blue will work."

"Gotcha," said the bartender as he began to turn away.

"Excuse me," said Eli, getting his attention, "would you double up on the vodka, and cut the juice in half, with only two cubes in the cup."

Eli looked at Lamara and asked, "Are your friends here?"

"Yep, see that table over there," she waved towards them.

Eli strained his eyes across the blurry room. "Looks like a lot more than six."

"Yeah, I guess you never know who will come out on a Wednesday night. Let's go say hello."

A man wearing slacks, dress shirt and tie, with black framed European style glasses, stood up to greet them. "Lamara, there you are, we were beginning to wonder when you two would make an appearance."

"Ah yes, well you can't throw a party and be expected show up on time."

"Of course not. So how are you? This must be Eli?"

"That's me," said Eli shifting his feet.

"It's a pleasure to finally make your acquaintance. Lamara has nothing but good things to say about you."

"What was your name?"

"Oh, my apologies, I'm Jeffery."

"He's the art professor at the university," chimed in Lamara.

"I see," Eli reached out his hand, "it's good to meet you."

"No it is my pleasure," said Jeffery, offering his flaccid hand-shake. "So I understand you are a bit of an artist yourself."

"Oh I don't know about that," said Eli, trying to avoid the subject. "I've only just started really, haven't put anything on display yet."

"Now there's no reason to be modest," replied Jeffery with an air of magniloquence, "some of the greatest artists in history weren't discovered until grass had taken root on the roof of their graves."

"Is that so?" asked Eli. He imagined Jeffery used that line in the classroom on the first day of every new semester. "Perhaps I shall go home and hang myself in the name of glory."

"That would probably do the trick," responded Jeffery with a laugh. "Placing humor aside, if you ever want to show me anything, just for some artist-to-artist feedback, let me know."

"Alright."

"Eli, let me introduce you to my friend Victoria," said Lamara, holding him by the hand and continuing to the table.

Victoria stood up and exchanged a hug with Lamara. She wore a colorfully eclectic selection of attire. She spoke with a French accent when she said, "Oh Eli, it is absolutely fantastic that we finally meet. Lamara has told me many wonderful things about you."

"Well, don't believe it all," he jested.

"Victoria and I met at the yoga studio. She's the instructor."

"I see. I didn't know you were doing yoga?"

"Yes, well I haven't had time to tell you everything I did over the summer."

"She is my finest pupil," praised Victoria, "I can only imagine the benefits that has for you."

Lamara blushed and said, "Oh stop it," while Eli nodded his head and looked away.

"So," continued Victoria, after realizing Eli's privacy of carnal affairs, "I understand you have just returned from a hermitage of sorts?"

"Yes, I suppose you could say that."

"So tell me about it. In France nobody does that anymore, there's simply no place for them to go and get away. The closest thing would be for an artist to give up their home and live on the streets. And believe me, plenty of people are doing that, you see them everywhere. It's quite the *factice* really."

"I agree," said Eli, saving face and pretending to know the translation. "So how long have you lived in the states?"

"I have been here almost five years. I enjoy it very much, there's so much country for people to escape in," she leaned towards him with prying eyes.

"Perhaps Lamara and I can take you to the property some time."

"Oh absolutely, you have to come," insisted Lamara.

"That would be lovely, I'm sure," responded Victoria. "So Eli, let me ask you this, were there any great epiphanies for you while living alone in the wild country?"

A faint grin crept onto his face, and his eyes twinkled mischievously. He took a pull from his drink, then replied, "I learned how to be a happy hypocrite."

She looked at him with a raised brow, "That sounds most pessimistic."

"But you're mistaken. In fact it is the most optimistic I have ever been." He couldn't judge if she were made more confounded or perturbed by his response, for she flashed him an evil eye, then promptly turned away to engage Lamara in a separate conversation.

Eli formed a personable smile on his face, and took a moment to study the people who surrounded him at the table. Earlier when he looked at the table from across the room, nobody stuck out, they all seemed to be blended into a larger single organism. Even at closer proximity, the most visible characteristic was their conformity. Their tongues and body movements dressed them in a persona of delight. But not their eyes. Each pair of eyes spoke volumes about the experiences and hopes their clothes and words denied. A vast and eternal realm of possibilities existed in this world. Yet it seemed as though everyone was trapped, caught in a happiness which was condescending to their ability.

The greatest question, which incidentally caused him the greatest dilemma, was whether or not this generation he was born into were capable of surpassing these superfluous behaviors, and acknowledging the supremacy of their individualism. It caused strain and sadness to disguise the despair in his eyes when he realized everyone who surrounded him seemed defeated by the simple fact they haven't taken the opportunity to discover their own wildness. Secretly everyone here saw this other hidden person in the spaces between the eyes and words of these familiar strangers who surrounded them. The only thing missing from their lives, the limiting factor of their absolute happiness, was they didn't understand their own capabilities; the power of their minds had yet to be explored. Somewhere deep inside, only known by words unspoken, was the knowledge they were better than what they were giving. But that's the price they paid for their civility. The price for simplicity was the sacrifice of originality. So they commingled in speechless conversation, never allowed to speak their minds, or so be banished from the circles that make comfort easy.

Eli searched their shifting pupils for a recognizable definition. It was difficult to focus on their eyes through the costume of personality. He wondered if they were as disheartened by the routine as he. The eyes were the only device remaining to display originality. There were as many versions of reality as there were eyes to see it. For all the other eyes in the world may never see, what another pair of eyes will see. He took a large pull from his drink, and decided to let it be.

"You ready for another drink?" he asked Lamara.

"Oh not yet, thanks."

"Alright, I'm going to go grab one." Eli approached the bar and looked around through tainted eyes. What was the secret? How could he wait patiently for the other life calling him while trapped here in an artificial happiness? He looked back at the table and saw Lamara laughing and conversing. She was the incandescence of this darkness. How does she do it? He knew she wanted the wilderness life as much as he, but she had configured a magic code which allowed her success in this waiting line. Too much thought. He needed to forget about it so it would come naturally.

Back at the table a young woman named Megan asked Lamara, "Who is that guy you're with? I don't think I've seen him before."

"That's my man Eli," she said proudly.

"Eli? So he's the one who has been living in the woods," asked Megan as she looked across the room.

"That's him."

"He doesn't look like the type. I would have expected someone different."

"Ah yes, well he's a master of disguise, isn't he."

"I guess, except for that outrageous beard."

Eli turned from the bar with a fresh drink in his hand. He felt a tap on his shoulder, and turned to see a middle aged man who looked familiar, but couldn't find the name in his memory.

"Excuse me, aren't you Eli?"

"Yes."

"Don't you remember me? I'm Lyndon, we met earlier this summer up at the resort. You were the fly fisherman who caught that big pike."

"Right, we met at the bar. You were sitting with the hotel manager. How's it going?"

"It's going good. Winter is coming so all of our summer help has gone back to school."

"Remind me, weren't you in the natural resources field?"

"That is correct. The thing is, just because winter comes around doesn't mean our work load gets any lighter. But we end up losing half our workforce when the interns go back to college. So we've been holding interviews all week, but most of them have been subpar. All these new kids fresh out of college have attitude problems. They get excited about saving the environment, but would rather sit at a climate controlled desk than be out in the field getting cold and dirty."

"Yeah, that's the way of the new world I suppose. I used to work in an environmental technologies position. I was an equipment analyst, and every new piece of environmental sampling equipment was designed to keep people indoors. I always found that ironic."

"So what kind of work are you in now?"

"Let's just say I haven't found the perfect job." Eli noticed a furrow develop on the man's brow, as if he were contemplating the existence of a perfect job. He sensed Lyndon was withholding a question, so he asked one first. "What exactly is this position you're looking to fill?"

"Entry level field technician. The person hired will be responsible for using a multitude of sampling equipment to collect data. It requires working in whatever conditions the weather provides."

"Doesn't sound so bad."

"It isn't, at least not for the right kind of person. Why, you interested?"

"Might be. You're doing interviews all week?"

"We are." The furrow on Lyndon's brow deepened. "You know, if I recall, seems like I gave you my business card last time we met. That was several months ago and I never heard from you. Why the interest now?"

"I've been out of contact," Eli took a pull from his drink.

"I understand, happens to the best of us. And you seem like the sort who could handle this kind of work, but there's more to it than that. We need a person who is committed and dependable. After not hearing from you for so long, I don't know what else to say."

"That's fair. You said you were holding interviews all week. If I brought my resume in tomorrow would you give me a shot? There will be no doubt of my commitment."

"I don't know. Today was our last scheduled interview. There's one candidate we are optimistic about. Technically speaking, since it is a federal position, we are not allowed to make a decision until the week is up. You stop by tomorrow morning at ten a.m., we'll see about getting you that interview. But no promises."

"I will be there."

"Good." Lyndon drained the last drop of his Irish whiskey. "Now listen," he said, looking straight into Eli's eyes, "it is a federal position, so appearances are important." He set the empty glass on the bar counter and rubbed his shaved chin.

"I understand."

"Good. I'll see you tomorrow."

Eli shook his hand and walked back to the table. He squeezed Lamara around the shoulder with a beaming smile on his face. The people sitting at the table suddenly became friendly and real. In his brief departure they transformed into something more comprehensible. He held up his drink and said loudly, "Cheers!" They joined in the ceremonious clanging of cups. Nobody knew why, but there didn't have to be a reason for unity.

"What's gotten into you?" asked Lamara quietly.

"Actually, I just got a job interview."

"What! How did that happen?"

"Oh you know, my charm and wit." She narrowed her eyes and smiled at him. "Well let's just say fishing has given me more than the occasional meal."

"Okay?"

"Let's do a shot. Shot's for everyone!" he exclaimed. The night spun away in dizzy excitement. The simple conversations took on the complexity of human involvement. Everything became interesting. All these people were so unique and mysterious. Everyone lived a life that deserved admiration. Eli felt like he was one of them, he had found his place in this magical world of fantasy. He forgot about the dissonance, and began to feel the harmony of just letting himself go.

"Thanks for the shot," said a young man who reached out and shook Eli's hand. He wore blue jeans with a checkered flannel shirt. On top of his head was a baseball cap with the logo of a moose. "I'm Allen."

"Good to meet you. I'm Eli."

"Yes, I know. So you've been living *Thoreau*, correct?"

"You got it buddy. And let me tell you, it was one hell of an experience."

"I bet. So did you see any wildlife?"

"All kinds of it. It's a wild world out there full of both serenity and danger."

"Oh believe me, I'm familiar with that. So do you hunt?"

"Nope, usually too busy fishing for that."

"Yeah, well I trap and hunt. I run a trap line on a river fifty miles from here. Last week I got two beavers and five muskrats. They pay pretty well, but otters get me the most."

"I see," said Eli, trying to ignore him yet feign interest.

"Yep, but the best part is I finally drew for a moose this year. Oh man, I was pumped. Two weeks in advance I went out and set up a trail cam, you know so I could learn their routine and see if there were any bulls around. Man, when I downloaded that footage and watched in HD on my big screen TV, shit was I stoked. It was like being right there in the woods. Here, I saved it on my smart phone, take a look." He flipped open the screen on his cell phone and played the video. Eli watched, and for a moment he felt far away, back in the forest, living as one with the animals.

"You should've heard the thud it made when I shot him," continued Allen. "So anyways, I took my dad and we went up to some state forest land just south of Canada. Man it was so cold, icicles were forming in my beard. No joke, second day in the tree stand this big old bull of a moose came grazing right in front of us. I had so much time, I watched him, you know, waiting for the perfect shot. I sighted him up with my high powered scope, and made the shot straight to the heart. Ten feet and he tumbled to the ground. It's a shame you can only draw for them once in a lifetime. I'd like to do that every year."

"You must be a great hunter," replied Eli, while adjusting his shirt collar. "I bet you got a lot of good meat out of that?"

"Oh yeah, enough to last me a year or more. You should see my deep freezer."

"Really?" Eli's eyes lit up.

"Yep, but the real thrill is the kill. Now I've got that mount with a big ol' rack that I can put on my wall to remind me the rest of my life."

"That's very impressive." Eli forced a laugh and shoved his hands deep into his pockets. Then Lamara rushed up, nearly out of breath with excitement, and pulled him onto the dance floor.

The music played loud and the room filled with energy. They danced ecstatically, kicked up their feet, shook their hips, twirled and jumped while flailing their arms. People were shouting and kissing, and blind with delirium. They made mockeries of themselves, and had a damn good time doing it.

"That was fun!" exclaimed Lamara as they walked away from the dance floor.

"Yes," said Eli, looking around the room with a new found sense of attachment, "I'm glad to be back."

"I hate to be the party pooper, but we should probably call a taxi and get home. I have to get up early tomorrow."

"Oh come on, we're just starting to have fun." Eli gave her another twirl beneath his arms.

"Yes, but tomorrow's going to be difficult."

Eli paused and said, "It certainly is."

25

The night covered the ground with several inches of fresh snow. Eli walked downtown to retrieve their truck, while Lamara prepared for work. Large yellow plow trucks removed snow from the streets and poured out sand and salt. Eli smiled and waved at the drivers as they passed, feeling a sense of admiration for these men and women whose job it was to ensure safe travel for the citizens of his new home town.

He pulled the truck up along the curb outside of their house and waited for Lamara with the engine running. "So what time is your interview?" she asked, brushing the snow from her boots and stepping into the truck.

"Not until ten."

"What are you gonna do all morning?"

"Try to act civil," he gave her a wink.

Lamara laughed and said, "I'm afraid to know what that means. You ready to drop me off?"

"Let's go."

Eli pulled the truck up alongside a downtown curb. As Lamara exited the passenger door he said, "So I'll pick you up at five?"

"Yep," she said and started to get out, "text me if your interview gets done in time to grab some lunch. I'll be curious to hear how it goes."

"Suppose I should upgrade my cell phone," he replied, after turning to look out the driver's side window. Lamara giggled and kissed him on the cheek. He watched her enter the dark glass office doors, and then drove away.

Eli pulled into the parking lot of the hardware store at five minutes to eight. He waited in the truck with the engine running until the store opened. Employees walked in wearing their uniforms and carrying their heads high. They greeted each other with smiles and friendly hellos.

He entered and wandered the aisles, admiring all the tools and supplies that could be used to better their home. So many brilliant conceptions designed for creating a happy life. He found the aisle stocked with ropes and chains, and as he walked by, his fingers reached out on both sides to gently touch each one as he passed. He paused to caress the serpentine coil of a thick poly-braid rope. The ground started to shift, as the aisles sprouted trees and the ceiling turned blue and bright.

A salesman approached and saw the distant look in Eli's eyes. He cleared his throat and said, "Excuse me sir, did you have any questions about that rope?"

Eli promptly returned the rope to the hanger and blinked his eyes several times before looking towards the salesman and replying, "Actually, I was looking for snow blowers but got distracted."

"That's alright, we like to consider our store a candy shop for men. If you follow me, I will show you to the snow blowers." He turned and walked as Eli followed him two aisles over. "If you want your driveway cleared with the most minimal effort, then you must have the *Snow Torrent 5000*. It is hands down the greatest model on the market. All your neighbor's will be envious watching the streams of snow shooting off your cleared pavement. And, if that's not enough, we're offering our *Welcome to Winter* sale until the end of the week."

"Looks impressive," replied Eli. He imagined how good it would feel to offer a tool for loan to his neighbor Martin. He could see his neighbors across the street pushing their shovel while wiping their brow and looking over at his impeccable driveway. Then he looked at the price tag and realized for the same cost he could buy a wood burning stove to heat their cabin that wasn't yet built. "I think I'll take this shovel instead."

He returned home and started scraping the pavement with the heavy steel blade. Martin came outside to start his car, and then saw Eli and walked across his yard. "That's a lot of driveway for that little shovel."

Eli wiped his brow and looked up, "Yep, but it'll keep me in shape through winter."

"You've got a lot of cracks in your pavement, maybe if you resurfaced it that job would be easier."

"It's not so bad."

"Okay. I just picked up a powerful new snow blower, the hardware shop down by the lake had a great deal. If you ever want to borrow it you just let me know."

Eli nodded and turned back to the driveway. The steel blade felt light as he lifted it and tossed clouds of snow into the air. The clouds separated and seemed suspended, and as they paused ever so briefly, the sunlight reflected off of each individual snow flake and created flickering rainbows of spectacular color. That's it, he thought, real magic, the magic of reality. It was a magic he could never replicate or understand. It was a magic more varied and infinite than there were eyes to see it. He knew he had found happiness; happiness in the ability to accept any scenario with a balanced sense of nonchalance. Nothing could destroy him now, the future waited with open arms.

• • •

Eli entered the workshop with snow on his shoulders. He stood before his new painting and viewed the barely formed image of a tree. He touched it with his fingertips but only felt paint. He could never travel there through this canvas. No image could ever replicate the power of reality. Life must be experienced through the senses of coexistence. Like his favorite song, it just didn't feel as strong, unless he was singing along.

With slow but deliberate movements, he unfolded a tarp and covered the paint cans, brushes, and canvas. He felt nostalgic for all that was lost. But you cannot lose something unless you love it. And love stays with us forever. True love always returns.

With focused footsteps, Eli walked out of the workshop, and pulled the door tight behind him. Tacked on the far wall beside a window was the brown crispy leaf. The vibrations in the wall from the closing door dislodged it from the tack. The leaf crumbled into fragments and silently fell to the cold cement.

• • •

Eli stepped into the brightly painted white bathroom. There were no spider webs in the doorway. The porcelain toilet was gleaming clean. The potpourri dish smelled exactly like the forest in spring. There were no mosquitoes. The shower was a perpetual torrent that would never go dry, with a solid stream of steady pressure, and a lever that could produce whatever temperature of water he desired. The mirror displayed an image of his entire upper body. Inside of the mirror was a man who didn't belong in this room. He watched that man as though he were a stranger. He saw him through the judgmental eyes of a more civilized passerby. He thought of the forest where his beard grew long and untamed. He felt the freedom of knowing nothing but natural sounds and peaceful walks, the sight of a deer, and the touch of a cool flowing river.

The top drawer slid open easily with the use of a brass handle. Inside he saw all of the aromatic potions with colorful labels meant to describe their scent and to conceal his own. He opened the next drawer down and saw all of the tools required to maintain a socially presentable appearance. He reached in and picked one up. He felt its cool black metallic structure in his hand, then unraveled the cord and plugged it into the socket above the sink. He flipped the switch up and felt its vibration in his palm. The teeth-like blades quivered at high speeds. He thought of a dragonfly's wings. It sounded like the mosquitoes. With his other hand he unconsciously swatted at the empty air. He brought the device up to his face and sighed. Then a faint smile formed on his upper cheek. His eyes turned to glass.

Someway. Somehow. Someday I will...

Daniel J. Rice was born in Wiesbaden, Germany, in 1979. He has lived in the state with the highest population density – New Jersey, and the state with the lowest population – Wyoming. He resigned from his position as a Hydrographer for the USGS in the wild and untamed landscapes of Wyoming, to begin his career as a novelist. He wrote *This Side of a Wilderness* while spending four months living alone, in a tent, isolated in a deep forest, with no running water, and the only electricity coming from solar panels used to charge a laptop computer. Currently he resides in northern Minnesota, with his wife Mayana, and daughter Amelie.